The Attic at Wilton Place

CE Rose is the pen name of Caroline England, the author of psychological suspense novels, *Beneath the Skin, My Husband's Lies, Betray Her, Truth Games* and *The Sinner*.

As CE Rose, Caroline has written gothic-tinged psychological thrillers, *The House of Hidden Secrets, The House on the Water's Edge* and *The Shadows of Rutherford House*.

D0264233

Also by CE Rose

The House of Hidden Secrets
The House on the Water's Edge
The Shadows of Rutherford House
The Attic at Wilton Place

c e rose

THE ATTIC AT WILTON PLACE

hera

First published in the United Kingdom in 2023 by

Hera Books
Unit 9 (Canelo), 5th Floor
Cargo Works, 1–2 Hatfields
London SE1 9PG
United Kingdom

Copyright © CE Rose 2023

The moral right of CE Rose to be identified as the creator of this work has been asserted in accordance with the Copyright, Designs and Patents Act, 1988.

All rights reserved. No part of this publication may be reproduced or transmitted in any form or by any means, electronic or mechanical, including photocopy, recording, or any information storage and retrieval system, without permission in writing from the publisher.

A CIP catalogue record for this book is available from the British Library.

Print ISBN 978 1 80436 297 6
Ebook ISBN 978 1 80436 296 9

This book is a work of fiction. Names, characters, businesses, organizations, places and events are either the product of the author's imagination or are used fictitiously. Any resemblance to actual persons, living or dead, events or locales is entirely coincidental.

Look for more great books at www.herabooks.com

Printed and bound in Great Britain by Clays Ltd, Elcograf S.p.A.

1

To Libby, Sam and Carolyn

I'm so lucky to ride the writing rollercoaster with such brilliant friends!

Prologue

Last night I dreamed of the attic at Wilton Place again. It's always the same, the climb up the stairs to the very top, the dusty curtain, the ancient lock, the sizzle of fear. And though I've been there many times in my head, that black wall of freezing fustiness hits me afresh.

I fumble for a switch and a dull glow lights the windowless room, made all the more claustrophobic by the looming timber rafters. Catching my shallow breath, I take in the weathered tea crates, the shrivelled bouquet of roses and grainy photographs. These items alone bring back dismal memories, but I steel myself for more and drag my gaze to the twin single beds.

My heart leaden, I know I must choose. Which will I settle on? The one adorned with a pink padded quilt, colourful cushions and a long-snouted teddy bear sporting a smile? Or the neatly made billet with the plain, scratchy blanket and a baby dolly, which stares at me malevolently through blue glassy eyes?

I'm fully aware that nothing is as it seems, yet I still agonise, torn between loyalty and love, autonomy and seduction. Then a scented cold breeze rises up through the floorboards. I make to rub my goose-bumped bare arms, but jolt in alarm at the sensation beneath my fingertips.

I'm wearing a fur jacket and... oh my God, it's real mink, ensnaring yet softly cocooning me.

That's when I wake, bursting from the dream with relief. Then I look around my golden surroundings and finally remember...

I've already chosen.

Part 1

Chapter 1

Although I had met Vanessa before, my first abiding memory of her was at ten years of age. She wasn't my real auntie, but Tim and I called her 'Aunt' on the rare occasions she visited.

'Good Lord, don't call me that. It makes me sound like an ancient spinster,' she always said. 'And when one is an actor of *international repute*, one can't possibly have that.'

That particular August day was no exception. On arrival she pulled out a chair, lit up a Gitanes cigarette, then casually dropped a French magazine on our kitchen table. 'There we go, little darlings. See if you can find me.'

I didn't know any grown-ups who smoked, and certainly no one who'd dare to light up indoors. I expected Mum to object, but she stood to one side with that peculiar expression she always had when her friend arrived. I could never quite make it out. Mum could be tense at the best of times, but there was something else behind her watchful eyes that didn't feel right.

Tim glanced at the central spread of our aunt in several provocative and barely-clad poses, then flicked through the rest of the glossy publication.

'Hmm. A lot of adverts for eau de parfum, don't you think, Aunt V?'

'Darling boy,' she replied. 'I believe you're now a teenager, so do stop calling me Aunt. It makes me sound as old as your mother.'

'You were in the same class at school, so unless you were a child prodigy, you are as old as Mum.'

Mum seemed to shake herself back at that point. She smoothed Tim's newly acquired quiff. 'Thank you, Timothy,' she said, elongating her vowels and sounding more like Vanessa than my northern mother. She flashed a triumphant smile at her. 'Just one reward of motherhood, especially with a son. Loyal to the nth degree.'

Mum's tone was a little barbed, but Vanessa lifted a shoulder and tapped the feature with a tapering finger. 'And yet this article says I'm *trente-trois*, so I must be. What did Shakespeare say? "Suit the action to the word, the word to the action."'

Her emerald eyes abruptly focused on me. 'I rather like the number thirty-three; I think I'll stick with it. What do you say, Ruth?'

She'd caught me ogling. Dumb from embarrassment, I pushed up my glasses and reverted to my sketching. But she hitched towards me and leaned so closely I could smell her perfume, an erotic heady blend of vanilla and jasmine and lily of the valley. Then there was her hair as it swept my bare arm; a shade of burned sunset, it was all I could do not to wrap it in my hands and bring it to my face.

'What are you drawing this time, sweetie?' she asked. 'Ah, a chrome kettle! You don't make it easy on yourself.' As she studied it, a tower of ash fell on the parchment. 'But do you know what? You're good, very good. And as an artist myself, I should know.'

She made to brush away the fine grey powder. 'Oh Lord, I've smudged it in. Sorry, sweetie.' She kissed my burning cheek. 'Maybe it helps with the shading?'

My heart whipping with pleasure, I eagerly nodded. A fragment of Vanessa was forever ingrained on my page.

–

That seminal moment was on the last Friday of the summer holidays before my final year at primary school. Mum had taken two days off work to drive Tim to the dentist and me to the opticians.

Luckily for Tim, his tooth decay was the fault of our local council.

'Why on earth did they stop putting fluoride in tap water?' Mum complained to Dad after discovering her eldest child wasn't quite perfect. 'His first filling at thirteen, poor boy. Don't tell me that's a coincidence.'

'Perhaps his addiction to fizzy drinks doesn't help,' Dad replied with a raised eyebrow.

Mum gave him the glare. 'Really, Clive? Is that your contribution when your son has to undergo a traumatic procedure in a week?'

Unluckily for me, my poor eyesight was my fault alone:

'If Ruth got out for more fresh air instead of having her head down in a book or scribbling away on her art pad, she might not have hyperopia and wear those dreadful magnifying glasses. Or have that unattractive slouch,' I heard Mum say to Dad, as though the walls of our house weren't paper thin. 'And goodness knows where the oddball musical gene comes from. Anything to avoid exercise, or indeed having friends, it seems. I wouldn't mind, but that cello cost an arm and a leg. Lord knows what we'll do with it when she gets bored.'

'I rather suspect that's unlikely.'

'Well, when she grows bigger and needs a full size one, then.'

'Perhaps use it for fire wood?' Dad answered, as ever not quite taking sides.

Still, neither Tim's genius nor my shortcomings were the focus of that particular evening as there was my aunt's social call to analyse and discuss. As ever it had been at ridiculously short notice, Mum stressed and excited and barking at me to help her dust and polish, straighten and sort within the allotted time.

Vanessa had stayed for only an hour, but it had been an electrifying sixty minutes, not just because she was sophisticated, exotic and attractive, or that she spoke so beautifully and smelled so sweet. It wasn't even because she'd slipped both Tim and I a twenty-pound note when Mum wasn't looking. It was her green appraisal and her words: *But do you know what? You're good, very good.*

Dad finally arrived home with a fish and chips supper on Mum's command. There was 'plenty of food in the fridge', so we were surprised at her gesture. But her cheeks were pink: though she tried to hide it, Joy Parker was always a little off balance from Vanessa's visits too.

'Give me chapter and verse then, Joy,' Dad said as we ate. 'How was *don't you know who I am*?'

I waited with bated breath. I was bursting with a million questions about my glamorous aunt, but I sensed it wouldn't go down well with Mum. When she'd shown Vanessa out, she'd pulled the front door behind them. Though I'd struggled to hear what was said through the crack, I'd gleaned they were arguing.

Mum pushed her fringe from her forehead. 'Well, you know Vanessa, she was—'

'Mutton dressed as lamb,' Tim replied for her.

Dad had already studied the central spread for some time to 'test his French', yet he glanced at it again. 'A little harsh if these photographs are anything to go by,' he commented with a skewed smile.

Mum frowned and tutted. 'Mutton? Not nice, Timothy. I'm only forty-two, not quite there yet.'

Dad pecked her lips. 'And a very tasty *Le Gigot d'Agneau* you are too, my love. Especially those shapely pins.'

A little pleased at my brother's rare fall from grace, my thoughts popped out loud. 'Well, I think she is just amazing in every single way.'

No one seemed to hear, least of all Tim. He was sporting a look of disgust from the parental kiss. But that was fine by me; I was in heaven, my chest still tight with exhilaration. *But do you know what? You're good, very good.* Vanessa had noticed me! She'd seen something in a solitary, introverted and invisible ten-year-old that no one else had, even if it was only my average talent for art.

Chapter 2

My self-esteem hadn't improved by the time I was twelve. My shortcomings now included being 'worryingly tubby', as Mum put it to Dad in a not-low-enough-voice. He tried to be kinder with 'it's puppy fat, Joy; it'll fall off very soon', but it all added up to the same thing: I was overweight. And no, that wasn't an attractive quality in anyone's eyes, least of all my own.

The boys' catcalls at school didn't bother me so much – some were pretty lardy themselves. Or spotty, or stick thin. And the good-looking few didn't come under my radar; even if flirting had been my thing, I'd never be in with a chance, so who cared what they thought. Alpha girls were more the problem. Though their derision wasn't spoken, the glances and sniggers, the sweeping looks from my head to my feet with wide, knowing eyes, or the pointing and covering their stupid mouths, were more insidious than that.

Then there was my cello. Was a musical instrument so very funny? In its case, it certainly seemed so. '*Ruth's violin got so fat she had to buy a bigger bag.*' '*What's the difference between a cello and a coffin? The coffin has the dead person on the inside.*'

But at least I did have a small group of friends. Though my music and art was still my *raison d'être* at high school, I'd discovered there were a few myopic oddballs other than me.

'Why don't you get in with Zoe or Beth?' Mum suggested after my crowd had been to our house one evening.

'And miss that sweet melody? I think not,' Dad murmured from behind his newspaper.

I wanted to say: 'Those three are my pals, Mum. I like them. We have a laugh and the same interests. So why would I want to do that?' Or perhaps, 'Do you think for a moment the popular girls would let me anywhere near their clique when I'm "worryingly tubby" and use an ancient cast-off Nokia phone?'

Yet as ever I shrugged rather than shape the words needed to express how I felt.

Mum scanned me, queen-bee-like. 'If you made more of an effort to be...' She searched for a word. 'More accessible, then you might be...'

Dad cleared his throat at that point, but the theory seemed to be that if I hung out with the likes of Zoe or Beth I'd become miraculously beautiful, sleek and slim overnight. Like my aunt Vanessa? Now there was a rousing thought.

Tim was on his Samsung. Though he spent whole chunks of time with his head down and absorbed with *something*, he had a knack of listening at the same time. Not just to the conversation around him, but to whatever was going on in my mind.

'So I'm guessing that you and Vanessa were part of a charmed circle at your school, Mum?' he asked.

My heart skipping a beat, I readied myself to learn more about their friendship. I was undoubtedly intrigued, especially after that frantic whispering the last time. I knew the two women had been best buddies back in the day, but that was pretty much it as Mum was tight-lipped about her childhood in general.

Clearly taken by surprise, she sharply inhaled. 'I wouldn't put it like that exactly...'

'Then how would you put it?'

His eyes wide with interest, Dad lowered his broadsheet.

Only Tim could grill Mum and get away with it. 'You were *meilleurs amis*, weren't you?' he pressed.

She seemed a little flustered. 'I suppose it takes more than two to make a *circle*, as you put it, but yes, we were very close.'

'Hmm,' Tim said. 'And you see her how often?'

My brother was Mum's golden boy, but occasionally his loaded comments went a little too far. Still, I was all ears, desperate to know more about my enigmatic aunt.

'As you know full well, she mostly works abroad, but we do speak regularly.' Cerise spots of annoyance had appeared on Mum's cheeks. 'As it happens, she's back from her latest filming in Paris. She'll be in touch very soon, just you see.'

—

I tried to keep the delirium of Mum's pronouncement under wraps, but Tim wasn't fooled.

'I don't get it,' he said elbowing in for the toothpaste later that evening. 'She's so actressy and superficial. And a bit weird, if you ask me, like she's wearing a mask. Why are you so giddy?'

Though I could see the excitement for myself through the mirror, I plaited my long tresses and did the usual shrug. 'Giddy about what?'

He rolled his eyes. 'Aunt V's impending appearance, of course.' He raked his hands through his glossy dark hair. 'I'm always up for a few extra quid, but you get so ridiculously… well, feverish.'

'No, I don't!'

'Yup, you do. Mum does too. I'm genuinely interested to know why.'

I studied my brother's reflection. Could he really understand what it was like to be me? He was laid back, clever and athletic; he was lean and had twenty/twenty vision; he was adored by my mum and our aunties; he'd clearly come from a cosmic egg. How nice it would be to explain how I felt and say: '*Aunt Vanessa noticed me, really noticed me on her last visit. I can't say why I'm so certain about it, but she thought I was special.*'

I didn't, of course. Tim would laugh me out of the bathroom. Besides, the Parker family didn't ever discuss feelings and now wasn't the time to start.

Chapter 3

Mum's 'very soon' stretched out from days into weeks and I gradually released my tight breath of anticipation and got on with approaching the ripe age of thirteen. Clearly hoping I'd miraculously befriend a queen bee or two, Mum suggested a gathering at our house to celebrate my birthday. When the usual three suspects turned up, she didn't bother to hide her look of disappointment, but Dad played a blinder by offering his credit card.

'What's that for?' I asked.

'To pay for a round of pizzas.'

I glanced at Mum. 'Really?'

Though she eyed the Victoria sponge she'd made and sucked in her cheeks, Dad got in first. 'Yes, really,' he said. 'Off you go and have fun.' He followed me to the front door and pecked my head. 'No beady parental eyes on you tonight, so there's no need to hold back, eh?'

—

Feeling grown up in the restaurant was fun. I had no intention of abusing Dad's trust, but the four of us pushed it as far as we could, ordering three courses and extra dough balls 'for the table'. Then some other kids from school appeared from nowhere and joined our group. Picturing Mum's frown of disapproval, I boldly offered another round of soft drinks, but Mohammed cut in.

'Nah, here's a better idea. You'll only turn thirteen once…'

His older brother was in the village with his mates; if we paid for it, Ahmed would buy us some bottles or tinnies of cider; we could go to the park and get drunk.

All eyes on me, I fingered Dad's plastic in my pocket. It was a seminal moment. Which way would I jump? Betray his faith in me or live in the moment? Do something outrageous for once? Like an out-of-body experience, I watched myself toss back my head, shocked at the words that came out of my mouth.

'OK, sounds good. Let's do it.'

—

Damp from both weeping and sitting on a grassy bank, I arrived home two hours later. I had managed to recover Dad's credit card eventually, but only after it had been used to buy far more than just cider, then passed around the older pupils 'for a laugh'.

It hadn't been a laugh, or even remotely funny. Though I had swigged the alcohol and tried to look nonchalant, I'd been twisted with worry and alarm inside. I'd disclosed Dad's pin code, I'd spent his money without permission. Mum's fury would be bad, but his disappointment far worse. I wasn't a rebel; I was a plain little mouse. I shouldn't have tried to be a person I wasn't.

Before I had chance to use my key, Mum yanked open the front door. 'It's eleven o'clock, Ruth. Where on earth have you been?'

'Just hanging around,' I muttered, shuffling past her.

But Dad appeared in the hallway, so any hope of being invisible – when I actually wanted it – was zilch.

Mum sniffed me like a hound. 'Have you been drinking?' Her face a picture of horror, she looked at Dad. 'They're not allowed to serve alcohol to under eighteens are they Clive?'

'No...'

'Which means she must have got it from somewhere else. Lord, please say it wasn't stolen.' As though I was an inanimate object, she pointed at me. 'And look at the state of her. Wild

hair and stained clothing. Bleary-eyed and as white as a...
You're not going to be sick are you, Ruth?'

'Teary too, Joy,' Dad replied as pointedly as he was capable
of. 'On her *birthday*. Perhaps we should let her go to bed and
talk about this in the morning.'

But Mum was speaking. 'Thank goodness she wasn't here
when—'

'Teenage jinks,' Dad interrupted. He patted my shoulder. 'If
there's one day it can be forgiven, today's the day. You go on
upstairs, love.'

Yet I knew what Mum had been about to say. That very
moment I had twigged it myself. The aroma of vanilla and
jasmine and lily of the valley still pervaded the air.

'Thank goodness she's already left,' she continued. 'Lord only
knows what she'd make of her in this dreadful state...'

I blocked out the rest of Mum's condemnation. Vanessa had
visited and I'd missed her. After all those days and weeks of
waiting, I'd been left out of the momentous occasion. I sniffed
back a fresh rush of misery. When I'd scurried up our road, I'd
thought the evening couldn't get any more dismal. It just had,
and quite honestly my heart felt broken in two.

As I swayed up the stairs, Mum called behind me. 'Wash
your face before you get in bed. Preferably have a shower. I
don't want you getting mascara on your pillowcase.'

What mascara? I thought as I stared in the mirror. Sure, a
little remained on my tear-streaked cheeks, but most had been
washed away. I had no idea why I'd used it in the first place –
make up didn't suit me; tight jeans didn't suit me; my hair, my
eyes, my own skin didn't suit me. And the one person who'd
seemed to look beyond that had been and gone. It wasn't even
that late and it was my special day. I was finally a teenager; surely
my aunt could have waited?

Trying to erase the whole night, I forced fingers down my
throat and puked in the loo. Then I stepped into the too-hot
shower, scrubbed my skin until it felt sore and willed half a stone
of flesh to melt from my body.

When I returned to my bedroom, I scooped up my new dressing gown, still in its packaging. Should I risk wearing it? Or would Mum take it back to M&S as punishment for the money I'd spent? The pyjamas and slippers too. As if I cared! Who wanted a matching set of nightwear as the star birthday surprise at thirteen? And yet I knew that person was undeniably me. Even if I wasn't swaddled in love by my parents at times, those mundane offerings made me feel safe. And I had let them both down. Oh God.

Fearful of causing more problems, I donned my old PJs and slipped under my duvet. It felt cold, unwelcoming and dank. Though that was me, in all likelihood, my hair damp from the shower and still snivelling with desolation. My momentous day had been a disaster; cider was revolting; I'd never drink it again.

I pushed my face against the pillow. What would tomorrow bring? Mum was notoriously tight with money as it was; no doubt my meagre pocket money would be docked, her general dissatisfaction with me would swell to new heights.

But after a few moments, my miserable thoughts were suspended. Something was pressing into my forehead, a hard item beneath the cushion. Intrigue overcoming the nausea, I flicked on the bedside lamp and glanced at the clock. It was ten minutes before midnight and still my birthday. Could this really be another present? Holding my breath, I slipped out the treasure and examined the foil-wrapped box. Had Tim's hints to my parents come good? The *'it's only fair, Mum. I got a new phone when I turned thirteen'* that I'd overheard? Mum's response had been, *'That would be wasteful, love. Your old Nokia is still working and perfectly adequate for Ruth's needs'.* Did I dare hope she'd changed her mind?

I tugged at the Sellotape, carefully peeled back the gold wrapping and clamped a hand to my mouth. The gift wasn't just a brand-new mobile, but a state-of-the-art iPhone. My stomach clenched with guilt and pleasure and worry. I'd thought badly of Mum and Dad, yet this was so incredibly generous. I'd completely messed up tonight; would I be allowed to keep it? Then another thought: running a smart phone was mega expensive; how on earth would I pay for the calls and texts, let alone any data?

Just knowing disappointment would soon replace the euphoria, I lifted the lid and lightly touched the black screen, jumping in surprise as it sprang into life. Hope and dread colliding in my chest, I studied the colourful icons, but the one marked 'SMS' drew my eye. Three messages were already waiting. Taking a deep breath, I opened them.

The first:

> Happy thirteenth birthday, sweetie!

The second:

> Don't fret about the cost or anything else as I'm paying.

The third:

> Love you lots, my special girl. See you very soon. Vanessa xx

Chapter 4

I couldn't shape why I wanted to keep my aunt's gift a secret from my parents. Vanessa had stolen their thunder, I reasoned. They weren't exactly poor, but my new phone was beyond their budget and better than either of theirs. They'd also been kind, treating me and my friends to the pizza and drinks. But the covertness excited me. When I was wracked with drunken anguish, Vanessa had crept into my bedroom and hidden it beneath my pillow. It felt only right that there it should stay, so when morning came I neatly made my bed and didn't mention it to anyone.

Blocking out the memory and sheer terror of the older kids chucking it around in the park, I returned Dad's credit card to him.

'I'm really, really sorry but I spent more than—'

He stopped my apology with a raised palm. 'It's fine, love. Lesson learned, eh?' Then with a crooked smile, 'Best not let on to Mum, though.' He seemed to sense my unspoken question as he continued, 'She didn't always have money growing up, so she worries about it far more than she should. OK?'

Dad's words stayed with me for the rest of the weekend. They made me feel bad; disloyal too. My mum wasn't the most affectionate person in the world, but she was still my mother. I frequently nipped to my bedroom, closed the door, pulled out my treasure and stroked and admired it like an item of jewellery rather than a tool, yet it got to the point where I felt so guilty I wanted to confess. I needn't have worried. When I came home after school music practice on Monday, Mum was sitting at the kitchen table, her face blanched with something I could only describe as fury.

'Where did this come from?' she demanded, brandishing my iPhone. As though it had been thrown, the box was dented. She didn't wait for my reply. 'You won't be seeing it again.'

Torn between anger and relief, I stomped and sulked for the rest of the week. Yet when I bashed my pillow into shape on Saturday evening, my present was back in its nesting place.

Why had my mum returned it? Had Dad told her to, or was it something to do with the telephone conversations she'd had curled up on the sofa, those same chats she'd had throughout my childhood which brought on her rare laughter and rosy cheeks? With Vanessa, of course, Aunt Vanessa.

As the days passed I was still inordinately pleased at her kind and lavish gesture, but in reality Mum had been right – the Nokia was perfectly adequate for my needs – so I continued to use that routinely, saving the iPhone for its sole, special and exhilarating purpose, which was to bring it out before sleep and check the internet for snippets of gossip about my glamorous benefactor. Occasionally finding a message from her too.

> Hope you are well, darling girl! Don your beautiful smile and keep dreaming. I promise you that one day all your wishes will come true!

Though I sent her appreciative emojis, my life was too dull and plodding to formally reply. Instead, I analysed and absorbed each and every word she composed. That she knew how seldom I smiled, especially.

Months marched on. Vanessa didn't visit us, but I heard from her now and then via my iPhone. There'd be a flurry of activity, then nothing for weeks. Most of her missives were postcard style, a quick 'greetings from' somewhere around the world with a scenic photograph and occasionally a selfie. Other times she made rambling statements that I'd stare at for hours, but still couldn't interpret.

I tried to play detective and equate the messages with what I could glean about her filming schedule, but they never quite matched. I longed to learn more about the real person. Other than a vague 'London based, I expect' from Dad, I didn't know where she lived or what her family circumstances were, and grilling Mum wasn't an option on so many levels, not least because I hadn't mentioned the exchange of texts in the first place. I eagerly read every article I could find, but I'd discovered from the horse's mouth that what the media printed wasn't necessarily true, so I decided my brother was the man for the job. Unfortunately, he'd turned seventeen and was rarely around.

'Don't be silly, Clive. He's studying at the library, of course,' Mum always said when Dad wryly asked if Tim had already left home for university. But I wondered what he was really up to. There was no doubt he'd smash his A levels, but no one spent *that* much time reading books. Still, he came good on the run-up to Dad's forty-fifth.

'I'm feeling creative,' he said to Mum. 'I'm going to make Dad a retro birthday card. Can you dig out some photos?'

Ever glad to oblige the golden boy, Mum yanked down a carton from the top shelf of her wardrobe and we spent an hour sitting on her bed and rifling through old images of our father, chuckling at his flowing mane, his long collars and bell-bottom jeans. Although younger, he hadn't changed a great deal – in each snap he sported a laidback stance and half a smile, including his wedding pose.

'I see you made him get his hair cut for the big day,' Tim commented.

Dewy-eyed, Mum picked up the portrait and looked from her groom to her son. 'So alike,' she muttered. 'Handsome, charming and clever.'

Tim rolled his eyes but let it pass. 'Come on then, show us more of your nuptials.'

Much like me and my iPhone, Mum pulled out another box and opened it as if the crown jewels were hidden inside.

'This is the official album, so please be careful.' I was no longer three years of age nor covered in sticky jam, but Mum squinted at me. 'No fingerprints, please.'

'Absolutely.'

Certain I was about to discover more about my charismatic aunt, I didn't take umbrage. Instead, I watched Tim turn the thick pages, keenly waiting for the group photographs to appear. Sure enough, there was Vanessa, auburn-haired beneath a huge hat and as resplendent as ever.

Tim thrummed his fingers, the usual prelude to an incisive observation. 'Hmm. So you didn't ask your *meilleur ami* to be your bridesmaid then.'

'Well, I wasn't sure if she'd be...' Mum pushed the hair from her forehead. 'She had commitments she couldn't break for the dress fittings and so on. But in all honesty not having a maid of honour suited me.' Her cheeks flushed. 'It was only a small event and—'

'And it was your big day,' Tim finished for her. 'I get that.'

Questions were threatening to explode from my chest. I took a breath to casually ask the paramount one, but Tim got in first. 'So what about her? Has she never married?'

'Ah.' Dad had appeared at the door. 'Call me Sherlock, but something tells me you're talking about *don't you know who I am*.' He raised the usual insouciant eyebrow. 'None that we know of. One suspects she scares everyone off.'

'Clive!' Mum admonished. 'No, not at all; she's had plenty of offers over the years. She just hasn't met Mr Right.'

'Any kids hidden away?' Tim asked.

'No, of course not! What a ridiculous suggestion.'

My brother pulled a face at Mum's pink consternation. 'One doesn't need to be legally wed to have a—'

'At one's mid-forties, one might deduce Mr or Ms R simply doesn't exist,' Dad interrupted.

'No Clive, that isn't at all fair.' Mum shook her head. 'Sometimes you go too far. As well you know, Vanessa lost her mother at a tender age, a mum she loved her dearly. I don't think she's ever got over it.'

Despite the central heating blasting out, she rubbed the arms of her cardigan and seemed to lose focus for several long seconds. 'Some voids you never quite fill,' she said eventually.

Chapter 5

Christmas flew by without any contact from Vanessa, but an envelope arrived in the post addressed to me and Tim on a Saturday in January. Though I scooped it from the doormat and clocked the French stamp, I dutifully padded through to the kitchen and passed it to my brother before I was told to by Mum.

Briefly pausing his breakfast, Tim glanced at the handwriting. 'Go for it.'

'As the eldest, you should be the one who—' Mum began, but he cut her short.

'Something tells me Ruth will get more pleasure than me.' He handed me a knife. 'But whatever lies within...'

Dad's lips twitched. '"Whatever lies within our power to do lies also within our power not to do." Our son is quoting Aristotle, Joy.'

Glad he'd diverted Mum's usual 'by the book' insistence, I carefully sliced the seal and pulled out a festive card. When I opened it, a folded letter and two fifty-euro notes slithered out.

'Hmm,' Dad said. 'Something tells me that the Bette Davis of our time is still working in Europe. Don't her undoubted talents stretch to playing a character in her native tongue?'

'Rude, Clive,' Mum replied. I expected her to defend Vanessa's thespian skills, but instead she frowned in thought. 'Bette Davis wasn't very pretty. If you insist on comparing my friend to a long-dead actor, then I'd say she's more Katharine Hepburn.'

I had no idea who that was, but Tim did, of course. 'Nonconformist artiste with sharp cheekbones and red hair? Yup, I can see that.'

'Not forgetting the trousers,' Dad added.

Mum tutted. 'I don't know why you're looking so amused Clive, so did your mother. Does in fact.'

He chuckled and pecked her lips. 'That must be why I like strong women.'

Tim pushed his cereal bowl away. 'What about yours, Mum?' he asked. 'Did she wear the proverbial trousers too?'

We didn't talk about Mum's parents, but the unspoken lore was along the lines of her dad dying young and her mum marrying again. Astonished at Tim's temerity, I held my breath and waited for Dad to smooth over the tension, but Mum tutted.

'Who knows,' she said. 'Who knows what went on in that woman's head.'

'Went?' Tim persisted. 'So she died?'

Mum seemed flustered by his question. 'I don't know and quite frankly I don't care, Timothy.'

Shrugging off her sharp tone, he picked up the escaped note and peered at the elegant handwriting. 'This is addressed to you.' He handed it to Mum. 'What does it say?'

Her cheeks pinking with pleasure, she turned towards the lounge. 'Wouldn't you like to know.'

Dad chuckled. 'Well that did the trick.' He gave it a few beats, then casually followed her out.

'He pretends not to be, but he's as intrigued as you are,' Tim commented. He scooped up his euros. 'Grandad didn't die, you know.'

'Well we did see him last weekend.'

'Not that one, you dope. Mum's dad.'

'Oh right.'

'He didn't exist in the first place.' Tim tapped his nose. 'This is between you and me, but it seems our strait-laced mother was a *bâtarde*.'

The contents of Vanessa's missive were revealed at tea time. Mum was still flushed and she even opened the packet of smoked salmon Dad had received in a Christmas hamper from a grateful client. I was allotted the smallest portion, but Dad noticed and passed over a slice of his.

'Ruth's a growing girl,' he mumbled, avoiding Mum's eye.

She didn't need to say, '*and don't we know it*' as her raised eyebrows said it all, and though I gave Dad a half smile of appreciation, I struggled to swallow it under her disapproving glare.

Once the delicacy was consumed, she washed her hands, smoothed down her skirt and cleared her throat.

'Is everyone sitting comfortably?' Dad interrupted.

Mum cast him a disparaging look. 'So, my missive from Vanessa…' She opened the note and read it out loud. '"I have news. Call me!"' She glanced at my brother. 'Are you listening, Tim?'

He placed his Samsung face down on the table. 'Of course, Mater. I'm all ears.'

Apparently satisfied, she nodded. 'So I called her.'

We already knew this. Her legs curled up on the sofa, she'd chatted for a good hour in the afternoon.

'And the winner of the Oscar went to?'

She shot Dad another frown of condemnation, then took a deep breath. 'Vanessa is getting married!'

That silenced us all, and though it was silly, I couldn't help feeling a little miffed that I hadn't already worked it out from my online stalking. Or heard it from my aunt first-hand.

Dad finally rallied. 'To Mr Right, I assume?'

Mum's eyes were wide with intrigue. 'I gather so. And what's particularly interesting is that he's a good ten years her junior.'

'Her real age or her media age?' my brother piped up.

'I didn't ask for chapter and verse, Tim.'

'But clearly a toy-boy.' Dad chuckled. 'I'd better start grooming. What do you think, Ruth? Maybe begin with that rogue grey hair which insists on sprouting from my left eyebrow?'

I smiled, but I was remembering the paparazzi snaps I'd seen of Vanessa with a dark-haired and attractive, aviator-clad guy. He'd appeared to be in his twenties and wasn't the type of man I'd expected her to date, so I hadn't added two and two.

'What does this youngster do?' Dad asked.

'He's an artist called Sergio Rossini. She wanted her portrait painted; he was recommended, so she commissioned him.'

Tim's head was down to his phone. 'Sergio Rossini,' he said. He read for a minute. 'Thirty-one-year-old Italian sculptor, illustrator and artist. Hmm, seems he's very well thought of.'

'Well, that goes without saying. So when is this wedding and are we invited?' Dad asked.

'As if we wouldn't be, Clive.' Seeming to drift, Mum rubbed her placemat. 'Yes, in June...' She eventually reverted to us. 'It'll just be a small affair, Vanessa said. Somewhere pretty, you know for the—'

'Photographs,' Tim finished for her. He nudged me. 'Hello, here we come.'

'Yes.' Mum bit her lip. 'She didn't say where, exactly, so I'm assuming she meant a venue in the UK.' She dragged her gaze to me. 'You'll be fourteen by then so...'

Her voice trailed off, but there was no need to fill in the blanks. *Photographs*. Perhaps fourteen was a magic number; maybe by some miracle I'd become the slim and sleek daughter she longed for by June.

She shook her head. 'Yes, yes. So at the end of the conversation, Vanessa made a suggestion...'

Dad and Tim leaned forward with interest, but to my surprise Mum looked at me. Her expression was terse, even angry. What on earth had I done now?

'Don't feel you have to say yes, Ruth. I'm sure she was just saying it to be kind.' She took a shuddery breath. 'She's asked if you'll be her bridesmaid.'

Chapter 6

Excitement overcame tiredness that night. Why on earth had Mum even doubted my reply? I didn't need to think about it twice; of course it was a yes; I'd been chosen!

I accepted via Mum then scurried to my bedroom as soon as was seemly, to text Vanessa.

> Mum told me about your invitation to be a bridesmaid. Are you really serious?

> Of course I am, sweetie. I only want one and that's you!

> Then yes please. I'd love to.

> Wonderful! Now we have to think dresses. Both yours and mine. Something matching or along the same theme would be nice, don't you think?

> Wow! Absolutely!

Then I'll have a big ponder. I'll be in touch,
sweetie. Until then, arrivederci!

My head held high, I basked in the exhilaration for several days.
An internationally acclaimed actor had selected me to be her
maid of honour! It was amazing, unbelievable! But as I trudged
behind a mini-skirted queen bee on my way to school, reality
smacked. Dresses. Me in a dress… Oh God. My go-to clothes
were combat trousers, T-shirt and a Parka, or leggings and a
baggy jumper which came down to my knees. The thought of
a party frock was bad enough, but a wedding-type of gown,
one that matched the svelte and beautiful bride's…

Bloody hell, what had I done? I already knew how exquisite
my aunt looked in a long flowing affair as a blushing newlywed.
I'd only ever seen a few grainy clips with subtitles online, but
Le Secret du Mariage was the film for which she was the most
famous.

Like a brick in my stomach, dread replaced my delirium.
It wasn't only what I'd let myself in for, but what my poor
aunt had done to herself by being 'kind'. I'd spoil the wedding
photographs; I'd be a thorn next to a rose, a veritable marrow
behind a leek. And suppose the images did find themselves
into the celebrity pages of a magazine? The humiliation for
us both would be unbearable. I could clearly picture the online
commentary: *It's usually an ugly bridesmaid's dress, not the bridesmaid… You'd have thought a noted starlet could have chosen a prettier
maid of honour… Maybe she did it deliberately to make herself look
even better… Or had to choose her, poor cow…*

Willing myself thin, I tried to reduce my intake of food,
but despite being faint from hunger at times, my dumpy reflection still ricocheted from window panes as I passed. Mentally
burying the whole thing might have been preferable, but Mum
was on a high, constantly chattering about the nuptials and
her own outfit plans. Both Dad and Tim gave the subject a

wide berth, so she had no alternative but to seek my opinion. Abandoning her usual frugalness, she'd sit me down at the kitchen table and spread out swatches of delicate cloth, or she'd take me through the dresses and suits she'd earmarked in magazines with a Post-it. What did I think about this style and that? Floaty or fitted? Off-the-peg or have it made? A two-piece or all in one? What fabric, what texture? And what about colour? Summer allowed for any combination, so long as it wasn't ivory or white…

That's when she'd peer at my pasty skin and bite her lip. '*White against white won't look good,*' I could hear her thinking. But then she'd catch her own glowing cheeks in the oven glass and revert to a smile. Joy Parker was in seventh heaven! She had a wedding to go to. Not any old wedding, but a celebrity do, the location of which turned out to be France.

–

Vanessa went off radar again for a couple of months. Although I habitually checked for texts the last thing at night, her lack of contact eased my panic. The midsummer's date was getting ever closer and there'd been no mention of dresses or bridesmaid's duties again, so I deduced Mum had had a word to her bestie on the QT, something along the lines of: '*Don't feel you have to do it. It was extremely kind of you to think of Ruth but we both know that an unattractive and overweight teenager isn't the look you really want.*'

The thought of not having to go through the mortification was a huge relief, yet there was an element of hurt or pique too. My aunt had offered this amazing invitation then pretty much ghosted me; it just wasn't right to make someone feel special one moment, then drop them the next.

In early April, Mum appeared in my bedroom one evening. 'Ruth?'

Turning from my cello practice, I was surprised, then dismayed, to see her brandishing a tape measure. 'Chop, chop, clothes off,' she said in a nurse-like tone.

I folded my arms defensively. My plump-in-all-the-wrong-places credentials were clear to see; I wasn't prepared to remove my protective layer and expose them in the flesh for her or anybody else.

'Come on, Ruth, up you get and let's get this done.'

Memories of being weighed and measured in primary school came rushing back. Some of my friends' mothers had declined to put their kids through the humiliation, but not mine. The word 'obese' clogged my throat.

'Why?' I managed.

Mum reflected my stance. 'I gave you the opportunity to politely decline, but you insisted on accepting so...'

I was nonplussed for moments.

'Measurements, Ruth. For the wedding. Vanessa has no idea of your... your figure. The seamstress needs them for the dress.'

Though relieved the examination wasn't medically-related after all, I held out my palm. Mum was very particular about her privacy when undressing, so why shouldn't I have the same curtesy?

'Fine. I'll do it.'

She held the reel away. 'Your actual measurements, Ruth. Underestimating them will do you no favours. Anything too tight will look, well, it will simply...'

Though her sentence trailed off I knew exactly what she'd intended to say: *exacerbate the problem.* Tears burned my eyes. How was I supposed to love my body if my own mother thought that? Should I back out after all? Send a private message to my aunt that I'd made a mistake and wasn't up to the task? But a sudden, blinding hatred overcame my self-pity, making me all the more determined to see it through. Whatever this mother of mine thought, Vanessa wasn't ashamed to be seen with me. On the contrary, she'd chosen me. Defiantly lifting my chin, I yanked off my jumper and leggings.

'So sorry I'm such a disappointment to you, Mum, but go for it.' I posed in the shape of a T. 'Measure away and feel free to do your worst.'

Chapter 7

Me and Mum didn't get back on track, or at least on the potholed path we'd been on up to then. Occasionally I found her looking at me with a bewildered expression, a 'what have I done?' look, which made me feel all the more aggrieved. Mothers were supposed to love and understand their daughters, not make them feel defective somehow.

'I can't seem to get anything right. She's gone straight from an extremely quiet child to a moody teenager,' I heard her say to one of Dad's sisters on the telephone. 'Without a... Well, the break one would hope for in between.'

A nice bit, I supposed, a fluffy mother-daughter bonding part. I would have enjoyed that too, but I simply couldn't remember her praising me for anything, ever. And if being 'extremely quiet' – in my book known as 'shy' – had been a cause for complaint, what hope did I have for the rest of my flaws?

Dad tried to mediate from time to time. 'I know Mum can be a bit... angsty at times, or perhaps say the wrong thing, but I honestly believe it's because she wants the best for you.'

Well, that was skewed logic. I wondered what he said to her in my defence. *'It isn't easy having a low opinion of yourself, then have your mother constantly reinforce it,'* might have been a start. Still, I loved my dad very much, so I made an effort when it came to Mum's continued wedding fever. It wasn't too difficult as I was excited too. Now my bridesmaid role was a fait accompli, I shelved that part and focused on the thrilling prospect of a holiday abroad and – even better – finally seeing Vanessa.

–

After weeks of deliberation, Mum decided that an outfit made from scratch was too convoluted, so my parents took a week off work and trawled the land for an off-the-peg ensemble. Dad accompanied her into every boutique, shop and store, and made all the right noises when he must have been bored to death, but Mum clearly twigged this as I was invited for the final selection.

'You have to be honest, Ruth,' she said when we arrived. 'And tell me which you like the best. I can't decide between the dress and the suit. Dad says I look lovely in both, so he's hopeless.'

'OK...'

Well, that was food for thought. Was honesty the thorn between me and Mum? Yet surely it paid to be tactful or thoughtful and kind at times? She disappeared behind the changing room curtain, and when she emerged, I didn't need to be any of those things. Dad had been right; Mum was sculpted, slim and elegant: she did look lovely in both.

Remembering my promise, I gave each my careful consideration. 'I can't decide either, but the suit jacket has long sleeves. Won't you be too hot?'

'I can take it off after the service.'

Though she illustrated the point by revealing an exquisite silk blouse beneath, the assistant held up a camisole. 'France, I think you said?' she murmured tactfully. 'Perhaps you could take both, then you can judge the weather and decide on the day?'

I inwardly smirked. Of course Mum had said 'France'. She'd undoubtedly mentioned the word 'celebrity' too. But she wasn't taking the *chemisette* bait; famous for complaining about her 'bingo wings', she always covered them up. They weren't remotely flabby – none of her was – but I understood these things were subjective; people had their own foibles and hangups and it was important to respect them. It was just a shame she didn't have the same insight when it came to me.

–

My gown arrived in late May. I happened to be passing the when the bell rang, so I idly opened the front door. A courier held out a huge cardboard box. 'Ms Ruth Parker?' he asked.

I immediately knew what it was. Both excited and terrified, I swallowed. 'Yes, that's me.'

As though he'd read my mixed emotions, the guy cocked his head. 'Just enjoy it, eh?'

'Thanks.'

I wanted to, I really did, but I had no idea of what I'd find inside. I didn't have imaginary flabby upper arms, I had an actual layer of extra fat everywhere.

Mum was at the kitchen sink. 'This has just been delivered. Should we take it—'

'Yes, to the lounge.' She looked down at her apron, then at my hands. 'Maybe give them a wash, Ruth. We wouldn't want to... Oh, how exciting – the grand unveiling! Should we call? No, you're right; I think this one is just for us girls, so let's go upstairs.'

Touched by her enthusiasm, I settled myself next to her on my bed, peeled off the tape and pulled out a solid white box. When I opened the lid, I was greeted by silver.

'What gorgeous tissue paper.' Mum lifted her eyebrows. 'Even that looks expensive.'

Knowing I'd have to keep even that for posterity, I carefully folded the layers, lifted a padded coat hanger and stood. A full length pale pink creation slithered out like an exotic fish. Both Mum and I gasped as we took it in. It was undoubtedly beautiful; the strappy affair would have looked stunning on a slim teenager with no spots on her back, the silky material a little sexy over a small bum and flat belly.

Mum eyes were moist. 'It's lovely, Ruth. Are you going to—'

'Yes.' I took a big breath. 'Yes, I'll try it on now.'

I had promised to send Vanessa a picture the minute it arrived, and though I'd have preferred to do a selfie in private, I could hardly ask Mum to leave. I stripped down to my undies, slipped it on and handed her my phone.

Though I avoided the mirror, her *honest* face and lack of comment said it all.

'Mum!' I quickly said to cover my upset. 'The photo before I freeze.'

'Oh, oh yes.' Her features scrunched, she adjusted my bra straps and stood back. Then with the slight shake of her head, 'Maybe try wearing different knickers and a pair of shoes?'

Vanessa was much kinder when her text arrived.

> You look wonderful, darling! That colour suits you perfectly. I can't wait to see you wear it in person.

Then:

> BTW. Have you found the matching Bolero at the bottom of the box? Cute, isn't it? The chapel might be a little chilly, so I thought it would be just the thing!

Yes, my aunt understood tactfulness too.

Chapter 8

June came around and Dad packed up his car under Mum's eagle-eyed inspection. His Volvo allowed enough room in the boot for their large suitcase and my tiny one, his suit, her outfit and hat carefully draped on the top. My box was nestled next to me in Tim's seat like a friend. He'd finished his AS level exams a couple of weeks before, so he'd gone ahead by train, touring Europe with his mates, Rav and Ed and some other school pals for the holidays. The cost had been funded by our parents, of course.

'It's *educational*, Clive,' Mum had said in support of Tim's case. 'So it's money well spent.'

I didn't disagree, it was learning as well as fun, but my music teacher's recommendation that I apply for a summer advanced cello course at the Guildhall School had been turned down.

'It's in London, Ruth! You're only fourteen, you're too young. And besides, you don't have the experience nor the confidence required,' Mum had immediately said when I broached it. 'It's a huge, scary city. Isn't it, Clive?'

'True,' Dad had replied. 'But let's listen to what Ruth has—'

'And where on earth would she stay?'

There'd been no 'well done for your hard work and talent', no praise for being the only pupil in my school to be nominated. 'Surely Vanessa has a base there? Or at least she knows someone who has…' I'd mumbled.

'Goodness knows what she has or hasn't got these days. She films in France and other countries abroad, so I believe she generally rents somewhere six months at a time.'

'I thought Vanessa had a place in the countryside,' Dad had commented.

'I wouldn't be surprised.' As though fibbing, Mum had been even more evasive than usual. 'She "invests" from time to time, so I lose track.'

'Couldn't we still ask her?' I'd said.

'Have you around, getting under her feet? And don't forget she'll be newly married. Even if she was kind enough to say yes, she'll have a husband to think of.'

That had been a fair point, but the fact it wasn't even considered, simply added to my ever-increasing resentment. I didn't say anything, of course, the Parker family never did. Instead, I wrote my angst out, and though the letters weren't addressed to anybody in case they were found, I promised myself that one day I'd have the guts to show them to my mum.

–

Setting off at dawn, the journey down south took four long hours, but at least I was armed with my iPhone and I napped, so listening to my parents' patter wasn't compulsory. From time to time, Dad turned on the radio and sang along to the given tune before Mum shut him down with a 'Must you, Clive?' or a 'Ruth needs her sleep and you'll wake her'.

When we finally reached Poole, we queued for the ferry.

'Much as you'd have adored all the attention, your voice wasn't quite up to the mark, love,' Mum suddenly piped up. 'A boy chorister is one thing, but I'm afraid when one's voice breaks—'

'I know.' His eyes crinkling, Dad turned to her. 'How about now as an old crooner?'

She laughed. 'No, Clive, sadly not even that.' She squeezed his knee. 'But you're a terrific accountant and I'm very proud of you.'

My ears pricked at my mother's mix of criticism and praise. Dad loved belting out a song, and I knew he'd been a long-haired psychedelic rock fanatic back in the day, but I'd never heard mention of a *chorister* before. The notion that he'd once had musical aptitude was interesting – and encouraging – but it chafed that he didn't make more of an effort to promote mine.

As though reading my thoughts, Mum turned. 'I'm afraid money makes the world go round, Ruth. Dreams are all very well in theory, but one has to be practical. I don't particularly like working in an office, but if we want nice things, it has to be done.' She paused for a few moments. 'A career in the arts takes exceptional talent. Then there's personality, luck and opportunity, let alone the financial wherewithal to pursue it. Few people have all these things, and it ultimately adds up to disappointment.'

Dumbstruck, I stared at the woman who was supposed to love me. She was listing my shortcomings again, personality included. And she'd clearly forgotten that an individual we were visiting had fulfilled her dreams. But I managed to shrug. 'Whatever,' I said, my standard reply.

Dad's eyes caught mine in the mirror. 'Fortunately, our youngest doesn't have to worry about those things yet,' he said. He cleared his throat and grinned. 'And we're on our jolly adventure. I have to confess, I'm rather excited to discover what's in store at Château Les Douves. Just four and a half hours until we hit foreign soil, then we'll be onward bound to seven blissful days of a lifetime!'

–

Entering France was thrilling in itself, but the golden sunshine and shades of green countryside made the third leg of the journey even more pleasurable. Tim had researched our holiday before leaving, so we knew a little of what to expect of Basse Normandie and the stunning château which would be our home for a week. Previous owners of the estate had been traced back as far as the fifteenth century and some records suggested a famous Abbot had once owned it. Dad was thrilled the location was close to the three 'local jewels' of Mont St Michel, Bayeux and the D-Day landing beaches, whereas Tim had been more interested in the accommodation's modern facilities – the complimentary bicycles, the gym and croquet lawn, the tennis courts, spa and swimming pool – all of which he'd eagerly enjoy after slumming it in Europe with a rucksack. Mum was still tutting and shaking her head, torn between delight and disgust at the prospect – and sheer indulgence – of an in-house Le Cordon Bleu trained chef. As for me, I'd discovered the château housed not one, but two grand pianos. Though I'd passed my Grade Eight exam with distinction, I'd never had the luxury of playing one, so my fingers itched at the chance.

I rolled down the car window and inhaled this new world. Mum fell quiet as the rolling scenery passed by and didn't even object to the balmy breeze which ruffled her hair.

Dad broke the silence as the clock approached six. 'Ah, methinks we're here.' He indicated left and drove down a winding, tree-lined drive. Finally bringing the Volvo to a standstill, he gestured ahead. 'Now that's what I call a sight for sore eyes.'

I don't know about my parents, but I simply gaped at the tableau. A stunning manor was set amidst immaculate lawns on one side and woodland the other. My days of princes and princesses were far behind me, but with its white elevations, shuttered windows and Queen Anne tower, it looked like a fairytale castle.

Dad continued his slow approach towards the paved terrace. My heart was already racing with excitement as I absorbed the sheer splendour of the château and its gardens, but it went up a notch when a graceful hand waved at us from beneath a huge parasol. By the time we parked up, the whole of my aunt had appeared. Wearing a wide brimmed hat, large sunglasses and a sarong, she looked the epitome of elegance and style.

Her three crumpled guests fell out of the Volvo. Opening her arms to my mum, she kissed both her cheeks. 'Welcome, dear old comrade! So wonderful you're here at last. Come and sit down; you can worry about the cases later. We expected you sooner, so we've had to top up the ice several times. We're on cocktails.' She smiled her perfect smile. 'Apparently The French 75 was created in the New York bar in Paris in 1915 during World War I.'

She moved on to Dad. 'Hello, handsome. How are you?'

Then finally me. 'My darling guest of honour.' She pecked the top of my head. 'You've grown so tall! I was exceptionally disappointed to miss you on your thirteenth, but you're here now, so we can make up for lost time. In the afternoons, preferably.' She chuckled. 'We were still fast asleep when Tim appeared this morning. I rather got the impression the poor boy hadn't eaten for several days.'

I could feel Mum bristle, but Vanessa took her elbow on one side and mine the other. 'Come and meet my fiancé, ladies. If you don't think he's the most attractive man ever – barring dear Clive, of course – you are commanded to lie!'

We crossed the pristine grass to a man at the canopied table. If his slick hair and cheek bones were anything to go by, Sergio was probably very handsome indeed behind his aviators. But affable, he wasn't.

'Darling, here we have Joy, Clive and our bridesmaid,' Vanessa said.

'*Ciao*,' he replied, barely interrupting the drag of his cigarette. 'Do sit.'

When we'd obeyed his clipped command, he poured what was presumably The French 75 into cocktail glasses and handed them out.

'Now you must excuse me,' he said, his accent rhythmic and alluring despite his moodiness. 'I have work to do.'

Vanessa caught his arm. 'Come back for dinner?'

He flashed a neat smile as white as his shirt. '*Ci proverò.*'

A tingling sensation burned deep in my belly, so I looked away, but I suspected Mum felt the same as she shuffled in her seat and positively trilled when he'd gone.

'As you say, not quite as dashing as my Clive, but not bad.'

Dad raked back his hair and cocked in an eyebrow. 'Quoi, moi?' He squeezed Mum's hand. 'Holiday on,' he said, grinning.

Chapter 9

Absently listening to the adults' chatter, I breathed in the aroma of cut grass and took in my exquisite surroundings.

'Yes, a dip before dinner sounds just the thing to cool us all down,' Dad said to Vanessa, bringing me out of my daydream.

'Really, Clive?'

I rotated to my mother. Her tone was sharp and she was rubbing her arms in that way she did when something was bothering her. Heavens knew what it was because the infinity pool looked so inviting that even I was prepared to reveal my lardy flesh.

But my aunt wasn't picking up on Mum's tense body language. She leaned over and squeezed her hand. 'Oh, let's do, Joy. We can pretend we're still splashing in those ghastly public swimming baths. Remember them?' She turned to me. 'Water safety, surface dives and lifesaving lessons wearing our pyjamas, can you believe. But Joy was by far the strongest swimmer in our class, so I was very lucky to be her partner and be saved every week.'

'Hair,' Dad said, finally rallying. 'Wouldn't do to spoil this *dashing* barnet until after the wedding. But we'll make a pool date for Sunday, eh Ruth?'

I took a breath to reply, but Vanessa's attention had moved on. 'What do you think of the cocktail, sweetie?' she asked me.

'Oh, I haven't...'

Mum's jaw tightened again but Vanessa persisted. 'Go on, you won't know if you like it until you have a little try. This is gin based, so it may seem a tad sour, but we can rustle up something sweeter if it's not to your taste.' She watched me take a sip. 'Hmm. Gin's an acquired taste. I know what you'll enjoy – a Kir Royale. It's champagne with crème de cassis, better known as blackcurrant liqueur. In short, fizzy Ribena with a kick.' She stood and held out her elbow. 'Come on let's explore and we'll make you one up on the way back.'

Feeling Mum's eyes burn my shoulders, I slipped in my arm and we ambled away. I madly searched for something to say, but Vanessa made up for my muteness by guiding me around the estate and giving me a commentary like a tour guide.

'So I gather you like to swim. I loved it as a girl and it pays to be a strong swimmer, especially outdoors. Of course this glorious weather makes it somewhat different to bracing oneself in the North Sea or even a reservoir, but there's something special about inhaling the fresh air, don't you think? Talking of which, let me show you the potager.'

Crossing another sun-bleached terrace, she led me into a walled garden. 'Organic fruit and vegetables. I fancy one of these at home. I rather think I'd be green-fingered given the chance.' She turned and studied me for a second or two. 'What about you? Do you think you'd like a country house with a folly, huge gardens and a vegetable patch one day? Be happy, self-sufficient and live off your own land with your babies and a man you adore?'

I was fourteen; my thoughts didn't progress much further than getting good results at GCSE and then at A level so I could escape to university to study music. 'What's a folly?' I asked.

'Traditionally it's a tower or similar constructed for aesthetic pleasure, one that has no real use. Some people build one as a monument. In my case it's a pavilion and my favourite place for contemplation.'

'It all sounds lovely.'

'Indeed.' She laughed. 'Especially if it includes a handsome spouse!' Raking up her shades like a hairband, she peered at me intently. 'You mustn't think he's rude. It's a question of artistry.

When one has that genius, that calling, one has to follow it. You understand, don't you, Ruth?'

A cold shiver brushed my spine. 'Yes,' I replied. 'Yes, I do.'

For moments she didn't break eye contact. Appearing satisfied, she finally nodded. 'Right, it's time to inspect the rotunda and see if you approve.'

'Great.'

Wondering what the *rotunda* was and why it would need my approval, I took her proffered hand, but it soon became clear when reached the thatched tower.

'This is where I will say my sacred vows with you right behind me on none other than Midsummer's Day.' Her mouth twitched with mischief. 'Traditionally a bridesmaid dressed identically to the bride – the same gown and most importantly the same veil like twins. Then if any evil spirits came to harm or whisk her away, the bridesmaid would act as a matching decoy and confuse the spirits long enough for the bride to become happily married.' She chuckled. 'Another old superstition suggests that if a bridesmaid stumbles, trips or falls during her walk down the aisle, a curse will befall her and she will never marry, but as you'll see it's tiny in here so I won't let that happen.'

Though I knew she was teasing, my anxiety about my role swelled up to new heights. But my aunt continued to speak as she took in the stony facade. 'It isn't officially a chapel but it reminds me of the three Romanesque round churches in Prague. The oldest one dates from the reign of Vratislav II in the second half of the eleventh century, so this isn't quite so ancient, but I thought it would be the perfect romantic setting. It's quite something, don't you think?'

Impressed by her knowledge, I took a breath to give a Tim-like erudite reply, but she hopped up the steps. 'Come in and see what you think.'

I peered around the worn timber door. From Vanessa's folklore, I expected something either spooky or religious, yet it was simply an empty circular space.

'It's somewhat dim with the shutters closed, but just you wait, my darling.' She gestured to the countryside surrounding us. 'There are sixty acres of park and woodlands listed as a *site classé* here, apparently.' Then pointing to a tree in the distance, 'And that rather majestic *Cèdre du Liban* is reputed to have magical powers. Shall we walk to it and make a wish?'

'Yes please.'

We followed the path to the cedar tree, its huge branches seeming to fold us in as we approached.

'Gorgeous, isn't it?' Once in its shade, Vanessa raked back her sunglasses. 'Do you have a wish?' she asked. Before I could speak, she put a finger to my lips. 'Of course you do, but you don't need to say it out loud.'

Her gaze indulgent and shiny, she watched me make my silent prayer, then cupped my face with her palms. 'Oh darling. You are beautiful. You don't know it yet, but you are.'

My throat clogged with emotion, I couldn't reply. But the moment was broken by my aunt's huge smile.

'Goodness, what are we like?' she said, dabbing her eyes. 'Come on, my love. Let's prepare that cocktail.'

Chapter 10

As though waiting for permission, Mum and Dad were staring at their empty glasses when we returned to the garden table.

Vanessa rubbed Mum's shoulder. 'Darling, do help yourself to whatever you fancy. The kitchen is choc-a-block with drinks and goodies, and everything has been paid for, so do fill your boots!' She placed a chilled bottle of champagne and another jug of icy alcohol on the table. 'We've just rustled up this concoction, so let me know what you think. Rum based this time. Or if you'd prefer fizz? Ruth's on Kir Royale, but it's weak, I promise.'

'I'm game for stuffing the old brogues,' Dad said. He turned to Mum. 'What would you like, my dearest wife? Another cocktail or...?' He grinned. 'A rather nice-looking Dom Perignon.'

Her whole demeanour was stiff, but with a clear effort she forced a smile. 'You choose, Clive. I'll have whatever you're having.'

'Excellent,' he replied, doing the honours with the cork. 'Rumour has it Raymond Blanc is popping by to cook our dinner.'

Vanessa chuckled. 'As it happens I've had the delight of being fed by Raymond, but André Maher's cuisine is of that standard.' She squinted in thought. 'Nope, I can't remember tonight's delicacies, but I can share the wedding menu if you keep it under your hat.'

'One moment,' Dad replied. He scooped up Sergio's abandoned straw fedora and placed it at a rakish angle on his head. 'What do you think, kiddo?' he asked me.

'Looks good, Dad.'

'Excellent.' He reverted to our hostess. 'Do tell; I'm all ears.'

'So we're having *langoustine dans un jus crémeux herbacé au safran, bœuf d'ici, Foie Gras, jus moelle & réduction.* Then *a tout chocolat en mousse soufflée, tuile et guimauve.*'

'It sounds delicious.' He theatrically cupped his mouth. 'Hmm, where's Tim to translate when you need him?'

'He and his friend were playing tennis earlier. Then they went off on bikes with a selection of goodies to picnic on.' Vanessa glanced at her watch. 'They promised to be back for dinner, so they're probably already—'

'Sorry?' Mum suddenly animated. '*They?*'

'Yes, Tim turned up with a friend. Rav, Jav, Mav? Some three-letter name. But he's a delight, they both are.' She wafted a graceful arm. 'Seems the travelling group have temporarily split, some wanting sea and sand, others culture. And it isn't a problem at all. We have plenty of everything, including bedrooms.'

Inviting someone to gatecrash wasn't something the Parkers would do, and most certainly not at an occasion like this. Even Dad appeared surprised at Tim's temerity. 'That's very kind of you, Vanessa. Thank you.'

'You're welcome.' She peered at Mum. 'It's really fine, Joy. The more the merrier. Yes?'

Her cheeks colouring, Mum dipped her head in acknowledgment. Part of me was glad that my brother had fallen from his golden boy status, but I could see she felt humiliated and I felt sorry for her. With a fixed smile she bravely stayed for another fifteen minutes, then she pulled back her chair.

'I'll just nip to the loo.' She looked at Dad meaningfully. 'Then when I return, perhaps we can unpack the car and get refreshed for dinner.'

Vanessa nodded. 'Quite right. Time is ticking. I'll show you to your room when you're back. The toilet is—'

'No worries. I'll find it.'

Falling silent, the three of us watched Mum walk away. Dad cleared his throat. 'Vanessa,' he began, his tone unusually serious.

'Yes, Clive?'

Anticipating an eloquent apology for Tim, I waited for him to say more, but he frowned thoughtfully and tapped the table top. 'I'm not sure if you know, but Ruth's a talented musician.'

My entire being tensed at the mention of my name, let alone the word 'talented'.

'Both Joy and I think she's still too young to venture from home just yet. But when she reaches eighteen, I want her to follow her dreams.' His gaze intent, he turned to me. 'I'm reading between the lines, love, but I'm guessing that will involve you studying music somewhere in London. Either university or music college?'

Breath stuck in my chest, I nodded.

He reverted to our hostess and smiled wryly. 'I know I'm mentioning this somewhat ahead of time, but you tend to be… well, somewhat elusive.'

Vanessa laughed. 'Fair point.'

'So if my Ruth does follow her dreams and goes to London, will you look out for her?'

'Well, that's an easy promise. I can't think of anything nicer, so I'd be absolutely delighted to do just that.' She took my hand and smiled. 'Excellent. London it is, then.'

Chapter 11

To both mine and Dad's surprise, Mum had ended up buying both outfits from the wedding boutique, and she wore the fitted dress for dinner that evening. Completely transformed from her earlier vexation, she looked truly resplendent. Though there were only twelve places set around the long dining table, so perhaps not the huge celebrity event she'd hoped for, she donned a Vanessa-like beam and graciously introduced herself to everyone, including an attractive man and woman, who turned out to be Sergio's parents.

'Good evening. I'm Joy Parker and this is my husband, Clive,' she said, holding out her slim hand and carefully enunciating her words. 'We've been friends with Vanessa for many years. Timothy and Ruth are our children.'

In fairness to her, the pair did have a bewildered demeanour about them which Mum had clearly interpreted as a struggle with the lingo, but Tim had other ideas.

'For God's sake, they're not idiots,' he hissed in my ear. 'Me and Rav played doubles with them earlier and their command of English is as good as mine.' He raised his eyebrows. 'I think they're a little gobsmacked by their son's union tomorrow. It seems they've only just met the... How should I put it? The less-than-spring-chicken bride. I still haven't seen the groom up close yet, but those two look around the same age as Mum and Dad. I'm intrigued about their attraction, aren't you? Geronto-philia, do you think?' He glanced at the mother. 'Or perhaps an Oedipus complex.'

The couple were probably in their late fifties, but wearing exceptionally well. With their chiselled features, dark gaze and glossy black hair, they looked much like their son. Well, from what little of him I had glimpsed, at least.

I eyed up my brother. I was curious about the backstory too, and if anyone could get to the nub of a mystery, it was him. But his tone was a little too waspish for my liking. Vanessa was beautiful, personable and intelligent; an acclaimed multilingual-speaking actor too. Why shouldn't she marry a younger man? If it was the other way around, no one would bat an eyelid.

'Maybe you should sit next to Sergio at the meal and have a good old gawp. Even better, subject him to your incisive psychoanalysis,' I said.

'Oops, touched a nerve, did I?' He sniggered. 'Your crush is still going strong, then.'

It was true, but not in the way he was suggesting. Yes, I did admire Vanessa enormously; indeed my wish beneath the cedar tree had been to replicate her one day, even in some small way. Yet it was more than just her physical attributes. My aunt had touched me like no one else had; she'd noticed me and made me feel special; she'd chosen me to be her sole bridesmaid, for goodness' sake. But there was no point trying to explain it to the boy who turned everything he touched to gold.

Mum was now amiably chatting to Rav, so I lowered my voice. 'If I'd invited someone home for tea without asking first, I'd be in huge trouble and in the doghouse for weeks. You flaming turn up with a friend at a posh wedding in France, and all is immediately forgiven.'

'We don't have a dog.'

'We don't need one; she has me to kick.' I shook my head. 'Rav has gatecrashed, basically. And you've got away with it.'

Tim laughed. 'I did get a bit of a mouthful as it happens, but I soon smoothed it over.'

'God, you're as bad as Dad. What did you say?'

'True friendship, allegiance and the like. That honour dictated I couldn't just abandon a mate.'

'And she fell for that?'

'She did actually.' He studied Mum for a few beats. 'She doesn't always show it, but I reckon her bond, love or whatever, runs deep.'

'To Vanessa?'

'Yeah. Strange, isn't it? A dark, dreadful secret from the past is my guess.'

'Haha, very funny,' I answered. Yet his off-the-cuff comment was certainly food for thought.

'Then I doled on a few compliments. You know – that Mum was looking great – just as good as her old pal.'

'You're a complete creep.'

'It's true, though. Mum's certainly the more natural beauty of the two.'

Surprised at his comment, I looked from her to Vanessa. It was true that our mother's appearance was more classical and refined, but on the glamour and sexiness side, there was no comparison. It felt disloyal to say that out loud, so I edged towards the waitress and had my flute topped up with champagne whilst Mum's attention was elsewhere.

'So who else is joining us for dinner?' I asked when I shuffled back to my brother's side. 'It'll be your fault if Rav takes the numbers to thirteen.'

'Triskaidekaphobia, you mean?'

'Exactly,' I replied. 'Then he'd be our very own Judas Iscariot.'

'Betrayal in Garden of Gethsemane? Or should I say, perfidy in the parkland of Château Les Douves. Nope, no fear of that or superstitions tonight; Vanessa's father can't make it, apparently. He's ill or similar.'

'Really? She has a father?' I had no idea why I was shocked. Perhaps because I'd assumed Vanessa came from a cosmic egg like Tim.

'It seems so. You know, like most mortals.'

A bell rang and our hostess cleared her throat. 'I think that's a sign for us to take our seats.' She glanced through the double doors. 'No Sergio tonight, it seems,' she said lightly. Her face lit when a hunched, older couple shuffled in. 'But here are lovely Eleonora and Francesco.' A pretty teenager caught them up. 'And Isabella too.'

She took each of their hands and exchanged a few words in Italian, then she turned to her guests with a chuckle. 'We can all relax! Sergio's grandparents say he will definitely be at the chapel tomorrow.' Though she beamed, I sensed worry behind it. 'And as you'll all know, any good Italian boy does exactly what his *Nonni* tells him to.'

Chapter 12

The dawn chorus woke me early the next morning, a cacophony of bird song which was gorgeous to doze to until it was interrupted by a sudden, loud screech. Weak sunshine was pushing its way through the shutters, so my imagination didn't go too wild. Sure, we were in the middle of nowhere, apparently without locks on the bedroom doors, but a murder at this hour seemed unlikely, so I prised open my sleepy eyes and padded over to the window. To my delight, a magnificent peacock was boldly strutting around the paved terrace.

All fingers and thumbs, I quickly took several snaps with my iPhone, but the blues and greens were so glorious that I felt compelled to share the moment with someone. Who else but my brother? He was in the next suite, and though he'd be mildly irked at being disturbed so early, he'd shrug and soon go back to sleep.

Still tingling with pleasure, I crept along the wood-panelled corridor, turned his ceramic handle and peered into the gloom. 'Tim? Are you awake? There's an amazing peacock outside. Come and have a quick look, then you can—'

Realisation struck me a moment too late. There wasn't just one person in the huge divan; there were clearly two. 'So sorry,' I muttered, quickly backtracking and closing the door.

Once I'd scuttled to my room, I covered my burning cheeks with a pillow. Oh my God, that was embarrassing. And did I really see what I thought I just saw? The erotic scene flashed in. Yes, two intertwined bodies beneath the crumpled sheets. But the visitor wasn't a waitress or a maid as I might have supposed; it was Rav.

Bloody hell! He'd been allocated a room of his own, so there was only one reason he'd be sharing with Tim. And that musty aroma of sweat and… I groaned out loud at my embarrassing faux pas. Sex; they'd clearly had sex, which meant my brother was gay or bi or at least sexually fluid. Yet was it really a surprise? Tim had never had a girlfriend or shown any interest in girls; his observation of women was purely descriptive or analytical, clinical almost. He couldn't see Vanessa's charisma, for God's sake!

I mulled for a while. It all made sense: the 'mates' he'd hung out with whose names I didn't recognise; the way he and Rav were so easy in each other's company; their tactile friendship over the preceding few months; their frequent glances and smiles.

When the shock had finally passed, I allowed myself some air and chuckled. The affair was actually romantic. I liked the blend of illicitness and secrecy, the boldness and tenderness of Tim inviting his love to this place of luxury. And a wedding, no less! Then another thought hit me: how would Mum take the news? Tim was her perfect son, the boy who walked a straight line and ticked all the proud parent boxes. She clearly had no inkling that Tim was gay. Or if she had, she was in denial; she'd swapped seats with him at dinner so he'd be next to Isabella, Sergio's stunning niece. And it wasn't the first time she'd tried to matchmake him with pretty young women she considered eligible.

I blew out long and hard. For once it wasn't my problem or fault; I wouldn't tell anyone; I'd keep my head down and worry about it if I had to. And anyway, I had more immediate concerns. Today was the day I had to wear *that* flaming dress.

—

With no prospect of more sleep, I eventually slipped from the mattress, showered and donned shorts. I hadn't had the opportunity of exploring the château's interior, so now was my chance.

The tits and sparrows still chattering outside, I pushed away thoughts of what I'd seen in Tim's bedroom and crept burglar-like past the closed doors, then down the elegant staircase to the floor below. Inhaling each flavour, I stepped into salons and solars I hadn't yet seen and absorbed each handsome setting. I wasn't usually moved by decor and furnishings, but I admired the pale sideboard and stripy chaise longue in one sitting room and shielded my eyes against the unforgiving red wallpaper in another. Finding my way to the tower, I hopped up the steps and discovered it was lined with books in every language. I was tempted to pull out a few glossy tomes to flick through, but art or architecture wasn't what I was searching for today. I finally found that in a bright and stately parlour at the far end of the house.

The double doorway was open, so I spent a few seconds on the threshold, staring in awe. Admittedly I wasn't an expert by any means, but I was certain the magnificent Steinway was a former concert grand piano. Creeping in closer, I peered at its fluted legs and filigree music desk. Taking in the eighty-eight-note keyboard and three-pedal lyre, I beamed with sheer pleasure. Yes, in my imagination at least, this beautiful rose-wood instrument was once the preferred choice of a superlative pianist.

I gingerly ran my finger along the polished wood, then perched on the leather stool, reached for the pedals and spread my hands. Would I press down the keys? Dare I, even using the una corda lever? But a rustling sound broke the mesmerising moment, followed by deep sigh. Oh hell, someone else was in the room. Slowly lifting my head, I met a pair of dark eyes. Still wearing yesterday's white shirt, his hair wild and chin stubbly, Sergio was on the chintz sofa and staring right through me.

Starstruck in his presence, yet mortified by my intrusion, I struggled to my feet. 'Gosh, I'm so sorry. I didn't realise anyone was—'

From the scatter of parchment paper and pencils surrounding his feet, I gathered he'd been working in here. This end of the building comprised a series of French windows, so from a light perspective it made sense. Yet it was only six thirty in the morning and his face was scored with pale purple strokes of tiredness. Perhaps he'd been napping, but I guessed he hadn't gone to bed.

His focus returning, he cleared his throat. 'You are—?'

'Ruth Parker.' Then tentatively, 'I'm Vanessa's bridesmaid?'

'Ah si.' Realisation apparently dawning, he smacked his head. 'The wedding is today.'

Not sure whether it was a question or a statement, I nodded.

He bounded to his feet. 'Merda!' Then raking his fringe, 'I must go to her immediately.' He gestured to the mess on the floor. 'Can you—?'

'Tidy up?' In that moment I felt ridiculously grown up. 'Yes of course I can. You go to your bride.'

He looked around distractedly for a further moment, then came back to me with an expression I couldn't quite interpret. Bewilderment? Desperation? Finally sighing, he lifted his arms and left.

My heart still thrashing, I knelt down to collect the abandoned artwork. Some of the sketches were shredded – from frustration, I supposed – whilst others were only torn into a few pieces, but I didn't need to study them to identify his muse.

Both joy and relief spread through me. From his absence at dinner and Vanessa's forced smile, I had worried that Sergio didn't truly love her, that he was a user, a gold digger or after fame on her shirt tails. But the certainty was hot and solid in my chest: this was a man who deeply adored his fiancé.

—

I took the drawings to my room and pieced them together on the floor until my aunt was whole again.

As if a little drunk, I felt lightheaded and giddy. The brief encounter with Sergio had been fortuitous – I already knew I'd been chosen by Vanessa, but here was a reason. For the last few years, she'd been in the background like a guardian angel, and though I'd rarely seen her in person, she'd been there for me, especially at low moments when I'd felt so unloved. Today I had returned the favour; I'd intervened at a seminal moment and sent Sergio back to her.

I pictured her too-bright demeanour at dinner. Yes, like the artwork before me, I'd patched up something that could have been smashed. And today I'd be her maid of honour, an integral part of the triangle again.

Mum's words from last night filtered in. 'Tomorrow is a special day for you as well as Vanessa, love. Did you remember to hang up the dress? Creases will spoil it.'

I'd nodded my lie, but I'd been touched too. Maybe it was the effect of the steady flow of champagne, but it was the first time Mum had acknowledged my special part of today. She'd seemed to be enjoying herself too, pink-cheeked and smiley as she'd chatted to Sergio's family, complimented the chef, held Dad's hand. At some point she'd leaned over to me and whispered, 'I believe there are two pianos here. I know Dad would love to hear you play. Perhaps we could surprise him.'

Her happiness had made me feel happy too.

Making up for my omission, I opened my wedding box, pulled out the silky fabric and stood on tiptoes to hook the padded hanger on the side of the wardrobe. It was more an evening affair than a traditional bridesmaid's gown, but I could clearly picture Vanessa in her grown-up version – curvaceous in all the right places but toned in the others, her slim, elegant arms and shapely legs made even longer by the highest of heels. And what about her glorious red tresses? Would she wear them up or down?

I lifted my own hair in the mirror. It had once been flaxen-white, but was now decidedly mousy. Was my aunt right? Was I beautiful? I snorted wryly. If I was, it was very deeply hidden. Mum had suggested a few curls around my cheeks 'to soften your angular features'. That had felt ironic; my face was the only part of me that was actually skinny. Still, my shoulders were slightly glowing from yesterday's sunshine and my blue eyes sparkled from my sense of contentment and pride. People said that real beauty came from within. Was there something in my reflection that hinted it could really be true?

Chapter 13

Images of what I'd witnessed in Tim's bedroom edged in again, so I was relieved to be distracted by my rumbling stomach. As she bid her guests good night, Vanessa had announced there'd be a champagne brunch at noon before the wedding service at three, but I knew I'd expire if I didn't eat something before then, so I made my way to the kitchen and furtively opened a few cupboards a crack.

'Can I help you to breakfast?'

I jolted around to the maid-cum-waitress from last night. She was holding an armful of white and pink freesias, and now I looked at her properly, she was older than I had thought, maybe around Mum's age.

'Sorry I took you by surprise. I am Claudette, the house-keeper. If there is anything I can get for you, you only need ask.' She gestured to a handsome range. 'Many of our English guests like a cooked breakfast so I'm happy to oblige.'

'Oh, no thank you.'

Her eyes crinkled. 'Sylvie – my daughter – isn't keen either. What do you like to eat? Perhaps a pastry?'

A tempting croissant or a pancake made my mouth water, but the thought of my belly protruding from the unforgiving silky material of my dress put paid to that. 'Maybe fruit or something from the fridge?'

'Of course. Help yourself. I will leave you to it.'

'Thank you.'

The first yoghurt made no impact, so I ate another two, quickly disposing of the evidence when I heard the creak of movement and voices from the landing above. I considered returning to my room, or even searching out the second grand piano, but I was on holiday in glorious Normandy for goodness' sake, a few photographs for Facebook was the thing.

It was already quite warm outside, the sunshine beaming down from a cloud-free blue sky. What a perfect day for a wedding it was! But my delight for Vanessa was swiftly replaced by worry. I was relying on the Bolero-cum-cardigan to cover my arms and spotty back. Would I be too hot? Mum had bought me some 'miracle cream', so the acne wasn't as bad as it had been, but my skin was far from blemish-free. Should I sod it and go for full shoulder exposure? Well, that wasn't an option, even though I'd be red-faced and disgustingly sweaty.

The breeze soft on my cheeks, I laughed my ridiculous conceit. No one would be looking at me, and besides Vanessa had mentioned the chapel might be cool. I could check it out now, so all was good.

Contemplating if I'd really be bold enough to sit at the Steinway and perform a small recital, I hummed Bach's *Prelude and Fugue in A minor* and ambled down the privet-lined path to the rotunda. As though welcoming me, the door was open this time, so I climbed the steps and peered in. A gasp of astonishment and pleasure escaped from my lips. The shutters were now open, allowing in shafts of sunlight and air; tied back by pretty posies, voile curtains decorated the stone walls, and six or so benches were covered in crisp linen with matching bouquets each end. Interspersed with flowers the pale pink of my dress, the white scene was simple but sophisticated, and undoubtedly romantic.

A fan of Orders of Service was displayed on a side table. Not wanting to disturb the artful array, I leaned closer to inspect the happy couple on the front. I knew Tim would think it naff and make a sardonic comment about the image being more suitable for a funeral than a wedding, but it had captured a moment. Her smile broad but natural, the bride was facing the camera, but the groom was looking at her.

The clear adoration in his gaze brought a burn to my nose. I was astonishingly part of all this... well, this *fantasy* was the best word I could think of to describe the heavenly surroundings and beauty and joy.

The patter of voices and crunch of pebbles outside broke the spell, so I moved further in and tried to get a handle on my childish snivelling.

I sharply inhaled. God, crying! I hadn't thought of that. Mum had bought me a cute satin clutch bag to match my wedding shoes. 'For a naked lip gloss,' she'd said to my surprise. But I'd definitely add a wad of tissues and a small mirror in there. And maybe not risk wearing mascara after the last disaster.

I chuckled to myself. Talk about first world problems.

The sound of footsteps approached, so I stilled and held my breath. Would Claudette burst in and tell me off? But whoever it was walked on by, so after a few minutes I stepped out of the shadows and rubbed the goosebumps from my arms. Vanessa was spot on; it was a little chilly in there.

Once again in bright daylight, I reverted to my musical thoughts. If I was to play something for Dad I'd need to practice it first. What piece did I know by heart? Absently warbling to myself, I strolled towards the 'magical' cedar, but when I got closer I stopped and squinted at the scene. From the marks on the grass it was apparent that someone had dragged over a chair from the kitchen. To climb the tree? To make a wish? But why was the seat on its side?

My mind was tortuously slow as I stared. No. No, it couldn't be. But a sixth sense and movement told me otherwise. I snapped up my head to the branches above. A twitching body; a rope and a ligature; a white shirt and dark hair... Immediately picturing the man's desperate glance in the salon earlier, I hurtled towards him.

Chapter 14

Sheer adrenaline took over. With a strength and determination I hadn't known I possessed, I belted to the chair, propped it upright and climbed on. Wrapping my arms around Sergio's legs, I pushed him up as high as I could and hollered for help.

Several events seemed to happen in at once. Claudette emerged from a shed, took one glance and vanished again. Moments later she reappeared with a pair of garden shears, ran over to me and cut the rope. The next thing I knew I had thumped to the ground, horribly winded and blinded and unable to move. Time stood still. The sheerest panic consumed me. This was the end. I was paralysed, even dead. Then sound filtered through and reality hit. I was trapped by the weight of Sergio's body. Just when I thought I couldn't cope a moment longer, hands prised him off me, and when I finally found the strength to raise my throbbing head, Claudette was performing CPR, and a distressed teenager was on her mobile.

Severely shaking from the shock, I went to suck in some air, but my lungs wouldn't work and the sharpest pain seared through my chest. I'd clearly damaged something badly inside, perhaps ruptured my heart. Would the life seep out of me? Too frightened to move, I squeezed my eyes shut and tried to battle the darkness closing in like a curtain.

A gentle hand on my shoulder and a voice brought me round. With a huge effort, I focused on the person peering at me. It was the girl on the phone, her gaze teary and concerned. '*Est-ce que ça va?*'

I attempted to form words. No, I wasn't OK. Something dreadful had happened on this perfect day, my chest was on fire and I was struggling to breathe. Was Sergio dead? Was it my fault? Tears seeped from my eyes. Where was my mum? I wanted my mum.

As though she'd heard my silent plea, the sound of her voice pierced the low chatter surrounding me. But instead of gentle murmurs of comfort and assurance, her tone was shrill, hysterical.

'I knew there was something going on yesterday, Clive. Oh Lord, what did she tell her?' Then her shadow was above me, her features distorted with anger. 'What did you say to him, Ruth? What have you done?'

Despite my stupor, devastating hurt stabbed me, deep in my soul. In my moment of need I had longed for this woman's tenderness; I'd stupidly thought I'd get it. But she couldn't bring herself to love me, not even now in my frightened and debilitated state.

'I... I don't know...' My throat was bone dry; I could barely speak.

But Mum was pushing a scrap of paper at me. 'This... I wish... I wish you'd never—'

Dad's drawn face replaced hers. He crouched down and gently pulled the hair from my cheeks. 'She's just upset, love. Whatever has happened, you're not to blame. Are you hurt? Shall I help you up?'

Perplexed by his comment, I gaped at his wet, hollow eyes. It was tragic and unbearable for Vanessa, especially on her wedding day, but why on earth would he be this upset for...?

Icy realisation seeped through me. Mum's hysterics; Dad's horror. I'd raced to help a dark-haired figure who I'd assumed was Sergio, but on reflection the legs I'd encircled were longer and broader than his.

'It was *Tim*?' I managed.

A painful bout of coughing took over. When I looked at my palm, it was spattered by blood.

I don't know how long I lay prone and stared at the deceitful blue sky. Once he'd realised I was bleeding, Dad wouldn't let me move and made urgent arrangements for a second ambulance. Though the French girl sat beside me and tried to offer halting words of comfort, none of the adults saw fit to tell me anything, so I strained to hear what I could — the sound of a siren and approaching vehicles, brisk footfall, a mix of urgent commands and exchanges.

Conversation filtered through the thudding in my ears.

'He has oxygen in the ambulance now.'

'Still unconscious but breathing.'

'The first twenty-four hours will be critical.'

'What does that mean?'

'This is a danger period for him. Very serious.'

'Oh my God, oh Lord.'

'But you said he was breathing. Please tell me he'll live.'

'One cannot know.'

'I am hopeful of life, as you say, but please understand that does not mean the same thing as recovery.'

'I don't understand what you're saying.'

'Survivors of suicidal hanging have… *variable* neurological outcomes.'

'Variable?'

'What exactly does that mean?'

'From complete recovery to irreversible brain damage and everything in between.'

'Oh Lord.'

'Please know that some patients stay in a coma and never regain consciousness, I'm afraid.'

Chapter 15

I never did get to wear the bridesmaid's dress and Bolero jacket, nor play that beautiful grand piano. Though my injuries weren't life threatening and nothing compared with Tim's, I sustained two broken ribs, a pneumothorax and a fractured left wrist.

My lung had been punctured and a large portion collapsed, so a tube was inserted into my chest and I had to stay in hospital for several days. Tim was in the same building on a psychiatric ward, and Mum remained by his side, but Dad split his time between his two children.

On the afternoon of second day, he reported with a wobbly smile that Tim had regained consciousness. So very weary and tired, he appeared to have aged ten years.

'Your brother had what they call "retrograde amnesia" when he woke, so he couldn't remember the act of...' He cleared his throat. 'When the doctor asked why he was here, he listed appendicitis, tonsillitis or sepsis as possibilities.' He blinked away his threatening tears. 'Only when I carefully explained he'd tried to... to take his own life did he believe it. But the rest of his memory seems to be fairly normal, so that's a good thing.'

I cried too. Since discovering who'd been hanging from the cedar tree, it felt as though a tap had been yanked on, and though I tried to turn it off, I just couldn't, not even when Claudette and her daughter, Sylvie, popped their heads around the curtain to bring me daily treats.

'That's so great,' I managed eventually. 'It's amazing news.'

'Yes.' Dad stroked his chin, then took a deep breath. 'The note?' he said. 'We haven't raised it with Tim – that would be inappropriate – but of course Mum needs to know what it said.'

A fork of electricity ricocheted through my torso from my sudden movement. 'What note?'

'Mum… gave… it to you when we were waiting for the ambulance? We haven't seen it since.' His tone was apologetic. 'We'd quickly read it, of course, but… Well, as I say, your mum needs to know what it meant.'

I frowned. Mum. My loving mother who hadn't yet bothered to visit me and check how I was. I could clearly picture her warped, scowling face beneath the cedar; indeed, it was a vision I'd never forget. And I did remember her throwing a scrap of paper at me, but I'd assumed it was connected to my stash of Sergio's torn sketches.

'I don't understand, Dad.'

His voice cracked. 'It was Tim's… goodbye note.'

A *suicide* letter? 'Oh my God. What did it say?'

'Only a couple of hurried phrases as I recall. Something about truth and shame. That you'd discovered it and would explain.'

I carefully lowered myself against the pillow and mulled on what Dad had just said. Whilst I was lost in romance and fantasy in the chapel, Tim had written to our parents, gone down to the kitchen, dragged a chair across to the tree, attached a rope to a sturdy branch and tried to kill himself. Of course I knew it already, but this news made my brother's actions real, devastatingly real. And now I knew the reason for them.

My brain seemed to rattle in my skull. My feelings were so confused, I couldn't hold onto any one of them for long. There was deep guilt for blithely barging into Tim's room that morning; sorrow he'd been so unhappy; alarm for not having noticed; frustration he'd done something so extreme. But mainly there was anger: why hadn't he trusted me to keep his secret? He was three years my senior, yet he'd dumped the responsibility of explaining it to our parents on me.

Then there was my mother. Dad hadn't given her the opportunity to say the words '*I wish you'd never been born*', yet they'd hung in the air like mustard gas. I finally had an explanation for her knee-jerk reaction, but it wasn't and would never be forgivable. And even now it was all about *her* bloody needs.

Dad was patiently waiting, but I couldn't give him the answer he needed. I hadn't had an opportunity to talk to Tim. When he'd written his note he'd expected to die. What did he want my parents to know about his sexuality? It was his call.

'I'm sorry, Dad; it's up to Tim to tell you if he wants to.'

'Understood. We have the first twenty-four hours under our belt, so we're heading in the right direction. Hope and prayers going forward, eh?'

'I thought he was fine now.' My heart clenched at Dad's grave expression. 'What do you mean?'

'It seems that survival from hanging is only the beginning.' He sighed. 'There are often complications, love. You know, neurological consequences that only become apparent as time goes on.' He squeezed my good hand. 'If it hadn't been for you acting so swiftly, then Claudette's CPR and the swift response of the emergency services... Well, without that vigorous and prompt resuscitation, Tim wouldn't be with us at all.'

My throat as dry as sandpaper, I pictured the scene in Tim's suite. Two naked bodies affectionately intertwined. Then Rav's stunned expression when he clocked I was there. In truth, without me, it would never have happened in the first place. That was something I'd have to live with forever.

Chapter 16

Back in Manchester, the summer trundled on. Tim's 'incident' was never mentioned, nor was our stay in France. From Mum's swift return of her wedding attire to the retailers and her donation of worn items to charity, I gathered Vanessa was now a *persona non grata*. Why my poor aunt was to blame, I had no idea, but my mother seemed to think that she, aided and abetted by me, had personally arranged the blight on our family.

Me and Mum rubbed shoulders day in and day out as usual, but despite my plaster cast being plain to see, she resolutely ignored it and acted as though I hadn't suffered any injury. I understood that part of her angst was frustration – neither of her offspring had spilled the beans about whatever the note had meant. As though willpower could make me relent, she glared at me frequently in lieu of speech, but I didn't much care; it wasn't my secret to tell and I was the child who should never have been born.

Tim and his recovery was everyone's priority. This was rightly so, yet it didn't stop my frequent self-analysis and pity. In the build up to France, and during the short period I was there, I'd felt myself crawl out of my dim shell and into the sunlight. Now I'd returned to that lonely place, more introspective than ever. It wasn't helped by my struggle to sleep at night. My physical injuries were still painful, and when I finally dropped off, the mental impact took over, forcing me to relive the trauma of that midsummer's morning: emerging from the rotunda to the smell of cut grass, the sun brushing my shoulders as I hummed a tune and ambled to the cedar. Then spotting the fallen chair. That was when dread spread in my stomach like acid. I knew exactly what was coming, but not who. Sometimes it was Sergio, other times Vanessa or Dad. Or someone famous, or from school, or even a stranger. Mostly I was able to reach the twitching, jerking body, but occasionally my fingers fumbled so badly that I couldn't force them to work, or the seat wouldn't righten or an invisible force pulled me back. But the ending was always the same: that stunning blow to my chest, the agony and fear and inability to speak, let alone inhale. And me inwardly screaming: '*Help me. I'm injured too. It really, really hurts. Why haven't you noticed? Why does nobody care?*'

That nobody cared wasn't strictly true. My dad didn't broach my inner feelings, but his soft gaze showed concern and he asked about my wrist and ribs when Mum was out of earshot. His weakness disappointed me no end. Why would he think Mum needed his love more than I did? But at least there was Sylvie. My new friend was the one silver lining from that darkest of clouds. She'd been the first person to worry about *me*, the one who'd stayed by my side and tried to chat in her hesitant English. She'd been the first to bring a gift to my hospital bedside, the first to make me smile. Even better than that, at just one year older than me, she was someone I could talk to, a teenager who understood me and made me laugh, despite our language difference.

Our friendship blossomed by FaceTime and text, and though our conversations were halting at times, our self-styled Pictionary and Google translate helped enormously.

'Why did your mother shout at you when you were lying on the grass?' she asked at some point. 'It was so mean of her. Me and my mum were really shocked.'

That was a query which loitered at the back of my mind. The note Tim had written was clearly about his homosexuality, but Mum's reaction had indeed been truly shocking. What exactly had she said as she spat out her angst? That something had been going on the day before. Maybe that was a reference to Tim and Rav's friendship, but she'd also said 'what did *she* tell her?'

There was only one 'she', and that was Vanessa.

Chapter 17

As autumn approached, Tim didn't give two hoots about me or anyone else. How could he when he didn't give any for himself? Though the medics thought he'd made a remarkable recovery in terms of their scans and physical examinations, his disposition changed and he became a shadow of himself. He increasingly withdrew to his bedroom to sleep or play computer games; he only responded to my attempts to chivvy or chat in monosyllables, and he neglected his personal hygiene.

It drove Mum to distraction. 'The doctors don't always give the correct diagnosis,' she said repeatedly to Dad. 'I think we should get a second opinion. He clearly has damage they haven't detected. Perhaps it's a condition they could cure with surgery. We have to do something, Clive, and soon. It's his A level year, for goodness' sake. He's already missed several vital weeks of study. What about his plans for university?'

Dad was careful with his reply. 'Maybe you're right, love, but we've been told that every brain injury is unique and that his personality may change in the short term, and possibly for longer, so we just have to be patient.'

'Well, that isn't good enough, Clive. I think we must—'

'Joy, listen. Irrespective of, or because of what happened in the summer, Tim's clearly down, unhappy, depressed. Until he's willing to acknowledge it and talk to the therapist, or indeed anyone, there's not a lot we can do. There's no magical remedy, I'm afraid. It isn't something we can rush, so we need to support him and be here when he's ready. Yes?'

Patience was not my mother's strong point, and in fairness it wasn't mine either. I hated being stuck in this frigid house, yet I had to wait for another three years before escape to university was in my sights. Thank goodness I had Sylvie to talk to; she was a disenchanted teenager herself and she'd been there when the unmentionable had happened, so I could complain as lavishly and honestly as I liked without being judged.

Though my aunt had been airbrushed from our lives, she was often in my thoughts. The château and chapel were indelibly tarnished, but I still kept Sergio's drawings beneath my mattress and carried a nugget of that fantasy in my heart. The moment Tim and I were discharged from the Normandy hospital, Dad had driven the tattered Parker family straight back to the UK, so we didn't say goodbye to the bride or the groom. I gleaned from Sylvie that the wedding was cancelled and the guests soon dispersed, but I had no idea if Vanessa and Sergio had later married. She intermittently made contact by text, sweetly enquiring how I was, but it didn't feel appropriate to ask. Sometimes I composed long replies explaining my sheer unhappiness, but by the time I had perfected what I really wanted to say, the moment had gone. Besides, her messages felt more like pearls of wisdom rather than a conversation warranting a response. In one she said:

> I know it isn't easy to communicate with someone who won't talk back when you desperately need it; I also understand it hurts when you feel wrongly blamed, but you have to keep trying.

Whether she meant my brother or my mother, I didn't know, but Mum was an adult and I was a child; she *was* the person I was yelling at in my dreams. As for Tim, my guilt was like a heavy cloak I wore every hour, every day, everywhere. My role in the whole mess had been unintentional, but I was inextricably

involved. I would *keep trying*, and despite the Parker's taboo
ways, I knew we'd have to address that dark day.

–

As winter set in, my life carried on as usual on the surface. I rose
at seven forty-five, plaited my ponytail and donned my blazer,
grabbed my lunch box and a banana, then made my way to
school with my head down. Most of the other kids congregated
en route and ambled in groups, gossiping, jostling and laughing.
I walked alone, blocking out the world by inserting earphones
and listening to music.

But my solitude was fine, even a relief. Fuelled by excitement
at the end of last term, I'd found myself bragging about my trip
to France. It was only a little – I was my parents' daughter, after
all – but I'd told a few people about our connection with a
celebrity, and the invitation to her wedding at a château. I was
now fearful – terrified, in fact – that someone would ask me
about it. How on earth would I reply? And what if word got
out about Tim and the unmentionable? I had no idea how I'd
handle it. Cry? Scream? Run away? Because my family never
discussed what had happened in the summer, it felt as though
a flannel had been stuffed in my mouth, then shoved down my
throat. The gag was now lodged high in my chest, a constant
ball of anxiety which sometimes stopped me from breathing.
When that occurred, I had to bolt outside or to a toilet cubicle
and talk myself round until the panic subsided. There had only
been two episodes during lessons so far, but the pupils who
hadn't already thought I was weird certainly did now.

I continued my daily attempts to connect with Tim after
school. I'd make two mugs of tea, climb the stairs to his
bedroom and knock on the door. At first I'd retreated when
he didn't reply, but after a couple of weeks, I went right on in,
yanked open the curtains and thumped down next to him on
the bed.

His mental and physical state was variable. Sometimes his pale face was lit by his phone or laptop, and there was evidence he'd opened a book or made himself a sandwich, but mostly he was beneath his duvet and the cooked breakfast Mum had made him hours before remained untouched.

I tried to focus on Vanessa's advice, blathering about something and nothing – the series I was watching on TV, the latest novel I'd finished, a new band or classical composer I'd discovered – but it wasn't easy with so little going on in my own life, and I became increasingly tetchy with his lack of response. I'd open the window even though it was freezing, tell him he stank and to get a shower, said he was bloody boring. Though I managed to hold back the word 'selfish', it was always on the tip of my tongue because that's exactly how I felt. Sure, I'd blithely entered that château bedroom without respecting his privacy, but the rest of it was on him. He'd coolly collected a chair and a rope, he'd made a noose and hung it around his own neck. I understood he must have been in a dark, desperate place and that he couldn't help the resulting fallout or his current condition, but it didn't stop me from feeling angry. And occasionally he engaged or gave half a smile, so I was sure he was capable of change if he just bloody well tried.

Chapter 18

My exasperation came to a head in November. Mum hadn't stretched to paying for individual cello tuition after school, so the group session for strings was at lunch time on a Friday. As I was leaving, Miss Shields called me back.

'Are you OK, Ruth? You seem to have lost your mojo this term.' She peered at me. 'It's as though you're only half here. Both musically and... Is something troubling you?'

It was the question I had dreaded. I inhaled to say I was fine, but she gestured to my arm and continued to speak. 'You seem to be struggling with your left side. Have you injured your hand?'

'No. Well, not recently.' Goodness knows how I managed to find my voice. 'But I broke my wrist in June.'

'Oh dear. I'm sorry to hear that, Ruth. You should have said.' She put a finger to her lips, clearly doing the maths. 'That's over four months now.'

I fought to hold in the tears of self-pity. At the hospital in France, a medic had explained that the scaphoid bone took longer to heal than others because of its peculiar blood supply. The guy had been sweetly attentive when Dad mentioned I was a 'musician', and yet my mother still hadn't asked about it at all.

'Apparently this type of fracture takes additional time to mend,' I muttered. 'More like twelve weeks than six.'

'Poor you.' My teacher scrunched her face. 'But that has passed too. Have you mentioned it to your parents? A visit to your GP might be sensible. You know, check that it's healing properly, perhaps get an X-ray? I'm no expert, but you might

75

need physiotherapy.' She patted my shoulder. 'You are such a talented cellist, Ruth. It would be a dreadful shame if you lost interest or if you had to...'

I didn't hear the rest of her commiseration. Her smile of solicitude was too much to bear, so I bolted from the room and the building. When I finally looked up through the playground drizzle, a gaggle of pupils were watching me, one or two with concern, but most of them with derision.

Sheer anger overtook the panic. My life was shit; the summer had been ruined; my own mother looked at me as though I was the devil; I had no bloody friends. And what did Tim do about it? The brother whose life I'd saved? Nothing. He just stayed in the sack all day.

Determined to shake him from his malaise, I stomped off the school premises and headed for home. Once there, I stormed into his bedroom.

'You are so selfish! You only think about yourself,' I yelled. 'Have you ever considered me? I have nightmares most nights. Do you know what happens in them? You fucking land on me! It hurt, it bloody hurt. My ribs snapped and punctured my lung, for Christ's sake. Have you any idea how agonising that was? Your twelve stone dead weight trapping and pinning me to the ground? I protected your precious bones from damage, Tim. Has it ever occur to you to say thank you or sorry?'

The tears belting out, my rant was unstoppable.

'But it's all about perfect Tim, isn't it?' I continued. 'We tiptoe around you, waiting for you to feel better. Well, not even that – for you to make the simple effort of speaking to us or a doctor or a therapist. Open your bloody eyes! You're not the only person suffering in this family. Because you won't tell them what happened in France, Mum and Dad blame me. I have no friends because everyone thinks I'm a freak. And do you know why? Because I'm not allowed to *say* anything; I have to swallow it down, including this urgent need to sob every second of my life.'

No response came. Just Tim's blank stare. I wanted to hit him, to pummel and smack him until he uttered something. Instead, I mustered all the strength I possessed, turned heel to my bean bag and bashed out my misery to Sylvie by text. Half way through, a message popped up from Mum.

> I've had a call from school. Apparently you just upped sticks and left without permission. Don't you think I have enough on my plate? Dad will be speaking to you later.

That almost made me laugh. Was reporting me to my spineless father supposed to be a threat? But the hilarity was soon replaced by the utter unfairness of it all. 'Escape' thumped through my head. I could pack a few belongings, leave this house and my family and never return. Vanessa would have me, I was sure of it. Reaching up on my tiptoes, I pulled down my travel bag from the top of the wardrobe and let it clatter to the floor. But when I threw back the lid and took in the bridesmaid gown I'd hidden from Mum, reality punched me. I couldn't go to my aunt. I had no idea where she lived, there was Sergio to consider and however much she loved me, her relationship with my mother went so much deeper.

For moments I put the silk to my face, then overwhelmed by disappointment, I shrieked out loud. Apart from all my other troubles, I had missed out on this special day. Yes, I had fretted about it, but it had felt like a sea change too, a chance to transform from shyness to boldness, from ugly duckling to swan, from childhood to maturity. They'd been snatched away, leaving me as… well, the very the same me I disliked.

Suddenly aware of a presence, I snapped around to the door. 'Tim!' I put a hand to my racing chest. 'How about knocking first?' I cringed at my own words. We never had growing up, which was why I'd casually entered that damned hotel bedroom. 'Sorry, you shocked me.'

'I was in the bathroom and I heard—' He frowned at the suitcase. 'What are you—?'

'Am I seeing things?' I asked, cutting in. My yelps of frustration were embarrassing, but this was more important – Tim was up and… 'You've actually had a shower?'

'Yeah.' His mouth gave the slightest of twitches. 'Thought it was time.'

I wanted to grab him and weep tears of relief, but something told me sentiment wasn't what he needed, so I fell back on my bed. 'Praise be. I'll make a note in my diary.'

He towel-dried his hair. 'Why were you shouting?' he asked eventually.

'*Where do I bloody start?*' I was tempted to reply, but my problems were nothing compared to his. Skinny, grey-faced and gaunt, he was a shadow of the guy who'd left for Europe in June. Ashamed at my tantrum, I shrugged. 'Oh, nothing much.'

His eyes burned into mine. 'What you said before; I don't think I can say thank you right now, but I should have said sorry and I am sorry.' He sighed. 'I can see I have been self-absorbed but it doesn't feel like that in my head. It's a real struggle to be, I don't know, objective?'

Hot with guilt, I nodded. My judgemental stance had been wholly wrong; he was in a dark, unimaginable place.

'And the thought of taking on other people's emotions feels… well, overwhelming.'

'OK.'

His brow creased. 'I know I ruined a wedding and a holiday, but I can't even go there, so I don't, but some things are unavoidable, especially if I leave my bedroom. You know, Mum and her expectations of me; her fears and fragility.'

Her fears and fragility? That made me frown; his description of her wasn't a person I recognised. What had she said about her own mother? '*Who knows what went on in that woman's head.*' That's exactly how I felt about her.

'Then there's outside this house,' Tim continued. 'Sixth form and…'

Though his voice trailed away, I sensed he wanted to say it, so I quietly asked. 'And Rav?'

'I thought it was love, Ruth. That I'd found someone who was completely on my wavelength…' His expression was wretched. 'I trusted him, Ruth, trusted him completely, so his reaction was unexpected, debilitating. If he'd dug in a knife and cut out my heart, it wouldn't have hurt so deeply or been so shocking.'

From Rav's absence at the hospital and since, I'd guessed something along these lines, but it didn't lessen my own culpability as the catalyst.

'So you came into the room and saw us,' he said after a while. 'Not ideal, but not a disaster. I knew you wouldn't say anything and part of me was glad I had someone to share the…' His voice broke. 'Sheer exhilaration, wonder, beauty, brilliance… and all the other amazing feelings I had. I'd genuinely thought he felt the same but he soon put me straight. Brutally. He wasn't gay; he'd deny it if challenged; sex with me was the price of a holiday. Other stuff too. Personal, vindictive. It was horrible.'

He fell silent for minutes. 'That's what I couldn't and still can't get a handle on. I was so sure yet so wrong. Elated one minute, devastated the next.' He cleared his throat. 'When he'd gone, the loneliness and hurt felt unbearable. I couldn't focus; my mind was blinkered, like I was looking through a straw. Right then, there was only one way to cope, to cure the inordinate agony in my head. So, I—' He stood and grimaced. 'Well, you know the rest.'

Though I was fearful of the answer, it was a question I needed to ask before he left. 'Do you still have those—'

'Cognitive restrictions? Acute suicidal moments?'

Holding my breath, I nodded.

'It was weird, as soon as I had made my decision, I had this overwhelming sense of release, of relief. I remembered Claudette's tool shed and calmly worked out what to do.' He glanced at me. 'All I can say is that I'm now in an odd place, languishing in some sort of liminal state. A black void most days but a glimmer of hope on others, so...'

'Hope is good, right?' Though I had more of an insight into my brother's psyche, it terrified me too. It was all I could do not to beg. 'But if you ever, ever... Please. Please just talk to me, OK?'

Chapter 19

Leaving a cuppa for Tim outside his door, I took mine to the beanbag and contemplated passion. *Sheer exhilaration, wonder, beauty, brilliance...* Just the words made my belly flip, let alone the thought of what happened between lovers in bed. Of late I'd tentatively explored my own body at night, and the idea of someone else touching me that intimately made my face burn. Would I ever experience the adoration and sexual attraction that had sparked so clearly between Vanessa and Sergio? The romantic in me certainly hoped so, but to have it snatched away so heartlessly, to discover one had been used and duped for 'the price of a holiday' was terrible.

The creak of our gate interrupted my musing. Inwardly groaning, I glanced at my watch. It would be Mum at this time, and though I couldn't be bothered with the confrontation, facing the music straightaway was the lesser of two evils.

I rattled down the stars but when I reached half way, I saw it was Dad, home two hours early. He looked up with an expression I couldn't interpret. 'Why didn't you tell me, Ruth?' he asked.

Tell him? I hadn't expected school, and especially Miss Shields, to snitch on me quite so quickly. Indignation shot to my cheeks. Up until now I had been a nerdy, goody-two-shoes student. I'd taken one step out of line and this was how my parents responded. So instead of replying, I folded my arms and clenched my jaw.

Dad put his hands either side of my shoulders and looked at me so strangely, I braced myself to be shaken. But his voice caught with emotion. 'I'm so sorry. I should have spoken to you sooner. I wanted to, but...'

My heart sank. Oh God, what had happened now? Yet he must have read my confusion. 'Spoken to you about what happened in the summer, love. Asked how you were, how you were coping. Mum and I have been so worried about Tim that we've overlooked you. On reflection, that's the dreadful truth and I'm so sorry, Ruth.'

He pulled me to him and kissed my head. 'The distress of seeing something like that, let alone your physical injuries. But we assumed you were OK, that you'd healed and made a full recovery because you didn't say otherwise.'

Pushing him away, I found myself shouting. 'I didn't *say* anything? That's a joke. No one is allowed to utter anything in this family. I get it wouldn't do to wash the Parker's dirty laundry in public, but I wasn't allowed to speak – or even bloody whisper – about anything even within these four walls. And anyway, I'm your *child*. I shouldn't have to *say* anything; you should know.'

I pointed a trembling finger. 'You're my dad; you're supposed to love me. You should have asked how I was, you should have cared. Instead, you acted as though my... my trauma didn't count.'

'I agree and I'm sorry. And I do care and love you very much. Never for a moment think otherwise.'

'*She* doesn't, though.' I glared at him. 'She doesn't love me, does she?'

'Yes, she does, Ruth, very much. Mum just has a different way of showing her feelings.' He squinted in thought. 'She's complicated and there've been things in the past that have shaped who she—'

'What things?'

'Oh, I don't know. But the point is she internalises her emotions.'

He was clearly just making the usual excuses. 'Whatever; I don't care. Love that isn't shown isn't love.'

'Then let me show it,' he replied. 'Let's start with your wrist, get it seen to by an orthopaedic specialist as soon as an appointment is available.' He hugged me again. 'I've been remiss, but I haven't forgotten your dreams, Ruth. Whatever it takes, I want you to achieve them.'

–

The breakthrough that Friday wasn't the miracle cure we'd all longed for, yet there was a profound change in my brother's condition nonetheless. Some days he still kept to himself, but on others he shuffled into the kitchen and briefly spoke to our parents. We continued our after-school chats which mainly revolved around Tim's frustration and his lack of answers about Rav.

'Why don't you write a letter to him?' I suggested. I still occasionally 'wrote' to our mum, but I wasn't about to tell him that. 'You know, just pen your questions and anger and all that shit, but don't waste the cost of a postage stamp. Either tear it up afterwards or keep it hidden for posterity.' I chuckled wryly. 'I believe it's very therapeutic.'

Over the next few weeks Tim took my suggestion to heart and became a prolific correspondent and poet. The outlet seemed to make him much brighter, but the downside was a severe case of too much information when he read them out to me. Added to that was Sylvie's graphic details about intimacy, intercourse and all the intricacies from her liaison with an older guy. Still, it was all adding to my learning as I most certainly wasn't having any sex education of my own – after my wrist rehabilitation, the cello case had returned and was putting boys off.

Tim didn't return to his old sixth form, but he surprised everyone in January by making an announcement. 'I've got a place at Craven College starting in a week. If I can catch up on what I've missed, I'll be allowed to take my exams as planned. If not, I'll stay a second year.' I knew the old Tim was long gone, but I was still surprised at the quaver in his voice. 'But I don't fancy studying law any more. Nor trying for Oxbridge. If I make it to uni, I want to read English.'

'Well done, son. I'm proud of you,' Dad said.

Recalling what Tim had said about Mum's 'expectations', I clocked his nervous glance at her. Until that moment I hadn't focused on how restrictive that might feel. I rubbed along with her and we'd dutifully exchanged Christmas gifts and put on a united front for Dad's family, but I didn't feel special or loved or appreciated by her. Yet I didn't have to worry about her projections for my future, and I recognised there was a freedom in that.

Her eyes were glassy. From disappointment or emotion, I couldn't quite tell, but she said the right thing. 'Studying the classics. How lovely, Tim. And somewhere local sounds perfect. If it takes an extra year, then we should think about repainting your bedroom.'

I could sense her mentally adding it all up. Her beloved son might be home for another twelve months; it wasn't completely bad news.

'And university?' she continued. 'Have you thought of where you'll apply?'

I watched my brother's flickering eyes. *'No! Don't do it, Tim,'* I wanted to yell. *'Cut the cord! Get away as far as possible! Be your own person!'*

But his reply was already out. 'Manchester has an excellent English department, so that might be a good choice.'

–

As things turned out, I didn't need to worry about Tim. He still had dark bouts, but after a haltering week or two at college, he discovered a 'like-minded crowd', as he quietly put it to me. He sat his A levels in the June and smashed them as only he could. And though he didn't move away for university, he did leave home, sharing a house with friends he could 'rely on'.

'Apart from everything else, Rav broke my trust, Ruth,' he explained to me. 'That still hasn't healed, so feeling safe is important.' Dad-like, his lips twitched. 'And if it makes Mum happy having me closer, it's a win-win, yes?'

My life trundled on. Even in Sixth Form I was still the loner who hauled my instrument to school and back, who kept my head down and studied hard. The 'freak' label had stuck and was nigh impossible to remove, so I didn't even try. All I could do was bide my time and wait for the day I'd be the new me.

Part 2

Chapter 20

I was finally eighteen, had sat my A levels and had London within my reach. For the last two years I'd regularly hung out at Tim's place, but I could hardly move in for the whole summer to avoid dreary evenings with my parents. Sylvie had the perfect answer: Claudette was always looking for extra help, so if I didn't mind cleaning loos, changing bedding and waitressing, I could stay with them in France over the holidays. Mum pulled a face, muttering something about my last summer at home, but Dad was all for it.

'I think she should do it, Joy. Adding a string to her bow by learning the language. Having fun with her friend. Earning an extra bob or two to spend at university.' He kissed her frown. 'And you'll have handsome me all to yourself. What could be better than that?'

–

Though none were as spectacular as Château les Douves, Claudette and her husband managed several properties in Normandy. They treated me like any other employee and laboured me hard. My palms took on a permanent tang of detergent and disinfectant, and my muscles ached from the lifting and bending, but they didn't charge me for rent or food, so everything I earned was squirrelled away. And when we had five minutes to spare, I chilled with Sylvie. It was a win-win, as Tim would say.

Sylvie and her mum still worked at the château, but they didn't suggest I help out there. I understood it was out of respect, but it felt too much like the 'unmentionable' in my own family, so when they needed extra hands for a party one weekend, I offered my services.

'Are you sure you don't mind?' Claudette asked.

'Yes, I'm sure. In fact, I think it might be a good thing. You know, facing demons and all that.'

Though I still had the nightmares from time to time, they had eased considerably, and I wanted to get a handle on what I inwardly termed the 'Vanessa niggle'. None of us had seen actual hide nor hair of her since that fateful summer, but I'd gathered from Mum's telephone chatter that she and her old friend were again in touch. I was glad the stand-off had been resolved, but no messages, nor photos nor emojis had appeared on my iPhone for at least eighteen months. Was I miffed? Hell, yes. But I hoped returning to the château would be a way to finally extinguish the remaining embers of that childhood crush.

—

Château les Douves was as magnificent as I remembered, but the August sunshine was even hotter and more people were milling the grounds for a French couple's silver wedding anniversary celebration.

Being a silent member of the domestic staff was interesting. Though the attendees were blind to my presence, I absorbed facial expressions and body language, heard gossip and whispered words; I judged people on the state of their bedrooms and bathrooms or whether they thanked me. It was a whole new eye-opening world, and I wondered what Sylvie and Claudette had made of the Parker family. Genial but weak husband constantly appeasing his wife? Gay son hiding his love affair? Plain Jane chubby daughter desperately dreaming? And what about the mother? What went on behind her brittle façade? Did she really have a dark secret in her past?

Of course, I was too fearful to ask them. I didn't like the impermissible approach my parents adopted, but I wasn't a masochist.

We turned up early the next morning for the after-party clear up, so I had a few minutes to roam the grounds before the guests awoke. Remembering my tears of romantic emotion, I put my head in the rotunda and said goodbye to that star-struck fourteen-year-old, then I inhaled deeply and steadied myself for the big one. Would I feel that thud to my chest, the heavy panic from my dreams? See a twitching body hanging from the sturdy branch? Part of me was tempted to turn tail and return to Sylvie, but I was a grown up now; it was better to face it. Though I kept my eyes on the arid grass as I approached, the cool shadows alerted me to my arrival. I slowly lifted my gaze, took in the proud *Cèdre du Liban* and blew out my trapped breath. It was just a tree, thank God, and a beautiful one at that.

I wryly smiled at the thought of its 'magical powers'. That day had been so blissful and surreal, I'd actually thought it could really be true. What had I wished for? To be like Vanessa, of course. An echo, an identikit, a clone.

What a very silly girl I'd been. The real goal was to discover the new independent *me* and I was finally on the precipice of that.

–

My new life at university was finally around the corner. Dad offered to drive the four plus hours to London, but I decided to start as I meant to go on, so I thanked him and said I was fine to travel by train.

'But you'll never manage it all,' Mum said, gesturing to the pots, plates and saucepans she'd sourced from every relative we had. Neighbours too, by the looks of it.

'I won't know what I'll need until I'm there,' I replied. 'And they do have shops in New Cross, Mum. I can buy anything I've overlooked.'

'Please don't, that would be such a waste of money when there's so much here to choose from.'

I squinted at the goods on display. A pressure cooker from the iron age. A hand whisk. And was that really rust on the cheese grater? Crockery was bad enough, but why would I want cast-off bedding or towels? University would be a new shiny start; I wanted gleaming possessions too.

'Thanks Mum, but I only need one of everything and I don't think most freshers spend their free time making fancy dishes for their dinners.'

'Well your bother enjoys it. He's become an excellent chef.'

He had and I was glad for him. Cooking was another therapy for Tim; it helped him fend off the occasional dips in his mental health. But of course I'd never say that to our mother; she was still in denial about that dark summer even though years had passed.

Dad knocked on my bedroom door and had a quiet word with me in the evening.

'Could you see your way to picking one or two of the items Mum's sorted for you?' he asked. He stroked his chin, the usual prelude to defending her. 'I think she feels a little rejected. She spent several weeks putting it all together for you, a sort of labour of love. And of course that's on top of you not wanting us to take you down and help settle you into your digs.' He cleared his throat and handed me a parcel. 'And here's a little something from me. It's nothing much so maybe save it until you arrive.'

'Thanks,' I absently replied.

I was still mulling his comments about Mum. Dad was so good at 'spin', he should have gone into politics. Tim lived only two miles up the road, yet he'd been bought everything new for uni, including a flaming duvet and pillows; there had never been any mention of Mum wanting to travel in the car with Dad and me. Other than dictating which hall of residence I should choose based on price, she'd shown no interest in my accommodation, and her only comment about my chosen degree was that I had higher grades than was required, so it 'seemed such a waste'.

It seemed to me that my mother put her fear of *waste* above happiness. I still enjoyed playing and composing classical music, but I'd chosen Goldsmith's College because there was scope to transfer into popular or electronic. Or maybe another subject entirely. I'd applied for the BMus (Hons) Music course because my dad had been so keen for me to show off my 'amazing talent' and follow my dreams. Now time had passed, I wasn't sure what they were any more, but I loved him very much, so for him I would give it a try.

Chapter 21

I was officially an adult and knew I couldn't continue through life blaming my mum for everything, yet I still couldn't help it. When I arrived at my halls, the reason why they'd been the cheapest soon became apparent. The alleged 'near campus' was actually a twenty-minute commute, so I didn't feel in the thick of things right from the start. Then, of the ten students sharing a kitchen in my flat, five were post graduates and three weren't even at Goldsmith's. Which left me and one girl called Li Min. She was smiley and friendly, but after two minutes she disappeared to share a room in other accommodation with her boyfriend.

Li Min kindly invited me to various freshers' activities over the first few days, but being a gooseberry wasn't ideal. Though I tried to join in with other group chatter, after my muteness at school, it didn't come easily. Even worse, I found people I had spoken to one night didn't recall or recognise me the next. Maybe everyone's excessive consumption of alcohol was a factor, but I couldn't escape the reality: I was possibly boring and entirely forgettable.

I hoped for better luck the next week on my course, but heads were down to take notes during the introductory seminars and everyone seemed to scurry off immediately after. So much for my exciting new existence. Something had to give. Drunk and teary after another disastrous night out, I looked at myself long and hard in the mirror.

What had Mum said when I returned from my summer in France? 'Goodness, you're as pale as when you left in July.'

'*I went there to earn some money because you're so tight, not to get a bloody suntan,*' I'd wanted to retort.

Yet she did have a point. If I appeared wishy washy, people would assume I was like that too. Who was I? What type of person did I want to be? I had checked out my fellow students in the lecture theatre and they'd all looked as strait-laced and as bland as me. Dramatic make-up and hair was the thing. Maybe a dash of dark lipstick and circle my eyes in black kohl. Dye my fringe purple and shave in tram lines. Buy alternative clothing or get a tattoo...

Knowing I didn't have the guts, I collapsed on the bed and fingered my iPhone. What I really, really needed was a friend I could turn to for reassurance and guidance, someone who'd tell me I was special and boost my self-esteem. Though I hated myself for it, I took a sharp breath and checked my messages again, hoping that by some miracle a 'welcome to London' text from Vanessa was waiting. It wasn't.

Absently listening to the beat pulsing through the partition wall, I fought back the tears. Eight years on and I was still bloody invisible. The one person who'd seen *something* in Ruth Parker had dumped me for her handsome husband. And why the hell wouldn't she? Why would she remember some long ago promise to my dad? But I was cross with myself for allowing her in, for still being that needy and impressionable girl inside. Determination taking over, I swung down my legs, marched to the neighbouring room and knocked.

'Who is it?' I heard.

'It's Ruth from next door. Can I come in?'

'I'm asleep.'

'No, you're not.'

'I'll turn it down.'

The occupant's music had vibrated through until the early hours for the past few nights, but I hadn't really minded. It had been company of sorts and I'd liked the eclectic mix, which had included the more classical Psychedelic rock. I hadn't yet

95

seen them in person; I knew he or she was from another uni or college, but that was pretty much it.

'It isn't the volume; I want to ask you something,' I said.

Nothing happened for several moments, then the lock turned and a tall, skinny guy appeared.

'So what's your question?' he asked, pulling the door behind him.

'An observation and a request.'

He dragged his shock of dark hair from his forehead and frowned. 'Right...'

'King Crimson's an unusual choice for an undergraduate.' His amber eyes widened in surprise, so I embellished a little. 'A genre characterised by extended instrumental sections and complex song structures isn't the usual millennial fare.'

I detected the hint of a smile.

'Secondly, do you have any scissors?' I gestured to my mousy barnet. 'I fancy chopping it off and giving it some colour. What do you reckon I should go for? Blue or red?'

It was a gamble, but my bold introduction won me an invitation inside number eight.

'I'm Ruth,' I repeated.

'Yeah, you said.'

Scooping up an acoustic guitar, my new friend flopped in its place on the mattress, so I perched on the chair. 'A Gibson 1960 Hummingbird,' I commented. 'Are you studying music?'

'Nope. Maths.'

From his appearance and lack of chattiness so far, I guessed this guy was introspective, a loner. Bloody typical he'd be an *oddball* like me. Searching for conversation, I swivelled to the desk and sat back in surprise. It wasn't every day one saw such a substantial and varied collection of vinyl.

'Wow, impressive! All originals, I take it?'

He nodded.

'Is it OK if I look? I'll handle them carefully.'

'Go for it.'

'Thanks.'

I spent a few minutes pulling a mix out and studying the immaculate covers. They looked like rare collector's pieces, which was probably why he'd been so loathe to let me in. 'Interesting Sixties and Seventies blend,' I said eventually. 'Prog Rock, Hard, Psychedelic, Blues, Free jazz… Not a bad assortment for a mathematician.'

He raked back his fringe. 'How come you know so much about that era?'

'My dad.'

I didn't want to talk about good old Clive. I'd almost forgotten his parting gift, and when I'd finally opened it, I discovered a music case made of the softest kid leather. The amount I was missing him was a huge self-revelation and it made me feel tearful again.

I changed the subject. 'You must have at least a hundred records here. Why have you brought them to uni?' I asked. 'I mean, there're nice to listen to, but they must be worth quite a bit. Suppose they get stolen?'

He shrugged. 'No way I'd leave them at home. My mother would have taken great pleasure in throwing them out. Or stamping on them.' His voice was surprisingly deep and eloquent. 'And anyway, I trade. Scout the internet and record shops, then sell them at a profit.'

That was impressive, but it felt soulless too. 'But what about the ones you really like? Do you keep them?'

'Nope. Doesn't do to get attached to anything in this life.' Her lifted his bony shoulders again. 'Need to make money somehow.'

I didn't fancy him one iota, but a mum he clearly disliked and a need to earn cash felt satisfyingly symbolic. I propped my weary legs on the end of his bed. 'So do you have a name?'

'Augustus Montgomery Avery. Take your pick.'

I sniggered. 'No. Really?'

'Yes, really.'

'Is your birthday in August or something?'

'Nope. My mother clearly loathed me the moment I was born.'

Bloody hell. I'd always disfavoured 'Ruth' because it was so plain and I didn't have a middle name to swap. 'So which one do you prefer?'

'Augustus. Gus.'

'At least you can shorten it,' I said.

'Still horribly posh.'

'Is that a bad thing?'

'What do you think?'

'You could tone it down.'

'What? And sound northern like you? A Manc, I take it?'

That made me chuckle. I wasn't aware I had an accent; Mum would be dismayed.

'Don't think I haven't tried,' he continued. 'Breeding and intonation are indelible.'

'It doesn't sound as though you like your family very much.'

'*Like* is an emotion. I don't do those.' His phone beeped and he yawned. 'Right, I'm tired now.'

The dismissal was to the point so I stood. 'OK. Night, then.'

'Black,' he said when I was halfway out.

'What?'

'We'll dye your hair black.'

–

Listening to the sound of Pink Floyd through the wall, I settled down in my narrow bed and smiled at the warm, fuzzy feeling in my chest. I had made a connection at last, maybe even a friend! Wondering if Gus slept to music, I bashed my new pillow into shape and reached for sleep, but just on the cusp I heard movement in his room, the click of his door and then the fire exit. When I peered at my mobile, it was twenty past two.

As though knowing I was there, a message flashed on the screen. My stomach clenching, I opened it.

It's fate, honey. I'm London bound! Now we can get to know each other properly. Arrivederci. Vanessa x

Chapter 22

I had mixed feelings about the contact from Vanessa. My body had a will of its own, my belly fizzing with the old excitement when I allowed myself to admit it, but my mind was more steely. Picking me up and making me feel special when it suited my aunt was not on. I wasn't a flaming toy to be played with at times and discarded at others. Yet I knew that was irrational too. She'd become quite famous, had no need to say '*don't you know who I am*' any more; she worked all over the world for many months at a time and had a husband to think of; she had quite understandable priorities over me, which included my mum and their long-standing relationship.

Either way, I decided not to reply to the text, but to focus on my own burgeoning friendship. Over the next couple of days I heard Gus come and go but didn't see him in person until he appeared in the kitchen on Tuesday evening. Dressed all in black – including dark Ray-Bans – he didn't acknowledge or say anything to our flat mates, but gestured me out with a flick of his head. Upgrading him from nerd to possibly cool, I followed him down the corridor.

'You're too pale for black,' he said when we reached my door. 'I decided on this.'

Though rich coming from someone equally as pallid, I delved into the carrier bag he thrust at me and pulled out a box of pink hair dye.

'Wow, thanks,' I replied, struggling to hide my delight.

'I thought Andy Warhol's Blondie circa 1980.'

'Really?'

'Yeah. Why not?'

Debbie Harry was an iconic beauty. Where would I begin my list of reasons *why not*? But the suggestion was still thrilling. 'Brilliant – thank you,' I replied.

I didn't know the form about offering to pay, but Gus's attention had shifted, so I watched him appraise my sparse room and bare walls. How I wished it was decorated with fairy lights and a million photographs hung on pegs like Li Min's, but my display would be limited to snaps of me and Sylvie from our summer, and the single one I possessed of the Parker family taken at Château Les Douves before all *that* happened. It reminded me of the happy couple, their Order of Service and that rousing image which had consumed me with hope and happiness and dreams.

I quickly pushed the thought away. I needed to take a huge dose of salt when it came to Vanessa. She'd sent a second message:

> Finally home with weary legs and desperate to see you!

I was determined not to jump puppy-like this time around, so I hadn't yet responded.

Gus had removed his shades and was looking at me curiously. He lifted a clump of my long mane. 'So, are we doing this?'

'What? Right now?'

He pulled a pair of scissors from his back pocket and shrugged. 'Have you got something better to do?'

Funnily enough, I hadn't.

—

I didn't have the time or inclination to reply to my aunt's text as my friendship with Gus grew in his room or mine. Or at least it blossomed as much as was possible when we were both so cagey about ourselves. Emboldened by my new quirky hair, I was the more inquisitive.

'So, you have a mother who wants to trample on your vinyls—'

'And anything else she can get beneath her Hunter's.'

I guffawed. 'She doesn't just ride horses, she owns them, doesn't she?'

'Yup.'

'And has awfully awfully nice friends.'

'So, you've met her.'

'What about your dad? Bet he owns an estate half the size of Hampshire.'

'Deceased.'

I smacked my stupid mouth. 'God, I'm so sorry.'

'No, *I'm* deceased as far as he's concerned.'

I peered at Gus then. He regularly claimed he didn't do sentiment or emotion, but the hurt was clearly there in his eyes.

'That must feel horrible. I'm sorry.'

'Don't be. His new wife forced him to pay the fees for my course and this place so I'm good.' He snorted. 'What else are fathers for?'

I could have mentioned a whole host of my dad's quiet qualities, not least his mischievous humour, but it also made me realise that my mum wasn't so bad. And I did miss her. I'd even had the good grace to mention the uncomfortable pillow in our weekly text exchange.

> I should have brought the bedding Aunt Paulette donated. The pillow I bought from John Lewis has given me a bad neck!

> Oh dear! Don't throw it out, will you. I'm sure it'll give with time. Or bring it home at Christmas and we'll do a swap.

Then there was my lovely big brother. Would we have been as close had his breakdown not happened? Probably not, but I was lucky to have him in my life. He still had negative periods when he'd call yet barely speak, but he'd finally moved on romantically as he'd met a 'body builder from Rotherham' whom he fancied 'like fuck'.

The pursuit and attention was exciting for Tim, if somewhat daunting for me. He hadn't 'come out' to Mum and Dad. What would happen if his heart was broken again? The thought of *acute suicidal moments* and *cognitive restrictions* brought on the old panic, and the only person I could confide in was Sylvie, via text.

> What can I do to help Tim? To stop it all happening again?

> The brutal truth? Absolutely nothing.

Chapter 23

A couple of weeks passed, and though I did make the effort, I didn't click with anyone on my course. When I tried to engage with either boy or girl, they stared at my pink locks and shrank away. It was disappointing, but I had to laugh at the irony – they were clearly made of pre-uni Ruth cloth, serious and intense and having the relationship with their instrument I'd once had. I still liked my cello, but it was no longer the precious possession I wouldn't let anyone touch. Indeed, I did temporary swaps with Gus's Gibson, discovering that classical guitar practice worked as excellent cross-training and helped the functioning of my bow hold.

Saying goodbye to the old Ruth was double edged. It was enjoyable to be carefree and relaxed, to listen to and enjoy 'pop' without picking the melody apart, yet there was high anxiety too. Reading and playing music had come easily at school, I'd been Miss Shields's clear favourite and the best virtuoso in my year, but the standard of both composition and performance was much higher here. My fellow string musicians were simply better than me and though I tried to work hard, I was already falling behind.

'I'm out of my depth,' I said to Gus in my room one evening. 'I'm literally dreading tomorrow's workshop. My heart is galloping even now.'

'Then don't go.'

'What? Skive it?'

'Yeah.'

'You're joking; I've never played truant in my life.' I pictured my dad's face. 'And anyway, that suggestion only makes me feel worse. If I don't pass the first semester, they'll kick me out and what then?'

'No, they won't.'

'You're not taking me seriously, Gus.' Tears pricked my eyes. 'This is important and—'

'Sorry.' He gave a crooked smile. 'I wish I had half your talent, Rue. You're just stressed. Get some beta blockers; they'll help chill you out. It's no biggie; everyone is on them.'

'Who's everyone?'

'City traders, high-flying executives, actors, professional musicians. Students under pressure, particularly medics and dentistry. At my school you could hear the rattle during exam times.' He shrugged. 'It's really no big deal. GPs give them out like Smarties. Just tell them you feel anxious.'

I shook my head. I hadn't had the cedar tree nightmare for several months and I didn't want to risk opening that can of worms. 'I don't fancy spilling my guts out to some random doctor.'

'Don't blame you; lots of people think the same. Or don't want it on their medical records.'

Feeling a fresh bout of palpitations, I groaned. 'And anyway, the workshop is tomorrow; even if I phone up the student health centre, I won't get an appointment for a week.'

Gus eyed me thoughtfully. 'I might have some from back in the day.' He stood from his comfy spot on my bed. 'I'll have a rummage and see...'

When he returned, he lobbed a large tub of pills in my lap. 'They can make you feel a bit nauseous and weird in a slow-limbed type of way. It says up to three a day when you need them, so don't go crazy.' He lifted his dark eyebrows. 'In the meantime, I have just the thing to help.'

'Oh, right?'

I expected him to produce the usual bottle of spirits, but instead he opened the window, returned to the mattress and patted the space beside him.

'What's that?' I asked.

'You've never seen a joint before? What part of Manchester do you come from?'

I felt my cheeks burn. 'I've seen one, just never…'

'You want the best way to ease tension? This is it.' He lit it and passed it over. 'Here you go. A compulsory accessory to psychedelic rock. I expect your dad was an expert.'

Though a little apprehensive, I lightly sucked and blew out.

'Maybe try inhaling?'

I did as I was told and gave it back.

Narrowing his eyes, Gus took a drag. 'As for creativity… Well, tell me when it hits and what you feel.'

'OK.' I waited. Nothing happened for moments, then I guffawed and sniffed him. 'I can smell your… What is it? Special shampoo for your silky hair? Deodorant? Oh God, don't tell me you wear aftershave!'

His lips twitched. 'Nope.'

Suddenly wanting to chat, I sat upright and crossed my legs. 'Do you have a girlfriend. Or maybe a boyfriend?'

'Nope.'

We continued to take turns with the spliff. 'What about sex?' I asked.

'What about it?'

'Have you had it?' I sniggered again. 'Not just DIY or a grope. You know, the full monty?'

'Why do you ask?'

'Well I haven't, so I was thinking…'

God, in that moment it made perfect sense! I was probably the only eighteen-year-old virgin in the whole of London, and losing one's maidenhood was just one of those things one had to get under the belt! 'You and I could do it, dear Augustus.

Intercourse *without strings*.' Christ, I felt witty. 'You know, like swapping our instruments and learning a new skill.'

'Thanks but no thanks.'

I wasn't the least bit offended by his rejection. 'Why not? It wouldn't even be friends with benefits but a one-off mechanical experimentation type of thing. See if we could achieve a *crescendo*. We'd just close our eyes and think of England.'

He studied me for a beat. 'There's no such thing as mechanical. Emotion clouds sex every time. That's why I don't go there.'

I flopped down next to his skinny frame. 'Okie dokie. So we're not getting married, then?'

'Afraid not.'

I chuckled. 'How about when we're forty? You know, if we're both single and desperate?'

'No can do.' He stared at the ceiling. 'By forty, I guarantee I'll be dead.'

Chapter 24

A brisk rapping sound roused me from sleep on Saturday. Trying to shake myself awake, I sat up and listened. Was it really my door? Who on earth would be calling for me? But when the knock was repeated, it sounded so official I tumbled from the mattress, took a nervy breath and opened up. My fur-coated aunt was standing on the threshold.

'Morning sweetie! Some nice chap let me in but for a moment I was worried I had got the wrong room.' Her eyes glowing, she fluffed my hair. 'Look at you, all grown up and simply adorable.' She took in the old T-shirt I wore for sleep. 'Interesting Jim-Jams.'

'It's one of Tim's castoffs,' I managed through the shock.

'Ah, sweet. How is he?'

I puffed out the air stuck in my chest. I had no idea why she was here, but at least it wasn't bad news about Tim. 'He's fine thanks.'

'Oh darling, don't look so worried. When I awoke this morning I realised I had a free day, so of course the first thing I thought of was you. Now she's settled in, my student niece will appreciate a day of indulgence, I reasoned.' She looked as immaculate and glamorous as ever. 'What do you say? Shall I whisk you away from these somewhat dingy premises?'

After all my internal wrangling, there was only one answer. 'Yes please!'

'Excellent.' She sat on the desk chair and gestured to the bathroom. 'I'll wait here. Take your time.'

Keenly aware of the mess surrounding her – including evidence of my new recreational habit – I grabbed some clothes and disappeared into the en suite. As I hurriedly cleaned my teeth, washed and dressed, I considered improving my reflection in the mirror by applying some make-up, but I'd look shabby in comparison with my aunt whatever I tried. Besides, despite her 'take your time', I didn't want to keep her waiting. When I tumbled out barely five minutes later, the bed had been made and the room tidied.

Wondering which of my two ancient Parkas to wear, I eyed up her exotic but worryingly real-looking mink jacket. 'This is only for the sake of appearances, darling,' she said, clearly reading my mind. 'And faux, I can assure you. A jumper will do. I have the car outside.'

'Oh, so we're not—'

'Going on ghastly public transport? As if! I don't do the winter outdoors unless absolutely necessary.'

'Oh, OK.'

As though a town crier had rung his bell, my flatmates all seemed to appear at their doors. Unsure if I was severely embarrassed or inordinately proud, I followed my aunt as she sashayed down the corridor, the scent of vanilla, jasmine and lily of the valley in her wake.

'Here's our lift,' she said when we were finally outside. She opened the rear door of a gleaming black Bentley. 'Hop in and shuffle over.' Then dragging on her seatbelt and chuckling, 'I told you I don't do the cold. At least not for long.'

Sergio's white smile from long-ago flashed in my head. God, I'd clean forgotten about him. Whatever we were doing, he was clearly in the driver's seat and joining us. Too nervous to speak, I inhaled the tang of warm leather and wished Dad was here to make a sardonic quip about taste and money. But this vehicle was extremely elegant; God knows how much it had cost.

The man himself was hidden by the headrest, nor did he speak. Instead, he smoothly drove down the Old Kent Road towards signs for the ring road. I had no idea where we were headed, but after half an hour, I recognised the imposing crescents of Belgravia. A blend of excitement and terror trickled down my spine. Vanessa couldn't possibly live here, could she? But when the car turned into Wilton Place and parked outside a handsome town house midway, I realised with a shock that she did. Bloody hell! My aunt owned a five story Georgian house in one of the most expensive areas of London. Why had Mum never told me?

'Home sweet home. So what do you think?' Vanessa asked.

'Completely amazing,' I replied. They were the only words I could find.

A blast of cold air broke the spell. A man wearing a dark suit had opened Vanessa's door. 'Thank you, Bernard,' she said, climbing out.

He did the same at my side. 'Thank you,' I muttered, quickly scuttling to join my aunt at the pillared entrance. Catching us up with keys, Bernard opened up and ushered us inside.

Vanessa patted his shoulder. 'Well done on circumventing those dreadful temporary traffic lights. Tea for two when you're ready would be lovely.'

The penny dropped then. Sergio hadn't driven us; this elderly man had; he was clearly something between a butler and chauffeur. The day was getting more and more surreal. I couldn't believe Mum hadn't mentioned any of this. Surely this splendour was something she'd either boast about or deride?

I somehow found my manners. 'If I'd known I was visiting I'd have brought flowers.'

'Not necessary at all, though I have to confess I do have a soft spot for roses.'

I took in the modern, bright foyer. I was no architectural expert, but the contemporary staircase and herringbone flooring, the wide entrances and high gloss white finish were far from the traditional style I'd expected from outside. I had never been to a boutique hotel, but this is how I imagined one might be – state of the art but tasteful and sophisticated. Yes, very much like my aunt.

I felt her eyes burn my back. 'Do you like it? I know it looks like open plan at first glance, but there are bifolds one can close if one prefers. But I hate to feel trapped, so...'

My flesh tingling, I turned. 'It's wonderful.'

'Think you could live here?'

'Absolutely.'

'Come on up.'

She slipped off her heels so I did the same with my trainers, stripping off my less-than-pristine socks for good measure, then I followed her to the first landing and into an equally trendsetting reception room. She flopped down on the plush grey sofa and yawned.

'I don't know about you but I had a dreadful night and I'm exhausted. Jet lag too, probably. How about a cuppa, then we both retreat to our rooms, have a rest and a shower and reconvene for supper at eight? Bernard doesn't like me to ask what he's making, but he never disappoints. Feel free to roam and have a nosy in the meantime. My home is yours. Anything you need, just ask.'

'My room?' Was she simply hinting that I hadn't had a shower in my haste or – 'Am I staying overnight?'

'Of course.' She laughed. 'I thought that was a given.'

Chapter 25

I expected Vanessa to chat, or at least ask a question or two about university, if not the last eighteen months, but when our refreshments arrived she put on Nina Simone and closed her eyes. Had it not been for the sway of her elegant fingers, I'd have assumed she was asleep. I slurped my tea and tried to keep my agitation at bay. I'd usually find listening to the 'High Priestess of Soul' relaxing, but it was as though I'd been airdropped from my tinny halls of residence room into this solid luxury, and it felt disconcerting. It was a relief when my aunt languidly stood and stretched after a good half an hour.

'Ready to see your bedroom?'

'Yes, I'd love to.'

Trying not to gasp afresh at the sheer splendour of the tiered stairway, I followed her sweet scent up another flight of steps.

'Apparently some of my neighbours have lifts as well as a resident phantom,' she said over her shoulder. 'Can you imagine getting stuck in one? Good old Bernard charging to the rescue? At least one hopes so. Can't bear confined spaces or the dark, can you?'

I chuckled nervously. 'I think I'd be more worried about meeting the ghost.' I peered up to the dusky garrett at the very top. 'There isn't really one, is there?'

'*Un diavolo?*' She paused, lost for a few moments, then shook herself back. 'One certainly hopes not.'

She led me to a guest suite and pointed to the ceiling. 'My boudoir is above here for anything cerebral. Everything else is catered for by Bernard, whom you can contact by dialling zero on the house phone. If he can't do it, he'll find someone who can.' Her eyes twinkled mischievously. 'Sometimes I think of a tricky task just to test the poor man, but he's never yet failed me. So if there's anything you want, you know what to do! See you at the table for eight.'

'Thank you,' I said, moving into the pastel-coloured chamber. 'It's beautiful. This carpet is so thick it feels as though it's growing through my toes. How long have you lived here?'

I rotated to my host, but she'd already gone, so I ambled around my digs for the night, lightly touching the velvet furniture, immaculate walls and crisp bedding. Opening various doors, I found closets and shelves and a stunning en suite complete with gold fittings, an exceptionally long bathtub, a walk-in shower and a million white fluffy towels. It was all very lovely, but what on earth I would do to fill the hours before 'supper'? I yawned and eyed the bed. I'd had a late night hanging out with Gus but it felt wrong to dent the ironed throw, so I moved to a teal-coloured chair my mum would call a 'love seat', dismantled the plethora of cushions and curled up my legs. When I pointed a remote at the huge television screen, I discovered it doubled up as a computer. How cool was that?

Though I passed some time flicking through the abundance of channels, I was parched and my stomach groaned for food. I glanced at the bedside telephone. Would I really have the gall to ring zero, make an order and have Bernard bring it up like a servant? No, I'd fetch something myself. After all, I had been given permission to explore.

Stepping out to the landing, I listened for sound. The whole house seemed dense with silence so I took a big breath, tiptoed down to the ground floor and tentatively pushed open a door on the right. Relieved that I'd found the kitchen first time, I moved further in, pausing to admire the sleek grey units and cupboards, the huge central island and glass ceiling above it. The American-sized fridge and chrome appliances looked unused, more a show display than a working room, and though I scanned the granite surfaces several times, I couldn't see a kettle.

A waft of tobacco alerted me to a presence behind me. My hand to my chest, I snapped around, but it wasn't *un diavolo*, thank goodness. His back as straight as a poker and eyeing me strangely, it was Vanessa's employee.

'I'm on zero if you need anything.' He gestured to a doorway behind him. 'But you'll find me in there if you don't like phoning.'

His accent was definitely more northern than not.

'Thank you. I was—'

'What can I get you?'

'Do you have any paracetamol or the like?' It was hard to make out his impassive expression. 'I have a bit of a headache, and I thought a mug of tea to wash them down, but there doesn't appear to be a—'

'Watch carefully.' His lips slightly twitched. 'It'll scald badly if you get caught.'

He produced a china teapot, threw in two teabags, stepped to the sink and added steaming water from the tap.

'Mod cons, eh? Not for everyone, though.' His piercing grey eyes seemed to read me. 'I take it you're hungry?'

'I am actually. Sorry, I haven't had any breakfast. Or lunch. Just a piece of toast or something easy would be great if you don't mind?'

He sucked in his cheeks. 'Aye. They're bad as each other. The two of them forget that folk need to eat.'

–

Perched at an oval glass table, I chewed the club sandwich Bernard had made me. He'd piled it high with deli meats, salad and pickles, and it was truly delicious, but his words 'the two of them' felt off. Was Sergio here or did he mean someone else? Vanessa hadn't said anything about her hubby being around and the dwelling was so eerily quiet.

Feeling somewhat unsettled, I took my plate to the sink and wiped off the crumbs. From the immaculate work tops,

I gathered Bernard liked to keep a tidy ship and it struck me that I'd left my 'bedroom' in a state of disarray, so I hurried out to address my lack of manners. But the distinct tang of chlorine caught me short.

Tracking the smell, I tiptoed down a set of spiral stairs to a basement area. My nose hadn't fooled me. It housed a small swimming pool, gym equipment and what appeared to be a media room. Laughing to myself at the sheer luxury of it all, I retraced my steps, but instead of returning to my room, sheer nosiness propelled me to Vanessa's brightly lit floor. Remembering she'd mentioned 'rest', I kept to the bannister and looked upwards. Dare I continue and explore the attic area?

My heart thrashing with intrigue and nerves, I crept up the final flight, but once at the top, the mood seemed to change. This part of the house clearly hadn't been refurbished. The wooden floorboards felt dank beneath my bare feet and from what I could glean through the gloom, any natural light was blocked out by a dark curtain on one side and a closed door on the other. Sure I had inadvertently crossed a line, I rubbed the goosebumps from my arms and made to retreat.

A noise made me still. Scratching? Movement? An eerie sigh? My ears pricked for more, but the icy moment was broken by the sound of my host's eloquent tones from below.

'Is that you, sweetie? I'm awake. You can come in.'

Somewhat shame-faced from my snooping, I caught my breath at her open door.

'Darling!' She watched me absorb the sumptuous suite and shades of gold decor, then she chuckled. 'I take it you approve of my boudoir?'

'It's stunning.'

'Just the thing for a siesta.'

'Absolutely.' In truth I couldn't imagine dressing in silk pyjamas, let alone be propped up by pillows during daylight hours in an equally silky bed.

She patted the space by her side. 'Come and sit. I've had a nap so I feel quite refreshed and able to conduct a conversation without rudely yawning. At least I hope so.'

I padded across the deep pile carpet. How old was Vanessa now? Late forties? Even fifty? But she still looked incredibly young and line-free.

'I've just ordered tea from Bernard. Will you join me, darling?' she asked.

It felt rude to mention my detour and lunch, so I blushed and nodded like the star-struck girl I had been the last time we met.

'Hop on then. Let's have a proper look at you.' She peered at me intently. I wasn't used to anyone getting so physically close, but after a few uncomfortable moments she smiled her huge winning smile. 'Sorry to stare, darling. You're just so perfect.'

My nerves came out as a guffaw. 'Really? Are you sure you've got the right person?'

'I have indeed. That porcelain skin and those bones. Talented *and* beautiful.' She chuckled. 'And though one shouldn't blow one's own trumpet, I'd like to officially take the credit for seeing it first!'

I was back in my ten-year-old shoes. Though I knew she was prone to theatrical exaggeration, the sheer pleasure spread through me all the same.

I covered my blushes with a quip. 'You are possibly deranged but thank you all the same.'

'And your gorgeous pink locks. How did that happen?'

I took a breath to explain but I didn't want to mention Gus to anyone just yet. I never thought I'd fancy someone with legs thinner than mine, but I'd had several erotic dreams about him, so maybe things were going that way. We'd definitely bonded since smoking together, and despite his claims about not doing emotion, I felt we were on the precipice of *something*.

Instead of answering her question, I self-consciously flattened my hair. 'What do you think? Do you like it?'

'I love it!' She elbowed me playfully. 'Maybe warn your lovely mum before you next go home, though.'

That was food for thought; Mum would not take it well; she was expecting me home for reading week in November, but perhaps I should re-think it.

I eyed my aunt. Was she currently in touch with her old friend? I considered casually asking but she swung out her long legs, strode to the fitted wardrobes and selected something from a shelf. When she turned, she held out a pair of sleek pyjamas.

'Tonight's supper outfit. Come and collect me in an hour.'

Chapter 26

Back in my room, I donned the PJs and twirled in the full-length mirror. My reflection wasn't a patch on Vanessa's easy elegance, but I smiled all the same. My mum would think eating dinner garbed in nightwear an anathema, but different rules clearly applied here. Besides, it felt like fun.

When the hour had passed I went to collect Vanessa, but she declared she couldn't be 'arsed' to traipse downstairs, so we ended up dining in her room. Hitched up against the pillows, she stayed in bed and ate from a tray on legs, and I sat on a button-tufted chaise lounge opposite.

Bernard appeared with a shapely tureen, placed it on a chest of drawers and served our soup into matching bowls. He added a swirl of pouring cream and a sprinkling of chives. 'Enjoy,' he muttered, stony-faced.

Vanessa dryly laughed when he'd gone. 'Not much of a conversationalist is he? But he doesn't need to say when I'm in trouble as his expression does it for him.' She lifted a slim shoulder. 'Best ignored, though. The important thing is to never eat alone unless one really can't help it.'

As the meal progressed, I wasn't surprised at the poor man's displeasure. He'd clearly put a lot of time and effort into the beautifully presented tiny portions. The haute cuisine was a huge improvement on my usual baked potato, but Vanessa didn't seem impressed or excited.

'This looks interesting, Bernard, but what is it?' she asked when he brought up another course.

His bushy eyebrows knitted. 'Cod on a latticed potato and spinach base.'

It appeared almost too good to eat. Only almost though, as I was starving. I managed to stretch it out to three mouthfuls and was mightily relieved when Vanessa enquired about dessert.

'What pud do you have for us, Bernard?'

He looked mildly surprised. 'We have an apple tart with cream or ice cream. And the tiramisu, of course.'

Though only a vague Italian connection, I stilled Sergio joining two pyjama-clad women for a meal had felt unlikely, but did the man even live in this house? I couldn't say why, but he felt like a taboo subject.

'And the sticky toffee pudding?' my aunt asked.

Bernard's frown deepened. 'It's bought.'

She reverted to me. 'The delightful dessert is from Cartmel. Of course we can buy a tray at any old time when we're home, but purchasing some at the races is compulsory.' She rolled her eyes. 'He still hasn't forgiven me. So what will it be, sweetie?'

'The tart sounds lovely. With cream please.'

'Very diplomatic,' she replied. 'I'll have the usual.'

The 'usual' was a crystal tumbler of whisky or brandy, which Vanessa slowly sipped as she watched me eat. When I'd self-consciously finished, she hitched to one side and puffed up a cushion for me.

'Let's watch something banal on TV and chat.'

'Sounds good.'

Though I focused on the television, I could feel her observe me again. 'No need for glasses these days?' she asked.

'They were only for reading and I—'

'Out grew the hyperopia. Excellent.' She continued to study me for another second or two. 'You were pretty in France but you've grown into a beauty. I knew you would.'

Though she'd said something similar earlier, Mum's words from long ago filtered back: *Don't feel you have to say yes, Ruth. I'm sure she was just saying it to be kind.*

Yet kindness was nice. Though free to give, it was rare.

Suddenly a shadow of herself, Vanessa shivered. 'She was always there for me. Always,' she said with a catch in her throat. 'Her loyalty knew no bounds.'

My aunt didn't mention who 'she' was, but it felt as if she had read my mind.

'After Mummy, those few months were devastating. Not everyone was nice; some were positively unkind and others… But Joy was the strong, smart one; she protected me and picked me up. It's a privilege to have a friend like that.'

Her account of Mum was at odds with Tim's description of her 'fears and fragility', not to mention her less-than-supportive relationship with me. My aunt's changed demeanour was undoubtedly odd, yet my old intrigue about their friendship was roused, so I decided just to ask. 'Protected you from what?'

She seemed to stare right through me. 'I know what she did but I never let on.'

'Who?' I involuntary shivered. 'Mum?'

'Yes, Joy.' Blinking the strange moment away, she pointed the remote control at the TV screen. 'Shall we see what else is on? It's always fun to spot an old pal. I can't tell you how many have popped up in *Corrie* or *Emmerdale*.'

What the hell did '*I know what she did*' mean? Though spooked, I longed to ask more, but my aunt had clearly changed the subject, so I went with the new one. '*Corrie?* Wow.'

'With a top-up methinks.' She reached for the decanter Bernard had left. 'Goodness, how rude. I didn't offer you a glass. Would you like to join me?'

'No thanks, I'm fine.'

'I'm sure we'll have cocoa or the like in the kitchen if you'd like to have a rummage. Talking of which, Bernard likes a lie-in on a Sunday, so I thought you could do the honours with morning coffee. I just can't get up without it. Oh, and open all the downstairs bifolds, would you? I like to greet a new day in the light.'

'Morning coffee? Yes, of course. No problem.'

Would I work out how to operate the damned 'kettle' tap?

Vanessa chuckled. 'I know; I hate it too. But you don't need to worry about second degree burns as we have a *café matinal* pretending it's a cupboard. Or perhaps it's the other way around. Anyhow, you just slot in your chosen pod and Bob's your uncle. Actually, I think it makes hot chocolate too.' She yawned. 'I'm super tired, so why don't you investigate it before bed? Have a nice glass of milk. Or even some of that sticky toffee pud whilst Bernard isn't looking. Just help yourself. My home is yours.'

I slipped off the mattress. 'Thank you for dinner and having me to stay.'

'No need for thanks. It's my pleasure. Nine o'clock tomorrow. *Torta Di Nocciole* for me and whatever you're having.'

When I emerged from the boudoir I moved to the bannister and looked down. I was still peckish so a milky drink, if not a slice of dessert, was very tempting indeed, but it was almost pitch black with the bifold doors closed. As I padded down the stairs, logic told me the sound of breathing was only my own, yet I couldn't shake off the feeling of being watched, so I scurried straight to my bedroom.

Buzzing with thoughts of my peculiar day, I didn't think I'd be capable of sleep, but when my head touched the pillow, I was out like a light.

–

Minutes or hours later, terror slapped me awake. Was someone in my room? Yes, the creak of a handle had been unmistakeable. Squeezing my eyes shut, I held my breath and listened to the swish of quiet movement, then… Oh my God, an exhalation above me, close to my face.

My mind thrashed with panic, but my body played dead. Moments later the door clicked. I gave it a few beats, then gasped out my trapped breath and flicked on the bedside lamp.

Ridiculously expecting to see footprints in the pile, I searched the plush carpet.

Oh my God. What had just happened? Did a person come in or was it simply my spooked imagination? A dream, it had to be just a dream. Yet hadn't there had been a smell? The distinct essence of cigarettes and brandy?

Chapter 27

It was dusky beyond the curtains when I woke, so I dozed for a while. When I eventually twigged I wasn't at uni but in my aunt's house, I jolted upright and snapped my head to the door. Had I really had a nocturnal visitor or was it a nightmare? The love seat I'd dragged over and shoved against it was still there, but a brand new morning was pushing through the small window panes and the modern room felt sturdy and safe. At the time I'd been certain the episode was real, but it was hard to summon up the terror I'd felt as I'd forced myself back to sleep.

I chuckled at my own ridiculousness. I'd simply spooked myself by thoughts of phantoms and devils. After France I was prone to weird dreams, to say the least, and I'd dropped off soon after, so clearly I hadn't actually regained consciousness in the first place.

Clocking the time and remembering my aunt's order of a *Torta Di Nocciole* – and whatever I was having – I hurried down to the kitchen, sliding doors open as I went. I found the elaborate coffee maker, and as I studied the choice of capsules, the aroma of tobacco and voices filtered through from Bernard's room. The butler was clearly enjoying his well-deserved lie-in by watching TV and taking his first drag of the day.

Having mastered both machine and tap, I poured milk and cream into jugs, arranged a tea pot and cup on a tray and made my way up the stairs. It was fun playing house. Vanessa hadn't mentioned food but I'd found a packet of Biscotti in the larder cupboard, so I'd added a couple to the saucers for good measure.

Gold-tinged daylight shone through her open door, so I tapped and entered. The divan was empty, so I moved further in to place my offering on the side table. The aroma of her soap or shampoo made me idly turn with a smile, but to my astonishment and shock, it wasn't my aunt who was stepping out of the en suite bathroom. It was her husband. Save for the towel he was using to dry his dark hair, he was emphatically naked.

He didn't rush to hide his modesty, but his scowl showed his irritation. '*Maledetto inferno!*' he said. 'Who the hell are you?'

Appalled and embarrassed, I struggled to form words. 'Ruth. Ruth Parker, Vanessa's—' What was I? Not even a real niece. 'I'm so sorry, I had no idea you'd be in here.' Recovering myself, I put down the tray. 'Coffee and tea,' I said, as though I was paid staff. 'If there's anything else you need, please give me a shout.'

–

I found Vanessa reading a magazine on a lounger in the basement. She thought it a hoot when I explained what had happened.

'Oh darling, I'm so sorry,' she said. 'Poor Sergio and poor you surprising each other like that.'

I didn't say I'd seen him stark bollock nude, but she'd clearly gathered it from my burning cheeks.

'I know you're embarrassed, sweetie, but it is a little comical too, don't you think? Sergio can be so very serious at times.'

On reflection he'd actually been bloody rude. We'd met before in France; I'd saved those scraps of his artwork; I'd been the sole bridesmaid, for God's sake.

'But you mustn't mind him,' she continued with a waft of her hand. 'He likes me to sit for him at a weekend so he's cross with me.' She tugged me down to the adjoining recliner. 'But you're here, so thank goodness I have an excuse. Holding my chin just so and not moving for hours can get extremely tedious. He's determined to finish a "collection", as he puts it, though why I don't know, as he says he'll never sell them.' She peered at me. 'Are you all right, darling? Fully recovered from the shock?'

Trying to shake off the memory of Sergio's glower – and the explicit rest – I finally laughed. 'Yes, I'll cope.' Then after a moment, 'So he's been here all the time I've—'

'Of course, darling! This is where he lives. Neither Bernard nor I can predict when he'll make an appearance, though. Sometimes it's hours, sometimes days. I blame the roof terrace. As you can imagine, the views are stunning.'

'Gosh, yes, they will be.' A roof terrace? Of course there was a roof terrace. Yet it felt at odds with that sinister top landing. 'So Sergio still paints?' Well, that was a silly question. Picturing his torn sketches, I quickly amended my question. 'I mean you're still his main subject? His... muse?'

'Absolutely.' She shrugged gracefully. 'It's a chore, but who else?' She looked at the door as Bernard entered. 'Being my hubby's sole inspiration is something of a task, isn't it Bernard?' She came back to me. 'But this wonderful man looks after me. He's a darling and ensures I'm properly fed and watered.'

Though Bernard didn't reply, he set a jug of fresh orange juice and two glasses on a low table, then passed his employer a vial containing several tablets.

'And vitamined-up,' she said with raised eyebrows when he'd gone. 'I think he's trying to spell out the alphabet. B for energy, C for the fight against free radicals, D for bone health through to Z for, well zinc, I suppose.' She brushed a finger across my cheekbone. 'E and K are also excellent for healthy skin but yours is as smooth as china, so you don't have to worry about that just yet. Though always remember removing one's make-up before sleep is compulsory.'

'Noted!'

She threw the pills back, then gestured to the sparkling swimming pool. 'Do go ahead. I've done my exertion for the day.'

If her dry and styled hair was anything to go by, her *exertion* wasn't from swimming.

'I would love to but I don't have a cossie,' I replied, crossing my fingers and toes that she wouldn't offer a size eight of her own.

'Actually, a sauna, I think, don't you?' she replied.

I'd never had one, but this morning I'd seen my first real penis since spying Tim's tiny todger around the age of ten, so I was up for anything.

'Sure, sounds good.'

'Excellent. Now in Asia, the soaping of one's body before a sauna is a must. It's a ritual that cleanses one's mind of stresses before one enters,' she said. 'Keep this in mind as you wash. Then thoroughly rub yourself dry with a towel as it doesn't do to be wet at the start.'

'OK.'

Vanessa's tone was schoolmistress style, so it was a relief she didn't follow me in to the shower to check I was obeying. When I returned, duly scrubbed, she motioned to the tinted glass unit.

'In we go. Now's the time to apply heat. Do sit.'

Bloody hell; was I supposed to remove my covering? Hanging onto it, I did as I was told.

'You'll feel the heat rising, then you'll break out into a full body sweat. Don't panic but try to stay in the room until it happens. I'll be here if you need me.'

'So you're not coming in?'

'Lord, no. They make me feel trapped. But it's important to try everything once. Yes?'

A far from pleasurable experience, I closed my eyes and willed the minutes away. I'd almost become used to the suffocating steam when a blast of cold air gave me permission to leave.

'How did it feel?' Vanessa asked as I stepped out. 'Describe it to me.'

Reminding me of Gus's similar question when I sampled my first drag of cannabis, I felt a stirring of pleasure. This bizarre weekend in Wilton Place had been amazing, but I was excited to see him and resume our bonding.

Vanessa was waiting for my reply. 'Honestly?' I asked.

'Of course. Always.'

Sweat was pouring from my skin and my heart was pounding like I'd sprinted a mile.

'Horrible. I have no idea why people put themselves through that.' I laughed wryly. 'Unless it miraculously melts off a ton of excess flesh.'

Vanessa tutted. 'Self-deprecation in a man is a charming quality, but for us women...' She seemed to think about it for a while. 'Self-belief, Ruth. If you don't believe in yourself, no one else will.' She looked at me pointedly. 'And if you're not quite there, you put on your poker face and damned well act. Now, you need to cool down to get that excess heat out of your body, then I think it's probably time for you to make tracks. A cool-to-warm shower or a dip in the pool?'

I very much wanted to believe in myself, to become that new person I'd determined to be in the summer, but I wasn't up to skinny dipping just yet, so I opted for the former. When I emerged minutes later, she'd gone.

—

Wishing I'd grabbed one of the Biscotti biscuits to fend off my hunger, I hurried upstairs to get dressed. My host's instruction to leave felt a little abrupt. Would a lift be on offer or should I travel back to my halls on 'ghastly public transport'? Should I quietly slip away or risk finding her with Sergio to say thanks and goodbye?

I needn't have worried. When I tumbled down to the lobby, both my aunt and her chauffeur were waiting for me.

Once ensconced in the warm Bentley, she slipped her arm through mine. 'What a wonderful weekend. You're such a breath of fresh air and fun to have around. Did you enjoy it too?'

'Absolutely. Thanks so much for inviting me.' My stomach embarrassingly rumbled. 'Dinner was delicious.'

'Then you must come again.' She chuckled. 'I might even remember to feed you breakfast.'

'That would be amazing.'

'Excellent.'

We fell silent as Bernard smoothly negotiated the busy London streets, but Vanessa animated again when we reached my block of flats.

'Saturday, then?'

'Sorry?'

'For our next date. We could make this a weekly thing if you like. A poverty-stricken student during the week and a dose of luxury to recharge your batteries at a weekend.' She nudged me affectionately. 'And to save me from sitting quite so long for my handsome husband!'

'Oh.' I looked up to Gus's window. He had a tendency to be somewhat elusive, but today his light was on. Quite frankly I felt torn. My time with Vanessa was amazing; her ability to make me feel special and valued hadn't diminished an iota. It was brilliant to sense her adoration. But I wanted the type of love which included romance, kisses and cuddles – and yes, sex. And what about my decision to be the new, independent me?

I took a breath to explain, but my aunt spoke first. 'Ah, a boy, I'm guessing?' She followed my gaze. 'In the room next to yours? How lovely. I understand completely.' She kissed my hot cheek. 'Bye for now, darling. You know where I am if you need me. I'm sure we'll see each other very soon.'

Chapter 28

Another week trundled by. The beta blockers helped me persevere with my course and Gus was right, the cannabis worked miracles with my creativity, at least until I studied my compositions later. Occasionally they were inspired, and some had nuggets of brilliance, but mostly they were like a puzzle I couldn't work out, a 'was that really me?' amazement.

It was a question I asked myself regularly. I don't know what I had expected of university – or myself – but this version of Ruth was a surprise. Other than a postgrad in our flat called Fayola, I was still fairly solitary, yet I was more at ease with it; in my mind I was travelling from being a boring oddball to a more interesting one. Or maybe it was just a reflection of Gus. When he was around we smoked weed and intensely discussed anything and everything from politics to movies to God – so long as it didn't touch on our personal lives. That suited me, but it didn't stop my intrigue in him, so I slipped in questions from time to time:

'Do you have any siblings?'

'None that I care to mention.'

'What does your father do for a living?'

'Nothing worthy.'

'Where do your parents live?'

'South.'

'When I leave the flat for my lectures, do you go to yours?'

'Sometimes.'

'Why are your answers so evasive?'

That brought a smile. 'Asks the woman who does the same.'

Late one evening, I tried again. 'Why does your mobile vibrate so often?'

'Why doesn't yours?' He held out his palm. 'Exactly how many contacts do you have? Come on, share with the class.'

'No way!'

Too fast for me, he grabbed my iPhone and held it aloft. 'If you give me your passcode I'll input my details.'

I tried to snatch it back. 'I'm no mathematician, but if I concentrate really hard, I might be able to *input* them myself.'

Secretly pleased to get his number, I eventually gave in. He laughed when he looked at my meagre list. 'Do you really only know thirty or so people?'

My state school was huge so I knew plenty of pupils in theory. Most kids had exchanged information over the years, but I'd been afraid of getting my precious phone stolen or smashed, so I'd feigned leaving it at home. And anyway, why would I have been pally with the A listers by text when they'd been so horrible to my face? Thank God I'd had—

'So who is Vanessa?' Gus asked.

The synchronicity of his query brought me back with a jolt. She'd sent me a sweet message only last night:

So lovely to see you at the weekend, beautiful girl. Missing you already!

Making a mental note to reply to it, I pondered how to describe her. 'She's my mum's childhood friend.' I felt a blush spread. 'A sort of godmother type of person, I guess.'

'A fairy one?' he asked, deadpan. 'The physical embodiment of hope; someone devoted to making dreams a reality by proclaiming the magic words: "bibbidi-bobbidi-boo"?'

Though he had no idea of how close that was to the truth, it did make me chuckle. And he'd clearly watched Disney's *Cinderella* animation at some point in his life, so surely his childhood couldn't have been all bad.

'Spot on. How about you?' I asked. 'Do you have one?'

'Have what?'

'Someone you'd call if you were ever in trouble.'

'A get out of jail card? Or maybe to arrange a happy ever after with a handsome prince?' he replied, evading the question as usual. He cocked an eyebrow. 'Or maybe a pretty princess?'

I stilled. Oh God; had he remembered my proposition about sex? What would I do if he made a move? Now the moment was here, did I want him to? Finally be loved and lose my virginity? Yes, possibly. Oh God, I didn't know.

The call for 'munchies' saved me from having to decide. 'Are you as starving as I am?' he asked.

Smoking dope made me feel both horny and hungry, but in the absence of satisfying the former, I was more than happy to give into the latter.

He dug in his rucksack and held up two packets. 'So what do you fancy? Crisps or crisps.'

Realising I was indeed happy, I put a finger to my chin and considered the options.

'Do you know what? I think I might go for the crisps.'

'An excellent choice.' He ruffled my pink hair. 'You know, for the wedding menu when we're forty.'

Chapter 29

I didn't become the culinary goddess Mum had hoped for, but sweet potato topped with tuna and cheddar had become my staple tea, so I used the donated cheese grater most evenings. This Friday was no exception.

'Lord, don't tell me you're eating that again,' Fayola commented when I reached for the can.

'Fibre, vitamins, minerals; omega-3 fatty acids and calcium. What's not to love?' I replied.

'Maybe mercury poisoning?' She continued to fry garlic and onions at the hob. 'Don't you get bored of the same old, same old?'

In all honesty I did, but by some miracle I seemed to be losing a pound or two of my 'puppy fat' despite the munchies, so I didn't want to risk departing from the magical formula. Plus, I was lazy and Fayola sometimes took pity and gave me a portion of whatever delicacy she'd made.

I peered at her cumin, paprika, chickpea and brown lentil ingredients today. I doubted my mum had even heard of them, let alone used them. Though a good cook, she was more a traditional type. Perhaps the cello-obsessed Ruth should have paid more attention, but how hard could a casserole or a Sunday roast be?

Fayola turned from her chore. 'The Man of Mystery graced us with his presence earlier.' She opened the communal fridge and gestured to his shelf. 'A box of orange juice, half a dozen eggs and a six pack of doughnuts.'

'Wow.' Even I was intrigued; it was usually empty.

'Interesting, eh?'

Fayola was studying an MA in counselling. She longed to get inside Gus's head, but whenever she tried to pry information from me I always laughed and said, 'No idea. Join the queue.'

She had a mischievous twinkle about her today. 'What do you reckon? Boiled, poached, fried? Maybe an omelette? Though steak might be an idea today.'

'Steak?'

'To soothe his shiner.'

'What? He's got a black eye?'

She tapped her temple. 'He's wearing the shades but nothing gets past Fayola. I wonder what he's been up to this time?'

'This time?'

She lifted her palms theatrically. 'When you find out, be sure to share.'

–

'So what have you been up to?' I asked when Gus allowed me through his portal the next day.

Instead of replying, he turned away, inspected a vinyl at the window, then slotted it back in its sleeve.

'That's a new one,' I commented.

'Yeah, I've been trading,' he absently replied. 'It's fairly rare, so hopefully I'll get a decent uplift.'

'That's good.'

I took a breath to ask where he'd bought it from, but he raked back his long fringe so I held the question in. The bruising was plain to see and the notion suddenly struck that he'd stolen the record and got bashed for his troubles. Tears shot to my eyes; my friend had been hurt and I was worried about him. I wanted to show my concern and ask what had happened, but it felt overly personal to pry. Instead, I sniffed away the emotion and groped for humour.

'The fridge Stasi have been.'

'Yeah?'

'I didn't have you down as a doughnut type of guy.' I wrinkled my nose. 'And filled with *custard*, too. Is that what they eat down south? An aristocratic delicacy?'

'I needed some change.' He carefully filed his new investment alphabetically. 'The guy in the booth didn't take cards.'

A booth? 'Oh right.'

He handed me a key. 'Yeah; thought I'd get a spare cut.' He gestured to his collection. 'You know; in case I'm ever away and the plants need watering.'

—

Gus was around on Wednesday evening, so we hung out in my room, ate stale doughnuts and shared a joint.

'You remind me of my sister,' he commented out of nowhere.

'You have a sister?'

'Yup.'

'You said you didn't have any siblings.'

'I said I had none that I cared to mention.'

Comparing me to a sister, and one he wouldn't care to mention put me straight on the romantic notions I was secretly harbouring.

'Thanks; I'm deeply flattered.'

'Because *mentioning* her makes me feel...'

I studied his shadowy face. The 'E' word, I suspected. 'Human?' I suggested instead.

'Something like that.' He sighed. 'It's complicated. I really miss her but I sort of resent her too, even though it isn't her fault she's the favourite progeny.'

Goosebumps chilled my arms. I inhaled to mention another spooky coincidence, but he continued to speak.

'So I never see her. Because when I do, the devil child emerges—'

'The devil child?'

'Yeah. It's my mother's fond name for me. Has been for as long as I can remember. Livia being the angel, of course. And so I'm not very nice to her. To my sister, I mean.' He paused. 'And I hate myself for being like that. Because Livia's the only person I ever—'

He abruptly stood and left the room, so I curled into a ball and tried to focus on his strange speech. My head was too fluffy to reach any firm conclusion, but on balance it felt nice, as though I'd been given a compliment.

I'd just drifted off when I felt him perch next to me. 'You're back,' I muttered.

He held out an envelope.

'What's this?'

'Open it.'

I did as he asked. 'It's your birthday?'

He nodded.

'Today?'

'Yup. I'm officially no longer a teenager.'

'Wow. Happy birthday!'

So Gus was a year older than me. I struggled upright. 'Why didn't you tell me? I'd have made you a cake. In fact, I'll do one tomorrow.' I chuckled. 'Or buy you one if Fayola doesn't have the right ingredients.'

I returned to the card and peered at the images of a smiley girl and a solemn-faced boy decorating the front. 'So this is your sister – Livia?'

'It is.'

They looked remarkably alike. 'She's your twin?'

'Yup.'

'Wow.' The twins at school had always seemed bonded, inseparable. A little creepy too. 'Did you send her one?'

'No.'

I read her affectionate inscription. 'Why don't you get in touch and say that you miss her? Even meet up?'

Falling back against the pillow, he sighed. 'Nope; too dangerous. She'll bring along our mother.'

'Why?'

'To reconcile us, restore harmony and joy.' He grimaced. 'It was never there in the first place. As soon as Livia's back is turned, she'll offer me money to stay away and I'll take it. So no, I won't be doing that.'

Chapter 30

I stirred mid-morning on Thursday. Nothing intimate had happened with Gus the previous night – not even a kiss – but instead of returning to his room as usual, he'd turned off the lamp, stripped to his undies and squeezed next to me beneath the duvet. Perhaps it was a recreating-the-womb type of thing, but after ten minutes he turned from our back-to-back position, slipped his arms around my waist and cupped me from behind.

My whole body had tingled and I'd held my breath. Would he make a move? Should I? But as his respiration became regular and deep, I gave into sleep too. When I stirred in the early hours, he'd gone, and I was left mulling about the power of mother love – or the lack of it – and the damage it could do to a child.

Now stretching my stiff limbs, I found myself smiling. There had been a shift in our relationship. It wasn't quite tangible yet, but it was definitely there.

Noticing a message waiting from Vanessa, I scooped up my phone.

> Spent the evening with Vivaldi and Mozart at the Barbican and thought of you. Divine!

> PS Do shout if you need some extra spends. I remember being a poor student all too well!

I couldn't help comparing my aunt's thoughtful generosity with my mother's frugalness. But there wasn't time to compose a suitably appreciative reply; today's urgent project was cake.

Consumed with positivity and purpose, I texted Fayola.

> Do you have any baking tins I can borrow please?

> Sure; help yourself. And there's sugar and flour in my stash you can use so long as you save some for me!

> Of course. Thanks!

> You are welcome. BTW I believe there's a six pack of eggs untouched on MOM's shelf :) Would be a shame to let them go to waste!

I so wanted to search her out and say something along the lines of: '*MOM slept in my bed last night and I think something's happening between us! I wish I'd turned to face him and find out. Even had the boldness to plant a kiss on his lips. I might have lost my flaming virginity at last!*'

I didn't, of course. My past was a closed book, and though Fayola was lovely, her kind but penetrating gaze would make the pages unstick and spring from the spine. So instead I focused on my mission. Anyone could whip up a basic Victoria sponge, surely, but who baked the best one I knew? Joy Parker, of course.

I texted her.

> Hi Mum, Any tips for making a cake. Maybe a chocolate one?

Even though she'd be at work, she immediately messaged me back.

> So this is what students spend their days doing?

A detailed recipe and instructions soon appeared. Then finally:

> Who are you making it for?

I stared at that for a while. Was this the question I had really wanted her to ask? God, I was pathetic, but with a stupid grin I composed a reply.

> It's for a friend's birthday. He was twenty yesterday.

–

Decorated with candles from the corner shop, my creation was looking pretty damned good by three, so I tapped on Gus's door to present it to him. I hadn't heard music or movement through the wall all morning, so it wasn't surprising when he didn't reply, yet I was still a touch disheartened.

'Someone has been baking. Are we sharing?'

It was Herman, the guy in the room next to the exit.

'No, it's for...' Gus was as private as me. 'I promised Fayola the first slice, so maybe try again later.'

'Thank you.' He pushed his glasses up his nose. 'I will look forward to it.'

Not trusting his snaky smile, I took the cake to my room and reverted to a half-finished essay. But my concentration was zilch. Where was Gus? I wanted to please him, to show him that someone other than his sister cared. More than that, I longed to recreate last night's surreal intimacy, and this time I'd turn and give him that kiss.

The evening stumbled by with no sign of Gus. Both exasperated and worried by midnight, I crept to his door and tapped again. Anxiety prodded; I knew better than anyone that young people were vulnerable, sometimes unexpectedly so. And how would I cope if something like *that* touched my life again?

I took a huge breath, inserted the spare key and stepped inside. It was empty, thank God. Wondering whether to bring in my birthday treat, I searched for space amidst the vinyls, empty coke cans, rolled joints, magazines and vintage musical newspapers, but on reflection the gesture now felt silly.

Deciding my other flatmates could have the damned thing, I took it to the kitchen, flopped down on a chair and absently picked at the icing. But my ears soon pricked at the click of the fire door and footfall along the corridor. Gus? It had to be.

Fayola put her head around the jamb. 'Hey girl! You didn't need to wait for me.'

She eyed my creation. 'Not bad for a first-timer. Do me a favour and cut me a piece for tomorrow? Those vultures will have it by morning.'

'OK.'

She peered at me. 'Hey Ruth. What's up? Why are you so sad?'

Choked by tears of disappointment, I shook my head.

'Come here.' She wrapped her arms around me. 'I was in two minds but you've decided it for me.'

'Oh yeah?' I managed.

'Tomorrow night. You and me are gonna go partying!'

Chapter 31

I gave myself a good shakedown when I woke on Friday. What had been wrong with me yesterday? Was I really so needy for affection that a backwards hug made me go all weak and snivelling? Well, yes, probably. But I had to get a grip. Gus going AWOL wasn't unusual. Hell, he might have even taken my advice and gone to see his sister.

I spent the day on campus, losing myself in a series of performances in the electronic music studios. The songs, improvisations and sonic adventures were bold and impressive, a melting pot of cultures and concepts, and I was particularly moved by the smooth soul sounds from a young woman who delivered explicit lyrics from the heart like Billie Holiday. How I wished that I could compose frank words to go with the rhythms and notes in my head, but where would I start? My sexual experience was zero and I'd never had a boyfriend or been in love. Unless this nervous fluttering in my belly about Gus counted. Or my old adoration of my aunt.

God, Vanessa. I felt a little guilty about her. Distracted by Gus, I'd forgotten to answer her texts, and last night's one asking: 'How's it going with the boy in room eight?' wasn't a question I was able to answer, so I hadn't. And anyway, would I? I sensed he wasn't the sort of polished person she would approve of.

Needing to fritter away more time, I ambled to 'Thirty-Five' cafe, drank coffee, exchanged messages with Sylvie and Tim, and sent a few pics with ironic comments to Dad. After demolishing a cranberry and brie baguette, I felt much better. My dodgy stomach had clearly been the need for food rather than the company of a chiselled but too-skinny posh boy, thank God. But when I reached our block at tea time, the churning recommenced. There was no light in his third-floor window. Even before I reached the flat, I just knew he wasn't there.

—

I followed the sound of Fayola's singing to the kitchen.

'Hey girl.' She wagged a finger. 'No long faces tonight. OK?'

I plastered on a smile. 'Absolutely.'

'So what are you planning to wear?'

I looked down to my usual uniform of black T-shirt, black combats and black Dr Martens.

'No! It's a party, not a funeral, girl!'

Quite honestly it felt as though I was going to one. Socialising with anyone wasn't the cure I needed right now, let alone with a bunch of people I didn't know.

'Surely you have something a little brighter?' She gyrated her hips. 'Or at least something you can shake a leg in? Because if you don't, I'm sure I can find—'

Bopping around in dazzling outfits was definitely Fayola's thing. It was joyous to behold but wasn't for me. 'I'm sure I have a dress at the bottom of my wardrobe,' I replied quickly before she decked me out in one of her own. 'I'll give you a knock when I'm ready.'

By the time I tapped on Fayola's door, I'd donned my favourite Calvin Klein underwear and my only frock, and imbibed several glasses of particularly disgusting cheap wine.

She looked me up and down. 'Wow, look at you when you make the effort.' She guffawed. 'Actually, am I crazy? Now I have competition!'

'I think not,' I replied dryly. The strappy summer tunic had looked cute during balmy evenings with Sylvie in Normandy, but the black tights did it no favours. 'You are most gracious, Fayola, but my wardrobe does have a looking glass.'

'Opaque tights and trainers?' She was looking at my feet. 'Are we sure about this?'

'We do live in London.'

'True. But we're only walking a hundred metres or so.'

'Other than my DMs they're all I've got.'

'OK, but off with the pantyhose.'

I sniggered. '*Pantyhose?*'

She pointed. 'Yes, those dreadful things.'

'And reveal my white northern legs?'

She laughed her deep laugh. 'Listen, I'm with you, but as strange as it is, some guys seem to like them!'

–

It was hard to be miserable with Fayola by my side. She slipped her arm through mine and teetered across the courtyard to another student block. On the basis we hadn't far to walk – or stagger – back, she forbade me from wearing a coat.

'Trust me, if you bring it you'll never see hide nor hair of it again. And though keeping it on all night might work in theory, you'll get too hot. Ever play that game of sardines? And I'm not joking.'

A replica of ours, it felt a little surreal when someone other than Herman let us into the flat. As we made our way along the corridor, I had an urge to try the handle of room number eight, or bang on the door and demand that Gus come out. Instead, I was propelled to the kitchen where ten or so people were gathered around the table.

'Ruth is joining us for prinks before we party,' Fayola said. 'Ruth meet everybody. Everybody meet Ruth.'

My heart fell. I had assumed we'd be hitting music and dance straight away, so I could be anonymous, but apparently I was to converse with these strangers, some of whom looked several years older than me. This was confirmed when they resumed their chatter about the horrors of clinical placement, their judgemental managers, the depressing tatty rooms and moth-eaten consulting chairs; they were clearly post-grad students on Fayola's counselling course.

It wasn't all bad once I'd sat, though. The alcohol on the side was a much better class than the plonk I had stashed in my bag, and the conversation flowed without any input from me, so I helped myself, half listened and drank.

The jargon they used was mostly double Dutch, so I drifted and let phrases such as 'psychodynamic, psychoanalytic and relational psychoanalytic perspectives' and 'ability to work with transference, countertransference and interpretation' wash over me. But my ears pricked when the discussion turned to people living with suicidal thoughts and behaviours. Discomfort hot in my chest, I tried not to tune in, but one guy with a loud, slurred voice dominated it.

'I disagree. In the vast majority of cases they occur in individuals with an underlying mental health condition.'

'But we know that's not the case, Giles. Many individuals with mental illness are not affected by those thoughts, whereas loads of life stressors such as death of a loved one, a debilitating illness, trauma, sexual abuse, rejection, relationship problems are associated with suicidal thoughts and attempts.'

'Agreed to a point. But "rejection" and "relationship problems"... Break-ups happen every hour of the day and most people get on with it. Come on, between these four walls, we all think it, don't we? When we sit there and listen to moaning Mabel or jilted John. They're just being self-indulgent and not actually at risk.'

I was gobsmacked that even a trainee therapist could begin to think that. I wanted to shout at the man's patronising tone, let alone his lack of insight, but Tim's grey-faced, gaunt and skinny image seeped in and I knew that if I didn't get a hold on the panic, the thud, the pain, the constriction of my airways would all return, so I lowered my head and puffed in and out.

The conversation continued to waft around me.

'It can absolutely be precipitated by the loss of a partner. Those who experience suicidal ideations don't do so by choice; they're not thinking of themselves but suffering from acute emotional pain or going through a life situation which is extremely difficult for them.'

'I'm only being honest and I'm not alone. Many people think that those who die by suicide or attempt it are selfish and take the easy way out—'

'Well, they're wrong. Those people have no idea of the reality of the pain. Take hanging, for example—'

At that point I knew I had to get out. I was back in my school uniform, breathless with anxiety, terrified I'd faint and make a scene. Dragging away my chair, I managed to mumble something and head for the door.

'Leaving already? Rude! How about a thanks for all my wine you've thrown back?'

It was that same condescending voice. Sheer anger overtaking the dread, I snapped around.

'Rude? Really? From a narrow-minded, judgmental shit who thinks it's OK to shame his own patients.' I jabbed a finger. 'You have no idea; you haven't—'

But what was the point even trying to explain? All eyes were on me as though I was the problem. And anyway, that old flannel was still lodged in my throat, so I threw my bag over my shoulder, turned tail and stumbled out to the black night.

Chapter 32

The wind whipping my bare arms, I stomped around the streets of Brockley for a period which might have been minutes or hours, but when I twigged I couldn't feel my face, hands nor feet, I decided it was time to retreat to the flat. It took several attempts to insert my key and heft open the fire door, but I immediately noticed a yellow Post-it attached to my number seven nameplate. Was it from Gus?

> *You weren't answering your phone so I came back here to find you. I'm going off again, so please text to say you are OK!*

Fayola. Was I embarrassed about my outburst? Hell, yes, but I was shocked and angry too. Tim's frail mental health was always just beneath the surface, but Gus's absence coupled with that prick's outrageous comments had triggered the past more vividly than it had since I was fourteen.

Once in my room, I wrapped up in my duvet and peered at my mobile. There were several missed called and texts from Fayola.

I composed a reply:

> Sorry my phone was on silent. I'm fine. Just needed to clear my head. I'm now at the flat and going to bed. Talk tomorrow.

My eyes and nose stung. Would I 'talk' tomorrow? Nope. Was I fine? No. No, I wasn't, I really wasn't. Where the hell was Gus? I needed to explain what had happened in France to *someone* before it literally burst from my chest.

I went back to my phone and typed a message to him.

> Are you around tonight? I really need to see you.

Willing a response to appear, I dragged off my trainers and paced around the confines of my cube. My head was spinning and my heart beating alarmingly fast; I had to stop this jangling agitation, calm down and get some sleep.

A thought suddenly struck. No reply from Gus, but he could help in a way... Picturing the spliffs on his desk from yesterday, I dug out his spare key, nipped into his room, helped myself and quickly slunk back. Perhaps it was simply my deep desperation, but the moment I took a drag, my mood seemed to lift and the tension drained from me.

I continued to smoke until my eyes drooped, then I slipped into blissful deep sleep.

A heavy thump to my torso jolted me awake. I tried to suck in some air but my lungs wouldn't obey. I couldn't inhale, I couldn't move, I was pinned to the mattress. The certainty I was dying seared through my whole being, but after a moment or two, a tiny part of reality kicked in. It was just a dream, the usual nightmare; I could climb out of the black tar, shake myself awake and everything would be fine.

With a tremendous effort, I hitched up the bed. My throat and eyes burned, my pulse raced; I was sweating excessively, the room spun and vomit was threatening to spill out. Getting to the bathroom was the thing. Puke in the loo, then quench my astonishing thirst.

I made to move but stopped in my tracks. Someone else was in here. I stilled and listened. Yes, scraping and wheezing and motion.

My urgent impulse was to hide, but recall nagged at the back of my mind. The noise, that sound of creaking, the impression of twitching, I'd heard it before.

Too afraid to face it, I covered my eyes. What the hell? My face was numb. I pinched my chin then my cheeks, my forehead, my ears; all sensation was gone. Oh my God, was I *dead*? Which meant the person in the room was...

As I slowly looked up, a scream blistered my windpipe like acid. Bare feet and pale legs. A dress covered torso, slack arms and slumped shoulders. A slim neck with a dressing gown cord tied around it. And finally a pink-haired lolling head.

Chapter 33

I stirred intermittently, trying to reach consciousness but falling back into blackness again and again. Eventually I managed to crack open my eyes. I was in a small, whitewashed room. It might have been a waiting area between heaven and hell, but the unmistakeable aroma of antiseptic and bleach pervaded both the air and the bedding. I peered at my itchy inner arm. Good God; I was clearly in hospital, taped to an IV bag.

A face bobbed beside me. A woman in scrubs. 'Hello Ruth. I'm Kama. How are you feeling?'

My throat felt as though it was stuffed with sawdust. 'Thirsty,' I managed to reply.

'OK, let's lift you up and check you out.'

She raised the top of the bed. Like a small child, I let the nurse fuss over me as she checked my pulse and temperature, then passed me a drink with a straw.

'Why am I here?' I asked when she'd finished writing her notes on a chart. I nodded to the drip. 'What's that for?'

'You were badly dehydrated.' She cocked her head. 'You don't remember?'

I squeezed my fuddled mind and scrambled memories surfaced: vomiting, screaming; loud knocking and voices; the scrape of keys. Then people and more puking.

'Your flatmates were worried about you.' She smiled a thin smile. 'Seems you'd been smoking cannabis and had a bad reaction.'

Full recall slapped back. God, yes. Confusion, paranoia, fear; the certainty I was dead. 'I thought I was… well, dying.'

'It's very common. An increased heartbeat feels like a coronary, then panic takes over and exacerbates it. It's a horrible, vicious circle.'

'It's never happened before.' I swallowed. Should I tell her about my vision? Not just any twitching, hanging body, but my own? I looked at my trembling hands. No; she might think I was crazy, the delusion some sort of psychiatric problem.

But Kama was peering at me intently. 'You told the paramedics you'd seen a person in your room. No one was there, so they assumed you'd been hallucinating.'

Hallucinating. Oh God, even the word spooked me out, let alone the terrifying memory. And someone in my flat had clearly called for an ambulance; I must have been truly freaking.

'Which suggests it was high potency cannabis or even a synthetic cannabinoid,' she continued.

'A synthetic cannabinoid? What's that?'

'Colloquially called spice or K2?' Kama pursed her lips. 'The THC chemical in the drug has been scientifically engineered to be many times stronger than plant-based cannabis. That's why users have psychotic episodes, agitation, vomiting, delusions, and so on.'

Anxiety and shame shot through my body. Even I had heard of the 'zombie drug' and its dangers. It was marked 'not fit for human consumption', and for good reasons too. Is that what I'd taken from Gus's room? Sure, I'd hoped for a 'new me' at university, but a druggie – because that's what people like my parents would think.

I covered my burning cheeks. I wanted the old, invisible Ruth back, not this being who'd made a public scene and humiliated herself. And suppose—

But Kama took the words out of my head. 'The authorities will want to talk to you about it, I'm afraid. A janitor was called so the paramedics could get into your room. They were both duty-bound to report what they found.'

The police, oh God. Almost dumb with panic, my voice emerged in a croak. 'What will they do?'

'Forensically test the item and if it contains illegal substances…' She spread her hands apologetically. 'They'll want to find out where you got it from, Ruth.'

'Will I be in trouble?'

'I'm just a nurse, so what do I know? But in my experience the authorities are far more interested in who you got it from. Spice is highly addictive and dangerous, so whoever is supplying it needs to be stopped. You'll understand that after last night's horrible experience.' She perched next to me and pulled me to her shoulder. 'Hey, don't cry. The important thing right now is your health and you're in the right place.'

'OK.' I nodded, but the tears of self-pity wouldn't stop. Why was this happening to me? Would bad luck always follow me around?

Kama passed me a wad of tissues. 'Here, wipe your eyes. You don't want your mum to see you like this.'

I gasped. 'My mum?'

'Yes, she's been here for several hours. She just popped out for a coffee.'

It was truly unbelievable. Just when I thought my miserable life couldn't get any worse, it had.

–

Anxiety overwhelmed me. The notion of a visit from the police was frightening, but facing my mother felt worse. She'd already know why I was here. A panic attack wasn't an illness; it had been self-inflicted by smoking an illegal substance. How angry would she be? And would Dad be with her? Of course he would; she wouldn't drive all this way – or catch the train – by herself. Oh God. Could I bear his disappointment?

But it wasn't just that. It was the unmentionable too. That dreadful day was the last time they'd visited a child in hospital. Though my admission was by no means as severe, it was wrong of me to put them through more grief.

Bad daughter; bad person; bad friend. I was getting Gus into deep trouble, wasn't I? But I couldn't think of that now; I had to focus on my parents and work out how I could begin to apologise.

I must have fallen asleep as a smell mingled with my waking dream. Not the mix of cleaning products this time, but that nostalgic aroma of vanilla, jasmine and lily of the valley. The long-ago happiness it evoked brought on an urge to weep, so I squeezed my eyelids and tried to return to merciful oblivion. But after a moment or two, I felt soft fingers stroke my forehead. The fragrance was real; so was the person peering at me. Vanessa.

'Hello sweetie. You're awake! How are you feeling?'

Too surprised to reply, I began to struggle up, but she gently restrained me.

'Let the bed do it for you, darling. Marvellous contraption; the only good thing about these godawful places. I'm almost tempted to get one for home. Tell me when to stop.'

'That's good, thanks,' I eventually managed. Then, too embarrassed to look at her, 'So, where's Mum?'

'Ah.' She chuckled. 'At home with dear Clive, one assumes.' She wafted an elegant hand towards the door. 'The powers that be sort of assumed I was your mother, so I didn't disabuse them.'

'So...?' Mortification spreading, I raked through the coals of last night − or this morning − but there were chunks I simply couldn't remember. Had I called her? In my hour of need, had I reached out?

'Someone from student support telephoned me, so of course I came straight away.'

I hardly dared to hope. 'Mum and Dad don't know?'

She took my hand. 'Not unless you want them to. You've always been a sensitive soul, so I expect you can do without all the... well, the drama it would entail.'

She was right about that. And *sensitive soul*. On some level it was heart-warming to hear her identify what was undoubtedly true, yet on the other it reinforced what a spectacular fool I had made of myself. Freaking out, hallucinating, for God's sake. Waking up the whole flat. Involving the janitor, paramedics and police. Then there was the rant I'd had earlier at Giles. Could I really go back and face Fayola? And what about Gus? Should I be alarmed or angry or apologetic about the spliff? I just didn't know; my brain was too addled to work it all out.

Vanessa raked a stray hair behind my ear. 'Here's the plan. As soon as they give us the all clear I'll whisk you away. We'll have another night of sheer indulgence at my place, then see how life looks tomorrow. In short, a step at a time.' She passed me a lacy handkerchief from her handbag. 'How does that sound?'

Chapter 34

Although frail both physically and mentally, I put on a brave face for Kana and she gave me the all clear for discharge an hour or so later. The clothes I'd arrived in were soiled by vomit, so I had nothing to wear.

'Are you taking this or should I bin it?' she asked, holding up the bagged frock.

I wanted to keep it. Throwing it out was wasteful – I was my mother's daughter after all – and I'd had such fun wearing it during my carefree summer with Sylvie. But this new version of Ruth was winded and meek; all the confidence I'd built since arriving in London had been knocked clean out of me.

Vanessa decided for me. 'I think dispose of it, don't you?'

'Yes, if that's OK,' I said to Kana. 'I'm so sorry for all the trouble I caused. Thank you again for your patience and kindness.'

Once she had gone, I tugged the cotton gown I was wearing. 'Do you think they'll let me borrow this?'

'On the faithful promise to return it, perhaps, but I do loathe hospitals.' Vanessa unbuckled the belt of her smart mac. 'Time is of the essence and neither of us want to come back, so pop this on.'

I could smell the stench of my own body odour. 'No, I couldn't possibly...'

'No buts,' she said, lifting it like a cloakroom attendant.

Thank God she was here. As I slipped in my arms, I couldn't quite dispel the notion that the warm, silky lining was a metaphor of this woman's protective love.

'I'm so sorry, I stink. I'll pay for it to be dry cleaned as soon as I can.'

'Darling, that won't be necessary.' Vanessa shivered theatrically. 'This room, this building, feels like a prison. Shall we escape?'

'Yes please.'

Though my pulse was racing and my legs insubstantial, I allowed her to firmly guide me past the nurses' station, along a corridor to a lift. Only when I looked back did I realise I'd been in a private room. My champion, of course, understanding me more than my own mother ever had.

When we reached the busy forecourt, she waved at the Bentley. I nervously swallowed as it smoothly made its way towards us. I was half naked and my hair was matted with puke. Could I really sit on the immaculate leather seat and be driven to the even more spotless Wilton Place? And would Sergio be there? Perhaps it would be better to return to my halls and face the music straight away. Or maybe I should hop on a train to Manchester and cook up some reason why I'd appeared at home without warning.

But my aunt seemed to read my mind. 'Come on darling, once we're back we can work everything out. This area is for ambulances. We'd better dive in before Bernard gets us arrested.'

I climbed in, and despite my agitation, I felt a strange sense of kismet as the handsome crescents of Belgravia came into sight.

Bernard parked in his usual spot. 'Home sweet home. Can you feel it, darling?' Vanessa asked with a soft smile.

'Yes,' I replied. 'Yes, I can.'

Though I'd been here before, the hallway and imposing staircase again took my breath.

'So what will it be?' Vanessa asked. 'A cuppa and a chat? Or straight up to your bedroom?'

The choice was a relief as I sensed she was curious about what had happened last night. I was also still wearing – and undoubtedly sweating – in her posh coat.

'Upstairs if that's OK. I could do with a—'

'A long shower and a nap? Of course.' As though I was an invalid, she took my elbow. 'Can you manage two floors?'

My jelly legs had been superseded by a thumping head, but I allowed her to guide me to the same suite as the last time. 'Thank you—' I began at the door, but my aunt put a finger to her lips.

'What did I say? No need for thank yous. And remember my house is yours. Give me a shout if you need anything.' She rubbed her temple. 'Rather think I'm due a siesta too. I'll see you anon.'

Reflecting on how life could astonishingly turn on a sixpence, I hung the mac on a padded hanger and made for the bathroom. I eyed up the walk-in shower, but the bathtub was infinitely more enticing, so I turned on the taps and sighed at the prospect of a good old soak; it was the one thing every student seemed to miss. That thought pierced my dream-like state. I'd almost forgotten why I'd been airdropped into this sheer luxury again.

Catching myself in the mirror, I stepped closer to look at my smeared, ragged reflection. Last night had been truly terrifying and at some point I'd have to face the consequences of it all, but for now I was safe, enveloped in this gorgeous palace and my aunt's tender and intuitive care.

I nodded. I'd be kind to myself and go with it.

Chapter 35

I stayed submerged beneath the bath bubbles for an age, but when my skin began to resemble a pitted Jaffa orange, I climbed out and wrapped myself in a robe I found folded amongst the snowy towels. My head was still thumping and my stomach churning with hunger. Some food was the thing, but what on earth should I wear? I couldn't remember a time I'd been without a debit card or a mobile phone – let alone clothes – and it made me feel ridiculously vulnerable. I sniffed my Calvin Klein bralet. Could I really put it on again? Absolutely not, but the radiator was pumping out heat, so I washed it along with my knickers. As I hung them to dry, I smiled wryly. Everything else was so pristine and white, they looked a decided shade of grey.

Trying to ignore the 'love seat' and the inevitable thoughts of Gus, I returned to the bedroom to hunt out a hairdryer. I searched drawers and closets but all were empty.

I stared at the phone. Despite the shorter style, my barnet was extremely thick and took hours to dry naturally. Was summoning Bernard appropriate in this instance? Or should I just borrow my aunt's? Deciding on the latter, I tightened my dressing gown and stepped onto the landing.

'Hello darling, feeling better?'

It took moments to locate Vanessa's far away voice.

'I'm up here but I'm coming down,' she called. I craned my neck to the very top floor, but all I could see was her shadow. 'Meet you in the lounge?'

'OK.'

I made my way down, sat in an armchair and studied the framed prints on the wall. With a jolt it reminded me that Sergio lived here. None of them appeared to be his work, but perhaps it didn't do to hang one's own art.

Picturing our last meeting, I felt my cheeks burn, then jumped a little guiltily at the sound of my aunt's voice.

'So how are we doing?' She opened a drawer and slipped in a bunch of keys.

'Fine, thanks. Do you have a hairdryer?' Even though my hair was clearly damp, she stared, perplexed. 'Sorry, I couldn't find one in my room. I thought I could borrow yours?'

She shook herself back. 'Sorry, I've been writing – a memoir of sorts – so I'm miles away. Or should I say stuck in the past. A hairdryer, got it. Mine's no more effective than blowing it oneself, but the Dyson in the basement will dry it in a jiffy. Shall we order tea? Oh, and a few sandwiches to see us through until dinner?' She chuckled. 'See? I promised I wouldn't let you starve.'

'Yes please, that would be great.'

She dialled zero and made her order, then she patted the sofa beside her. When I took my place, she peered at me carefully. 'How are you really feeling now? You look a whole lot better than early this morning. I was quite worried when I arrived at the hospital and found you out for the count on a trolley, waiting for a bed. The room I sourced wasn't a great deal better, but I was quite shocked at their casual attitude.'

I was holding my breath from her close inspection. 'No more than I deserved,' I managed to wheeze out. 'I shouldn't have wasted NHS resources on—' I was too ashamed to mention the cannabis. 'Well, a panic attack I guess.'

'I'm very glad that you did. And better safe than sorry.' She raised a sardonic eyebrow. 'I almost had to say "don't you know who I am?".'

The thought of my dad brought a lump to my throat. As though she knew, she pulled me to her shoulder. 'Would you like to talk about what happened?'

I inhaled to say no; it would involve mentioning the unmentionable. With a jolt, it suddenly dawned that I could if I wanted to. She'd been there; she'd witnessed the awful events of that day. But could I share how I felt, even so? I'd hidden the trauma deeply and was afraid of how I'd cope, so I shook my head.

She cleared her throat. 'That lovely nurse—'

'Kana.'

'Yes, Kana. She thought you'd had more than just a panic attack. As nasty as they are, of course. I had them quite often at one time.'

My Alpha female aunt? That was a surprise. 'Really?'

'Yes, when I was twelve. It was that horrible period I told you about.' She eyed me a little strangely. 'A horrible bully at school.' She shrugged. 'There's always one you have to shake off, isn't there? And of course some actors have terrible stage fright.'

'You had stage fright?'

'No, not me, but I believe it's akin to a creative block, which is particularly debilitating for any artist and must be treated with patience and understanding.' Bernard appeared with a tray so she paused until he left. 'As for acting, fully inhabiting the role of the character is the thing. Become them and you're not putting yourself on the line, which is actually perfect for real life too.' She squeezed my hand. 'But back to you and what brought on your anxiety...'

Oh God, she'd returned to my mortifying episode.

'A terrifying hallucination?' she prompted. 'A body hanging in your room?' She rubbed my back and spoke calmly. 'It's fine; you're safe. You can tell me anything, sweetie. Nothing you say will shock me and it'll stay inside these four walls.'

I sucked in some air. 'Since Tim...' Traitorous tears spurted out with my words. 'Since then I've had nightmares. Seeing him or others at the end of a rope.' I patted my ribs. 'Then the crushing. It had almost stopped, but last night—'

'Oh darling.' Her green gaze shone with emotion. 'I'm so sorry. I should have been there for you. It was a difficult time for us all, but your mother thought—'

'It's fine,' I quickly interrupted. I didn't want to get into the failings of my mum. Or how I'd felt abandoned by Vanessa too. She was here for me now and that's what counted; the past had gone and there was nothing anyone could do to change it.

She sniffed. 'But now we've reacquainted, I can make up for it.' She handed me a plate and gestured to the tiered cake stand piled with triangular sandwiches. 'First up are these delicacies and tea, followed by your hair, then we'll find something for you to wear. Sound OK?'

I blew my nose and almost laughed at her knack of making everything seem better. 'Thank you, it does.'

Chapter 36

When I'd finished in the basement, I met Vanessa in her boudoir. She'd already opened several wardrobe doors and was raking through the hangers.

'So what do we think?' she asked.

I inwardly guffawed at the notion of wearing this slim and exotic woman's clothes. 'I'm sure they're all wonderful, but I'd have to lose a stone to fit in a pair of your loose joggers.'

'Joggers? I think not.' She sized me up. 'Pah. A few pounds at most.' She selected several items and threw them on the bed. Then she rustled in a chest of drawers, lobbing over various pieces of underwear.

Seeming satisfied, she turned. 'It would be fun to play dressing up like your mother and I did back in the day, but I mustn't get carried away or embarrass you. Have a gander and hold onto what you fancy. These might not be quite to your taste, but I hope something is suitable for later if not for tomorrow. It wouldn't do to return you to your halls in a dressing gown.'

My smile fell at the thought, but she was having none of it. 'Chop chop! Take them all away now I've decided I'm over them. You'll be glad to hear supper will be served in the dining room tonight, so I'll see you at eight.' She called after me. 'By the way, I believe Bernard has laundered and returned your pyjamas.'

I went through Vanessa's castoffs, carefully folding or hanging them. Each sported a designer label and was undoubtedly exquisite, but none of them were for me. After last night's disaster I no longer knew who 'me' was, but she certainly wasn't someone who could carry off the red satin maxi, the emerald 'bondage' dress, nor the skimpy black number. The wide-legged trousers, crisp shirt and stripy blazer would have been perfect if I'd been in my thirties and off to Ascot for the races; the white skinny jeans were all right, or at least would be if I lost those 'few pounds' and dared to wear them in winter, and the cashmere sweaters were simply divine, but would I even wear the black one when I trudged to my lectures next week?

That thought made me groan, but I checked myself short; I wouldn't look further than this weekend. I'd keep these precious items and when I felt down, I'd pull them out and remember that light sometimes glinted in the darkness when one least expected it to.

I moved onto the underwear my aunt had donated. The knickers were new, so that was OK, but would it feel weird wearing a second-hand bra? Yes, probably, but I had time to spare, so I spent a few minutes trying on the lacy, balcony, halter and plunge selection and inspecting the results in the mirror. They were inevitably too tight, cutting into my back, but they were too expensive to throw out. Not 'wasting' them brought on thoughts of my mum. After Vanessa had talked about her in such glowing terms the last time I was here, I had decided to ask more about their friendship when the opportunity arose, but in all honesty the subject alarmed me today and I was glad when she shut it down. Shrugging the discomfort away, I turned my thoughts to dinner. Was this another pyjama event or not?

Rather than risk looking stupid, I decided to ask, but half way up the stairs to Vanessa's bedroom I heard talking filter down, not from her floor but the attic area above. Pressing myself against the wall, I stilled to listen to the low male and female voices. A cold shiver passed through me. Was the tearful whispering really my aunt's? Followed by the creak of a door, the conversation soon stopped, but a moment later the sound of footsteps approached. My heart in my mouth, I darted away, managing to hop into my bedroom before Bernard passed.

The peal of the telephone from behind me made me jump from my skin. Somewhat shaky, I answered.

'Hello?'

'It's Bernard.'

Bloody hell. Did he know I'd been eavesdropping? Not that I'd been able to make out the hushed yet urgent tones. 'Oh hi.'

'I'm afraid Vanessa is indisposed for dinner. Would you like yours in the dining room or would you prefer me to fetch it up on a tray?'

Indisposed? What on earth did that mean? My mind thrashed with uncertainty. I was sure Vanessa had been crying. Should I find her and comfort her? But that might be overstepping the mark. Oh God, there was a thought – were my own troubles intruding her routines or upsetting her?

I inwardly nodded. It was best to stay quietly here and not encroach further. Yet I'd definitely ask her about it and apologise tomorrow.

I reverted to Bernard. 'Here, please, if that's OK.'

Chapter 37

'Morning!' My aunt dragged open the bedroom curtains. 'Did you rest well?'

I was so deeply asleep I didn't hear her come in so it took a moment or two to adjust. She chuckled when I covered my eyes from the light. 'Sorry, darling. But it is eleven o'clock.'

I struggled upright. 'Really?' I was truly shocked; sleeping in late in the Parker household was considered very rude even for people who lived there.

'I expect you were making up for Friday night.' She arranged several cushions and sat next to me on the bed. 'I'm so sorry about dinner. I got an unexpected call and had to go out. Did Bernard look after you?'

It felt at odds with Bernard's 'indisposed'. And that teary murmuring from the attic landing had surely been hers.

'He did, thanks.' I gestured to the tray by the love seat. 'I wolfed down his delicious offerings and then pretty much fell asleep.'

'Excellent. So you didn't miss me too much.' She patted a pile of clothes on her lap. 'I've brought you these for later.'

Oh God, today's return to the flat. 'Thanks so much.'

'Jacket, top and,' she pulled a face, 'leggings.'

'I take it you're not a fan.'

'For yoga yes, but otherwise no. Still, each to their own. The denim is a Levi's from back in the day. Vintage is what the young call it, apparently.'

'I love it. Thank you.'

She twisted the ring on her wedding finger. 'Your mum and I used to imbibe a dreadful faux champagne called Babycham and think we were the bee's knees back then. But life moves on and your lover becomes your *meilleur ami*. Like Joy and charming Clive. And of course my own talented *bel homme*. He hides it behind that serious demeanour, but he's an absolute sweetie. Extremely sexy too.'

Perhaps I blushed as she chuckled. 'Oh yes, I'd forgotten you'd seen that for yourself. Trust me, you'll completely understand one day when you fall in love.' She slipped off the huge diamond. 'I couldn't decide between a solitaire or a cluster. Try it on.'

I knew it wouldn't fit, but to please her I tried. 'It's gorgeous,' I said, quickly handing it back. Remembering the old Disney song, I smiled. 'Someday my prince will come.'

'I'm sure of it.' She gave me a peculiar look. 'It was a surprise to get the callout on Friday. Or should I say Saturday morning. When I thought about it, it made sense, though.'

Why *had* she turned up at the hospital? 'Oh right—'

'Your not wanting to worry your mother unnecessarily.' She cocked her head. 'Having my name as your next of kin?'

With a flash it suddenly made sense:

'*So who is Vanessa?*'

'*A sort of godmother type of person, I guess.*'

'*A fairy one?*'

'*How about you? Do you have one?*'

'*Have what?*'

'*Someone you'd call if you were ever in trouble.*'

Gus. The one person with whom the best part of me flowed out – funny, flirty, chatty. Even attractive. Hiding the hot swell of pleasure, I looked at my bitten fingernails. 'The call from Student Support?'

'Yes, a helpful and well-spoken young man.'

So Gus had remembered our Cinderella chat and contacted Vanessa. Which meant he'd returned to the flat and was fine.

Relief surged through me. I'd see Augustus Montgomery Avery later and talk everything through.

'You'd be no good at poker, darling.'

'Oh?'

'You're like Bernard. Everything shows on your face.'

I felt my deep flush. I'd always thought I hid my feelings well, but I clearly had to work harder at it. Or maybe it was just this woman who seemed to have an uncanny ability to look into my soul.

My stomach loudly rumbled.

'Oh darling, you're hungry. Get dressed and let's see what we have. I'll meet you down there in five.'

My Calvin Kleins had clearly been scooped up with the wet towels, so I donned the whole Vanessa ensemble and hurried down to the kitchen. Pulling items from the fridge and piling them erratically on the granite island, she seemed tired and distracted; perhaps her *bel homme* wasn't happy having me around.

'I can prepare something for us both,' flew out of my mouth. 'A light brunch if you fancy?'

'Would you, darling?' She peered at the goods on display. 'Yes, whatever you're having, I'll have too.'

When she'd wafted away I spent a good ten minutes fretting about what to make now I'd made the hasty offer. Something egg-based seemed safe. Yes, I could manage poached or scrambled with mashed avocado. Or perhaps I could top the pumpkin bread with the olives, pine nuts and feta, then grill it. But those dishes really needed to be served immediately.

I ended up measuring out muesli, Greek yoghurt and berries, followed by a cured meat platter with figs and sliced ciabatta. Then I set the table for two, displayed the food in matching ramekins and plates, and patiently waited.

By twelve forty-five I gathered Vanessa was otherwise engaged. My appetite somewhat dampened with disappointment, I desultorily ate the delicacies alone. Then as though he'd been watching me swallow my last mouthful, Bernard appeared, asked if I was ready to leave and ushered me to the Bentley. I politely sat in the back and stared though the window as the streets of Belgravia sped by, yet I felt bundled out. Had I outstayed my welcome? Or was it just Bernard wanting to resume his free day? Would my aunt think I was rude not saying goodbye after all she'd done for me? I'd text, of course, but it wasn't the same as a thank you in person.

Shaking off the mixed emotions, I focused on my return to student life. To my surprise I didn't feel too horrendously anxious; indeed, there was a glimmer of optimism, even hope, deep in my belly. And if things didn't go to plan, I'd remember my aunt's wise words by putting on my poker face and I'd 'damned well act'.

Chapter 38

I'd felt vulnerable beneath the hospital gown and had the same sensation at the entrance to my flat. I pressed the buzzer, but no one answered, so I knocked until it finally swung open.

'Thanks,' I said to Herman's retreating back.

Not daring my eyes to Gus's door, I hurried to mine and tried the handle. It was locked. A good thing in terms of safety, but it meant I couldn't hide in my room and adjust. I inhaled to take a steadying breath, but Fayola appeared at the end of the corridor.

'Ruth! Thank goodness you're back! Are you OK? I've been so worried. Why didn't you reply to my texts?'

Her excitable voice alerted my flatmates in a way the flaming doorbell hadn't, as everyone seemed to appear at once.

'Sorry, I left my mobile here.' Trying to ignore the gawkers, I focused on Fayola. 'I don't suppose you've got my keys?'

'Yes, I have them somewhere. Where did I put them? One minute...'

The onlooker's curiosity clearly couldn't stretch for that long, as they vanished as quickly as they'd come, yet one person was noticeable by his absence. But there was no need to panic; eagerness wasn't Gus's style, and Fayola had returned and was opening up like a busy mother hen. Almost clucking, she gestured to my bed.

'I stripped it for you but I didn't like to dig into your drawers for new bedding.' She smiled thinly. 'I gave the bathroom a clean and the carpet a scrub, but I was fairly gone myself, so I think you'll need to give them both another go.'

The room smelled rank. 'Thanks so much. It was really kind of you and beyond the call of duty.' I opened the window and glanced around. 'Thanks for keeping my keys safe; I don't suppose you found my phone?'

'Sorry, no.' Her eyes didn't quite meet mine. 'I don't know how much you remember, but you were screaming the place down. It was all a bit hectic, what with the janitor and the paramedics.'

I looked at my feet. God, it was too, too embarrassing. 'All for a stupid panic attack. I'm really sorry,' I muttered.

She peered at me then. 'It was more than that though, wasn't it, Ruth?'

Bloody hell, how much was she aware of? My stomach churning, I considered how to reply but she squinted in thought.

'*He* was in here. He had a mobile in his hand.' She clenched her jaw. 'A thief as well as a bloody drug dealer, then,' she said at full volume.

'What? Who?'

She jabbed a finger at the wall. 'Him. I've lived with him for – what? Four weeks now? And I don't even know his name.'

Her boom was so loud, Gus was bound to hear, so I lowered my voice. 'You can't go around making accusations like that, Fayola. As you say, you don't even know what he's called, let alone anything about him.'

'Don't be naive, Ruth. Out during the night, sleeping in the day. He'll have been dealing.'

Indignation bubbled on Gus's behalf. 'What the hell? You have no idea what he does when he goes out, nor in the privacy of his own room,' I hissed.

'And he's probably helping himself along the way by the looks of him.'

'What the hell, Fayola? You're judging people on what they *look* like?' Good God, she was as bad as that prick who'd started this whole nightmare. 'You're accusing someone you don't know of being both a dealer and an addict?'

Her hands on her hips, she jutted out her chin. 'Who gave you the joint on Friday night then, Ruth? You were howling and scared. You told the paramedic that you'd seen your own dead body. You were clearly hallucinating. Whatever you'd been smoking was bloody dangerous. People like him should be locked up for that.'

I couldn't believe she was being so judgmental. Up to that point I hadn't decided what to say about the cannabis, but a desire to protect my only real friend pulsed through me.

'You're wholly out of order here, Fayola. As it happens, I bought it from some guy after I'd left you on Friday.'

'Really?' She lifted her eyebrows. 'Is that why the police raided us yesterday?'

'What?'

'You heard me.'

Though gobsmacked, I managed to splutter a few words. 'A raid? Like a search of the flat?'

'Yeah, exactly like that.' Her expression was triumphant. 'Didn't you notice that everyone's pissed off with you? We had to gather in the kitchen while they foraged our rooms.'

I groped for an excuse. 'It must have been a coincidence.'

'After the paramedic bagged what you'd been smoking? I think not.'

'Christ. I'm so sorry.' Then after a moment, 'Did they find anything?'

She shrugged. 'They didn't arrest anyone, put it that way.'

'That's good.'

I breathed through the shock. A drugs raid was truly unbelievable, something that happened in films, not in my dull little life. But the police clearly hadn't found anything illegal which meant that Fayola's suggestions were still outrageous.

'Look, I am really so sorry about the search, but you can't make blind accusations about people, especially when there's no evidence.'

'Evidence?' She folded her arms. 'Well, there wouldn't be any would there.'

'I'm sorry, I don't—'

'He cleared out before the police came.'

'What?'

'Come and look for yourself.'

I followed her to Gus's room. She gestured to the stripped bed, record-free shelves and empty desk. 'The facts speak for themselves. Guilty as charged.' She must have clocked my dismay as her tone softened. 'Look, I'm sorry, Ruth. I understand you and him hung out, but friends like that aren't worth having. He clearly wasn't a good person.'

A sharp blend of disappointment and anger took over. It wasn't Fayola's fault, but it felt like it just then.

'Don't lecture me about good people,' I snapped. 'Take a proper look at your own bloody friends.'

Chapter 39

Returning to my room, I flopped on my bed and tried to process the information I'd just gathered. So many different emotions fought for dominance, it was difficult to concentrate on any one. I really liked Gus – I might have even loved him – so I didn't want to think badly of him. But he'd scarpered without saying goodbye; he'd probably stolen my mobile. And what Fayola had said about his nocturnal habits did make sense.

Was he really a drug supplier? Were his record collection and trading just a front? The word *dealer* had sounded horribly grubby coming from Fayola's mouth, but was it really a surprise? Gus's parents had all but abandoned him; he'd clearly faced financial hardship and had to support himself somehow.

Perhaps I was naive, as Fayola had put it, but even I knew there was a ready market for illegal substances at uni. Better to buy from a fellow student than some local tough nut. And was it so very bad? University was a time when people experimented with sex, sexuality, ideologies and binge drinking, as well as drugs. Bloody hell, even me.

My nose stung. Gus wasn't a bad person, he wasn't a violent criminal on the fringes of society, but an unloved son with rejection issues. It was forgivable, wasn't it? And yet... How would my dad react if he knew? I'd been hospitalised, traumatised, poisoned. He'd be furious; he'd want to invoke the full force of the law. And what about Sylvie? Fearful of her disapproval, would I even tell her about it?

I pressed my face into the pillow. I didn't know the answer to anything; the only certainty right now was my despondency and sadness: I had so looked forward to seeing Gus, to hanging out with him, touching him, perhaps even kissing him, but instead he'd abandoned me.

–

The next thing I knew it was dark outside. My first thought on waking was my sheer bloody loneliness, the second was the essay I had to write by midnight. Part of me said 'fuck it'; I was probably the only goody-two-shoes who submitted coursework on time. But what else could I do to fill my empty life? Gus had done a runner, my flat mates clearly hated me and I'd ballsed-up my tentative friendship with Fayola. Even my blissful weekend in Belgravia had gone awry at the end. Was it simply me? Was I so boring or uninspiring, that this would be a pattern in my life?

Suddenly aware of the cold, I shuffled to the wardrobe. When Bernard had asked if I was ready to leave, it hadn't felt appropriate to belt up two flights of stairs for my new clothes. How nice it would be to slip on a soft cashmere top and transport myself back to at least some semblance of feeling loved. Instead, I reached for one of Tim's discarded sweaters. Mum had been delighted when I'd taken on her 'waste not, want not' ethic, but in truth I wore them to hide the unattractive roll of fat around my waist. As I yanked out the navy jumper, a large envelope tumbled too, which I quickly caught before it fell to the ground.

My heart pounding with expectation, I sat on my chair and swivelled to the desk. Gus used these cardboard cases for his postal sales; he'd clearly left it for me. There'd be a note, an explanation of why he'd gone. A new address; perhaps even a suggestion that we meet. Maybe his leaving would be a good thing; we could cultivate a relationship outside this miserable, judgmental flat.

I opened the flap and slid out the contents. My iPhone – thank goodness – and the King Crimson LP I'd first heard through our mutual wall. He'd told me this was a first edition and worth a fair sum of money, so he'd had no plans to sell it unless he was 'made an offer he couldn't refuse'. Both relief and pleasure spreading, I smiled at his sweetness. It was a really thoughtful gesture and showed he didn't blame me.

Looking for clues to his whereabouts, I went back to the packaging then carefully inspected the inner sheath and the vinyl itself. Nothing was apparent but Gus knew my passcode; he must have left a message on my phone.

I retreated to my bed and turned it on. A voicemail was waiting, so I took a quick breath and listened to it. Her tone crisp, the speaker was a detective constable from the Metropolitan Police who asked me to call her back. Oh God, this was exactly what I had dreaded; I was in big trouble, wasn't I? And I'd put Gus in jeopardy too.

I slowly inhaled and focused. It was fine, actually. I had already told my lie to Fayola and that would be the story I'd stick to: I'd bought the drug from some random man in a dark corner of London. Bloody hell; it wasn't as though it didn't happen all the time.

Returning to my phone, I systematically went through the missed calls and texts over the last two days. When I reached the one Gus had made to Vanessa, I smiled. Bless him, he'd done absolutely the right thing. Involving Mum and Dad would have freaked them out initially, then been swiftly followed by all sorts of maternal alarm, reproof and reprimands.

A sentimental bravery overtook me. Save for that once, I'd never messaged or telephoned Gus, but I now had two excuses – to thank him for contacting my aunt and for leaving me his precious LP. What should I say? Something light and sardonic, but a comment that warranted a reply so I could get a dialogue going. It wasn't too late to meet now. I'd happily ditch the essay for him.

Stupidly grinning, I searched my contacts. Though I frowned and looked again there was nothing under A or G, not even M. I stared, perplexed, for several moments, then realisation finally dawned. Augustus Montgomery Avery had deleted his number.

Chapter 40

Over the next few days I functioned like a robot, doing the bare necessary to get by. Each morning I caught the bus to campus, doodled in the library, half listened during lectures and practised my cello on autopilot. I ate a desultory sandwich in a cafe at lunch time and returned again for tea, but I had no other option than to skulk back to the flat each evening. Initially I was fearful about a confrontation with my flatmates, but I needed have worried as they all seemed to avoid me.

By Friday afternoon my despondency was so raw that I sat on my floor and cried. How had it come to this? I was still the same friendless girl who'd trudged to high school and back, listening to music in lieu of company. I was nearly nineteen years of age and supposed to be living the dream, yet a whole twenty-four hours had passed without me speaking to a single soul. I'd exchanged a couple of texts with Sylvie and she'd sensed I was low, but the convoluted situation was too difficult to explain.

Unanswered questions and negativity consumed me. Why had Gus deleted me from his life? Would a police officer turn up with a warrant for my arrest? I tried to focus on my weekend in Belgravia, but there'd been no word from Vanessa since, so that sensation of rejection loitered. Besides, it now felt as though it had happened to someone else.

The hallucination, on the other hand, remained fresh. I wasn't by any means a danger to myself, yet I couldn't help unpleasant thoughts edge in. What if it wasn't so much a delusion as a premonition? Suppose I couldn't go on feeling this abandoned and wretched?

Forcing myself upright, I reprimanded myself for the pathetic self-pity. My parents would be horrified, Tim too. I'd never put them through that debilitating turmoil again. I had to shake myself down and escape the four walls of my cell.

I considered the options. Contact Li Min? Go to the student union and force conversation on someone? Try Tinder? Or maybe slink back to Manchester? None of the options felt right, especially the latter: though I longed to be hugged by my dad, he'd sense something off and Mum would see me turning up unexpectedly as another failure.

Despite my misery, my lips twitched. There was clearly only one option left: Netflix, a shed load of unhealthy treats and as much cheap wine as I could throw back.

—

Loud knocking rattled me from sleep the next morning. I had no idea of the hour but it felt like dawn.

The sharp rap again, then Herman the doorman's clipped tones. 'Ruth, you're wanted.'

I slithered from the bed. Oh God, my head; it felt as though my frontal lobe had come loose. 'Who wants me?' I asked through the door.

'See for yourself. They're waiting for you on the landing outside.'

'What?'

I fumbled with my dressing gown and opened up. Doorman was retreating to his room.

'Herman,' I hissed. 'Who is it?'

'How should I know?'

So it wasn't Gus. God only knew where the ridiculous hope had come from.

'An official type, if that helps.' He lifted his fair eyebrows. 'It looks to me like they want a private word.'

'OK, I'm coming.'

Bloody hell, the police. Alarm jangling through me, I tightened my belt and pulled open the fire door. His hands clasped behind his back soldier-like, a suited man was looking out of the window. Oh hell, it wasn't just a constable but a senior officer.

'Hello?' I called, absently noting dull daylight through glass. 'I'm Ruth Parker. Did you want me?'

Surprise overcame my terror when he turned. 'Bernard!' I exclaimed. 'What on earth are you doing here?'

—

I was all fingers and thumbs as I washed and cleaned my teeth. My emotions had jerked from shock to pleasure to deep, deep worry. There could be only one reason why Bernard was here in person: something bad had happened to Vanessa. An accident, an illness, even death. Quite honestly it would have been the final straw; though flaky in some ways, my aunt had been the most constant good thing in my life. She'd invoked hopefulness and romance, and somehow she still had that flair of making me believe dreams could come true.

Bernard had been perceptive, thank God. 'I'm here to drive you to Wilton Place,' he'd immediately said. 'Another visit, I believe.'

Dumbstruck, I'd looked down at my state of undress.

'I expect I'm a little early.' He'd cleared his throat. 'Sometimes Vanessa makes arrangements in her head, but gets so busy with other things that they don't get communicated, if you take my meaning. No need to hurry; I'll wait outside in the car.'

I yanked open my wardrobe. Exclusive Belgravia again. What on earth should I wear? As if that would matter to my indulgent aunt! More than a little giddy at my unexpected good fortune, I threw on Tim's jumper and dragged on my leggings, shoved a few bits and bobs in my bag, grabbed the denim jacket and left.

Chapter 41

I breathlessly watched the bustling London streets pass by as Bernard drove. Good things didn't happen to Ruth Parker. Or if they did, they were soon followed by a nasty curve ball of one sort or another. But he duly turned into Wilton Place, pulled up the Bentley outside the handsome building, opened my door and marched up the pathway to let me in.

I was greeted by the smell of chlorine, shortly followed by the sound of Vanessa's eloquent voice. 'Darling! There you are.'

Wearing a robe and a turban, she was half way up the spiral stairs. She'd clearly just had a swim, and it was a little odd to see her face without her auburn locks framing it. Still beautiful, of course, but different somehow.

I proffered her the bunch of roses I'd bought en route. 'Thank you for having me again,' I said.

She sniffed them theatrically. 'Aren't you sweet. They're the same shade of pink as your lovely hair and they're still in bud like you are.'

I was stuck for a suitable reply. Her description was exquisite, but I'd never seen myself as a bud, or indeed anything as delicate as a flower.

'And you are very welcome.' She put her manicured hands either side of my shoulders and peered at me intently. 'However, now this is a regular thing, we need some ground rules.'

The naked image of Sergio flashed behind my eyes, quickly followed by that odd whispered exchange in the garret, but I focused on the heavenly words 'regular thing'. 'Yes, of course, fire away.'

'What did I say both times? My home is yours. And it is.' She glanced at Bernard behind me. 'So that means you don't have to wait to be fed if you're hungry; if you fancy a dip in the pool or a session in the gym, you help yourself. And you don't need to stay like a prisoner in your bedroom all day. Agreed?'

I couldn't hide my beaming smile. 'Absolutely. Thank you so much.'

'Good. And you mustn't mind if I have other things to do.' She rolled her eyes. 'They know full well I've taken a final bow, but the manuscripts keep coming, sometimes several in a week. Naturally I can't resist having a peep.'

'That's understandable.' It was the first I'd heard about Vanessa's... well, retirement, if that's what she meant. If Mum knew, she hadn't said anything to me.

She slipped her arm through mine. 'In all aspects of life, it's better to call it a day when one is at the top, don't you think? Come on, let's chat whilst I dress.'

Her bedroom was as golden as ever, the central heating blasting out and the weak sunshine filtering through the Georgian window panes. And, thank goodness, the en suite was open and vacant from what I could glean.

She flung open a wardrobe door, spent a moment or two raking through the hangers, then threw a colourful kaftan on the bed. 'I don't know about you, but I have no intention of leaving the house today, so comfort is the thing.' She looked me up and down and chuckled. 'Tim's sweater, I take it? Here.' She pulled out four or five items and laid them on my lap. 'Add those to your collection. Right, I'm off for a shower. When you've changed, I'll see you in the kitchen. I thought we might partake in a little cooking.'

'Sounds great. Thank you.'

Fleet-footed with cheerfulness, I went down to my 'bedroom' and opened the closet to hang my new clothes. Smiling at my aunt's incredible talent of imparting her wishes without seeming critical, I looked down at my attire. What had my mum said at some point? '*I'm all for recycling, Ruth, but wouldn't it be better to lose weight rather than trying to hide those extra pounds?*'

With that thought in mind, I stepped in front of the mirror. A clump of melted chocolate was stuck to the front of Tim's castoff. Along with my hangover eyes, Bernard had collected a veritable ragamuffin from Brockley. I nodded to my reflection. My aunt had standards; from now on I'd make an effort to reach them.

—

Studying a display of vegetables on the island, Vanessa was already in the kitchen when I arrived.

'Look at you!' she said when she turned. 'As pretty as a picture. How are you at cuisine?'

To my delight a tunic not dissimilar to Vanessa's had fitted. Even better it had clearly pleased her too, so I shifted my mind to the next challenge. *Cuisine.* Something told me it was more than just shoving a sweet potato in the microwave. 'Ah, not my strongest talent.'

'Why on earth not?'

I thought about her question. We weren't really that type of family. Mum baked a good cake, a tasty casserole and an excellent Sunday roast, but both she and Dad worked, and though Tim had become a foodie in more recent times, meals had been more a means to an end rather than an event. 'I suppose I just haven't tried it.'

'Excellent.'

I wasn't sure why that was a good thing, but Vanessa handed me a chef's apron and turned back to her chore, fingering onions, tomatoes and peppers before deciding which ones passed the test.

'Right,' she said eventually. 'We'll start with a classic Italian beef ragù that's easy and packed full of flavour. It takes only a few simple ingredients and can be used in many ways.'

'OK.'

Italian. Did that mean Sergio was around this time? That we'd – or maybe just she – would be dining with him later? But my aunt was still speaking in her authoritative tone.

'For example, one can toss it with fresh tagliatelle pasta, make it into lasagne with béchamel sauce or use it as a filling for homemade ravioli.'

'Perfect.'

'And we're starting early because one slow-cooks ragù to ensure it has time to develop all the incredible – and healthy – flavours. People not in the know rush it, but it needs a minimum of two and a half hours on the hob. Understood?'

'Absolutely.'

That seemed a very long time. No wonder my mum had never favoured 'cuisine'. Her world was full of brisk activity and action rather than lolling around, and I was like her in that respect, which was why my non-life at uni was driving me nuts. But here it felt as though I was on holiday where I could relax and be someone else, where I didn't have to think about my broken heart, my lack of friends or the rest of the shitstorm.

Vanessa placed her chosen onion on a wooden board and handed me a sharp knife.

'The ragù starts with *Il Soffritto*, which is basically finely sliced carrot, celery and white onion which one sautés slowly with a little olive oil for about ten minutes until soft but not browned. Chop, chop, off you go.' She watched me peel away the skin. 'Finely, but do watch those lovely fingers! It wouldn't do to send you back tomorrow with one missing.'

'Righto,' I replied.

I'd been at such a low point, I'd have accepted an offer to be imprisoned here forever, but the confirmation I was staying for the whole weekend was sublime.

I continued to follow my aunt's crisp instructions until all the ingredients were bubbling in a pan. Appearing satisfied, she finally nodded. 'Good work. So long as we top it up with water or stock, it can simmer away while we relax and sip a glass of vino.'

Hand on hip, she considered her extensive collection of wine, opened one and poured two inches into huge goblets like a sommelier. 'Let's get comfortable and talk about you.'

Bloody hell; talk about me? That would either be a shedload of doom and gloom or take thirty seconds. We made our way up to the lounge, but by the time Vanessa had put on background music and curled up her slim legs on the sofa, she seemed to have forgotten her suggestion.

'Sometimes one has to draw a line,' she said instead.

Was this more culinary advice? 'Oh right.'

'I drew mine when I was sent not one but two manuscripts for a middle-aged supporting role,' she continued as though we'd been on the subject for some time.

Her expression was aghast. Whether it was it the 'supporting' or 'middle aged' which appalled her the most, I had no idea, but it threw me back to her comment about remaining *trente-trois*. In fairness, she didn't look a great deal older even now.

'Yet still Fabian sends them, hoping to tempt me. He wants his commission, of course, but I have a mind to write and produce something myself just to spite him. Cast me and Joy as the beautiful and *young* leading characters. Perhaps have a Shakespearian-style character swap so one doesn't know whom is who or what whom has done. Because of course it's the many acts of deception which provide the dramatic devices to inform the action.' She stretched gracefully. 'You could vet them if you're bored. Allow the ones through that won't bring me out in a sweat.'

Vanessa in a sweat? That was something I could not imagine. 'I'd love to read them.'

She wafted her hand dismissively. 'Help yourself. There's a whole heap of scripts upstairs.' Then, 'You've barely sampled your drink. Don't you like it?'

I took a breath. Be honest about last night's pathetic boozing session on my tod? Confess my sheer loneliness? 'I don't think I have the palate for red. And I probably drank a little too much last night.'

Immediately sitting forward, I thought she'd ask me to elaborate on where and with whom. 'One doesn't *have* a taste for wine, darling. One acquires it.' She looked at me pointedly. 'And one starts by not drinking plonk.'

'Well, I am but a mere student—'

'Not here you're not. Go on, have a sip.'

I did as I was told.

'What do you think?'

Like all red wine, it tasted sour, so I wasn't a fan. 'Better than last night's cheap rosé.'

'Praise indeed. Still, this is a fairly inexpensive bottle.'

Well, that was a relief. I tried it again. Still sour. 'So, what is this one?'

'A Brunello di Montalcino. Cost around thirty quid.'

I nearly spat out my mouthful. 'Thirty pounds?'

'Ruth Parker, you have a lot to learn.' She tucked a lock of hair behind my ear. 'But don't worry, darling, we'll get there.'

Chapter 42

The afternoon pleasantly drifted by. Humming to Nina Simone and Ella Fitzgerald, Vanessa bobbed in and out of the lounge to check on the ragù and I slowly sipped my *vino*, trying to detect the flavours she described.

'This one is made in central Italy,' she said. 'Of course the taste is unique to the individual, but people speak of sour cherry, dried oregano, aged balsamic, red pepper flake. Then there's brick, fig, sweet tobacco, espresso and leather…'

So I hadn't been wrong about the 'sour'. And even if brick or leather had been part of anyone's diet, I still thought it was a load of old baloney. Yet I understood Vanessa was trying to educate me, so I tried to pay attention despite my need for food.

'The other Italian wine you've probably heard of is a Barolo.' Lifting her glass to the light, she demonstrated. 'See? Brunello is a much darker colour than Barolo. And with this rich brilliant red hue on the rim? With time, Brunello softens out and becomes paler. Most professional tasters recommend drinking it after a decade, but that's only a rule of thumb. This one is eight. Apparently it was a good summer weather-wise.'

There it was again – the drifting of time. I was ten when this vintage was bottled and Vanessa was 'thirty-three'. The kettle sketch was still in my bedroom at home, ingrained smudges and all. She'd been smoking that day but there was no sign she still did. And hadn't her fingernails been badly bitten? Nothing like their shaped and painted elegance today.

The woman herself now stood. 'My creation has had long enough now, don't you think?'

Thank God, food at last. I tried not to nod too manically. 'I expect so.'

She languidly moved to the door. 'We'll dress properly for supper today. I've done the hard part, so Bernard can do the rest.' She cast a beam over her shoulder. 'Remember my house is yours, darling. I'll see you in the dining room for *cena per due alle otto.*'

When she'd gone, I breathed out a huge sigh of relief. I didn't know much Italian, but even I could work out that *per due* meant 'for two', and though the 'properly' dress for supper was a little alarming, a try-on in my bedroom would be fun and pass the time. My more imminent concern was my hangover hunger – I couldn't possibly manage until eight, especially if I'd be *experiencing* more wine.

I peered down to the front door from the landing. I could nip to the shops for a chocolate bar or a bag of crisps; I wasn't an inmate, after all. But I felt the weight of Vanessa's expectations on my shoulders. They actually felt a little like Mum's. I'd never thought of the two women being similar before, but in a way they were. Vanessa's direction and advice was reams more subtle, but eating or drinking calorific crap clearly wasn't the way forward.

As though the food police had visited, a tower of sliced carrots, cucumber and celery was waiting in the fridge along with a collection of clingfilm-covered dips, so I perched at the island and sampled them. Beetroot and dill? Definitely something and avocado. A salsa, and thankfully, hummus.

Finally replete, I cleaned and tidied, then ambled upstairs and flopped down on the bed. In fairness there was plenty to do: text Sylvie and update her; phone Mum and Dad; watch a film or surf the internet; explore the gym or have a swim. Instead, I closed my eyes, and moments later I slept.

–

When I awoke I felt horribly groggy. I'd clearly been functioning on adrenaline all morning and afternoon, and it took quite a while to adjust. But after a long, brisk shower, I finally perked up and turned my mind to what to wear for my dinner date. Vowing that one day I'd be brave enough to wear the red silk, thin enough to don the little black number and sexy enough to sport the bandage, I opened the wardrobe and raked through the frocks. There were four more additions since I'd looked earlier, so I hooked them up and stood back to consider each one.

'So which will it be?'

Vanessa's voice from the door made me start. She was already dressed in a wide-legged cream jumpsuit.

'Sorry,' I said, catching my breath. 'I didn't hear you come in.'

I gestured to the blue maxi dress, an outfit I'd never dream of wearing in normal life, but I liked its simplicity and the fact it had sleeves. 'This is my favourite but it'll be too long. I'm not as tall as you are.'

'Aren't you?' She stood next to me in the mirror. 'What size are your feet?'

'A five and a half.'

'Wait there.'

She returned a minute later with a pair of silver mules. 'They're a six but maybe worth trying the ensemble?'

As she made no sign of moving, I stripped off my bath robe and self-consciously struggled into the gown. When I'd finished with the heels, she gestured to my pink reflection and laughed. 'See?' she said, lifting her chin and elegantly stretching her neck.

'What?' I asked, unconsciously doing likewise.

'Just look. Who says that I'm taller? A little attention to those cheekbones and lips, then I think we're done.'

Chapter 43

Feeling quite grand, I hooked arms with Vanessa and sashayed down the stairs like a debutant. Sadly there were no handsome suitors to greet us in the dining room, but I immediately noticed the roses I'd bought were displayed on the sideboard, and – with a jolt of dismay – that the polished table was set for three. A trio with Li Min's boyfriend had definitely been a crowd, but at least he was pleasant. The same couldn't be said for my aunt's husband. Though his toned torso had flashed in my mind more often than was comfortable over the past weeks, I'd replaced it with his 'Who the hell are you?' comment, and outrage had soon bubbled: I was the person who'd saved her brother's life at his flaming wedding. I might have been completely forgettable, but surely any decent person would have remembered that.

My aunt gestured to one carver chair and pulled out the other. 'Let's do opposites like Lord and Lady of the manor.'

'Perfect,' I replied, hoping the seat beside her might be for Bernard. But a moment later he appeared with a tray, placed a silver charger centrally and disappeared as silently as he'd come.

'Oh dear; I must have said something out of turn. I rather think it means we're serving the antipasto ourselves. What do we have today?' She peered at the display. 'Prosciutto, salami, pepperoni, peppadew peppers – which are the best thing ever – artichoke hearts, olives and focaccia. Oh, and almonds, which always have to be Marcona.'

'Oh, really? It looks lovely.'

'Shall I be mother?'

'Yes please.'

A notion suddenly struck: I'd thought of this woman as my godmother, an older sister or even a friend, but perhaps she saw me as the daughter she'd never had. Presumably she'd left it too late, which was why she was showering her love and affection on me.

Sniffing back the emotion, I watched her efficiently scoop a little of everything onto my plate, move on to the 'guest's' and her own. She lifted a wine bottle from a cooler and showed me the label. 'Both Pinot Grigio and Sangiovese – the Chianti Classico grape – are perfect with antipasti, but see what you think of this young Friuli and do tuck in.'

Chatting intermittently, we ate and drank, then as though he'd been watching, Bernard appeared the moment we'd finished our appetiser, whisking away our dishes but leaving the spare.

'So,' Vanessa said from her end. 'How's the romance going?'

My shock – and dismay – must have shown on my face.

'Oh darling, what happened? Not a broken heart, surely?'

I found an abridged version popping out. 'He decided to quit uni.'

'Ah, disappointing. But surely it won't stop you remaining pals.'

'I have no idea where he lives, so...'

'Not with his parents?'

'I doubt it. He doesn't even bother with his twin sister, so I think it's a safe bet I won't hear from him again.'

'Ah, twinnies. The unique closeness and perception. And of course that enduring elastic. Despite stretching and separation it never quite breaks.'

Surprised at her rogue comment, I pulled myself out of my brimming self-pity.

'You have a twin?'

Her eyes seemed to lose focus. 'Yes, it's an indelible bond others don't fully—'

Bernard's loud clearing of his throat interrupted her sentence.

'There you are, Bernard,' she said, snapping back from wherever she'd been. 'We were so engrossed in conversation, we didn't hear you come in.'

He carefully lowered bowls of spaghetti ragù on our placemats.

Vanessa pulled a wry face when he'd gone. 'He thinks I'll spill on the linen if I serve it. Eat up whilst it's hot. Eating cold food's a monstrosity.'

'I agree,' I said, pleased it would be the two of us after all. But the instant my shoulders relaxed, the door swung open and Sergio appeared, damp-haired and wearing a bizarre combination of smart jacket and jogging pants. The aroma of shampoo or shower gel in his wake, he swiftly moved to Vanessa and kissed both her cheeks.

'*Scusa il ritardo, tesoro.*' He held out his palms apologetically. 'After you left I lost track of the hour.'

That was interesting; they'd clearly been together whilst I'd been napping. It was the first time I'd seen them interact since the garden at Château Les Douves, and though I tried not to stare, I burned with embarrassment as they drank each other in with their eyes. I longed for the ground to swallow me whole, but Vanessa eventually sighed and raked back Sergio's shock of thick hair from his forehead.

'Better late than never, my love.' She swivelled to the sideboard, but instead of choosing the wine as I expected, she pulled out a flower, snapped its stem and threaded it through his button hole.

'A rosebud just for you.' She motioned to me. 'You remember Ruth, don't you? She was a darling and helped me to prepare dinner tonight. She's a very quick learner; I was impressed.'

He turned to me. Would I have recognised him if we'd passed in the street? Chiselled features, dark colouring. But today he was neither the smooth model-type I'd met in the French sunshine, nor the deranged artist I'd encountered the next day. Nor, thank goodness, was he naked.

'Hello,' I muttered. Fearful he'd greet me with social kisses, I froze, but I needn't have worried.

'Ruth, yes of course,' he replied. And though his tone was polite, he looked clean through me.

–

Vanessa chatted graciously for the hour or so Sergio remained at the table, including us both in the conversation, but her 'bigging up' of my artistic and musical talents was excruciating, made all the worst by Sergio's disinterested, monosyllabic replies.

She eventually pecked his cheek. 'It's fine, darling. I know you're busy, so do go.'

'*Grazie*. Then I will bid you *buona notte*.' He finally had the good grace to meet my eye. 'Good night, er—'

'It's Ruth,' I replied, emboldened by my second shot of *Liquore Strega*.

'Yes, darling, our rosebud is called Ruth,' Vanessa repeated. She yawned extravagantly. 'I think I'll retire too.' She made her way to my end of the table and kissed the top of my head. 'Night, sweetie. Beauty sleep is a-calling, so I'll see you when I see you.'

Feeling unaccountably piqued at my aunt's swift exit, I drank another measure of minty liqueur and contemplated what she'd said about the scripts sent by her agent. Writing her 'memoir' too. Did one of the guest rooms double up as a study? Deciding to investigate now, I ambled to the door, but when I entered the lobby, all the bifolds were closed and the darkness felt foreboding.

That sense of someone or something nearby brushed my spine again. Was the wheezing sound just the wind from outside? And was there a shadow on the landing above? I forced myself to look up to the very top. No lights, no movement, no whispering tonight. I shook myself down; ghosts and phantoms or even *un diavolo* did not exist and I couldn't stay here all night.

Taking a big breath, I scuttled up to my room, threw off my dress and hid beneath my bed covers. The groans and creaks which pierced the silence were just the echoes of an old house, I sensibly reasoned. Yet I kept my breath shallow, listening for footfall until I slept.

Chapter 44

When bright morning awoke me at ten, the spooky sensations from yesterday felt silly. In reality I'd been tipsy from the wine and too many helpings of *Liquore Strega*. Though I couldn't recall it, I'd clearly got up in the night to wee, as I was make-up free and the bedside lamp had been extinguished. Why this place felt so different in daylight I couldn't say, but hunger took me downstairs to the kitchen. When no one had stirred for a good fifteen minutes, I decided to embrace the 'my home is yours' ground rules.

Feeling a little giddy at playing house, I started by making myself the egg and avocado creation I'd thought of last week. If Vanessa appeared and fancied partaking, I'd happily share. Heck, I'd even make a portion for Sergio, despite his lack of friendliness. What had Vanessa said back in France? '*You mustn't think he's rude. It's a question of artistry. When one has that genius, that calling, one has to follow it. You understand that, don't you, Ruth?*'

Completely starstruck at the time, I had nodded enthusiastically, but I wasn't so sure any more. Still, whether the guy liked me or not, I felt good about myself today: I had actually admired my own pink reflection in the mirror last night; I was about to imbibe a healthy breakfast and fresh coffee; I'd let it settle by flicking through a couple of magazines on the sofa upstairs; then I'd hit the gym and finish off my routine with a refreshing swim.

I didn't see hide nor hair of my aunt or her husband all morning, but moments after I had taken my last mouthful of a green salad for lunch, Bernard appeared from nowhere again.

'Are you ready to leave?' he asked.

I took a big breath before replying. Dare I go to Vanessa's room to bid her goodbye rather than suffer the sense of dissatisfaction I'd felt the last time? But suppose Sergio was there? And it was her private space; if she'd wanted to see me, she'd have summoned me. Knowing I'd kick myself for not getting some kind of assurance or closure, yet too cowardly to try, I nodded. 'Yeah, sure.'

But on the way out, she called from above. 'One moment! I'm coming down.'

She waited until her butler had quietly disappeared. 'There was something I meant to ask. Bernard said you looked, well, somewhat frightened when he called for you yesterday. Were you expecting someone else?'

'It's a bit complicated to explain.'

'Oh darling.' She led me to the stairs and sat down. 'I have time. And if I ever haven't, I'll always make an exception for you. Tell me.'

Tears pricked my eyes. 'I was taken to hospital after smoking—'

'Cannabis, I rather gathered that.'

'But it might have been something stronger so the police raided our flat. So when Bernard called—'

'Ah his black suit. I have to say I prefer him in grey.'

'And I got a message from a PC asking me to call back. Do you think I'm in trouble?'

'No, certainly not if I have anything to do with it.' She tapped her nose. 'I have an old pal high up in the Met. I'll smooth things over with him.'

'Really?'

'Yes, really. So you're to stop fretting about it.' She peered at me knowingly. 'I don't suppose your flatmates are terribly pleased with you?'

'No, they pretty much blanked me all week but I'm going to try and make it up to them, especially my friend Fayola.' I smiled thinly. 'Beg if I have to; June's a long time away.'

She patted my hand. 'You're sweet.'

There was something in the way she said it. 'You don't think I should?'

'Darling, it's up to you. But the words "blanked" and "beg" say it all, don't you think? Self-worth is the key, remember? Friends should be people you can rely on.' She stood and kissed my forehead. 'I shall see you next Saturday, my beautiful rosebud! We'll buy you a pair of Jimmy Choo's.'

'Wow, sounds wonderful! Thank you for everything.'

'My pleasure, darling, but perhaps don't mention it to your mum.' She raised an eyebrow. 'She might not approve of my profligate ways.'

'OK.'

'Oh, and we mustn't let you get behind, so don't forget to bring your cello!'

—

I was soon back in room seven. Although the prospect of another lonely week nagged, Vanessa's parting words spurred me on. Already I felt different; a little taller, slimmer and prettier somehow. Sure, those things were superficial and shallow, but Vanessa had a way of imbuing confidence and yes, self-worth. Perhaps a touch of self-importance too. The latter was reinforced when I braved the kitchen at dinner time.

'Saw you earlier,' someone said amidst the general chatter.

Naturally I didn't respond. Who'd be talking to me?

'Ruth? I saw you earlier.' His eyes wide behind his glasses, Herman the doorman was clearly intrigued about something.

'Oh right?'

'Departing and returning in a chauffeur-driven Bentley, no less. I didn't have you down as that sort.'

Everyone fell silent. 'What sort is that?' I asked.

He had the good grace to blush at my challenging tone. 'Rich, I suppose,' he muttered.

'And that's a bad thing?'

'Er no, I guess not.'

In fairness it probably was; genuinely wealthy students were unlikely to let on about their privilege in the culture of university, but there was no doubt that he and the others were regarding me through a different lens.

For good or for bad, I found I liked it.

Chapter 45

As October trundled by, my routine stayed the same – days on campus in New Cross, evenings at the flat in Brockley and weekends in Belgravia. Although I had an occasional exchange with Herman in the kitchen, I didn't pursue my friendship with Fayola. From time to time I caught her studying me with an analytical frown, but in truth I was happy with my own company. My aunt sent me messages ranging from flattering to educational to funny every evening, and if I lost some of my poise during the week, it was topped up within minutes once I saw her.

More often than not Vanessa accompanied Bernard in the Bentley to collect me and we headed straight to Harrods to effect something of a trolley dash in the womenswear department where she selected clothing, accessories and footwear – including the promised peppermint-coloured Jimmy Choo sling-backs – with astonishing speed without trying anything on.

'Let's hope something fits one of us, sweetie. Shopping is such a bore. If only Bernard was as proficient at selecting and purchasing as he is at returns,' she said dismissively, even though the man himself was at the wheel. 'Let's now do the fun part.'

The 'fun part', it turned out, was akin to sixth form, albeit at finishing school standards. During those Saturdays, we studied masterpieces by da Vinci, Rembrandt and Van Gogh at the National Gallery, took in Shakespeare, Elizabeth I and the Brontë Sisters at the National Portrait Gallery and admired Andy Warhol, Pablo Picasso and Salvador Dalí at Tate Modern.

It was a little embarrassing when Vanessa tested my knowledge in front of other viewers, but I understood she wanted to educate me, so rather than take her arched-browed reprimands personally, I swatted up in my uni room and was thrilled when rewarded with a 'Well done you!' proud smile when I got it right.

—

One weekend we visited an exhibition of nudes at Tate Modern.

'What are your thoughts, darling?' Vanessa asked me after a good fifteen minutes of silent study.

'He—'

She gave me that schoolmarm look. '*He* is Modigliani! An artist with a unique and instantly recognisable pictorial style. His emotionally intense portraits and seductive depictions are among the best-loved paintings of the twentieth century, Ruth.' She gestured to the artwork. 'But what do you think of his muses?'

I inspected the long-faces and blank, almond eyes of his models. 'I don't know,' I replied, wanting to be honest despite her admonishment. 'They don't look very happy.'

'I disagree. They have amazing sensuality and they are using it. They were paid far more than their peers who worked long, demanding hours in factories. Which makes them the strong ones with the power, no?' She stepped closer to a painting of a woman glancing over her shoulder. 'And now she's immortal. How amazing is that?'

I still struggled with the thought of stripping off for a love interest, let alone for payment or art. As ever, my aunt seemed to read my mind as she chuckled. 'Food for thought, sweetie. As is his famous quote.'

'Oh right, what's that?'

'"*You look out at the world with one eye and into yourself with the other.*" What do you think that means?'

I had no idea. 'That people are hypocrites?'

'Mmm, perhaps. Of course one's eyes are the gateway to the soul and reflect what's really going within us. No one really knows, do they? How did Shakespeare put it? *"Look like the innocent flower, But be the serpent under it."*'

I couldn't say why, but I thought of my mum and gave a little shiver. But Vanessa's attention had shifted. 'Time for a coffee, methinks.' She glanced over her shoulder as we headed for the cafe. 'Maybe he's suggesting there are two versions of ourselves.'

'I suppose there are inwardly.'

'How about outwardly? They say everyone has a "double-walker."'

'A what?'

'German for doppelgänger.'

'Isn't seeing your doppelgänger an omen of death or similar?'

'Or one's spiritual double, according to the Egyptians.' Her eyes sparkling with mischief, she chuckled. 'Don't worry, I have no plans to meet mine today.'

Chapter 46

November and reading week came around but I didn't go home as planned. Though Vanessa had been too polite to say it in terms, she'd been right about Mum's likely reaction to my hair. Dad would make a candy floss or similar quip, but she was bound to say something critical or hurtful, so I made excuses and said I was visiting a friend.

I had expected an invitation to stay at Wilton Place. None was forthcoming. Even worse, my aunt's usual plethora of cosy night-time texts simply stopped, so I spent a lonely few days in room number seven fretting I'd done something wrong. But to my sheer relief all came good on Saturday at ten when I looked through my window. The Bentley, thank goodness, was reassuringly there.

—

One Sunday morning, Vanessa made a rare appearance in the lobby and announced we were to visit Hampton Court Palace to 'converse with Henry'.

'Which wife would you be if you had the choice?' she asked me as we ambled around the Tudor elevations.

'Preferably one who didn't die,' I answered dryly.

'How about Jane, a demure spouse who was completely subservient to his wishes?'

An image of Sergio immediately swam before my eyes. I suspected he took pains to avoid me in the house, but on the few occasions we'd briefly rubbed shoulders, the glance he'd given me was either blank or dismissive. 'Hmm; I think not. Didn't she die giving Henry a longed-for son?'

'Yes indeed and we can't have that. Both you and your gorgeous babies will thrive and survive.' She shaped her hands around a horror-filled face. 'It's said her phantom, a "white wraith", appears on the anniversary of her death. Romantic, *non*?'

I still occasionally had that goosebumpy sensation of being watched at Wilton Place and wondered if it did have a resident ghost or *un diavolo* who walked the landings at night, but in daylight it always seemed too ridiculous to mention it.

I chuckled. 'Romantic? If you say so.'

'So Anne, perhaps, a woman with sophistication, confidence and charm?'

'Well, that didn't work out well for her.'

'True. But I like her feistiness. She knew what she wanted and set out to get it.' She gave me a sidelong glance. 'Promise me you won't be a wilting wallflower when the time comes.' She theatrically inhaled. 'When a woman has "*black and deep desires*" why shouldn't she act on them like a man would? As Anne illustrated, life is very short, so one should seize the day.'

'If only it was that easy.' I thought of my almost-interlude with Gus. If I could turn back the clock, would I now have the confidence to initiate sex?

'See?' she said, clearly reading my mind. 'You are beautiful, intelligent, interesting, fun. Sensual too. You have the power.'

Though deeply flattered, I adopted a wry tone. 'Well, seeing as you insist…'

'I do. And of course we mustn't forget Anne of Cleves. Apparently, Henry fell in love with her portrait.' She affected a dreamy look and laughed. 'Now you have to agree there's something rather spectacular in that.'

—

I didn't mind a dose of culture, but it was always a relief when Vanessa abruptly said she'd had enough, was tired or hungry. She'd call for Bernard and he'd appear in the car minutes later and whisk us back to Belgravia.

Once in the foyer she would generally say, 'See you in five,' then vanish for an hour or many hours. But I was happy to idle away the time after cello practice by making myself smoothies and healthy titbits in the kitchen, or working out in the gym and swimming lengths in the pool. As if I'd been hiding she'd finally reappear with a, 'So there you are! Let's do girly stuff,' command, which generally involved her dressing me up like a doll and experimenting with different make-up styles.

'You have such a fabulous facial structure,' she'd say, showing me her artwork in the mirror. 'Eyes, colouring and hair can be changed, but those bones make the perfect base for a chameleon.'

In fairness she was right: each time I looked I was someone different, a person even I barely recognised.

Chapter 47

When I arrived at Wilton Place on the sixth of December, I was greeted by the distinctive and refreshing scent of woodland pine.

'Isn't it beautiful?' my aunt called from the landing above. 'It took four of them to get it in and three hours to decorate it.'

I wasn't surprised; the Christmas tree was huge.

'Look.' She stretched over the bannister. 'I can almost touch the angel from here.'

Bernard cleared his throat beside me. 'Careful!' I said, reading his thoughts.

'Isn't it pretty, though? I just adore fairy lights.' She had a child-like glee about her. 'Following family tradition we had it installed on the first, didn't we, Bernard?'

'How lovely.' I pictured Sergio's parents at the Château Les Douves. Did he ever visit them or they come here? I didn't know Italians put up Christmas trees like the British, but clearly they did. My mother was a stickler for tradition, so even though ours was artificial, it wasn't dragged out of the garage along with the dusty old baubles until twelve days before the twenty-fifth.

'Come on up then, sweetie.'

'OK.'

When I reached my aunt she slid her arm into mine. 'Sorry there was no detour today. I couldn't bear the thought of all the hustle and bustle and busyness everywhere. December is a time for hibernation, don't you think? Except when we hunt for your pressies darling girl.' She tapped her temple. 'I'm still giving those a great deal of thought. What would Ruth wish for, I keep asking myself.' She brightly laughed. 'Well, one isn't supposed to say a wish out loud, but I rather think I already know the main one and I'm working on that.'

I'd been so spoilt by my aunt over the preceding few weeks, I had no idea what I'd actually ask for. Yet my stomach still flipped with excitement. She was clearly one of those people who enjoyed and embraced every aspect of the festive period and it was infectious.

When we reached her boudoir she flopped back on the bed. 'How do you feel about a JimJam day?'

'Sure.' She was still wearing her silk dressing gown. Although I'd have preferred to be somewhere well out of her husband's way, I picked up a large soft toy sitting in his place and hitched beside her.

'Nice teddy bear,' I said.

She seemed surprised to see it. 'Oh, that isn't supposed to be in here.'

Perhaps it was a Christmas gift for a child. It was certainly in good condition and plush, but its extended snout and jet beady eyes seemed a little old fashioned for a modern kid. Still, Harrods sold pretty much everything. And did the thought of her treating someone else really give me a tiny jolt of jealousy?

'It's Sergio's fault.'

That brought me back to my aunt's slightly petulant tone. 'Oh right.'

'His fault that I'm so very tired and headachy.' She theatrically yawned. 'He's had me posing for hours. You know, for the last portrait he's so flaming obsessed about.'

I nodded as though I understood. She'd mentioned a 'collection' before, yet save for a reference to the roof terrace, I had no idea where she modelled or he worked.

'Darling, could you do it for me?'

'Do what?'

'Sit for Sergio in my place. You'd be doing me a huge favour.'

I couldn't help laughing at the ridiculous suggestion. I ruffled my hair. 'Apart from all the obvious physical differences, lack of experience and so on, something tells me Sergio wouldn't be best pleased if I appeared in—'

'His attic studio.'

'Yes, there, pretending to be you. I'm not sure he even remembers my name. So as much as I'd do anything you ask of me, I'm afraid that isn't something I can help you out with.'

I was still chuckling at the notion, but my aunt didn't smile back. 'You wouldn't do that for me after all I've done for you?'

Her mood was so peculiar, I couldn't quite tell if she was teasing me or not.

'I would, of course I would but… well, I'm hugely flattered you think I'd be suitable but—'

'Funny girl.' She seemed to flip to her *don't you know who I am?* stance. 'Darling, it would simply be about perspective, proportions and light so the Hunchback of Notre Dame could do it, but you are absolutely right. Only one person could replicate me and that's my—'

A knock interrupted. Bernard was at the entrance, holding a tray. 'Time for upstairs?' she asked.

He nodded. 'I think so.'

She slipped from the mattress and padded over the carpet. At the door she turned and eyed me witheringly. 'Leggings, Ruth, honestly? And you really do need to attend to those nails.'

—

Sure I'd let my aunt down somehow, I collected my cello from the hallway and skulked down to the basement. When I'd first brought it to Wilton Place in October, she'd asked how my uni course was going and I'd probably been too honest with my reply by describing my musical inadequacies in comparison to my peers. Instead of the 'don't worry everything will be fine' response I'd expected, she'd looked at me pointedly and said, 'Well that isn't good, Ruth. Have you told your parents?'

'No, I don't want to—'

'Disappoint them, which you certainly will if you don't pull up your socks. You're an artist, young lady, and I want you to shine.' She'd smiled and kissed my forehead. 'Practice makes perfect. At least two hours a day when you're here, please!'

'Absolutely,' I'd replied. Because above all other things, I did want to please her.

—

I smelt rather than heard Vanessa come into the media room. The aroma of her vanilla, jasmine and lily of the valley scent usually evoked feelings of light-hearted pleasure, but today I felt anxious.

'Was I out of sorts earlier, darling?' she said from behind me. I stopped playing my instrument and turned. 'I see from your face that I was. Sorry Rosebud, the last thing I want to do is offend my favourite girl.'

'You haven't, not at all.' I looked at my nails. I'd practised for three hours and my whole hand felt sore. 'It's just that I need to keep them short to play, so...'

'Understood.' She lifted an arched eyebrow. 'But perhaps trimming them by biting isn't the best way to groom, and it isn't a terribly hygienic habit either.'

'Point taken. But the leggings...' I gestured to my cashmere jumper. 'It's long so I thought they went together quite well.'

'They're for yoga, but if you say so.' She laughed. 'My own fault for handing them over; I must take greater care.' She looked at her watch. 'Goodness, it's three o'clock. Are you hungry?'

'I am actually. Starving, in fact.'

'You and your huge appetite.' She tugged me from the chair. 'Come on, let's see what healthy snack we can rustle up to keep you going. I'm not for a moment recommending you take up smoking, but when I was your age I managed until dinner on cigarettes and thin air!'

Chapter 48

The final weekend before the Christmas holiday soon came around. I was sad there'd be an intermission of three weeks before my next visit, but I was excited to go home. I had unsurprisingly pined for Dad and his affectionate humour, yet I'd missed Mum too.

Vanessa had texted to say we'd go shopping, so I'd carefully dressed in suitable attire for Harrods. I'd planned on using her usual trolley dash to glean what she might like as a festive gift, but Bernard turned up alone at my flat, saying that Vanessa felt 'quite under the weather'.

When we arrived at Wilton Place, she was dismissive of my concern. 'Silly man; I woke up and simply couldn't be bothered,' she said. 'And besides it's far too cold to venture outside.'

Either way, we stayed in the lounge and chatted all day. Before supper she raked her fingers through my hair. 'Your natural colour is making quite a comeback. Maybe keep it a little longer this time? It's a shame not to show it in its full glory,' she said. 'So thick; you're lucky. I know someone who has alopecia. Great chunks of hers falls out because of an autoimmune disease. Can you imagine how distressing that must be. One's body attacking itself?'

'God, poor woman. That's really horrible.' In comparison to my aunt's vibrant locks, there was nothing 'glorious' about mine. 'I'm not sure anyone would describe my "mouse" as beautiful, though.'

'You're still fair, and when one is born blonde, one is entitled to retain the label for life. It's a rule,' she said. 'All you need are a few highlights running through. Right, a trip to my salon is now on our new year's list. I'm excited already.'

'Fabulous, thank you! If one was to find someone a Christmas pressie to thank them for their incredible generosity,' I asked, 'what on earth would one buy?'

She kissed my forehead. 'If you're referring to me, darling, you've already given it.'

'Given what?'

She gazed, her eyes shiny. 'Yourself. Your company. Your willingness to learn. You couldn't offer me anything I'd want more.' She sniffed and changed the subject. 'So, tell me, what have you purchased for dearest Joy?'

I was still fretting about that. 'I'd love to treat her to something really nice, but she'll think it's a waste of money and insist I take it back,' I replied.

Even as I said them, the words felt dreadfully unkind, and my guilty feelings weren't assuaged by Vanessa crinkled brow.

'You mustn't be so hard on your mum, Ruth. Her heart is surely in the right place. I've told you before; she's the most loyal person I've ever known.'

That old discomfort about their friendship churned in my stomach. Yes, Vanessa had described Mum as loyal, yet she'd also mentioned the word 'bully'. Then there was her strange comment '*I know what she did but I never let on.*' Quite honestly the whole subject disturbed me.

Vanessa misinterpreted my frown. 'I'm sure she loves you very much, Ruth. Maybe she just struggles to show it.'

That was all right, then. Dad had said something similar, but it didn't lessen the old sensation that it was me who fell short in some way. I took a breath to change the subject, but Vanessa was gazing at the bouquet of roses I had brought.

'Fear,' she said. 'Fear is a horrible, insidious emotion. It plays with the mind; it can make the very thing one dreads actually happen. Yes, we both understand that very much.'

An icy shiver trickled down my spine. I thought she'd say more, but she remained as still a statue for several alarming seconds.

I touched her hand. 'Hey. Are you OK?'

Her face animated again. 'Of course. What were we talking about?'

I intended to brush over the strange blip, but words popped out. 'Fear. How that can make the worst happen?'

'Do you mean your mother?'

'Well, yes, I suppose so.'

'Oh darling.' Vanessa stroked my cheek. 'Little Joy loathed her mother with a vengeance; my guess is she's terrified that history will repeat itself.'

–

When Bernard brought in tea at three, he cleared his throat.

'Are we still set for the ballet this evening?'

Vanessa looked at me. 'Oh golly, I'd completely forgotten about your treat. *The Nutcracker* at the Coliseum, of course. It's a Christmas must.'

'And the Clos Maggiore for dinner at six?' he murmured.

Vanessa bounced up from the sofa. 'Goodness, look at the time; we need to get ready. Bring it up to Ruth's room, would you?' She held out a hand to me. 'Come on, sweetie, time is of the essence. You take longer to transform, so let's sort you out first.'

My closet was chock-a-block with dresses these days, so it took my aunt several minutes to decide what I should wear. There was no doubt I'd lost weight since my first visit in September, yet she pulled out a dress I immediately knew wouldn't fit.

'Let's give this one a go,' she said, handing it over.

'It's a size eight, it'll be too small.'

She gave me a disparaging look. 'Not crisps again, I hope.'

I'd tried so hard with my intake of food that a single flaming crisp would be have been a veritable treat, but she relented with a twitchy smile. 'Okie dokie. You choose. So long as it isn't sporting a Sweaty Betty label I'll cope.' Patting the stool beside her, she perched at the dressing table. 'Come on then, make-up, young lady.'

Her eyebrows knitted with concentration, she spent some time applying my foundation and concealer. She lightly applied bronzer with a huge fluffy brush. 'Paying attention to these stunning cheekbones is vital, remember?'

I couldn't help smiling at her usual description. 'Yes, Aunt Vanessa.'

She looked at our reflections in the glass. 'Not quite there yet.' She studied the colours on the eyeshadow pallet. 'But soon you will be.'

—

It was exhilarating to accompany my aunt as she sashayed into the restaurant and later the theatre. All eyes were on her but I couldn't help basking in her reflected glory. I tried to do her proud by emulating her straight spine, the set of her shoulders and angle of her neck as I followed like a bridesmaid. I inwardly guffawed at the irony of finally fulfilling that particular aspiration, yet I felt so elated and positive, it seemed entirely possible I could find love and romance, too.

Of course the best person to consult on matters of the heart was Vanessa. I'd never seen *The Nutcracker* but she had explained the moral of the story in the car:

'Clara learns that she possesses the power she needs to make her dreams come true. Confidence and execution are key!'

Ready for a dose of Tchaikovsky, I flashed a Vanessa-like smile at the person sat beside me. Next year was going to be amazing; I couldn't bloody wait.

Chapter 49

Dad's face was such a picture at the railway station, it brought tears to my eyes.

'Welcome home, love,' he said, hugging me tightly. 'We've missed you. The house has been so quiet without you.' I already knew what he meant, but his next comment confirmed it. 'No cello?'

I'd left it at Wilton Place. 'Christmas presents, so something had to give. Don't worry, it's securely locked away.'

'I'm sure it is, love. Just thought we might have a few carols as usual.'

A pang of guilt struck. I had thought of bringing it home, but as well as safety, Vanessa had suggested a 'refreshing break' from my instrument would do me good. 'And we will. I still have my old violin and that dented flute which refuses to work. Assuming Mum hasn't sold them, of course.'

He raised his eyebrows. 'Best behaviour please, young lady. She's so excited to see you.'

—

Mum was in the kitchen when we arrived home. She turned when I entered. 'Your hair!' she immediately exclaimed.

I tried not to rail, but it was hard to keep the clipped tone from my voice. Dad hadn't said anything about it, bless him, but my mother had done exactly what I'd predicted.

'A friend cut it and dyed it for me,' I replied, somewhat challengingly. I immediately felt bad as she seemed to shrink. 'The pink's nearly out now, though.'

I was excited about becoming blonde, but I pushed that thought to the back of my mind. It was brilliant to have Belgravia and all the excitement it invoked under my belt for January, but now was the time to focus on my family and to practice what I'd promised myself – to be kinder and more patient with Mum. I glanced around the familiar surroundings. Compared with Vanessa's palace, everything seemed a little shabby, including my mother.

'How are you, Mum? It's so nice to be back.' I tentatively stepped forward for a hug, but she seemed to stiffen, so I dug deep for a smile. 'I bought you something for Christmas.'

She looked alarmed; my mother did everything by the book. 'It isn't for a week, Ruth. You can't—'

'It's fine, Mum. This one's for now. Sort of for us both.'

She opened the envelope as if it might bite. 'Oh, it's a—'

'A high tea for two with a glass of champagne.'

She bit her lip. 'How lovely. But you're only a student; you can't—'

'I got it on Groupon at a really good price, Mum. Maybe we could go this weekend?'

As though counting the calories I'd imbibe, she seemed to look me up and down. Bloody hell; I'd been here five minutes and I was already holding onto my vow by a thread. I took a steadying breath. 'I thought it would be fun. Just you and me.'

'And it will.' She abruptly smiled; a huge, neat beam which transformed her face from shrewish to quite stunning. 'Thank you, Ruth. What a lovely gesture. I'm looking forward to it already!'

–

I hopped on the bus and visited Tim in the evening.

He gave me an easy hug. 'Wow, look at you!'

Had we always embraced? Nope, this was a new thing; the adult siblings slowly peeling off their set childhood ways.

'Which means?' I asked wryly.

'I can't quite put my finger on it. Sure, there's your fab hair and how you've done your make-up, but...'

I discarded the denim jacket. Other than this, a couple of tops and a pair of designer jeans, I'd left all my 'Vanessa' clothing at hers. 'Careful,' I said. 'I've already had Mum assessing whether a cream scone will tip the scales to obese.'

'Nope, not that. You've definitely lost a good half stone, but it's something else.'

Only Tim would mention my weight loss so directly, but it was great to know it showed. 'Lack of one of your sweaters, maybe?'

'Hmm, don't think I'm letting you off that lightly. Come on through.'

I followed him to the tiny kitchen and watched him taste a dish on the hob. 'Nearly done. I only had time for a mushroom risotto, but I figured that would be counted as luxury food for a student. Am I right?'

I pulled out a chair and sat at the table. He'd clearly gleaned some change in me and assumed I'd met someone romantically. I felt a small stab of loss about Gus. Falling in love – and all that went with it – was the one thing missing from the past heavenly weeks.

My brother was observing me. 'You didn't answer the question.'

'About?'

'Luxury food.'

I paused before replying. Could I tell him about my weekends at Wilton Place? But Vanessa had suggested we keep it between us so as not to offend Mum, and it was an exquisite, secret life I didn't want to share.

'Absolutely! So, how's it going?'

After all he'd said about teachers over the years, Tim was training to be one himself, but that wasn't what I was asking about. Keeping me posted by text, he'd moved his affections from the 'Rotherham adonis' to an 'even more beautiful' colleague at his school.

214

His cheeks deeply coloured. 'I still can't tell whether he's into me or not.'

'Is he mirroring your body language? Does his smile get bigger when he sees you, does he move in close when you speak, leans towards you and makes eye contact?'

'Err, maybe. God, I'm not sure. He's friendly but—'

'Do you even know if he's gay?'

'Yes. No. I don't know!'

'Is he aware you are?'

Tim didn't reply.

'OK, does anyone outside your close circle of friends know?'

He raked his newly cropped hair. 'I can't exactly go public to everyone except, well, you know who.'

I nodded. Our mum. Poor Tim. Any fall from grace by me wouldn't be far, but for my brother it was a whole other thing.

Chapter 50

Mum dressed in her best for our trip to the Lowry hotel. She looked classically beautiful, serene.

'Is that an actor from *Coronation Street*?' she asked whilst we were waiting to be seated.

Her eyes were shiny with intrigue; she phoned one of Dad's sisters most evenings, and it would be something to discuss. I was glad they loved her as much as he did, but it was interesting to note that her only longstanding friend was Vanessa. It reminded me of her comment about Mum and her mother. Could I casually ask about their relationship? Nope; 'loathe' was a very strong and uncomfortable word.

I came back to her question. 'Maybe. In fact, yes it is,' I replied. 'Should I sneak a picture?'

'Ruth!'

But her reprimand was in an excited, animated way, so I stood. 'I'll go to the ladies and take a snap. I'll be very discreet, I promise.'

When I returned, she was sitting at our linen-clad table. She shook out her laundered napkin. 'This is fun. I haven't had afternoon tea since being invited to the Savoy.'

My antennae twitched. 'That sounds lovely. By Vanessa, I assume, with it being London?'

She sipped her champagne and nodded. 'Yes, but back in the day, of course.'

'Oh?'

'She lived there until she was taken on by the French! She was a jobbing actor then, accepted whatever work she was offered to pay the bills, and not a lot of it was acting.' She lowered her voice. 'Dad suspected it was because she wasn't very good at her art.'

I bridled at his unsporting comment. But maybe he'd been bigging-up Mum rather than putting Vanessa down. After all, it was what he did all the time for 'his Joy and his joy'.

'But she could still afford to eat at the Savoy?'

'That's a good point. But Vanessa never did anything by halves. As soon as it was earned, it was frittered.'

'It was nice of her to spend it on you.' I leaned back to make way for the stand of crustless triangles. 'You must have been close for her to spoil you like that.'

Mum frowned. 'And still are.'

'Absolutely.' The huge garland which now adorned our front door was evidence of that. 'That holly wreath is something else.'

'And the usual Harrod's hamper. I haven't peeped yet as I'm saving it for Christmas Day.'

'Quite right.'

I offered Mum the sandwiches and helped myself to a selection. She watched me take a bite. 'You have to be in it to understand it.'

I'd expected a critique about my manners or diet, so I was thrown by her comment. 'Sorry?'

'A young friendship like that. One born of—' she thought for a moment, '—deprivation, dependency and need.'

'Deprivation' seemed an odd word to use. Dad had mentioned Mum's poor upbringing, so perhaps Vanessa had one too. It was very much at odds with the glossy Alpha girl I imagined she'd have been.

'Such foundations of mutual trust are rock solid.' Mum looked at me meaningfully. 'Even if you don't see each other all the time.'

I nodded in acknowledgment. Vanessa had disappeared from my life after France, and although I'd felt let down during those long lonely months, the moment I saw her, I knew the attachment had always been there.

Mum poured tea into our cups. Her set jaw suggested the conversation was at an end, so it was a surprise when she resurrected it.

'Have you heard or seen anything of her?' she casually asked.

I spent a moment sipping my drink. My time with Vanessa was relaxed, enjoyable and treasured, not ambivalent and testy like now, but I didn't want to completely lie, so I went for a middle line.

'A little,' I replied.

Carefully spreading the jam on her scone, Mum fell silent for some time. When she lifted her head, she eyed me strangely. 'If I ask you a question, will you answer it honestly, Ruth?'

'Of course,' I replied, breathlessly scanning the possible options.

'It's something I can't ask. Not because I'm disapproving or being judgmental.' She put a trembling hand to her chest. 'I just can't.' She took a sharp breath. 'Is Tim gay?'

Gobsmacked, I just gaped.

'It's fine, Ruth,' she said. 'Your expression says it all. I suppose that's what the note was all about?'

'Yes…' I didn't need to ask which 'note' she was referring to, but what on earth had she thought it meant back then?

She played with her napkin for a moment or two. 'Could you tell Tim that I know, please?' Her clear anguish showed how difficult her query had been, let alone asking me, of all people, to broker an understanding between them.

'Of course I will. What would you like me to say? I mean, will it be OK for him to discuss it with you if he needs to?'

'If I'd wanted to talk about it, I wouldn't be asking you, would I, Ruth?' she said sharply.

'Right, got it.'

And I had. It was another unmentionable. How Tim would feel about it, I had no idea.

Chapter 51

When I rocked up at Tim's on Sunday morning, I made to ring the bell, but the door swung open and a man strode out. It might have been a new flatmate, yet my brother's beam from the hallway suggested otherwise.

'Hi,' I said to the guy as he passed.

He ruffled his sandy hair. 'Morning,' he replied, turning at the elevator with a sheepish smile.

'So he's—'

'Ssh. He'll hear you.'

'So he's Welsh.' I made my way to the kitchen and pulled out a chair. 'Go on, what's he called?'

'Cadwgan.'

'Cah-doo-gan. Well, that's a name I won't remember.'

'He answers to Cad.'

'Not "darling" or "my love"?'

Tim filled the kettle. 'Unfortunately not.'

'What? You're joking. He's so into you I could feel the flipping heat. I take it he stayed overnight?'

'I made dinner, we drank and talked. I offered him the sofa, so yes, but that was it.'

'Did he laugh at all your jokes? Does he like everything you post on social media?'

'Yes.'

'And you didn't make a move?'

'Friends do all those things too, Ruth.' He sighed. 'I really wasn't sure; I wasn't going to take the risk.'

My grin falling, I nodded. Once bitten…

I took a quick breath. 'Mum knows you're gay, but she doesn't want to talk about it,' I blurted. Then hurriedly, 'Sorry to say it like that; I understand it's disappointing, but I didn't know how else to dress up the second half.'

He fell silent, his brow furrowed, so I made two instant coffees. He sipped the proffered drink and pulled a face of disgust. 'What did she say?'

'Just that she knew and I was to tell you she did. That she wasn't being disapproving or judgmental.'

'Right.'

'I tried to—'

'It's fine, actually.'

'Really?'

'Yeah. Mum knows, so that's good.'

It was my turn to frown. 'OK, great, but... Well, suppose you wanted to bring your handsome Welshman to Mum's for a cuppa? What then?'

'I have no idea, Ruth. Besides, he isn't mine and probably won't be.'

There was an irritated edge to his voice. Yet I felt irked too. As ever it was Mum's way or the highway.

'Look, I get it's your decision, but is this the—' A flash of Tim's twitching body hit the back of my eyes. Anticipating the thump, I put a protective hand to my chest. 'Is this the healthy way going forward? Another elephant in the room we all ignore?'

'It's her call, Ruth. We all have things we'd prefer not to speak about or want to hide.'

Surprised at his hostility, I lifted my palms. 'OK.'

'Like whatever you're getting up to in London. I'm guessing it's a bloke?'

Sergio's moody glance shot in. 'Life doesn't revolve around men, Tim.'

'A woman, then?'

It was, I suppose, but not in the way that he meant. And how could I even begin to explain the lure of Vanessa? 'Don't you feel let down by Mum?' I asked instead.

It was a somewhat direct question from a Parker family member, but I did want to know. She was our mother; she should want the best for us, be loving and concerned rather than constantly thinking of her own needs.

'Yes I do, if I'm honest. But there's stuff about her we're not privy to.'

'Like what?'

He smiled wryly. 'Well, as you're aware I've tried to glean what I could over the years and it doesn't add up to a lot. But sometimes Dad lets snippets slip out.'

The hairs on my neck stood erect. 'Go on.'

'After I was born she had severe post-natal depression, apparently. Dad didn't elaborate, but the symptoms include all sorts of things, including low esteem, feelings of hopelessness, rapid mood swings...'

It took several moments to digest what he was saying. 'Right.'

'Then she went on to have you. Maybe against doctor's advice.' As though deciding something, his eyes seemed to flicker.

'What else?' I asked.

'Have you ever noticed those marks on her upper arms?'

The silvery lines had always been there and looked like fine scratches from childhood scrapes. 'Yeah, but—'

'I think they were from cutting herself. And even recently she's worn a shirt or long sleeves when you'd least expect it...'

Oh God, I knew where he was going with this.

'I reckon that's when they've been fresh.'

–

Though I tried not stare at my new-found mother, Tim's revelation prayed on my mind. Was he right? Did my polished, upright mum really self-harm? It was shocking of itself, but Joy Parker had a secret life I knew nothing about. There were the crumbs I'd gleaned from Vanessa – including the *loathing* of her mother – and now a mental illness. Were they connected?

Her penchant for cardigans and layers of clothing, even in summer, now made sense. 'You know me, I'm cold-blooded,' she'd say if Tim asked if she was too hot. But she hadn't been able to cover up at the beach or in the swimming pool when we were kids, at least not all the time. Those holidays were long ago, yet if Tim was right, she was still doing it now. It would explain her refusal to wear a *chemisette* in France and her reluctance to take a dip at Château les Douves.

'Look, we don't know if that's what they were – or are. Don't you think you're just jumping to conclusions?' I'd said at his house.

'Maybe, but after Dad mentioned her illness, I... Well, I paid more attention, I suppose, and it struck me that when she was uptight or upset, she changed clothes from the smart stuff she likes to wear to a long-sleeved T-shirt and joggers.' He'd lifted his hands. 'I know, it's a tenuous connection, but one time I noticed blood seeping through the cotton.'

'Did you say anything?'

'Yup, I pointed it out. She said she'd been pruning and got scratched.'

'Well, it could—'

'It was here, Ruth.' He patted the fleshy part of his upper arm. 'And she hadn't been in the garden.'

'When was this?'

He'd smiled apologetically. 'The day you left for London.'

'Really? She was upset?'

'Of course she was, Ruth! You'd basically left home. Both Mum and Dad were devastated.'

Chapter 52

Fuelled by affection for both my parents, I offered to cook on Christmas Eve.

'Seeing as we're having the full works tomorrow, I'm happy to rustle up something a bit different. What do you think?' I asked Mum.

'Just being catered for would be lovely. Thank you, Ruth.'

My efforts to be nice were paying off, and it felt heart-warming, a joyous upward spiral. Taking over the kitchen, I recreated the *Braciola* Vanessa had taught me, and though I didn't mention the cost, I'd bought a *Vino Nobile di Montepulciano* to go with it.

'This is delicious, Ruth,' Mum commented after savouring her first mouthful. 'Where did you get the recipe?'

'Just off the internet.'

'Take me through it, then.'

I ignored Tim's sceptical rise of his eyebrows. 'It's quite simple really – you combine bread crumbs, herbs and seasoning with a little olive oil, spread it over the meat and roll it up.'

Mum nodded attentively. 'And the sauce?'

'I fried carrots, onions, celery and garlic until caramelised, added a splash of white wine, then when it reduced, I stirred in tomatoes and herbs.'

Though she twitched at the 'splash of white wine', it was lovely to see her so interested.

'I might give that one a go. What do you think, Clive?'

'Absolutely, so long as we replicate this red, too.' He had a playful twinkle in his eyes. 'How much did you say it was, Ruth?'

'It was on offer, so actually a bargain.'

The twenty-three pounds I'd paid was far from that, but perhaps it was a secret nod to my teacher. Or maybe it was the good-looking guy in Casa Italia who'd chatted to me about the options for a good twenty minutes. Had he actually been flirting or simply gunning for a sale? I'd left with such a bounce in my step that I'd texted Sylvie.

> I think someone in the next village actually fancies me!

> You are gorgeous, Ruth, why wouldn't they?

> Hmm. Have you looked at my case history?

But it was nice to feel attractive, light and carefree. Even nicer to spend a relaxed adult evening with my family. After mine was finished, Dad procured the next bottle, encouraging us to 'explore the rest of Europe'.

Mum gamely met us glass for glass until ten, then gracefully excused herself. She kissed Tim and I on our foreheads. 'I'm suddenly shattered. A little too much alcohol, I suspect. Thank you both for a lovely evening. What wonderful children I have.'

I had to remind myself that this was my mother, a person who had reason to self-harm. 'Love you, Mum. See you on Christmas Day!' I called, as the door closed behind her.

I was pretty gone myself. So were Dad and Tim if their bleary eyes were anything to go by.

'Anyone up for a small tipple of aged port?' Dad asked.

'Yeah,' Tim and I said in unison.

Dad cracked it open. 'I see you've picked up your old dad's bad habits, Ruth.'

'As in?'

'Lying to Mum,' Tim answered for him.

'I was going to say having a taste for fine wine,' Dad said with a chuckle. 'Which is precisely what fibbing is for, as my daughter ably demonstrated earlier.'

Tim's voice was slurred. 'If you say so.'

Dad's smile became wry. 'Or when it's for Mum's own good.'

We all selectively lied to both her and each other, but it still made me uncomfortable. Tim clearly felt the same. 'The trouble with deceiving people for their benefit is where you draw the line.'

'Cheers to my two grown up children!' Dad said, passing over our glasses. 'How on earth has that happened when I'm still so young and dashing?'

Tim ignored his attempt to lighten the conversation. '*Grown up* being the imperative words,' he muttered.

Dad sat back. 'What do you want to know, son?'

There were so many variables. Mum's mental health, my brother's sexuality, let alone what had happened in France. But Tim pushed his port away. 'Actually, I think I've had enough. I'll get off for my yearly sojourn in the old bedroom. Night night, dear family.'

When he'd gone I puffed out the air trapped in my chest. Bloody hell, that was close. But Dad turned to me. 'How about you, love?'

His expression was sincere, apologetic almost, and quite honestly it freaked me out.

'No, I'm good thanks,' I replied. 'I'll stick with this delicious...' I peered at the label. 'Warre's 1980 Vintage.'

'So what do you make of it?'

Vanessa's 'bitter chocolate', 'nutty caramel' or 'roast prune' descriptions came to mind. I still took the view that some expensive wines were 'Emperor's clothes', but I was getting the knack of detecting smells and flavours.

'My nose says figgy pudding. As for the palate, I'd say blackcurrant, moss and newly mown grass.'

Dad chuckled. 'Very good. And how much did I pay?'

I had no idea. My finishing school education – thus far – was limited to Italian *digestivo*.

'Fifty?'

Dad lifted his eyebrows.

'A hundred?'

'Spot on.'

It was a lot of money in this world but commonplace in Belgravia. 'Actually,' I said. 'I do have a question.'

'Hit me.'

'Vanessa.'

Dad pulled a droll face. 'OK.'

'Don't you like her?'

'No, I do. But I have to deal with the fall out.'

'They argue?'

'No, nothing's ever said. You know what Mum is like, it's mostly in her head, but even I would overthink the long periods of silence. Still, it always comes good in the end. Some friendships are like that.'

I looked at him questioningly.

'Durable.'

'That's true. Mum mentioned something about trust and dependency from when they were kids.'

'Hardly surprising when they were together twenty-four hours of each day.'

'Sorry, you've lost me.'

The porto was paralysing my mind, but the truth pinged and made perfect sense. Boarding school, of course. Not popular girls necessarily, but those entitled posh types I'd come across at Goldsmiths. Yet...

'Didn't you say Mum's family were poor?'

'No dad on the scene, so "family" was just a mother. And not a very good one.' He lifted his shoulders. 'Which, I guess, was why she was taken into care.'

–

Stunned by Dad's revelation, I made my way upstairs and forced down several glasses of water. My attempts to discover more had been futile: Dad only knew the basics himself; it wasn't something Mum talked about; he had a vague notion the children's home was in the Lake District and that Vanessa's parent or parents had died, but that was all.

My head clanged from too much alcohol and too many thoughts, but the one thing that stood out as I stared into the black night was that my mother had been dealt a tough hand. Sure, she was challenging and unloving at times, but I had to make allowances and give her more leeway. Certain I'd never sleep, I closed my eyes. The next thing I knew, it was morning.

Chapter 53

Finally roused by my throbbing temples, I peered at the bedside clock. It was nearly half past ten, but I reasoned I'd get away with another five minutes on a—

Realisation struck. It wasn't a Sunday but Christmas Day.

My fingers sweaty and fumbling, I quickly dragged on my dressing gown and stumbled down the stairs to the kitchen. Dad shot me a warning look but Mum got in first.

'Nice of you to make an appearance, Ruth.'

I glanced at the work surfaces. The potatoes, parsnips and carrots had been peeled, the sprouts were prepared. From the aroma, the turkey was already underway in the oven.

'Sorry, you should have woken me.'

'Tim was considerate enough to set his alarm.' She gestured to a tray of stuffing and meat balls. 'And was here to help. Food doesn't just make itself.'

'I know. I'm really sorry but I'm here now. What can I do?'

Mum threw down her tea towel. 'Nothing. Why don't you just go back to bed and sleep for the rest of the most important family day in the calendar?'

My brain was rattling and I longed for a hot drink, but her expression was furious. Desperate to make amends, I glanced around. 'Why don't you go into the lounge and have a breather while I wash up everything so far?' I asked. 'I'll bring through a nice coffee.'

'You're not even dressed yet, Ruth.'

'It'll take me two minutes.'

'And you reek of alcohol; I can smell you from here. Goodness knows how much you drank before bed.'

I caught Dad's raised eyebrows. He was slowly backing out of the room, the coward. Part of me wanted to chortle, but I was offended too: surely most mothers were a little indulgent of their young adult children during the festive season; I doubted they hurled insults. But I checked the usual hurt; tolerance and helpfulness was the thing.

'Right, I'll have a super quick shower and be back before you know it. For the rest of the day your wish is my command. OK?'

I pulled on a dress Mum had bought me last year. It was way too big and not at all something I would dream of choosing myself, but I wanted to smooth over my faux pas. I took two paracetamol, brushed my hair into a sensible style and dashed back downstairs to clear up the kitchen.

Once my chores were complete, I made cappuccinos and carried them on a tray to the lounge. I paused before going in. My hands were trembling. Why did I feel so culpable? Why was there a host of other curdling emotions in the pit of my belly? I couldn't quite describe them, but none of them were good.

Composing a bright smile, I opened the door and absorbed the flavours and sounds of Christmas. The evocative aromas of pine tree, gingerbread and mince pies, the background hum of *Carols from King's* should have made me happy.

'Merry Christmas, everyone!' I passed Mum her drink. 'Pots and pans washed. The surfaces are now gleaming and I've mixed the bread sauce. Let me know what's next.'

Dad and Tim were in their usual armchairs. My brother looked as rough as I felt, but he appeared sheepish, too. My eyes followed his to the discarded wrapping paper on the carpet.

'Oh, you've started opening the presents, then?'

'It's nearly noon, Ruth. I have to get back to lunch preparations if we're to eat at one thirty.' Though Mum's tone was reasonable, her spine was defensively straight.

'Of course.' I sniffed away the smarting at the top of my nose. 'Anyone got anything nice?'

Dad lifted a shirt to his chest, then added the tie. 'From my beloved. Suitably debonaire, don't you think?'

'Absolutely. Lovely fine silk.'

Tim gestured to the pile at his feet. 'Loads of really nice things—'

'Including a pair of cords.' Dad chuckled. 'Essential uniform for teaching.'

Mum tutted. 'They're back in fashion actually, Clive. Besides, they were on Tim's list.'

She had asked Tim for a list. Of course she had.

I pulled out my offerings from beneath the tree. Mum's was in a Harrods bag, so I'd hidden it at the far side to save the surprise. I presented the first to Tim. 'Careful, it's heavy.'

He made a show of shaking it. 'Not bath salts this year, then?' He ripped off the wrapping. 'Wow, a Le Creuset casserole dish. Thanks, Ruth. This must have cost you a fair sum.'

It did, but I'd dug into the last of my savings from France. 'I found an outlet shop, so…'

'Still, that's so nice of you on a student income. Thanks, sis.'

'I'm taking my time with this one.' Dad grinned and carefully peeled off the sticky tape. 'You've set a precedent with Tim, so I'm expecting great things.' He peered at the contents and frowned in confusion.

'It's a mini amp and microphone,' I explained. 'I thought you could progress from singing in the shower.' I pointed to the jack. 'That's a line out for recording directly to your computer.' Though I wasn't looking her way, I knew Mum's expression was tight. 'You know, just for fun. Maybe we could experiment with a few carols later?'

'You are thoughtful.' He gave me a tight hug. 'Thank you, love.'

I popped Mum's gift on her lap. 'Happy Christmas, Mum. I hope you like it.'

'Thank you, Ruth.'

She pulled out the box, tugged at the gold ribbon and peeled back the soft tissue to reveal the cardigan I had taken an eon to choose.

'It's cashmere,' I said hurriedly. 'I thought the pale silver grey because that goes with most things. And ignore the price tag because I found it in a sale.'

But she was already folding it and replacing it in its nest. 'Thank you, but I actually have one almost identical.' Clearly clocking my dad's glare, she patted my shoulder. 'I wouldn't want you to waste your money, Ruth. Not on something I won't ever wear.'

Part 3

Chapter 54

My lectures didn't start until mid-January, but I told another 'fib' and returned to London on Twelfth Night. Though I had already mithered my conflicting emotions to death in the privacy of my bedroom, I did it some more on the packed train. I loved my mum because she was my mother and occasionally I almost liked her. I'd discovered she'd had a difficult childhood and that she self-harmed, which were clearly good reasons for her mood to be low or prickly. But why did she take it out on me? Even though I was an adult, she could still humiliate and hurt me in a single swipe. She made me feel unattractive, unloved, rejected. When I tried to do something nice, she pushed me away – I had her Christmas present in my rucksack so I could return it to Harrods, for God's sake.

I turned to the smeared window and watched the saturated countryside pass by. It looked much like I felt – despondent and flat. I was exhausted; acting a brave face and bright smile were all very well for appearances and smoothing family tensions, but they were bloody tiring. Then there was my dad. He'd tried to corner me and make excuses for Mum, but I hadn't wanted to go there; my relationship with her was 'it is what it is', an expression I hated, yet which covered the problem to a tee, so there was no point raking over the coals. And besides, I hadn't wanted to threaten my façade – better to keep my honest feelings firmly in situ rather than risk them bursting out. Still, I'd come to a decision: Joy Parker was my mum and I'd dutifully love her from arm's length, but other than for short visits, I'd never live with her again.

I sniffed away the threatening tears. During my last Belgravia sojourn, I'd felt so optimistic and excited to see my family, but in truth I was closer to Vanessa than to my own mother. She'd once said, 'I don't think anybody understands you quite like I do, sweetie', and she'd been proved right. I considered texting her to say I'd be back earlier than planned, but it felt too needy and desperate. I just had to knuckle down in my uni halls and get on with it. It was for less than a week; I could manage that.

–

Though light was shining from beneath Herman's door, the flat felt dank, cold and unoccupied. Needing something to fix my hunger, I dumped my bags and headed for the kitchen, but the best it could offer was solidified milk and out-of-date cheese in the fridge, and a bag of rotten carrots in the veg rack, which had spilled out their juices like acid.

Knowing I couldn't live with the stomach-turning smell, I filled the sink with hot soapy water and set to work scrubbing the lino, but after a minute I sat back on my haunches and sobbed. This felt too much like Christmas Day when everything had turned as sour as those damned carrots. But I eventually shook myself down. I wasn't at home any more; I didn't need permission to order a takeaway or explain why I was going out and where. Hell, I could even eat at a cafe or treat myself to a meal at a restaurant if I fancied. I had the money after all – Dad had given me a tight hug at Stockport station, then squashed something into my palm.

'Unless it's a fine port, don't spend it all at once,' he'd said.

Though he'd given a skewed smile, his eyes had seemed sad, and when I'd finally opened my fist on the train, I'd discovered ten twenty-pound notes.

Pushing away a new wave of misery, I collected my coat and doggedly stepped into the cold night. Determined to walk in my aunt's shoes, I lifted my chin and strode across the forecourt. I'd swan into to the *Le Querce*, graciously sit at a table and I'd order the *bruschettina diversa*, followed by samphire pappardelle with prawns, queen scallops and nduja, in perfectly enunciated Italian as she had taught me. But half way there my lips twitched at my own ridiculousness. I was certainly more confident than I'd been in September, but that was definitely stretch. A thin-based take-out pizza as a return-to-London special treat would do me just fine.

—

When I woke in my freezing room on Monday morning, it felt strange not to immediately glimpse my cello, but I felt upbeat. Rather than wishing my life away until Saturday, I decided to be proactive. First up was food, and now was the perfect time to experiment with a few delicacies I could try out on Vanessa. Researching the recipes, buying fresh ingredients and cooking them in the mostly-empty kitchen took up a pleasurable chunk of the week.

On Wednesday, I returned my mother's cardigan to Harrods and scoured the sales for a little gift for my aunt. It wasn't easy; what did one buy the woman who had everything? Some-where along the line Vanessa had mentioned that Sergio came from the island of Sardinia, so I settled on a hamper stuffed with Sardinian-sourced pasta. It was a half price bargain and the reusable basket satisfied my ingrained waste-not-want-not upbringing; plus I could add a few extras to it.

Then there was project hair. The mousy roots were very noticeable now, and though I was wistful about the end of my pink days, I decided to spend Dad's cash at Vanessa's salon and surprise her at the weekend. My hopes were nearly scuppered by the lack of appointments, but they called with a cancellation for Friday.

Bethan the junior stylist greeted me with a hint of disdain. Though not a great deal older than me, a uni student clearly wasn't her usual clientele. She fingered my thick hair with a 'what am I supposed to do with this?' look, but when I mentioned my *actor* aunt, she immediately warmed to me.

'Ah, Vanessa's one of Pierre's clients,' she said, looking at a colleague with raised eyebrows.

I glanced around for a male employee, but Bethan read my mind. 'Pierre works upstairs. Doesn't do to have people looking in through the window and telling tales, if you get my meaning.'

A puff of pride swelling, I nodded. I did get her meaning. Despite her retirement, Vanessa still had no need to say: '*Don't you know who I am?*'

—

Herman was shredding cabbage in the kitchen when I returned to the flat.

'Hello,' he said over his shoulder. Then, doing a double take, 'Wow, you look... well, head-turning.'

'Aw, thanks.' I struggled to stifle my grin. Bethan had tutted each time she'd checked to see if the pink had completely stripped, but the final result looked pretty damned nice. Indeed, I'd found myself admiring my blonde reflection in every shop window. Would Vanessa approve? Well, I knew the answer to that.

'You are positively glowing,' Herman added. 'I take it you have a date tonight?'

A date? Ridiculous though it was, that's how my excitement about Belgravia felt. 'Yup, though it's tomorrow,' I replied.

His pale eyes lit with intrigue. 'Ah. One of your chauffeur-driven expeditions?'

'Yes, but no driver tomorrow.'

As Vanessa had put it back in December, Bernard was taking 'a well-deserved rest' during January. She'd offered to pay for a taxi, but I was more than happy to make my own way.

'Ah, interesting.' Clearly keen to hear more, Herman abandoned his sauerkraut and pulled out a chair.

Doing likewise, I flicked back my new hair. 'So sadly for me, darling,' I said, Vanessa-like. 'I'll have no option but to travel on ghastly public transport.'

Chapter 55

Though sharply cold, it wasn't raining when I hurried for the train on Saturday. What with the hamper, a bunch of roses and my overnight bag, I'd have struggled to carry an umbrella, and it wouldn't have done to squash down my crowning glory with a hat.

When I finally emerged from Hyde Park Corner station, I was earlier than I'd planned, so I headed for the broccoli trees of Belgrave Square Garden. Vanessa and I had visited in December, and we'd spent a happy hour arm-in-arm, sauntering around the 'Christmas Kingdom for all the family'. She'd indulgently watched little kids have their faces painted, eat festive treats and prod their damp fingers through the wire gauze at the petting zoo. It had been on the tip of my tongue to ask if she wished she'd had children, but that would have been invasive and rude. Despite all the time we'd spent together, I'd never asked about her personal life, her past or her family. She'd given that one hint about having a twin and she'd offered the occasional wafted comment about Sergio's 'allergy to babies', his 'snip' and his mother's disappointment there'd be no '*bambino artista*', but otherwise the subject had felt taboo.

Intending to walk the frosty paths, I hovered at the gate, but all my new winter clothes, including the lush cashmere coat Vanessa had bought me, had remained at Wilton Place, so I was wearing my Levi's jacket and my fingers were icy with cold. We hadn't actually agreed on a time for this week's visit, but Bernard had delivered me at ten-thirty in the past, so I'd only be fifteen minutes early.

When I reached the handsome building, I took a deep breath of anticipation, pulled back my shoulders and rapped with the knocker. There was no reply, but after a minute or two of worry I saw sense. The house was huge, five storeys in fact. Unless Vanessa happened to be hovering in the hallway, she most definitely wouldn't hear.

I pressed the intercom, glancing up as I waited. Her third-floor window was in darkness, but a glow of light shone from mine. That brought on a buzz of excitement. More elegant outfits, undoubtedly, and maybe the Christmas present she said she was 'working on'? I squeezed the handle of my own gift. As well as chocolates and biscotti, I'd added four homemade delicacies and I just knew she'd approve of my perfected Italian 'cuisine'.

Hoping none of the other wealthy residents would think it odd that I was hovering on Vanessa's step, I gave it another minute. But just as I reached up to ring again, the door swung open and Sergio appeared.

He looked as surprised as I felt. 'Hello?'

'Hi.' I gritted my teeth; he clearly didn't twig who I was. Again. 'It's Ruth. Vanessa's niece. I'm here for the weekend?'

He slowly took in me and my baggage. 'She isn't here.'

'Oh right...'

He pulled out his mobile and peered at the time. From his smart attire, he clearly had somewhere to go, which was a good thing; I could prepare for my aunt's return knowing he wasn't around to cast his usual gloom.

I nodded beyond his shoulder. 'It's freezing out here. Is it OK if I wait in the kitchen?'

He stared for a beat. 'She's away.'

'Away? Vanessa is away?' Though I repeated the words, did some part of me already know that? Had I stood here for several minutes in denial?

'Yes, she's away. She isn't here.'

'I see.' Disappointment burned the back of my eyes. 'I brought these… things… for her,' I managed to croak. 'Could I just leave them inside? They're fairly heavy so rather than—'

'Sure.'

Trying to hold onto my dignity, I strode into the warm foyer and quickly deposited my offerings on the console table, but tears had escaped by the time I returned.

Sergio spoke again when I reached the railings. 'She should have told you.' I couldn't quite interpret his expression, but irritation was there. 'I can't work with kids. She knows that.'

Though there was no sign of life from the neighbouring properties, it felt as if eyes were on me as I scrambled away. My cheeks burning from sheer humiliation, I wanted the ground to open up and swallow me. But at the end of the street I remembered my cello. I sorely wanted to leave it; that man had dismissively just called me a 'kid'. I may have been a gushing, immature fourteen-year-old in France, but I was an adult now and I'd be nineteen in a month. Yet I had to go back; I couldn't start a new term without my instrument.

He was at the gate by the time I rotated, so I pelted along the pavement to catch him up.

'Hello,' I called. 'Sergio.'

He stopped and turned. 'Yes?'

I had to catch my breath. 'I have to go back inside.'

'Why?' He seemed alarmed. 'I've already explained—'

'My cello's in there.' He looked at me as though I was speaking double Dutch. 'Vanessa suggested I leave it over Christmas for safekeeping.' God knows why I was justifying myself. 'And I need it for uni.'

He glanced at the parked vehicles. 'Right.'

'My new term starts on Monday.'

He nodded. '*Vedo.* Tell me where it is and I'll get it.'

Chapter 56

Back at my flat, I paused at the door, hoping and praying that Herman wouldn't be there to witness my mortifying – and now sodden – retreat. He was. So, it seemed, were the rest of my cohorts, back for a fresh semester and gawping at me.

I was just being paranoid, of course; I held no interest for them, and in fairness to Herman, he only cast me a questioning look rather than say anything out loud.

'Tell you later,' I managed, fumbling with my lock.

Willing myself into oblivion, I stowed beneath my duvet, but the events of the morning repeated on a loop in my head. Once we'd returned to the house, Sergio had all but shut me out so I hadn't even felt welcome to step into the hallway.

'This instrument. Where is it?' he'd asked me.

'My bedroom, I assume, but I'm not sure as Vanessa said she'd put it somewhere safe.'

'*Maledetto inferno*,' he'd muttered under his breath.

Rubbing my arms from the cold, I'd remained outside and watched the windows illuminate as he made his search. A light had eventually flashed at the very top of the building and he'd returned with the cello shortly after, so presumably my aunt had left up there.

Annoyance fired in at that thought. *Maledetto inferno* indeed. The man was so clearly self-obsessed that he hasn't noticed a cello in his flaming workplace. And how hard would it have been to let me down gently instead of implying I was some sort of toddler who'd get under his feet. Yet he'd clearly been shocked to see me. Why on earth hadn't Vanessa warned me she wouldn't be there?

I tried to logically examine the facts. Had I got the date wrong? No, we'd definitely agreed the thirteenth, a number one didn't easily forget, even if it hadn't been etched in my memory. And when we'd exchanged brief festive messages on Christmas and New Year's Day, she hadn't said anything to the contrary.

'Away', Sergio had said. What did that mean? On holiday? Surely that was unlikely without her beloved husband's company. Maybe with Bernard as her chauffeur? No, Sergio had been heading for the Bentley this morning. Filming? She'd told me she'd retired. Perhaps a manuscript had fallen on her doormat for a leading role that wasn't for someone 'middle-aged'. She'd be pleased about that. So thrilled she'd forget to send me a simple text? Probably; I wasn't the most important person in her world.

I deeply sighed. Yes, that was the problem; it was precisely how she had made me feel.

–

For the rest of the weekend I stayed in my room like a hermit. Before leaving Manchester I'd stuffed an old travel kettle sourced by my mum in the top of my rucksack so I was able to brew up, and the twin pack of digestives she'd insisted I take were still on my desk, so if my appetite ever returned, I wouldn't starve.

Though my body stayed inert, my Vanessa thoughts continued to churn. She wouldn't have knowingly been hurtful; something else had cropped up; she'd been inadvertently remiss. And if it had been a working opportunity, who could blame her?

I repeatedly fingered my iPhone to call her or text, but chasing her felt demanding and needy. And yes, too much like a bloody kid. She'd be sure to contact me soon. Her husband had been distracted on Saturday, but surely he'd mention me at some point, even if to reprimand her for putting him on the spot.

I just had to be patient; she would get in touch, I was certain of it.

—

When I looked at my mobile first thing on Monday morning, my forbearing flipped to anger. There might have been a mix up with dates, but Vanessa would know about my visit from Sergio by now. And even if he hadn't seen fit to tell her, she'd have seen my offerings on the foyer table.

Fuelled by mix of frustration and disappointment, I strode, bashed and bustled through the rest of the week. I didn't need Vanessa nor Wilton Place to make my life meaningful. I was at a London university, for God's sake. There were hundreds of resources at my disposal I hadn't yet tried. And I was only one term in, so it wasn't too late to make friends or at least to interact and collaborate with other students on my course.

Sustaining my resolution, I visited the recording studios on New Cross Road and took in the Yamaha grand piano and the variety of synthesisers, mics, amps and other high-end equipment. The next day, I attended the Electronic Music Studios, and peered at the iMacs and other software for mixing and creating sonic sounds. On Thursday, I tried loan instruments for my course project and composition module, and on Friday I jotted down the details of an orchestra, a creative string ensemble and a collaboration looking for a cellist from the department noticeboard. Then for good measure, I put my name down for various extracurricular topics, including African & Asian music, Sonic Arts and Jazz techniques.

I felt bloody good about my efforts, yet heartache still prodded. Why had I been dropped by Vanessa?

Chapter 57

My determination was still thriving on Saturday. I rose early, painted my face, styled my hair and left my room. If, by some miracle, Bernard appeared, I wouldn't be here.

'You look very nice,' Herman commented through his open door. 'Is your weekend... assignment... back on?'

He clearly thought my 'assignment' was with a lover, a married one, probably. But that was hardly surprising; there'd been a huge smile, a sparkling demeanour and an overnight bag in the past.

'Nope,' I replied. I considered leaving it there, but none of this was Bernard's fault. If he did happen to turn up, it wouldn't be fair to keep the poor man hanging around. 'But if my ride happens to appear, could you do me a favour?'

'Sure.'

'Pass on the message that I'm...' What should I say? Of course: 'That I'm *away*.'

His eyes filled with intrigue; Herman pushed up his glasses. 'Absolutely. It will be my pleasure.'

—

The hours in the city dragged. I wafted aimlessly from gallery to gallery, and though I tried to view the art objectively, I heard Vanessa's commentary and saw each piece through her critical gaze. My early dinner in a Bistro was tainted by her too; I'd deliberately chosen French, but I scanned the menu as she might have done, looking at the food and the wine list from expensive to cheap rather than how an impecunious student should. Then there were her sage words about eating alone…

In the end I called the waitress and glanced meaningfully at my phone. 'Sorry, an urgent message has just arrived, so I have to go. Should I pay for the water?'

'No, it's fine.'

Her expression was sympathetic. Did she think I'd been stood up? Well, that was a silly thought. I had.

—

I skulked back to the flat. I hated myself for needing to know, but had Bernard or even Vanessa turned up?

Herman was in the kitchen, tucking into his dinner, and though I tried to affect the nonchalant pretence I had left with, he saw through it.

'Sorry,' he said before I'd even opened my mouth. 'No show.'

'OK,' I said, turning away. 'No worries.'

Maybe it was the smell of traditional home cooking, but when I returned to my room, I was hit by a desire to hear my mum's voice. Call her mobile or the landline? Well, that was a no brainer; I didn't want to risk further rejection by her seeing my name on the screen.

Hoping my deep misery wouldn't spurt out if Dad answered, I inputted our home number.

'Nine one zero three.' It was her, thank goodness.

'Hi Mum.'

No reply for a few beats, but that was fine. She was clearly orientating herself; I rarely called home and certainly not on a Saturday evening.

'Ruth?'

'Yes, it's me. Thought I'd say hello.'

'Is everything all right?'

'Yes, of course.' Oh heck, my voice was cracking. I took a steadying breath. 'I was after a recipe actually. One of my flatmates had cooked and the smell reminded me of your homemade pie. The one with beef and onion that Tim used to saturate in HP sauce.'

Silence again. Then, 'It's Vanessa, isn't it?'

'No!' I replied, not wanting to alarm her. 'Sorry no, not at all. I'm sure she's—'

But Mum's tone was gentle. 'Oh Ruth,' she said. 'Has she let you down already?'

Emotion clogged my throat. It would have been so nice to share my unhappiness and confusion with my mother, but could I with her, of all people? Yet she was the one person who would understand, wasn't she? But a rat-a-tat-tat saved me from having to decide.

'I'm just missing home, that's all,' I said hurriedly. 'And there's someone at the door, so I'll call another time. OK?'

'OK.' A hesitation and then, 'Always remember, we do... Well, we miss you too.'

My visitor was Herman. His expression read, *'Are you all right? I know you were upset in the kitchen just now.'* But he actually said: 'I saw you eyeing up my Mince Muttischen. I have a slice left. Will you join me?'

His invitation was so sincere, I wasn't sure how my erratic mind would react, but a chuckle bubbled out. 'Mince Muttischen? Well, that's an offer you don't get every day.'

He held out his elbow. 'Then allow me to escort you.'

The table had been commandeered by Fayola's pots and pans, so I sat on the hard sofa and accepted the proffered food on my lap.

Herman held out a sleek bottle. 'This Riesling is from the Thorn wine estate in Limburg. I first tasted it at the Rypp festival in June last year.' He poured some for each of us. 'What do you think?'

'I think it's... highly aromatic with a distinctly floral aroma. How about you?'

I inwardly groaned at the irony of another flaming wine lesson, but his reply wasn't lecturing and the food was tasty, albeit more spicy that I'd expected. His eyes, I noticed, were pale blue and feminine behind the lenses.

'Limburg: do you come from there?' I eventually asked.

'Maastricht.'

'That's in the Netherlands, right?'

'Yes, the principal city in the south-eastern appendix. You might have heard of the Maastricht Treaty and it's the birthplace of the Euro?'

Maybe he was a bit preachy after all. But at least he was topping up my glass, and the more he talked about himself, the less likely he'd ask about me.

He cocked a fair eyebrow. 'At least that's what an internet search will tell you.'

'Ah, so tonight you're my very own Google.' I wiped my mouth with the folded kitchen roll he'd provided. 'So take me through your recipe for this—'

'Muttischen.'

'Yes, that.'

Though he gave a step-by-step account, I gradually twigged he wasn't as serious or as dour as I'd assumed, but had an appealing dry humour. And when he removed the wire-frames, he wasn't bad looking either. Perhaps I had 'beer goggles' from the second bottle of *Limburg* Riesling, or maybe I was simply desperate to feel wanted and loved. Either way, I didn't object when he leaned forward to kiss me, nor did I resist when he tugged me to my feet and led me down the corridor for '*toetje*'.

Chapter 58

It was a struggle to function the next day. My life was a disaster. As things had turned out, I wasn't even a notch on Herman's bedpost. After twenty minutes of surprisingly nice kissing and cuddles, he'd retrieved his glasses from his desk and said, 'I have to stop.'

'OK.'

What on earth had that meant? Was it code for something? Going for a pee? Finding a condom? Did he have an STD he'd forgotten to mention?

He'd gestured to his aroused nether regions. 'Believe me I want to, but I have to stop right now, so if you could please go back to your room.'

A very low point, so low it had been almost laughable. Sadly, humour hadn't been in my repertoire just then, so I'd shuffled across the corridor, collapsed on my mattress and cried until the merciful anaesthetic of alcohol took over.

In the morning I stayed submerged, hoping the mortification would miraculously disappear. It didn't, and was made even worse by a 'rat-a-tat-tat' on my door.

'Go away, Herman,' I called.

'A quick word.'

'No thanks.'

'Please.'

'Really?'

'Yes.'

With a groan I thumped over and opened up.

'So my predicament—' he began.

So that's what one called an explicit rebuff. 'What about it?'

'I have a wife.'

'Right. Congratulations.'

'Ruth, I—'

'It's fine, no worries,' I replied, quickly shutting him out and retreating to my duvet.

I tried to be as positive as the shitty situation allowed. I'd been humiliated yet again, but it was a good thing I hadn't lost my virginity to a married bloke. Apart from it being such a dreadful cliché, it went against my romantic moral code. A bit like karma, my principle was that if I didn't betray the sisterhood by sleeping with their men, they wouldn't do it to me.

But negativity soon took over. If I ever got a love interest. Who the hell was that positive, romantic person at the ballet? And was Herman's excuse even real? Then there was me. He'd changed his mind when I was all but naked. Were my boobs inadequate or my body revolting? On some level I was still the chubby, unpopular girl on the inside, but was my exterior still not good enough too?

Desperate for validation, I pulled out my mobile and composed the first words which came to mind.

> HI, Happy New Year! I must have got my dates muddled as Sergio told me you are away. Hope you are having fun and that I'll see you soon! Ruth xx

I quickly pressed send and scrunched my eyes for several minutes. When I looked again, the message had turned from 'delivered' to 'read'.

—

A new week on campus didn't improve my despair. My attempts to network and connect with my fellow musicians miserably failed, and the certainty that my musicology, performance and composition weren't as good as theirs flared. Anxiety fizzing, I hovered at practice room doors and listened to their brilliance, knowing I couldn't match it. I eavesdropped on conversations about choirs, orchestras, ensembles, music theatre and groups they were joining. By all accounts, some had even been scouted by 'names'.

My peers were moving forward, yet I was falling back. My left wrist seemed to ache and my right hand felt cramped when I held my bow. Even looking at my cello brought on a nauseous feeling so I hid it away in the wardrobe at night.

With no one else to confide in, I texted Sylvie.

> I think I might have to give up my degree. I'm just not good enough.

> That's ridiculous, Ruth! It's just imposter syndrome. I bet everyone feels the same.

> No, really. These guys have been headhunted for projects outside uni.

> Headhunted? Really? But even if it's true, they'll be putting themselves out there, looking for opportunities, Ruth. You need to do the same.

She was right, of course. Sure, some people were lucky, but most had to work for success. More to the point, they had to want it. But I had no idea who I was, let alone what I *wanted*. It felt as though I had slowly evolved from a chrysalis to cracking the pupal shell during my weekends in Belgravia, yet I hadn't quite got around to pulling out my wings. There was now a huge void in my life, and as ridiculous as it was, I needed Vanessa to fill it and tell me what species of fully formed adult I should be.

But I'd somehow offended her, I was sure of it now: she'd read my text and hadn't replied. I spent hours desperately reviewing the time we'd spent together before Christmas, trying to work out what I had done wrong. Was it something to do with my declining her request to sit for Sergio? Was she even 'away' as he had said, or had she been hiding from me in the house? Whatever it was, I was swamped with agitation and I had no one to blame but myself.

Needing something to calm me, I dug out the beta blockers Gus had given me and fingered the tub thoughtfully. Suppose I had a propensity for alarming reactions and hallucinations when I was unhappy or stressed? Conditions that were exacerbated by any kind of drug? But the mental threshing about my course had now become crippling.

I threw a pill back, held my breath and waited. Like before, my heartbeat slowed and I felt rational enough to go into uni that day and the next. But as the week passed, I became increasingly lethargic and tired, my functioning robotic and my appetite gone.

One afternoon merged into the next, the only thing piercing the fugue being Herman's daily raps at the door and his pale blue look of concern. He hadn't seen me in the kitchen; had I eaten? He'd made *poffertjes* or *stamppot, oliebollen* or *erwtensoep;* would I like a taste?

'It will pass,' he said one evening.

'What will?'

'Your unhappiness.'

Emotion constricting my throat, I shook my head.

'My heart was once broken too,' he said. 'I thought it would never mend, but it did.'

I took a breath to explain he'd got it wrong, but I paused. In all honesty, he hadn't.

Chapter 59

Herman's tapping dragged me from gluey sleep early one morning.

'I'm asleep. Go away.'

'I need to speak to you about something.'

'Can't it wait?'

'No.'

'Tell me later.'

'Later will be too late.'

Once he was in, I retreated to my bed.

'So what's so urgent?' I muttered.

'You need to consider this very carefully before making a decision.'

Oh God, what now? I knew he had a soft spot for me, but I'd heroically shelved our near miss, and he was firmly back to geeky doorman in my mind.

'Ruth? Are you listening? I'm serious.'

'OK.'

'You promise you'll really think about it?'

Nope. 'OK.'

'Your driver is here, but I think—'

'What?' I bolted upright. 'What day is it?'

'Saturday.'

'And what date?'

'February the third. Why?'

The month couldn't be coincidental. Vanessa had warned me that Bernard was away during January. Perhaps he'd been chauffeuring her in a hire car abroad or accompanying her on a shoot as her batman; they'd been away together; that was why there'd been radio silence.

'What time is it?' I asked, trying to catch up on this amazing development.

'Ten o'clock. But I think you should—'

'It's ten already?' I took a deep, steadying breath. Focus, Ruth, think. Clothes, my mobile, a shower. 'Right. Please could do me a favour? Could you tell him that I'll be ready in fifteen minutes. That I'm sorry for the delay, but I'll come to the car. He'll be warmer waiting there.'

'Ruth.' Herman put a hand either side of my shoulders. 'You promised to give this some thought.' He pulled a wry face. 'Admittedly I may well be biased, but this person you visit... They let you down badly. They made you deeply sad. You've barely eaten for three weeks, let alone smiled.'

His tenderness brought a lump to my throat. 'I understand what you're saying, but I have to go, Herman. It's really hard to explain – a cliché, I know; but it's like the missing piece of a jigsaw. Once that has slotted into place, I'll have the tools to be...' I hesitated. To be me? An adult? That fully formed butterfly? 'To be happy again.'

He sniffed and pulled me into a hug. 'OK, but please be careful.'

'I will.' I playfully pushed him away. 'Off you go and deliver my message. And don't look so worried! I'll be back tomorrow.'

–

Throwing a few toiletries and a pair of undies in a bag as I dressed, I was ready in no time. As I reached for the handle to leave, my heart thrashed so hard I had to lower my head. I wouldn't need the beta blockers once my aunt had calmed me down, but I slipped them in my pocket, just in case.

I wanted to say goodbye to Herman, but his door was closed, a clear sign of his disapproval. Or perhaps it was because he knew wild horses wouldn't have stopped me from pelting down the stairs with a huge grin on my face.

Once outside, I glanced around. Somewhat incongruously, the gleaming Bentley was parked next to the line of overflowing bins. Bernard stepped out and it was all I could do not to throw my arms around his neck and thank him for erasing the past miserable weeks from my memory.

Instead I said, 'Thank you,' and climbed in. 'Did you have a nice holiday?'

A nod through mirror. 'I did, thank you. All belted up?'

That was as far as our conversations ever went, so I managed to hold my tongue and save my questions for Vanessa. The journey was slowed by road works, and by the time he'd parked up, the weak sunshine had been replaced by heavy rain. I considered how to cover my 'new' hair, but I needn't have worried; holding a huge umbrella, Bernard escorted me to door and let me in, then disappeared as usual.

The first thing I noticed was how chilly and dark the hallway was; the second were my Christmas offerings, exactly where I'd left them on the console table. Perplexed, I walked over. The roses were still in bud and preserved, yet they were old and wrinkled too. I opened the hamper lid. My Tupperware boxes were where I'd left them, nestled at the top.

Reasoning the silent spookiness was just a question of closed bifolds, I rubbed the goosebumps from my arms. My aunt hated them shut, but perhaps Bernard hadn't had time to open them this morning. I made to do it myself, but a slamming door from high above, then the sound of approaching footsteps stopped me short. Vanessa? But somehow I knew they weren't hers. Trying to dispel her comment about *un diavolo*, I swallowed and looked up.

A shadow emerged from the gloom.

'You're here.'

His voice a croak, it was Sergio.

He beckoned me to him. 'Come on up.'

Alarm charged through me. Something was very wrong. Where was my aunt? Where was Bernard? I inhaled to ask, but he spoke again. 'Please come.'

A 'please' was certainly a surprise. And there was something about his tone. Was Vanessa ill? Was she ailing in her bedroom? Was that the reason for her lack of contact?

My legs like jelly, I climbed one set of stairs, stopped to catch my nervy breath, then took the second. I headed for her boudoir, but Sergio spoke again.

'This way please. To my studio. I need your—'

Apparently stuck for words, he patted his own cheeks. I couldn't help gawping. Close up, I barely recognised him; the black, sleek hair was no more; though a dusting of regrowth was emerging on his scalp, he'd clearly shaved his head.

His face was etched with grey and purple shadows. 'Your… I need you to sit for me.'

'Pardon?'

'She is still away. Which is why—' He seemed close to tears. 'Without a model, I can't—'

Fearful he'd weep, I cut him off. 'OK, I see. But…'

His request was astonishing; he couldn't be serious; he'd been nothing but rude since the moment I met him. Besides, I didn't have the confidence required.

Recall trickling back, I glanced at my aunt's door. Sitting for Sergio in her place… '*You'd be doing me a huge favour*'. Then: '*You wouldn't do that for me after all I've done for you?*' And the certainty I'd let her down. This had to be the reason for her ghosting me. A flicker of hope spread in my chest. Here was my opportunity to make amends.

I watched Sergio continue his upwards journey. I was hardly my aunt's substitute, but the woman herself had said it was simply about perspective, proportions and light.

The thought of that dank garret brought on a cold shudder, but I nodded to myself. I could and I would do this for Vanessa.

Chapter 60

Sergio was waiting on the dusky top landing. He stared at me for several seconds, then having no option but to use plain old me, he disappeared through the door I'd first seen in September.

Remembering that tearful whispering I'd heard from up here, I drew in my breath and followed. Almost gaping in surprise, I looked around the bright open space. I wasn't sure what I had expected, but it wasn't this blend of traditional and modern with the Georgian panelled windows on the street side and contemporary French doors on the other.

I turned to the famous roof terrace. The heavy downpour was bouncing off its wooden furniture and decking. 'It's still raining,' I commented, for something to say.

Clearly not interested in British chatter about the weather, Sergio gestured to an ergonomic, yet exceedingly plush leather chair. Despite my nerves I inwardly smiled at Vanessa's undoubted insistence of comfort and took her seat. Were the coffee cup, cigarettes and lighter on the side table hers or her husband's? Or had he used another 'model' in her absence?

In contrast to Sergio's erratic countenance and his attire of soiled T-shirt and jogging pants, the room was tidy and ordered. Artwork had clearly been hung on the white elevations, but there was now only one piece, a headshot of my aunt which I studied with a frown. Painted in black, white and greys, it was clearly of her and yet it wasn't at all. The facial structure, the cheek bones and lips were there, but none of the glamour I saw when I admired her. It was certainly wholly different to the paintings I'd seen in magazine articles, so perhaps those more classical portraits were once hung on these walls. Had they been sold? It seemed at odds with Vanessa's comment that Sergio had refused to sell his 'collection', whatever that comprised.

My contemplation was disturbed by the man's sudden proximity. Without asking for permission, he cupped my chin and adjusted my head, then he moved on to my torso, rotating my shoulders and positioning my arms for several moments. When he finally stepped away, he took photographs with a long-lensed camera, then studied the images. By the time he looked up, cramp was setting in.

'You must learn to relax,' he muttered, striding back and repeating the process.

Anxiety rose as he prodded and poked me. *Relax?* How was that supposed to happen when my body was pulsing with nerves. Why didn't he talk to me? Tell me what to do, what he hoped to achieve? Be bloody nice when I was doing him a favour.

He finally disappeared behind his huge canvas, so I listened to the drum of my heartbeat and tried to contain the threatening panic. God knows how long passed, but a knock at the door broke the cusp of sleep. I turned to Bernard's obvious disapproval.

'It's past two o'clock. Folk need to eat and drink,' he said in the direction of the invisible artist.

'*Cosa intendi?*' Sergio appeared and shrugged when he spotted me. 'I was unaware she was still here.'

Bernard tutted loudly and ushered me out. 'You have to let him know who's boss. Come on, lunch has been waiting for you.' He peered at me. 'You look hungry and parched. Next time, you call me, eh? Where should I fetch it?'

His kindness brought tears to my eyes. 'Thank you,' I managed. 'Would my bedroom be OK?'

'Right you are. I'll make a fresh pot of tea.'

Relieved, I scuttled away. I needed to take some beta blockers before my heart burst through my chest.

After Bernard's club sandwich, my intention to swim and exercise in the gym, or even go for a walk and breathe in fresh air were stymied by lethargy. My racing pulse had slowed, thank goodness, but my energy was zapped. A tiny corner of my mind railed against how I'd been misled into coming here, indeed almost ambushed, but it was a relief to do something rather than stare hopelessly at my cello and fret about my course. Besides, what else did I have to occupy my weekend? Return to Herman's sympathetic yet knowing smile? Just exist in my dingy room again? At least I was in beautiful surroundings and comfort here, and if the opportunity arose, I'd hunt out the manuscripts Vanessa had mentioned. If I vetted them as she asked, it could be another peace offering to add to my bow.

Interspersed with napping, I played games on my phone, watched television and drank whatever Bernard supplied on the hour.

'Anything in particular you'd like for supper?' he asked at some point.

Supper. Such a Vanessa word. Where on earth was she? Her reply seemed to slide from my lips. 'Whatever you decide will be delicious, thank you.'

'Very good. I'll serve it in the dining room at eight.'

When he'd gone I groaned at my own ineffectiveness. Why hadn't I just said to bring it in here? Was I supposed to dress up as usual? And would Sergio be joining me? As if reading my thoughts, the telephone beside me loudly rang.

'Hello?'

'I'm ready for another sitting.'

I folded my arms and didn't reply.

'So if you could come up now.'

I stayed stonily silent. The man might have been born in flaming Sardinia, but he knew the English for please.

He audibly exhaled. '*Per favore.*'

'Fine.'

I veritably stomped up the stairs. Sergio's sigh had said the word 'kid' as clearly as he had three weeks ago, but which of us was behaving like a spoilt child? I'd done him a good deed and he hadn't had the decency to say thanks. He'd treated me like a malleable object or some plastic dolly rather than a human being with feelings.

Determined to tell him who was 'boss', I took a deep breath at the top, but the heavy curtain on the right-hand side caught my eye. The last time I had briefly looked at it, I'd assumed it was covering a fire escape or similar view from a window, but it was slightly pulled to one side and revealing what looked like the panels of a door.

'Ruth?' Sergio's voice made me jump. 'This way please.'

It was on the tip of my tongue to say something sarcastic about him actually knowing my name – and indeed saying please – but his wretched demeanour as I sat caught me short. This man was clearly in a deep and dark creative hole. What Vanessa had said about 'a calling', 'making allowances' and having 'patience and understanding' suddenly made complete sense. My own meagre calling had gone awry, but the thought of helping someone else's gave me a profound and much needed sense of purpose. Whatever he needed I'd be here for him for as long as it took. University and lectures could wait.

Chapter 61

Over the next week a Groundhog Day pattern set in: listening to music and watching inane television, long soaks in the bath, the deepest of both daytime and night-time sleeps, peppered by summonses to the attic. I never knew when they would be, so I fended off the thrashing heart and anxiety Sergio's scrutiny induced by imbibing the beta blockers every few hours.

He worked mostly in silence behind his canvas, but occasionally he'd appear and surprise me with a terse command.

'Tie back your hair,' he said at some point.

'OK, but with what?'

He stared as though my question was off-the-wall, then scrabbled in a drawer, found an elastic band and tied my mane into a knot. That seemed to please him as he muttered 'better', adjusted and bent my plastic head and limbs as before, then took a new series of photographs.

As the minutes and hours passed, I did learn to relax. I'm sure my self-prescribed medication helped, but I gradually mastered the right slant of the shoulders or angle of chin required without Sergio asking or manhandling me. It didn't evoke the praise or a smile that I found myself desiring, but at least my sense of incompetence lessened. I became a little braver too, just upping without permission if I fancied a drink, was peckish or needed the loo. I even dared to pull back the dusty curtain on the landing, only to discover the door behind it was locked. But in truth a strange compulsion or connection was developing within me, and I wanted to stay every second until I was dismissed. What was the artist doing behind his screen? Was his creation fine art or another abstract? How far had he got? A painting of Vanessa he needed to finish for his 'collection'? Whatever it was didn't matter a jot – I was breathless with anticipation. Would there be a hint of Ruth Parker in it? Would the invisible girl be forever ingrained on a page?

–

Interspersed by Bernard appearing in the studio with a face like thunder if meals were missed, time passed. I finally roused myself to do some exercise on Saturday, and when I emerged from my room, I was surprised to spot a smart and shaved Sergio in the hallway below. He looked up at me with that same tortured expression I'd seen in the parlour at Château Les Douves. Astonishing myself, I felt a surge of heat deep in my belly. I'd adored Vanessa, of course, but could it be that I'd been a touch smitten with him too? My cheeks burned at my own shocking train of thought. I'd hurtled to the *Cèdre du Liban* to save him. Could I do the same in his workplace today?

But Bernard stepped into view. 'We're going out for a few hours. Do you need anything fetching on the way back?' he asked me. 'Maybe a treat of some sort?'

Chocolate or crisps would have come to mind in the past, but it felt as though Vanessa was invisibly sitting on my shoulder these days. 'No thanks. I prepared some crudités last night.'

'Right you are. We'll get off then.'

Though I very much doubted it was for an afternoon pint in the pub, I wondered where they were going. My lips twitching at the chalk and cheese twosome, I ambled down to the kitchen. I knew a little about Sergio but nothing about his butler. Dare I find out more?

Once I had checked the Bentley had gone, sheer nosiness propelled me towards Bernard's quarters. There was no apparent lock, yet I was still caught short when I pressed down the handle and the door swung open. Feeling a touch guilty, I stepped into the sparse and tidy space. The expected smell of tobacco pervaded the air, and my suspicions that he'd been in the military were confirmed by two framed photographs on the wall, one of an army squadron and the other of a much younger Bernard in uniform. I studied the woman by his side. A wife or a sister? Either way, a child with cropped hair was clutching her skirt.

I glanced around the rest of the room, surprised to see he didn't have a television, so perhaps he'd been talking to someone on his phone the original Sunday I'd visited. Short of opening wardrobes and drawers, which felt too much like snooping, there was little else I could glean, but as I turned to leave, a bunch of keys on the bedside table caught my eye. They very much looked like the set Vanessa had slipped into the lounge drawer. She'd called down from the attic landing that day. Would one of them fit the hidden door?

My stomach clenching, I spent a moment or two deliberating whether to satisfy my curiosity. From my very first visit, the garret area had felt sinister and out of bounds. The strange noises and whispers had exacerbated that sensation. Yet I'd been wrong about Sergio's bright and comfortable studio. There was no harm in exploring, was there? After all, Vanessa had told me to make myself at home and look around many times. I might not get another chance, and it *was* broad daylight...

Fuelled by adrenalin, I belted up to the top of the house. When I'd finally caught my breath, I gingerly drew back the old drape and inserted the key which looked the oldest. I expected some kind of resistance, but the lock easily turned and the portal yawned open.

A black wall of fustiness hit, so I fumbled for a switch and was rewarded by a dull glow which lit the windowless area. Puffing out my trapped breath, I squinted ahead. Beneath the looming rafters there were two single beds, the first adorned with a somewhat dishevelled padded quilt, colourful cushions and a plethora of soft toys. I peered more closely at the biggest teddy in the centre. Seeming to grin at me, it was the one I'd seen in

Vanessa's boudoir. As though it was alive, I tentatively stroked the tawny mohair and felt a chilled curiosity run through me. What had she said all those weeks ago? *That isn't supposed to be in here.*

The other billet was a much plainer affair. Neatly made with a blanket and turned-down sheet, a baby dolly with cornflower blue eyes was sitting on top. Dragging my gaze away from its malevolent stare, I rubbed the chill from my arms and glanced around. In comparison with the rest of the refurbished house, this room felt so eerie, so out of place. What was it for? Did anyone use it? And what did the clear distinction between the two mattresses mean?

A single framed photograph hung above each headboard. The quality wasn't great, so I guessed they'd been taken by an old instamatic camera and been 'blown up' from their original size, but they were of two girls posing in a walled flower garden with a smallish stately home in the background. It was difficult to make out the identical grainy images, but they had the same bobbed hairstyle, the same height and build. And the same ginger shade of hair. A notion took my breath. Could this be Vanessa and the twin she'd mentioned?

Though I couldn't say why, icy thoughts of resident phantoms, night time visitors and doppelgängers prickled my skin as I leaned in to study their features. Then, as if I'd crossed an invisible line, a scraping sound from behind made me jolt and spin around. The door was bouncing against the jamb, which meant a breeze... Oh God, that was quick; the men must have returned already. All fingers and thumbs, I flicked off the light, locked up and hurriedly dragged back the curtain.

My heart thumped loudly as I tiptoed down the stairs. How the heck would I return the keys without either of them noticing? Yet when I reached the lobby, the house was inert and still deathly silent. I peered through the window. Bernard's parking space was empty; the Bentley wasn't there.

Chapter 62

By Monday morning, I'd shaken away my ridiculous disquiet about the children's room in the attic. It was simply another bedroom with side lockers, a desk and a sink. Maybe Vanessa or Sergio had nephews and nieces who visited from time to time. Or perhaps they housed temporary staff for big occasions. That seemed to make sense; it had probably been used for young maids back in the day.

That niggle sorted, I turned to another. The beta blockers tub was now empty, I'd got used being Sergio's temporary model and I couldn't ignore real life for ever. Taking a steadying breath, I checked my iPhone. The lack of communication from Vanessa brought on the usual pang of loss, but there were several other messages, including a couple from uni.

I stared at the music department's missives for several long seconds. The emails were the standard 'you haven't swiped into lectures' fare, so I wasn't too worried about getting into trouble. What gave me more pause for thought was how generic they were. My tutor was brilliant, but he didn't really care whether I was there or not; if I abandoned the course he wouldn't give two hoots. It confirmed what I already knew: I wasn't suffering from imposter syndrome; I was bang average at both composition and my instrument. I wasn't good enough to be noticed or excel at either, which was precisely why I'd stayed in Wilton Place, hidden away from the stress and my cello.

Maybe my new 'calling' here was a sign; perhaps a higher deity was telling me to stop battling my performance anxiety and simply give up. I took a breath to compose a reply, but

Vanessa's words flashed in: '*You're an artist, young lady, and I want you to shine. Practice makes perfect. At least two hours a day when you're here, please.*'

The need for her approval burned deep in my chest. I'd been remiss in not bringing my cello last Saturday; it absurdly felt as if she knew. But there was no need to panic. I was helping her husband's creativity for now; when she returned and we resumed our weekends, I'd be sure to bring it every visit.

–

As the week drew on a small flare of anticipation flickered in my belly. I'd been so focused on my 'calling' that my nineteenth birthday had crept up unawares. There was no rationale for it at all, yet I just knew Vanessa would be in touch on the day. I tried to dampen my hopes of an actual meeting, but they were there nonetheless, so I spent each afternoon doing all the things she'd approve of – a long workout in the gym, swimming several lengths and 'cleansing my mind of stresses' in the sauna. And, of course, carefully grooming my appearance, including my nails.

–

Infused with energy on Saturday morning, I jumped from my bed, curled up on the love seat and responded to a heart-warming number of birthday wishes on Instagram and Facebook. After a long exchange with Sylvie, I considered pre-empting Mum by calling her first, but she might have sent a present to my flat and ask if I liked it, so I sent a text to say that my phone was on the blink, and not to worry if I didn't answer.

My ears pricked at the sound of conversation breezing up through the open window. Could it really be Vanessa? I dashed over to witness her arrival, but it was Sergio, climbing into the passenger seat of the Bentley. The two men on another day trip seemed unlikely, so... Realisation struck: they were clearly off to Heathrow or Gatwick to collect my aunt.

Positivity pumping through me, I spent a good hour preening, shaving and plucking, styling my hair and applying make-up just as she would direct, then raking through the wardrobe and deciding what to wear. When I'd finished, I veritably danced down for breakfast and opened the fridge for the usual mixed berries, but I was too hyper to eat. What should I do to occupy myself for another hour? Walking off my exuberance was an excellent idea. I looked up to the skylight above the table. No rain today, so perfect for a stroll – or I could try the roof terrace and take in the view.

I wryly laughed at my ridiculous self-deception. Who was I kidding? What I really wanted to investigate was Sergio's studio, most specifically the easel at one end. The thought of what I might discover both thrilled and terrified me, yet I might not get another opportunity before Vanessa returned and reclaimed her chair.

I slipped off my heels and trotted up. My plan had been to walk straight on in, but as I caught my breath on the landing, another debate raged in my head. This was Sergio's personal and creative space; he'd never invited me to look at his artwork; it didn't take a genius to work out that he was loathe for me – or anyone – to view it. Maybe I'd see something I couldn't unsee; I should turn away and retrace my steps. And yet... What was the harm of having a quick peep? I'd been modelling for him for hours; surely I was entitled to see the results? He'd never know.

The 'buts' prevailing, I strode to the easel, took a sharp breath and turned to look. For moments, I stared, perplexed. Save for a few pencilled outlines, the canvas was blank.

Certain this couldn't possibly be *it*, I hunted around the brightly lit room. The other frames were empty, so I opened the tall storage unit and peered inside. The likes of turpentine, brushes and primer were lined on one side, unused parchment and boards on the other. Lost for ideas, I idly stepped behind the photography screen, then pulled back in surprise. A burgundy velvet curtain was covering a window? No. The property was a mid-terrace; I'd already made that mistake with the creepy children's room across the way.

I stood stock still. Should I explore further? No, going beyond this point was wholly wrong. Yet I found myself squeezing through one side of the heavy drape nonetheless. The smell of linseed alerted me to the missing painting, so I threw caution to the wind and groped for a light switch. Similar to Bernard's annex downstairs, the area was sparse and tidy, but every inch of lower wall was covered with artwork facing in.

I wasn't an expert by any means, but I had learned from school – and my gallery education with Vanessa – that masters who used techniques such as impasto or paddling had to wait at least a week for the oil paint to dry. Indeed, something similar to the abstract of Vanessa would take several months, which surely meant Sergio hadn't been working on these.

A little disappointed, I took in my surroundings. A double bed, a sink and a few pieces of furniture. Feeling that strange tingle from before, my eyes rested on the stripy duvet. Was this where Sergio slept? The dent in the pillow and his rare appearance in other parts of the house suggested so. I tentatively opened the wardrobe and peered in; a few items of clothing were dotted on shelves, but there were no hanging outfits – or indeed a hidden portrait.

Wholly baffled, I pulled back one of the frames. As anticipated, it was a painting of Vanessa, but I did another take, then looked again, moving on to the next, then the next until I'd seen enough. Unadulterated shock rattled through my very being. Perhaps I was a 'kid' after all. Each was of my aunt in a different pose, but what I hadn't naively expected to see was her nakedness, and more particularly the erotic and highly explicit denotations of it.

Chapter 63

In a state of high anxiety, I clattered down to my bedroom. Why the images had disconcerted me so badly, I couldn't say. After all, I'd seen similar of my aunt in magazines and on the internet over the years, and she was particularly known for the soft porn nudity in her early films. And she did have a beautiful body – why shouldn't she show it to the world in all its glory? She had the self-assurance, the confidence, the charm. Modelling *au naturel* was hardly salacious; it had been a preoccupation of the ancient Greek artist and gone on from there, for goodness' sake. No one batted an eyelid these days – including the sight of pubic hair. Indeed, the Tate Modern exhibition from last year had been a case in point.

For a moment I struggled to summon up the artist's name. He was Italian and had gone to Paris at eighteen where he'd become a bohemian 'bad boy' who'd been condemned for his dissolute ways.

My unease racked up another notch. Were these parallels significant? Was I missing something? Was Sergio a man with less than 'artistic' intentions? Had he and Bernard colluded somehow? Did Vanessa even know I was here?

Slowly inhaling and exhaling, my heart soon slowed in tandem with my head. Bloody hell, what was wrong with me? The portraitist's name was Modigliani; similarities between him and Sergio weren't exactly mind-blowing. A million creatives had lived in Paris and painted naked women over the years. I was nineteen now, and yes, I had to grow up and stop behaving like a...

That thought made me pause. Is that what he'd meant at his front door five weeks ago? That I was a 'kid' and thus ineligible to qualify as Vanessa's temporary *nude* substitute? Now he'd changed his mind, did he expect me to strip? I covered my burning face. I could never do that; my body was disgusting; I was still haunted by the memory of Mum measuring me up for my bridesmaid's dress, that look of pity on her face. I hadn't even shown it in full to a love interest yet. The fumble with Herman was as far as it'd got, and look what had happened then.

I puffed out the hot panic. I was being absurd; Sergio had barely shown interest in me fully clothed, let alone given any hint that I should undress. And my aunt would be here any minute; she'd take back her rightful place and everything would revert to how things were before Christmas. My tremulousness was just hunger, that was all.

Relief easing through me, I made for the door, but something from Sergio's quarters flashed into my mind. I frowned at the fresh wave of agitation. Did I really see what I thought, or was I completely losing the plot? I looked at my watch. Time was ticking on, but I had to find out.

I hurried up the stairs, paced to the annex and took a moment to catch my heaving breath. Then I cracked open the wardrobe and picked out the items I'd subconsciously seen. Oh God, my eyes hadn't deceived me: the discoloured Calvin Klein bralet and knickers were the very ones that had gone missing on my second visit. Why on earth—?

A voice splintered the silence behind me.

'What are you doing in here?'

I spun around to face Sergio. 'These are mine. Why do you have them?' I asked, my challenging tone sounding far braver than I felt.

He shrugged and rotated, so I followed him to the studio.

Anger overcame my nerves. 'What's wrong with you? Don't you have the power of speech?'

As though to reply, he inhaled, but instead shook his head and began to move away.

'What's going on?' I gestured to the canvas. 'I've sat in here for hours. You've moved me around like a mannequin. But that… Well, it's basically nothing. Is that really it?'

His cheeks filled with irate colour and I tensed, certain he'd shout or even lunge at me, but after a beat he turned tail and strode out.

–

Grappling with mixed emotions, I remained motionless for a time. What the hell was going on with that man? I looked down at the garments still gripped in my fist. He'd seemed perplexed when I'd showed them to him, but there'd been a shiftiness too. If he had nothing to hide, why didn't he just explain? And what about that flash of sheer defeat on his face when I challenged him about the painting?

Dismay and failure fizzled in my chest. Whatever he'd wanted from me, I'd been unable to give it. Yet it was hardly surprising; I could never hold a candle to—

Comprehension dawned: Sergio and Bernard were back, which meant…

I flew down the first staircase. Vanessa's door was closed, so I continued my journey to the lounge. It was empty, but the distinct tang of her perfume hovered as though she'd just left the room. Composing myself, I took the last flight more elegantly. This was, after all, a big moment. I hadn't seen her for weeks and I was excited for her to admire my slender figure and new hair.

Bernard was quietly preparing food in the kitchen. He turned when I entered, and though his expression was as deadpan as always, I sensed a furtiveness behind his grey gaze.

'A light early dinner this evening,' he said. 'I'll bring it through shortly.'

I couldn't help smiling. *Early* was unheard of here; it was actually teatime, the hour one magically whipped out sandwiches and presents and cake. 'Okie dokie. Thank you.'

Donning my heels, I all but skipped to the dining room and checked myself in the mirror. My tresses were still styled, my make-up just so, and though Sergio's lost countenance seemed to hover like a layer of responsibility, I was pleased to see the table was set for two. Tonight I'd celebrate my nineteenth with the very best company, and in the meantime I'd call Mum.

Smiling fondly at her tiny icon of the Parker foursome in Cornwall, I waited as her mobile rang out, but to my surprise, it was answered by Dad.

'Ruth! Hello, love. Happy birthday.'

It was so lovely to hear his voice. 'Thank you! Is this what happens when I'm not around to keep an eye on things? You've become Mum's receptionist? Is she there?'

A beat of time passed. 'She's just busy right now.'

Heat shot to my cheeks. Surely not a strop with me today of all days? Yet I frowned. Dad's cheery opening had sounded off, subdued, almost strained. And hadn't there been an echoey ring?

'Dad?'

'Yes, love?'

'Where are you?'

A pause, then, 'We're at the Royal Infirmary, but it's—'

'What?' I pictured those faint scars on Mum's arms. 'In *hospital*?'

'Yes, but it's nothing for you to worry about. Not on your birthday.'

'Why? What's happened? Why are you there, Dad?'

'It's fine, Ruth, really. Mum was struggling with her breathing, but she's already feeling much better.'

'Her *breathing*. What do you mean?'

'Apparently she has something called pleurisy.'

'What's that, exactly?'

'It's a form of pneumonia, I suppose. The tissue between the lungs and ribcage gets inflamed.'

Remembering the pain of my own pneumothorax, I put a hand to my chest. 'I'm coming home.'

'You really don't need to, love. Mum wouldn't want to spoil your celebrations and they've already started her on antibiotics, so—'

'I want to, Dad.'

'Righto. Then I'll keep you posted about what's happening. They want to keep her in tonight, but they're locating a bed, so...'

I ended the call and looked at my shaking hands. I had to focus and move, pack up my stuff and head out to Euston. As I scraped back my chair, I almost bumped into Bernard.

'Is everything all right?' he asked.

'Please could you call me a taxi? I need to get the next train to Manchester. My mum isn't well.'

'No need to do that; I can drive you.'

'Thanks, but it's fine.' I gestured to his tray. 'Vanessa will be hungry.'

'She's still away, love.' The pity in his eyes was unmistakeable. 'So a lift to the station is no trouble at all.'

All I could do was nod. My child-like anticipation had been nothing short of preposterous. Yet I couldn't help remembering the scent of her perfume in the air, and wondering what on earth it meant.

Chapter 64

Finally back in Manchester, it was too late to visit Mum, but I spent a nice half hour with Dad, sipping a brandy before bed. I was inordinately weary from the highs and lows of the day, yet I couldn't sleep. My mind was in full torment mode. How pathetic had my neediness for Vanessa been? And so extreme that I'd thought I had *smelled* her. From my research on the train, I'd discovered sufferers of phantosmia conjured up odours, and that the condition was classified as an olfactory *hallucination*. On top of those imagined night-time 'visits', it was very scary indeed. Then there was Bernard's look of concern and commiseration. He'd witnessed my adoration of Vanessa first-hand and it made my cheeks burn from the deepest humiliation.

─

Dad dropped me off at the Royal Infirmary en route to work on Monday.

I made to climb out, but he lightly held me back. 'Ruth?'

'Yes?'

Mum hadn't woken for the whole of yesterday's visit, so alarm gripped my chest.

'What? What is it? Is Mum more ill than you're letting on?'

'No, not at all.' He cleared his throat. 'It's you I'm worried about.'

I swallowed. What had he heard? Quite frankly it could be all manner of things ranging from my own hospital stay to abandoning my cello or skiving two weeks of lectures. 'Why?'

He peered at my intently. 'Are you eating properly?'

'Of course. Why do you ask?'

He sighed. 'I know it doesn't do to comment on someone's physical appearance, but you look very thin.'

I tried for a smile. 'Just healthy, Dad.'

'And you don't seem yourself.' He turned off the engine. 'Come on, Ruth. You can talk to your old dad.'

'Nothing, honestly.' My nose burned. Part of me wanted to sob the whole sorry saga out, but when it came to my performance anxiety, Dad was the one person I couldn't confide in.

'OK.' He took my hand and squeezed it. 'Do me a favour, will you?'

'Of course.'

'Stay at home this week and get some rest. If there's anything on your mind, however small, just talk to me. OK?'

–

Her skin waxy and pale, I found Mum in a similar state to Sunday. After a good five minutes of me fretting that she might actually be dead, her eyes flicked open.

'Ruth! What on earth are you doing here?' she croaked. 'You should be in London and having fun rather than coming to see me.'

Despite her brittle words she looked small and vulnerable. I proffered the bag of goodies I'd brought. 'It's a good job I know you're pleased to see me really. How are you feeling? I came yesterday but you were—'

'Resting.' She patted my hand. 'I know. The nurse told me. She described you as slender and extremely pretty.'

I felt myself blushing. 'Thanks.'

'Don't thank me, thank Sister Kerry-Ann.'

'OK.' But it was a rare compliment of sorts from my mother.

'Still sleepy and short of breath. And though they're hard to describe, I get sharp chest pains when I inhale, let alone when I cough, sneeze or move around,' Mum said, answering my question. 'When I talk too much as well, so it's best to keep this visit short.'

'OK,' I replied again, working hard not to let the old feelings of rejection rise to the surface. Her lack of insight too: they were the very symptoms I'd experienced myself from saving her precious son.

She sniffed. 'If the pleural effusion doesn't clear up with the antibiotics, they'll drain the fluid by inserting a needle or tube through my chest wall, so either a local or general anaesthetic might be on the cards.'

Yup, I'd been there too, at just *fourteen* years of age. Grappling with the need to leave, I lowered my head and fell silent, but Mum piped up with a question.

'How is your brother?'

I looked up, surprised. She was examining her fingernails, so I gathered teacher training was not what she meant. 'He's in a really good place. It's early days, but he's met a nice guy. He's Welsh and called Cad. Short for—'

'Lovely. He's happy, and that's what counts.'

Her eyes closing, she drifted for some time. Longing for a spark of her love, I examined her sculpted features. Such a complicated woman, but she did adore her son, and that was a good thing.

As I stood to get a drink, she stirred again. 'The secret you learned in France...' Her expression was so angst-ridden, a shiver passed through me. 'Was that it?'

I paused. We'd already discussed this at the high tea before Christmas.

'Tim's... note. It said you'd discovered the truth. Was that it?' she asked again. 'That he was gay?'

'Yes, it was. I'm sorry I couldn't tell you at the time, but it wasn't mine to share and I didn't know what he'd want me to say. Obviously, if he'd... Well, I'd have explained it to you and Dad, but that didn't happen, thank goodness.' I was blabbing, but her intensity was freaking me out. 'He recovered and he's in a really good place. As you say, that's what's important.'

A tear splashed down her cheek. I was almost too frightened to ask, but I took a shuddery breath. 'Why do you ask, Mum? Did you think Tim meant something else?'

She gazed, hollow-eyed, then finally shook her head. 'I'm very tired now. I think it's time for you to go.'

Chapter 65

It was just me again at the Royal Infirmary on Friday. The fluid in Mum's chest hadn't shifted, so she was to undergo a procedure to drain it when a slot next came free. She and Dad had argued over her choice of a general anaesthetic, so I knew to veer away from that particular debate.

'Morning.' I offered the magazine I'd bought on the way and sat in the visitor chair. 'It's celebrity gossip rubbish, but I think we've exhausted all the other options.'

'Thank you. I'll have a flick later.'

Mum's breathing was laboured, but she seemed to appreciate the gesture. In days gone by, she used to scour them for a mention or a photo of my aunt. Needless to say, I'd done the same. Pushing the uncomfortable thought away, I noticed a large box by the bed that hadn't been there yesterday. It sported the green logo of Harrods.

Bloody hell; talk of the devil.

Mum raised her eyebrows. 'It arrived this morning. A hamper, of course.'

My chest tight and stomach churning, I pictured my heartfelt Christmas offering on Vanessa's console table. I had disposed of the food, but the flowers, the wicker basket and dry contents had remained there, waiting for the woman who could effortlessly arrange the delivery of an expensive gift to her hospitalised friend, but who hadn't had the time for even a short explanation about her absence to me.

But it wasn't all bad. Some might have thought her offence was trifling, yet for me there was a profound sea change in my very being. The emotion bubbling in my gut was anger. I liked anger. It was far easier to shape than the spectrum of sensations I'd suffered for the past six weeks. Yes, *suffered*, like an infectious disease.

Yet today I'd been miraculously cured and it felt bloody good; from this moment onwards, Vanessa, Wilton Place and all that went with it were behind me.

Mum was speaking. 'Sorry?' I asked. 'What was that?'

'Feel free to have a look and choose something. There isn't much left.'

'Sorry?' I repeated.

'The nurses and cleaners have taken the wine, biscuits, preserves and the like. I imagine we're down to the teas.'

I was literally stuck for words. My penny-pinching mother had shared her much beloved Harrods gift with the ward staff?

She chuckled, then coughed. 'Your face, Ruth. Don't make me laugh. It hurts.'

'Wow, that's really kind of you, but it's a... well, a surprise.'

Her smile fell. 'Not really. I do this from time to time. One of my tiny protests.'

My flesh tingling, I waited for her to elaborate.

'You know as well as I do that she does this. Goes silent for months, then love-bombs with gifts and the odd personal appearance. It's easy to send presents by courier or buy the most costly item of clothing in the shop when you have the money. But that's not real friendship, is it?'

I had carefully selected Mum's cardigan and paid for it with my summer earnings, but she wouldn't have known that, so her cold rejection at Christmas made sense.

She patted her chest. 'No doubt I'll soften the next time she deigns to visit, but I'm rather enjoying my insubordination just for now.'

I understood completely. My personal rebellion would not be temporary, though.

'Shall we get a drink?' Mum asked, startling me again. 'Apparently there's a cafe here. A little expensive, I'm told, but who's counting?'

–

Though loaded with calories, we both chose a whipped cream and marshmallow-topped hot chocolate.

Sensing Mum's willingness to talk, I just asked: 'How did you and Vanessa meet?'

She sighed and rubbed the table top. 'It's not something I'm proud of, but I had a spell in a children's home.'

Being placed into care was hardly anyone's fault, but I knew better than to interrupt.

'I was the plump, dowdy girl no one wanted to know, then Vanessa appeared.' She smiled thinly. 'You can imagine my excitement when she needed... when she asked to be my friend. I did what I could to help her settle in.'

Needed. It was an unusual word to use. Remembering Vanessa's '*I know what she did but I never let on*', I gave a little shudder. Did I really want to learn what had happened back then? Yet I was still intrigued. 'She told me she'd been bullied.'

'Did she?' Apparently thrown, Mum rubbed her flushed neck. 'Yes, I suppose she was.'

I took another shallow breath. 'So, why was she—'

'Oh, her hair. You know, the colour.' Mum raked her fringe from her forehead. 'So yes, she arrived when her mother passed away. They were incredibly close and she was devastated. I was old for my age and she was young, so I tried to be a substitute, a protector, I suppose.'

'What about your own mum?' I asked gently.

'She's not worthy of a mention, Ruth. She got the end she deserved.'

Her tone was sharp, but I wanted to discover more. 'She died?'

A nod.

'And the people in your wedding photographs?'

'My foster parents. Not everyone wants to take on damaged goods. They were elderly so...'

Poor Mum. It made sense of Dad's all-embracing loyalty to her; he'd become the family she'd never had.

The fusty attic room at Wilton Place flashed behind my eyes. 'Vanessa mentioned her twin. Presumably—'

'She told you about that?'

'Vaguely.' My mother's already pallid face had become a shade paler. An icy sensation trickled down my spine.

She looked at her hands. 'What did she say?'

'I can't recall exactly but it was something about indelible bonds and enduring elastic that never quite breaks.'

Mum nodded but didn't speak. I knew I was pushing my luck, but my curiosity was piqued. 'Presumably he or she was in the children's home too?'

'No, she wasn't.'

She. I was right about the photographs; Vanessa had a sister. She was such a dominant force, I couldn't believe there were two of them. 'Gosh, what was she called?'

'I'm not sure I can remember.' Mum coughed. 'I think it's time for a nap.'

'Yes, of course. I'll walk with you.'

Linking arms, we ambled back.

'What happened to the twin?' I asked at the ward door.

'Rose died long ago,' she muttered, and though she cast it over her shoulder, a sixth sense told me she was lying.

Chapter 66

Dad must have been psychic as Mum had an allergic reaction to the anaesthetic. For the first couple of days she suffered from nausea, vomiting and violent shivering, but her confusion, or what the doctor called 'postoperative delirium', lasted even longer.

Dad tried to encourage me back to London.

'Look love, Mum's condition is fairly rare, but it's not life threatening,' he said. 'She will definitely get better given time. Right now she has no idea of what day it is, and I know she wouldn't want you to miss out on all the fun.' He looked wistful. 'The first year of uni should be the best of your life.'

Should was the operative word. 'It's fine, Dad,' I replied. On the journey home I'd been sensible by messaging the department and explaining my mother was ill. 'I'm doing as much of my course as I can online.'

'Not quite the same as having your cello to hand though, is it?'

'Instrumental is only part of it. And I can make up for lost time when I go back.'

'Righto.'

He didn't sound convinced, but at my tutor's behest I *was* attending lectures and seminars remotely, and I'd surprised myself how much I enjoyed it. Participating from a distance suited me: there was less scope for competitive peers, their bragging and the inferior feelings which followed.

'Oh how lovely, you're here,' Sister Kerry-Ann said whenever I visited Mum. 'She's been asking for you again.'

Her condition frustrated Dad and Tim no end. They constantly corrected her befuddled comments, yet I rather liked this version of my mother. As though we were on the same team, she whispered asides, raised her eyebrows or rolled her eyes when the men attempted to put her straight.

When we were alone, I let her prattle without cutting her short. Some things I gleaned, such as her poor relationship with her mother, but others made no sense:

'*I'm sorry, love. I only ever wanted you not to be me.*'

'*I didn't want to become her, but I did, didn't I?*'

'*It was dreadful jealousy. Did she guess, do you think?*'

'*The water was so very cold. I felt her let go.*'

'*The fear never goes away, never. One day they'll find out.*'

Sometimes she laughed like a child, yet at others she keened and covered her face, so it was difficult to hear. I was sure there was something she needed to tell me, but her agitation alarmed Dad, so I backed off.

One day when I was leaving, Sister Kerry-Ann pulled me to one side.

'How did you find Joy today?' she asked.

'A little downcast, even furtive, as though she… Oh, I don't know.'

She titled her head. 'The letters? She wants to apologise.'

Nonplussed, I gazed. 'What letters?' Then the penny dropped. The teenage vitriol penned by my own hand. She'd obviously found them and read them.

Guilt shot to my cheeks. 'They were written—'

Kerry-Ann put a reassuring hand on my arm. 'Believe me, mums don't always get it right, not least having a nosy in our daughter's private things. But Joy's sorry she made you unhappy. Perhaps misguided, but it was her way of making you better than she was.' She smiled. 'Beats me why not. You both seem lovely people inside and out.'

Joy Parker returned, reinhabiting her body one evening and her home the next day. Dad and Tim breathed a huge sigh of relief, but that strange connection we'd had disappeared. I missed it, but at least my letters – and all the angst that went with them – had been avoided by a whisker. We were back in our safe *unmentionable* zone.

I was in a much better place with my course in terms of theory, but the notion of playing my cello in public still brought me out in hives, so I decided to broach it with Tim; he, of all people, knew that life threw out curve balls and that the expected trajectory wasn't always the right one. As I had most evenings, I cycled over to his flat on Friday night.

'Where's Cad?' I asked.

'He's popped out for some booze.' Tim looked at the bottle I offered. 'I don't think it'll be quite up to this standard, though. How much did you pay?'

'You can't ask about prices! Just one of many things the Parkers don't talk about.' I took a quick breath. 'Actually—'

But he spoke at the same time. 'That's true.' He shuffled his feet. 'I've been thinking about it a lot.'

'Oh right?'

'What you did for me in France. You saved my life.'

I grappled for humour. 'Annoying little sisters have to be good for something.'

'I never said thank you.'

'Oh, that's fine.'

'I should have straight away but I was pretty pissed off you'd intervened.'

'I know. I understood.'

'Then I suppose I forgot, or felt embarrassed, so I'm saying it now. Thank you.' His sincere look was so intense, I struggled to return it. 'Of course I knew you were physically hurt, but it wasn't until I talked it through with Cad that I realised it must have had other impacts on you.'

Tears stung my eyes, but the beep of a text saved me from embarrassing myself. Wafting my mobile aloft, I made for the lounge. 'Back in a mo. I'd better look at this.'

I perched on the sofa and spent a moment orienting myself. My brother was inviting me to talk about the consequences of that horrendous day beneath the French sunshine. I'd resented no one asking me, but in truth I was as repressed as my parents.

Mouthing a silent thanks for the interruption, I glanced my phone. Sure the unrecognised number would be spam, I casually opened the message.

> It's Bernard here. Text or call when you need a ride home.

As I stared, disbelieving, another popped up.

> As soon as you're ready. Sergio needs you.

—

I raged internally all night. The bloody cheek! Did the two men really think I'd return to London at the drop of a text? They had another think coming. I wasn't a dummy to be used and abused for the sake of art. And what about my hidden Calvin Kleins? That felt pretty damned pervy.

But as the wakeful hours passed, my contemplation became more seductive. Bernard had used the word 'home'; Sergio had seemed both perplexed and dismissive about the under-wear; he'd never propositioned me sexually, nor made me feel uncomfortable in that way. Then there was his expression when I asked about the blank canvas, his slumped and hopeless stance.

Sergio *needed* me. It was tremendously exciting. Ruth Parker was special after all; she was wanted; she'd been asked for.

And there was now a guiding light through my floundering uncertainty about the future. What could be better than having my image replicated by a famous artist? Be forever ingrained on the page? Be immortal, in fact?

Taking a deep breath of resolve, I flicked on the bedside lamp and composed a reply.

> Will Vanessa be there?

Though it was now the early hours, Bernard responded immediately.

> No.

I considered asking where she was, when and if she'd be back, but the new me said no. She'd been like a festering wound that wouldn't heal. Thank God the Harrods hamper had put an end to that. The cut had scabbed over; I was not going to pick at it.

> Then I'll see you tomorrow. I'll text you the time I'll be at Euston.

> Very good.

I thrummed my fingers. I couldn't shape why, but this destiny had to include my cello.

> I'd like a favour first, please.

Of course.

My uni keys are in my bedroom. Please go to my flat and collect my cello and music bag.

Of course. Consider it done.

Part 4

Chapter 67

Mum declined Dad's suggestion she accompany us on the short journey to Stockport station, citing the need to vacuum and clean my messy bedroom. It seemed that whenever we reached an understanding or a sense of affection, she swiped it away. After opening up a little during her hospital stay, she'd closed down again and that peep into her soul had raised more questions than answers in my mind. Maybe one day I could ask them, but I doubted it.

The train journey was restful and my reunion with Bernard felt like an everyday event. True to his word, he'd collected my cello and other 'bits and bobs' which he'd packed into large leather bag. I wondered what Herman had made of his visit, but at the end of the day he was a married man; like Gus, it was better to leave him in the past.

When we arrived 'home' and stepped into the dark foyer, I glanced at the console table. The hamper basket and the flowers had gone.

'It's so much nicer when the doors let in the daylight,' I commented. 'Could we open them up?'

I wasn't up to giving a 'you' command quite yet, but I was determined to start as I meant to go on.

'Of course.' Bernard gestured to the holdall. 'Shall I put this in your bedroom?'

'Yes please.'

'Are you hungry? Or just a pot of tea for now?'

'Tea would be wonderful.'

'Where would you like it?'

I was certain Sergio would be listening out for my arrival, so there was no point procrastinating. 'In the studio, I think.'

Absorbing the elegant interior afresh, I ambled to the top floor and inhaled deeply at the door. Then I straightened my spine, stepped in and met his eyes.

He raked his growing hair. '*Benvenuta.*'

'You have me for a couple of hours,' I said. 'I want to get in some cello practice before dinner.'

'OK. *Grazie.*'

I gracefully took my seat and looked around. There were none of the tell-tale aromas one might expect if Sergio had been productive, but he'd pegged several headshots on a wire line. With a jolt, I realised they were of me. Angular features, arched eyebrows and huge eyes, all of which were emphasised by the lack of hair around my face. It reminded me of Mum's comment about softening my features with curls for the wedding; she'd been right, but there was no doubt the woman in the photographs was striking, even beautiful.

With a rare smile of conceit, I inserted my AirPods and chose *Cello Suite No. 1* on my phone. Then I loosened my shoulders and jaw before setting them again, taking the same position as I had in the photographs.

With the help of Johann Sebastian, I could do this.

—

As the week went by I attended lectures online in the morning, became lost with Beethoven, Brahms, Britten and Bruch as I sat for Sergio in the afternoon, then went downstairs to the media room and tried to emulate the fabulous cellists I'd just heard perform. I was certainly rusty, but the area was soundproofed where no one could listen, condemn or criticise, and slowly I regained the standard I'd been before Christmas. I so wanted to surpass that, but it was a start.

Though Bernard set the dinner table for two at eight each evening, the man of the house didn't appear. Was I a tad disappointed? After all, this was the artist who needed me.

'Doesn't he ever eat?' I asked.

'He does when he's ready, so don't worry, he won't starve. I leave it on a plate in the oven.'

I wasn't convinced. Whilst I only saw Sergio when he bobbed his head around his canvas or approached me with a pencil and a frown, his face was hollow-cheeked and his body lean beneath his T-shirt and jogging bottoms. I wasn't sure if he slept either. From time to time I saw him emerge from Vanessa's room with the smell of shower gel in his wake, but otherwise the bedroom door remained open night and day.

—

When I helped myself to breakfast on Saturday, Bernard appeared from his back room.

'Would you like a ride out?' he asked.

'Oh. Where?'

'Anywhere you like.' He gestured to the window. 'Spring sunshine's out. It's only weak but it's there. Hatfield House or Chartwell? Or how about Hever Castle – the childhood home of Anne Boleyn? Have cake and tea while you're at it?'

Remembering my chat about Henry and his wives with Vanessa, I paused for a moment. Was there anything in my heart resembling love or affection for her, even just wistful nostalgia? No. Glad there wasn't even a whiff, I glanced at my watch. A day trip was tempting, but I'd become a little obsessive about my cello practice, let alone my modelling duties.

'He's not here,' Bernard said, reading my mind. 'He got off early.'

'Where's he gone?'

'Here and there, I expect.'

'Oh, OK.' I felt ridiculously miffed that I hadn't been told, but another thought struck: the maestro was out, so now was an opportunity to see how the painting had progressed. 'Let's do it, then. An outing would be fun. Apparently Hever has a magnificent yew maze. I just need half an hour to sort myself out.'

'Very good. Shall we say ten-thirty?'

'Perfect.'

I sauntered until I was out of sight then dashed up the rest of the way. Tingling with expectation, I stopped on the top landing to have a moment, then entered the studio and strode to the easel.

Disappointment settled on my shoulders, self-reproach too. Pride had come before a fall; I'd been so enamoured of my own image in the pegged photographs that I'd been certain the me in person would unleash Sergio's creative beast. It wasn't so. There were additional strokes in charcoal, but still no more than a framing guide.

My heart went out to him. He'd barely spoken during this week's sessions, but he hadn't revealed his frustration either. Was there such a thing as artist's block or lack of inspiration and confidence? Well, of course there was, same as in any creative endeavour. Indeed, I'd experienced the debilitating, vicious circle myself, which was precisely why I was in a good place now – for whatever reason, I'd recovered my musical mojo; I was back in the *zone* and it felt bloody brilliant.

Then another thought struck. Did his passive stance suggest he'd lost hope? He was a brilliant artist; I couldn't let him give up.

Searching for solutions, I paced the old floorboards. Sergio needed the original model, his actual muse. She clearly had other priorities but… Inspiration pinging, I cast my gaze to the heavy curtain. He might consider it a huge overstep, but nothing ventured, nothing gained. I picked up the phone and called Bernard.

'Put our outing on hold for an hour,' I said. 'For now, come up to the studio and bring some ladders.'

Chapter 68

After a bottle of fine wine with dinner, I woke late on Sunday and stretched. Bernard and I had enjoyed our trip to Kent, and after some persuasion he'd accompanied me around the castle and its grounds.

'Are you having a day off tomorrow?' I'd asked.

As though I'd caught him out, his cheeks had pinked. 'I thought I might. If you don't need me for anything…'

I didn't. It was amazing to have a butler around for domestic chores and cooking, but I felt I invaded his space when I made food for myself. I had adopted a more confident tone when I asked things of him, but I was still on best behaviour around the house, cleaning up after myself so he didn't have to, keeping my room neat and the music down.

I suddenly remembered his handiwork from yesterday. How on earth had I forgotten? I'd been buzzing about it before sleep, swinging from excitement to worry. Would Sergio be pleased about my concern and desire to help his creativity? Or would he see it as a major transgression and be annoyed with me? I raked back the duvet and peered out of the window. The Bentley had gone, so both men were out. Upstairs first or my cello?

I had been itching to perform and record Dvořák's *Cello Concerto in B minor* somewhere other than the basement to compare the acoustics, so I did that for a while, grinning to myself when I played it back.

'*You're an artist, young lady, and I want you to shine. At least two hours a day when you're here, please.*'

My jaw set, I pushed my aunt's voice away. Yet in fairness the old adage was right: practice did make perfect.

An hour or so later, I took the stairs two by two, chuckling to myself as I entered the studio: more positive progress; I no longer panted or had to recover my breath from the sprint. A sense of anticipation building, I walked to the wall and studied the eleven nudes Bernard had hung. It hadn't felt seemly to ogle them with him by my side, and I hadn't been sure of my own reaction, so I'd left him to it. I could have come later, but even now I was loath to visit the attic landing at night.

I slowly moved from one barely clad Vanessa to the next. Her initial 'reclining' or 'draped' poses seemed to progress from innocent to demure to alluring, but the last three were embarrassingly uninhibited. I checked my emotions again. Was I sad or regretful? Even jealous? None of them; it felt as though this woman was a stranger, or perhaps a veneer of the actual person. I took a step closer to peer at each face, but the swish of the curtain made me spin around.

Bloody hell, it was Sergio.

'Oh, I didn't realise you were back.' My heart thrashed as I tried to gauge his response to the artwork. Was he angry? Did I want him to be angry, to react to my interference and shout? Or even just talk to me? But other than weariness, nothing seemed to be behind his blank gaze. Had he even noticed them?

I gestured to images. 'We hung them yesterday,' I said. I didn't mention why, but I was desperate to elicit some sort of reaction.

Rather than look at them, he moved forwards and studied me. '*Sei dolce.*'

For a frozen moment I thought he'd touch my cheek, but he dropped his hand and stepped away. 'Will you sit?' he asked. He smiled thinly. '*Per favore.*'

I had to swallow back the urgent need to cry. Or perhaps shake him. Or yell and demand a response. 'Sure,' I said instead.

I fretted as I posed. What on earth did he do behind his canvas? Sure, he opened cupboards and drawers occasionally, but presumably he mostly sat in his chair. What went on in his head? How frustrated must he be? How deeply unhappy? Would his muse now surrounding him bring him out of his low mood? Help him to find a creative flow?

This man's stance, his whole depressed bearing was way too similar to my brother's after France. So God, I really did hope so.

Chapter 69

It was more of the same over the following days. I went upstairs for my afternoon sessions and Sergio did *something* behind his canvas. On the rare occasions I glimpsed him, his expression was neither elated nor despairing, yet my stomach still churned. Did Vanessa watching him from the walls help his vision? I'd certainly felt her eyes on me at first, judging and appraising me, but I was used to them now.

Though I tried to distract myself by listening to music, the artist's silence felt oppressive by Friday.

'Don't you ever eat?' I found myself asking.

'*Scusate.*' He emerged from the easel and motioned to the door. 'Are you hungry? Feel free to—'

'No. I'm talking about you. You don't appear to eat,' I snapped. 'You don't seem to sleep either. You need to do both to stay well.'

Instead of replying, he scooped up the packet of Marlboro from my side table and stepped out to the terrace. After a moment he turned. 'Do you want one?'

Bloody hell, if it took a cigarette to start a conversation, I was all for it.

I accepted his offering. 'I didn't know you smoked.'

'I don't any more.' He moved to the railing and gestured out. 'St Paul's Church. Wilton Crescent's Private Gardens.'

'Wow what a view, this place must have cost a fortune,' I said when I joined him. I pointed to the far end of the street. 'Presumably that's the Berkeley Hotel and there's Hyde Park?'

'*Si.* Somewhat different to the vista at *Gola Su Gorropu.*'

The name rang a bell. It had been part of my finishing school education, but I couldn't recall more. 'In Sardinia, I assume?'

'Yes. *Sardegna.*'

'*Sardegna,*' I repeated using his pronunciation.

The crow's feet above his cheek bones crinkled. 'Very good. Of course *Sardegna* has many beautiful beaches with white sands and crystal clear waters settled between the mountains, but my heart is in *Gola Su Gorropu*. People call it the Grand Canyon of Europe.' He glanced at me. 'It's a limestone gorge with some difficult yet *stupefacente* trekking routes. If you look up from inside, you can follow a thin ribbon of blue sky which snakes its way to the hidden rock pools. And from above there are many fantastic photographic opportunities. You should go sometime.'

I'd never heard him speak for so long and I could have listened to his mellifluous tones all day. But he abruptly turned and frowned. 'It's a beautiful afternoon. You should go out and enjoy it instead of being stuck in here. Motcomb Street is just around the corner for boutique shops and restaurants.'

I shook my head. Eating out would be nice, but I already had more clothes in my wardrobe than I'd ever use.

'If you need money, please say.' He stroked his growing stubble. 'I'm sorry I haven't thought that through. A salary, I should have arranged something before now.'

'It's fine; there's nothing I need.' I felt quite put out at the suggestion of payment. I wasn't doing it for money but for... What exactly? Feeling a hot blush, I moved away. 'I might walk to Belgrave Square Gardens though, so thanks.'

'*Buona.*' He took a breath. 'I do eat and sleep. Not as much as I should, but...'

His eyes flickered to his easel but he didn't need to say it. When I'd walked past it just now, the portrait had barely progressed.

Words bubbled up through my chest. 'Look, everyone gets a creative block sometimes.' As if I'd hit him, he flinched, but I doggedly carried on. 'Freaking out and starving yourself won't help.' My tone was sharp, but I had to spit out my concern. 'Your calling is one thing, but your mental health is more important and you need to look after it. Why don't you take a proper break? Go out with your mates, chill out and have a pint.'

I cringed at my own hypocrisy.

'Or if you're intent on staying inside, try something different, draw just for fun. Put your current project aside and go for another angle or idea. Even if it's rubbish, at least you'll have achieved something.'

Clearly unconvinced, he gazed at me steadily.

'I know I'm just a *kid* but—'

'No. No, you're not.' He sighed and reverted to the scene. 'I was wrong to offend you that day. Selfish. I've been selfish. It's just—'

'It's fine; I understand. I can't hold a candle to your talent, but I had the same thing; I lost all my confidence and was sort of paralysed, I suppose.'

He surprised me with the white grin I first saw in France. The one which had flashed behind my eyes more often than was appropriate. 'Your cello on Sunday morning. I thought I was dreaming when I woke and heard music wafting up.'

The thought of him listening was highly embarrassing, but my deep flush wasn't so much from that as the stir of attraction, deep in my belly. 'I'm not saying that it won't happen to me again,' I said stiffly. 'But right now it's... well, it's good.'

'I'm pleased for you, Ruth.' He looked away. 'If you find the magic formula, please sprinkle some on me.'

Chapter 70

Both men went off in the Bentley the next morning, so I did end up ambling around Belgravia in the March sunshine with a coffee. Not having any 'dress down' clothes these days, I wore designer everything from top to toe – including a pair of Dolce and Gabbana sunglasses I'd found in my bedroom drawer – but in this neck of the woods I was not out of place.

My mind, however, was elsewhere. I kept playing back my conversation with Sergio, a man with a *heart*, who'd trekked in a ravine, looking up at a ribbon of blue sky. The lightness about him when he'd described *Sardegna* accentuated his current malaise in my mind. I so wanted to make everything better for him. Why hadn't I wrapped my arms around him and hugged him tightly? Even put my lips to his troubled frown?

I deeply blushed at that particular thought. He'd mentioned magic, but it felt as though Puck had sprinkled a love potion on me in the night. It was wholly improper and taboo, but I'd had erotic dreams about him, not only kissing his mouth, but moving down his chest and along the tapering line of dark hair I'd glimpsed last year.

I laughed at myself. What was I like? Just because I'd managed a three-sentence conversation with the man, I was all a-flutter! It was obviously some sort of Stockholm syndrome-type of psychological response and best ignored. What was of greater concern was his safety: when he'd gone indoors yesterday, I'd leaned over the terrace railings and looked down, and for an awful moment I'd imagined the thud of his body hitting the ground. He hadn't said anything to suggest he'd do something so desperate, but his demeanour had seemed to.

I increased my pace along the busy high street. How to find a way to release Sergio's artistic block? My facial structure, the pegged headshots nor the paintings of Vanessa had helped, so what next? As I passed a shop window, I briefly glimpsed my reflection, but after a few steps, I turned around and looked again. A person I didn't recognise stared back. I rotated one way, then the other; so did my mirror image. Willowy, long-limbed, slim and striking. I pictured the nudes hanging on the attic wall, and more particularly the blank space where the final one should be.

An incomplete collection. Sergio clearly required 'more' of me to create the twelfth.

I binned my paper cup and marched happily for home. I couldn't say why, but instead of cringing at my inspiration, I felt emancipated. I didn't want to dwell on Vanessa and her regular pearls of wisdom, but what had she said about Modigliani's models? They were using their sensuality to be the strong ones with the power. Sure, I hadn't had actual sexual inter-course with another person, but that didn't stop me from being epicurean or tapping into the sensory pleasure I experienced when I touched myself. And these days I was the woman I'd just seen in the glass, so why couldn't I do the same?

–

I had a salad for lunch, then set up my cello in the lounge. The downside of a solitary life and remote learning was the lack of fellow musicians, especially as I needed a piano accompaniment for some pieces. Determined to improvise, I connected Vanessa's speakers to my iPhone and blasted out Beethoven's *Cello Sonata No. 3* to give the feel of a keyboard in the room.

It wasn't exactly a duet or completely in time, but I soon became lost in my endeavours, moving on from Ludwig to Sebastian. As dusk settled beyond the windows, I turned to my favourite composition, Camille Saint-Saëns' *Le Cygne*, listening to a slowed down and extended version of it, then joining in myself.

Just as the swan was dying, the hairs on the nape of my neck stood erect. A waft of perfume, *her* perfume was creeping in from behind me. Certain my aunt was watching from the doorway, I grimly continued until the end of the piece. When I finally took a deep breath and looked around, no one was there.

Chapter 71

Unsettled by the old sensation of being watched, I slept fitfully and awoke late on Sunday. I had already checked the basement and Vanessa's room before retiring for bed, but I looked again in the morning. Her door was ajar and there were no rumpled covers, discard clothing or other signs she'd been home, but to be sure, I peered into her en suite. The Bentley had returned at some point yesterday, so I was at risk of being caught, but I'd been so certain of her presence, I wanted to test my own sanity. Quietly opening her bathroom cabinet, I studied the contents. A contact lens box, her array of vitamin pills, a huge selection of face potions and products, make-up brushes, bronzers and a whole lot else was still there.

Ignoring my guilty pink reflection, I frowned. When I allowed my mind to consider her whereabouts, my guess was a film shoot in France. Was it odd she'd left these items here? Probably not; she wouldn't think twice about buying everything new and graciously donating it to someone at the end.

I shook the bountiful image away. The transient aroma had been clearly my imagination, an olfactory hallucination sparked by my own feelings of culpability. It was certainly unsettling, but I was only planning to do what she'd asked of me. Determined to see today's mission through, I tightened the belt of my dressing gown. Onwards and upwards, both literally and metaphorically.

I lifted my chin at the studio door. All was fine; I had it within me; in an artist's eye my body would simply be shape, shadow, texture, colour – like the veneer I saw when I looked at the nudes. I just needed to be bold and suggest it in a suitably professional manner. With a nod I strode in. Sergio wasn't behind his easel as usual. Surprised and frustrated, I flopped down on the chair, but after a few minutes it occurred that I might not be the only person who'd overslept.

I cleared my throat. 'Hello?' Then after a beat, 'Hello!'

A voice echoed back. '*Ciao?*' Then Sergio's dark head and shoulders appeared around the velvet partition. 'What is the time?'

'Half past eleven.'

'*Scusate.*' He looked sleepy and exceptionally handsome. 'Two minutes.'

As I listened to the creak of taps and splashing water, I rehearsed what I planned to say: '*I have an idea to help your creativity! I know I'm no substitute for your wife but—*'

Damn, nothing sounded right; it would be better, and far less embarrassing, to show rather than tell. Satisfied with that notion, I dragged a beanbag from the corner, draped over a faux fur throw, then positioned myself with my legs to one side like Copenhagen's 'Little Mermaid'. Taking a breath of resolve, I unbelted my silk robe and let it slither from my arms.

Despite my sheer nerves, I chuckled to myself. What the heck would the popular crowd think of me now? Shocked but a little envious? And my nudity didn't feel too bad. Though a little chilly, I was reasonably comfortable, my nether regions were hidden, and if I kept my eyes fixed on the view beyond the patio windows, I might have been wearing a bra.

After what felt like an eon, I heard the swishing sound of the drape. Rather than witness Sergio's response, I kept my gaze on the skyline and prayed he'd disappear behind his screen and get to it without the awkwardness of words or any acknowledgment of my nakedness.

'No. No, Ruth.'

His words stung like a sharp slap. The next thing I knew he was scooping up my gown and pushing it at me. 'Get dressed,' he said.

With fumbling hands, I did as I was told, and though the hurt and humiliation was already unbearable, I still needed to know.

'Why not?'

He studied the images of his muse on the wall. 'It wouldn't work.'

'Why not?' I asked again. My voice was petulant, cringingly shrill. 'What's wrong with me? I have feet, arms and legs. I have shadows and creases and curves like she does.'

He finally turned. 'It isn't as simple as that.' His expression softening, he sighed. 'It wouldn't be,' he seemed to search for a word, '*adeguata*.'

'What does that mean?'

'Appropriate.'

Oh my God; I'd only offered to model for him. Did he think…?

Clearly having the same notion, his cheeks flushed with colour. '*Scusate*. That wasn't what I…' He gestured towards his stand. 'And I've started a new, well, something. I was up until the early hours with it, so…'

Though I couldn't shape why, this was the worst blow. *Something new*. Yet I should have known. I'd been so absorbed with myself I hadn't noticed the heady blend of turpentine, paint and linseed in the air. And when I looked, the old canvas was propped against the side table, clearly surplus to requirements, like me.

–

Groping for some semblance of self-respect, I had left the attic with my head held high, but I was a blubbering mess by the time I reached my room. Wishing I was invisible, I stowed beneath the duvet, but there was no hiding away from my thoughts.

What *was* wrong with me? Had I really asked that out loud? But it was a question which had hounded me for bloody years now. I was defective, not good enough somehow; I'd been deserted, discarded, abandoned again.

Mortification flooded back. Had Sergio really thought I was offering him sex? It was ludicrous and yet, if I was honest, wasn't that why I'd felt guilty in Vanessa's bathroom? Hadn't some part of my mind fantasised about it when I awoke this morning? Hadn't his naked body been my focus as I'd touched myself? But that made it all the worse. He hadn't just declined my modelling services, he'd spurned me too.

Then there was his new project; the words '*you are no longer needed*' had dripped from his '*So…*' far more clearly than spelling it out. What would I do now? Could I really return, broken and humiliated, to either Brockley or Manchester? As my mother would have said, pride had come before a fall.

Christ, what a spectacular plunge it had been.

Chapter 72

Exhausted by my tears, I fell into dreamland and was soon led by a softly smiling Vanessa up the stairs to the attic. Instead of turning to the studio door, she tugged me to an open sash window on the right.

'Come and look at this spectacular view, sweetie,' she said.

The breeze on my cheeks, I began to step forward, but a sudden fear of heights overtook me.

'No, I can't,' I said, cowering away.

Then just as her lips shaped into a terrifying snarl, I jolted upright, certain she was there for real in my bedroom.

His expression apologetic, Sergio sat forward in the loveseat. 'Sorry, I didn't mean to—' He gestured to the bedside table. 'I brought that up but it's probably cold now.'

I took in the mismatched mugs, jug and teapot. Bernard was clearly not here to oversee perfection, and the image of this man trying to make British tea brought on a small smile. He'd silently watched me sleep, too, which felt a little romantic. Then the humiliation from earlier hurtled back.

'I upset you. I'm sorry,' he said. His palm on his chest, he frowned. 'I should have come down sooner but I'm not used to dealing with—'

Irritation surfaced. 'I'm not a child. Or a kid, as you put it. I'm nineteen, an adult. You don't need to *deal* with me.'

'I know you're not. I meant me. Coping with emotions is not my strong point. I can paint them, yes, but in person...' He raked his hair. 'Your offer to... to pose was touching but—'

'But what? I'm not slim enough, pretty enough, sexy enough?' What the hell was I saying? But anger was bubbling.

'You are all those things, Ruth. You are a beautiful woman. But it's complicated. Some artists portray what they see, but there are layers behind the—' He swept a hand by his face. '*La facciata.*' His dark eyes seemed to search for an explanation. 'Like an onion. And I paint those too.'

'So what are you saying? I'm too insular, too boring, too pedestrian to have *layers*?'

'No, not exactly.'

'Then how, exactly?'

'You are young and sweet, and—' He shrugged. 'I don't know you. That is the problem.'

Sweet. Again. I didn't want to be sweet; I wanted to be desired; I wanted him. The tears suddenly falling, I lowered my head. Why was I humiliating myself like this?

'So basically I'm being dumped,' I muttered. 'You're telling me to leave here.'

'No, absolutely not.' To my astonishment he grinned, knelt by the bed and waited for eye contact. 'You did it,' he said.

'Did what?'

'*Il blocco creativo.*'

'Really? How?'

'I don't know yet.' He stood, clearly eager to leave. 'But give me a few hours and we'll see.'

—

I was truly pleased Sergio had somehow perforated his creative block, yet I felt displaced and unsettled. On a Sunday I was usually lolling in the studio with my AirPods and music, pretending to be a model and stupidly thinking Ruth Parker could make a difference.

Searching for positives, I padded down the stairs. Anyone could have told him to 'try something new', so it was nice of him to give me the credit. And today was all mine to do as I pleased: the weather was bright and inviting; I could head out for a walk, take the bus or a train to a gallery or the shops. Yet I didn't want to miss any summons from the maestro. I knew I was hanging on by my fingertips, but whatever he was creating, I wanted to be involved.

A few hours, he'd said. What could I usefully do in that time? As I ambled into the kitchen, the cardinal red tomatoes gave me the perfect answer. Cook a ragù, of course.

–

That first tutorial by my aunt played in my head like a film reel, yet I didn't follow her recipe completely. It felt important to leave my own mark, a tiny act of defiance similar to Mum and her hamper.

The sun shining in through the panelled window, I peeled and chopped and sautéed. Once the sauce was on the boil, I inspected the fridge for appetiser inspiration and decided on mini meatballs. It was one of the dishes I'd lovingly made for Vanessa, so exorcising the connection felt apt, and after the angst of the morning, immersing myself in the chore was relaxing.

An hour or two passed, and though I tried to disregard the neat pile of onions in Bernard's vegetable box, I eventually gave in, scooped one out and studied it. *Layers*, Sergio had said. And *I don't know you. That is the problem.* It was very true. Over the past weeks we had barely conversed. Something had shifted when we had the cigarette on the terrace, but that brief chat hardly counted as a friendship.

With a sigh, I shook my head and made to replace it, but the deep, harmonic flavours from the tureen made me pause. Vanessa was right about never eating alone unless one couldn't help it, and although it was a long shot, I rang the top floor extension.

To my surprise Sergio answered. 'Hello.'

'Food will be served downstairs at eight,' I said. I didn't give him the opportunity to reply. 'I'm tonight's chef and this is your notice.'

A pause and then, 'Do I need to dress for dinner?'

Was that a hint of humour? 'Yes, it's spaghetti, so a bib and tucker would be sensible.'

Chapter 73

Dressed in the little black frock from my wardrobe, and veritably tingling from the heady mix of guiltiness and excitement, I was waiting at the table for eight. From my one previous experience of dining with Sergio, I didn't expect him to be on time, so I opened a bottle of Masseto and slowly sipped. By eight forty-five, I was getting a little drunk. Deciding on food to soak up the alcohol, I scraped back my chair, but as I made for the door, he rushed in. He hadn't changed from earlier, and his feet were bare.

'Am I late?' he asked.

'It depends on your definition of late.'

He smiled. 'Which means yes.' He kissed both my cheeks. 'My apologies. Believe it or not, I don't own a watch.'

It was ridiculous. This man had been in my personal space many times, yet his close proximity brought on butterflies. 'I've heard worse excuses. Right, sit and don't move. Hopefully there's some wine left. Antipasti will be served shortly.'

Puffing out my trapped breath, I hurried to the kitchen, donned oven gloves and returned with the oven proof dish.

'Don't blame me if these are overcooked.'

Sergio was pacing.

'Are you OK?' I asked.

'Yes, absolutely.' He moved to his chair and pulled it out. 'So what do I have the honour of eating?'

'Meatballs.'

Agitation steamed from his body; so much for getting to know each other.

I inwardly sighed. 'Why don't you have yours upstairs? Actually, take the whole pot. If you keep on the lid, they'll stay warm for a while.' Despite my disappointment, I tried for humour. 'That might not stretch until breakfast, so tonight's the thing.'

'Good. Yes, that's good.' He accepted the mitts and picked up the tureen. At the door he turned and flashed that white grin. 'We'll need wine glasses. Should we go for Masseto again?'

–

A bowl in one hand and a spoon in the other, we sat on beanbags in the studio.

He savoured his first mouthful of my delicacy. 'My grandmother is the cook of our family and these are—' His eyes crinkled. '—almost as good as hers.'

'Why thank you!' Although I pictured the old couple at the villa in France, I was determined not to let thoughts of my aunt spoil these sublime moments. 'Your *nonna?*'

'Yes. My grandparents lived a few houses away when I was a boy. My parents moved away, but they are still there. A village near *Urzulei*, so many beautiful places to see and things to do as I grew up. The *Villaggio Nuragico di Or Murales*, for example.'

Similar to when he'd described the canyon, it was as if he'd removed a veil to reveal the Sergio before Vanessa. I yearned to discover so much more, but he patted his mouth with a napkin. 'Delicious. *Grazie.*'

That clearly was my cue to leave, but I wanted to stretch it out a bit longer. 'Maybe you'll sample my *ragù alla bolognese* tomorrow if Bernard doesn't get there before you. I wonder what he does on his days off. Do you think he has a girlfriend stashed somewhere? A Mrs Bernard in the pipeline?'

He didn't reply so I followed his gaze. Vanessa, of course, not a nude but that huge, startling abstract of her face. Even in her absence, his muse was clearly inspiring his new project and he was itching to get on with it. Indeed, he'd eaten and drunk so fast, he was sure to get indigestion.

'I'll leave you to continue the good work.' I reached for his empty dish, but he tugged it back.

'Don't go.' He leaned forward and peered at me so intently, it was all I could do to breathe. But he didn't move in for the longed for, yet terrifying kiss. 'It keeps changing. The new piece. Evolving, I suppose.' He gestured to his wife looking down on us. 'Like that one. The beginning and the end were wholly different.'

He seemed lost for a while, but finally regained focus. 'So I need your help.'

Stuck for words, I waited for more.

He massaged his forehead. 'It started with the *musica* and that's what I painted all last night. You know, replicating the colours of it?'

Understanding what he meant, I nodded. Music was auditory with tempo, pitch, timbre and rhythm, yet it also had colour properties of lightness, vividness and hue. The reverse had to be true.

'But sound doesn't exist by itself.' He shaped it with his hands. 'So I need an image of your cello.'

Surprised laughter burst through my nerves. 'You want to photograph my cello?'

'Paint it.'

'You want my cello to sit for you?'

'Yes.' He flushed. 'But here's the thing. Sound doesn't exist by itself, nor can an instrument create it alone. So, if you are prepared to... if it doesn't embarrass or inconvenience you... I'd like you to play it for me.'

My instinct was to guffaw. I'd offered to model for him naked, yet he was obviously struggling to ask me this favour. But my smile soon fell. I'd been crippled by my perform-ance anxiety. Since then I'd hidden away and only practised in private. Posing with my cello would be one thing, playing it for him another. Could I go that far out of my comfort zone? And yet...

'It was you. You watched me in the lounge yesterday.'

'Yes.' He spread his arms apologetically. 'You were so rapt, I didn't think you'd notice. You were accompanying recorded music.'

'Yes, in lieu of a piano.'

'You play that also.'

It was a statement rather than a question, and I cringed at the thought of that gauche girl fingering the Steinway in France.

'A few other instruments too. Badly,' I said, to cover my embarrassment.

His brow creased in thought, he drifted for a while. 'So, what do you think?' he eventually asked.

I was my turn to fall silent. This was exactly what I'd wished for – not only to be part of this man's creativity, but to stimulate it. Yet I craved more, didn't I? As wholly wrong as it was, that was the honest truth. I wanted *him*. I wanted to touch him, stroke him, feel his lips on mine; I longed for him to invade me, take me, make me moan with desire.

'I want to know you first,' I said simply.

That's what he'd meant, wasn't it? Looking behind his muse's façade by exploring her intimately? But for me was more a matter of trust: if I could trust him with my fragile self-worth, I could trust him with anything.

His eyes almost black, he took my trembling hands. This was a make-or-break moment; my whole life would be defined by his acceptance or rejection.

'God knows I'd love to, what fool wouldn't? You're beautiful, accomplished, charming, caring, funny...'

My whole being tensed, I waited for the 'but'.

'But I'm thirty-four, Ruth. It would be wrong to... to take advantage of a woman so much younger than me.'

I was thrown, then relieved, then finally empowered. 'Isn't that my decision to make?'

'Yes, yes, it is—'

I stopped the next 'but' with my lips. Though the moments of resistance felt like an aeon, he finally took me in his arms and kissed me back. After a while, he gently pulled away and peered at me intently.

'Are you sure about this?' he asked.

I was breathless and rattling with a million emotions, but the overwhelming sensation was that fate had brought us together and that *this* was meant to be. 'Yes,' I said, both trembling and grinning. 'As sure as I'll ever be.'

Chapter 74

I thought Sergio would guide me to his room beyond the curtain, or even use mine, but he firmly grasped my hand and led me down to the *boudoir*. I should have felt deeply guilty; it should have felt duplicitous to be stripped of my clothes and have every last inch of my body kissed by my aunt's husband in her huge, silky bed. I didn't experience any of those sensations; I had already detached myself from the woman and spread my wings many weeks ago. Besides, I couldn't have stopped the pivotal moment if I'd tried. I was finally losing my virginity to this achingly attractive man who was attentive and tender, and although I didn't reach a dizzy orgasm that first night, he certainly did.

The feel of my *nuovo amante's* lips from my earlobe, down my neck and along my shoulder roused me from deep sleep in the morning.

My cheeks burning with sheepishness, I hitched around to him. Had I really propositioned this man last night? Pretty much coerced him into having sex with me even though he was married? But he didn't seem the least bit perturbed, certainly not if his smile and erection were anything to go by. He continued his journey from my mouth to my breasts, loitering there for a minute before making his way to my belly button. My loins were already on fire, but when he moved lower and lingered there, I couldn't help the stunning climax coming out as a moan, an embarrassingly loud one.

He surfaced with a grin. 'I take it you like that?'

Tingling, breathless and zapped, I eventually found the power of speech. 'It was simply—'

But my reply was cut short by a tap at the door, then Bernard a second later.

'Morning,' he said, placing a breakfast tray on the side table. Daylight flooded in as he opened the curtains. 'Tea for two. Crumpets, a pot of jam and butter. Anything else for now?'

Bloody hell, he was looking at me. 'No thank you,' I replied, my voice emerging as a squeak.

'What the hell!' I hissed when he'd gone. 'How did he know we'd be in here?'

'I don't—' Sergio began. He frowned thoughtfully, took my hand and kissed it gently. 'Perhaps he saw this – us – before we did.'

The notion was appealing; I really liked Bernard, and his quiet 'business as usual' offering felt like an assurance of his discretion. Then another mortifying thought flew in: 'Oh my God! Do you think he heard me?'

Sergio laughed. 'Who cares? It was a joyous sound I'd like to hear every day.'

'Cello music too?'

'Just half an hour here and there.' He kissed my nose. 'You don't need to devote *all* your attention on me.'

'That's all right, then.'

'And I have been known to get a little… agitated or forgetful on occasion when I'm in the throes of—'

'You don't say!'

It was Sergio's way of telling me he'd need time on his own, but that was good; I still had my lectures and practice to do, and if ever I got over my ignominy, I'd resume the trips with Bernard in the Bentley.

Pulling the sheet with me, I hopped from the bed to collect our food. Sergio wasn't nearly as coy about his own nudity; his body was beautiful, his proud penis on full display. 'I didn't have you down as a tea and crumpet type of guy,' I said to cover my blushes.

He gave a lazy smile. 'The first of many surprises, I hope.' He caught my arm and gave it a tug. 'But for now, I think *frittelle* can wait.'

Chapter 75

I was so utterly contented, April and May flew by. Each morning began with a long lie-in with Sergio where we'd cuddle and chat about his early years in Italy, his family and his friends from those days, his *nonna's* cooking and solid but strict love. He was fascinated by my ability to play and create music, so I showed him how to hold a bow and construct the triad of C Major chords. I taught him about themes and variations in classical compositions, and I introduced him to an eclectic mix of prestigious composers, both dead and alive.

When the hours weren't filled with performing and sitting for Sergio, coursework or cello practise, I donned silk pyjamas, lolled in the golden boudoir and let Bernard spoil me with the tasty titbits he'd lovingly prepared. Or I'd have a sauna and swim, then dress in the red silk or green bondage dress and partake in pre-dinner wine tasting with Nina or Ella crooning to me in the lounge.

From his frequent offers to drive me to Knightsbridge, I gleaned Bernard missed the trips to Harrods, so I went once or twice, traipsing around the store and peering at the ridiculous prices. The men's watches were the only thing which caught my interest, and though I didn't have the funds for an expensive one, what Mum had said about thoughtfulness stuck in my mind, so on a whim I bought Sergio a James Bond ^{2}Q Swatch as an affectionate hint about dinner times. I expected him to leave it by his easel or in a pocket, but he declined to take it off, even in the shower. Perhaps I was misguided by my infatuation, but it felt like a symbol of our growing closeness.

Bernard's Sunday off extended to the whole weekend. It felt overly familiar to enquire where he went, but I enjoyed the freedom in the kitchen, branching out from Italian cuisine to other countries for my love.

As Sergio had warned me, he wasn't always communicative, light-hearted or even in the same world at times, but he'd be at the table for eight if I'd cooked a meal and he always awoke in our bed. I took care not to invade his artistic space nor check on the progress of his project, but he came to fetch me late one Friday evening.

'Come.' He held out a hand. 'It's ready.'

His arm around my waist, we made our way up the stairs. Quite frankly I was terrified I wouldn't like it. Suppose I couldn't just 'damned-well act'? Life in this old house had been so perfect with him, I was afraid the Ruth Parker curse would raise its ugly head and smash my happiness to smithereens. Yet the moment I stood at the threshold, I knew my worries had been needless. Replacing the headpiece of Vanessa, the painting wasn't as abstract as I had feared. Surrounded by rolling clouds of colour, the woman's top half was a slim, naked back, the bottom half a cello. But its emotive purity was what made it stand out.

Emotion burned behind my eyes. That was what he must have seen when he'd silently watched me play in the lounge. Was I still that innocent girl? Hardly, when I was in love – and sleeping – with a married man. *Le Cygne* had been the thirteenth and penultimate movement of *The Carnival of the Animals*. Why did that feel significant?

'It's wonderful,' I managed.

'Good, good. I'm pleased that you like it.'

He seemed a little distracted. A canvas was on his easel; he must have started something new. He kissed my forehead. 'You go to bed and sleep. We have a delivery in the morning.'

A horrible sense of foreboding trickled down my spine, and though I hated being needy, I had to know more. 'Some art supplies?' I asked.

'Something for you. A thank you present.'

'For what?'

'For waking me up. Bringing me back from oblivion. And because...' Taking me by the shoulders, he peered at me intently. '*Ti amo*, Ruth.' He pulled me into his arms. 'Hey, don't cry. I promise, you'll like it.'

—

Sergio sent me to the studio when the intercom rang in the morning. Keeping my eyes averted from his artwork, I made for the terrace and stared at the pillow clouds, but my agitation was so strong, I searched out the Marlboro and lit up.

What exactly was I worrying about? Was I afraid the finished cello painting made me redundant? That he'd need a new muse? Yet surely that was sheer paranoia; he'd bought me a gift he was excited about; he'd told me he loved me for goodness' sake!

When telephone finally rang, I stubbed out the cigarette and took a deep breath.

'Your present awaits in the lounge,' he said.

'OK. On my way.'

Anxiety rising, I ambled downwards. Sergio was waiting at the bi-folds. He beamed and waved me in. 'After you.'

'Thank you.' It took moments to see what was before my very eyes. The sofas had been pushed back to the walls, making room for...? A Kawai baby grand piano had replaced the marble coffee table.

Sergio searched my face. 'Do you like it?'

I gaped, stuck for words. I guessed a price tag of around ten thousand pounds, but this wasn't just about money, it was an incredibly perceptive, thoughtful and supportive gift. Only last week I'd muttered about the possibility of hooking up with a local pianist, and Sergio had asked if it was feasible to record the keyboard parts myself and use it as accompaniment.

'You don't like the colour,' he now said. 'I could have bought black, but it matches...' He gestured to the bright gloss bannisters and doors. 'And I thought the white was more you.'

Innocent again? Was that really how he saw me?

'I do like it. I love it. It's beautiful. It's incredibly generous of you.' Needing to hide my throbbing unease, I buried my face in his chest. 'Thank you. Thank you.'

He eventually pulled away. 'A good surprise?'

It was, it really was, yet my stomach churned. 'Absolutely. An utterly wonderful surprise.' I peered at him intently, needing to say it: 'Promise me they'll only ever be good ones?'

Chapter 76

It didn't take a genius to unscramble my disquiet. Vanessa. When she'd elbowed into my thoughts over the last few weeks, I'd blanked them out and just enjoyed the here and now. From confidence to culture and clothes, she had done so much for me, I hadn't wanted to risk sensations of guilt seeping in, so I'd mentally floated above her furnishings, her ornaments and other personal possessions. Considering I was sleeping in her bed with her husband, it was perhaps illogical, but I took care not to pry in her wardrobes and drawers, and I used my old bathroom as my base.

In the early days of her absence my fingers had itched to search the internet or check the gossip pages as I had as a child, but after Mum's illness I'd avoided them at all costs. I had no idea if the two women were in touch. When we chatted on the phone, Mum didn't mention my 'aunt' and nor did I.

It was denial, of course. Pure and simple denial. But the delivery of my piano had changed all that. Like the Harrods hamper, it felt like a significant wake up call, and as I spread my fingers across the keys each morning, reality nagged. Five months had now passed since Christmas. Time was ticking on. The Kawai was a fixture which matched its surroundings, but I wasn't; I was a temporary guest.

Sergio's young lover wanted to stay here forever, happily trapped in this fantasy, but the real Ruth Parker was more pragmatic. She couldn't completely bury her head in the sand. When would Vanessa return?

I was still fairly certain she was working abroad on a film shoot. In the past she'd described back to-back productions, but the mention of six months had stuck in my head. Renting somewhere for that term made sense, wherever she was. Which meant I had a month.

The prospect of her reappearance brought on waves of nausea. Even if she offered, there was no way on God's earth I'd stay here and pretend everything was the same as last year. I'd have to pack my rucksack, take my cello and music bag and leave. Where could I go? It would coincide with the end of my first year at university, so I couldn't retreat to my old room in Brockley; I didn't have the resources to rent anywhere in London, which meant I'd have to return to Mum and Dad.

The idea of parting from Sergio brought on a physical ache, but I knew I had to prepare myself. The obvious solution was to simply ask him or Bernard about Vanessa. I could have done that since the Bentley turned up to collect me in February, but Parker habits died hard. My aunt was another unmentionable, made even more taboo by the two men's reticence. There had to be documentation or other clues about her filming where-abouts, and her likely return, somewhere in this property. The time had come to unearth the information myself.

–

Bernard was away and Sergio busy in his workshop, so Saturday morning was an ideal time to explore the house. I tried to eat breakfast, but my stomach felt off, so I lifted my chin and got on with it.

My heart jangled in my chest even on the first floor, so I held onto the bannister to recover my breath and looked down to the zigzag parquet like Vanessa had before Christmas. So open plan, so modern for a property built – when? Maybe the early eighteen hundreds? And when, exactly, had she moved in? Remembering her comment about *un diavolo*, I gave a little shudder. If there was one, I hadn't felt it for some time, just the occasional mild aroma of her perfume which was clearly embedded in the fabric. Or perhaps just in my head.

Admiring my beautiful piano as I passed, I continued upwards and popped my head into the bedroom opposite mine. It was a pristine suite with a bathroom attached. Had anyone ever slept here? A friend of Vanessa's, a colleague? Sergio's family? From its soulless, chilly feel, I doubted it.

Moving onto the next level, I glanced into the boudoir to ensure Sergio wasn't around, then stepped across the landing to the other door, opened up and peered in. It was another guest chamber with nothing to suggest Vanessa kept her paperwork in there – or indeed where she 'wrote'. Casting my mind back to several weeks ago, I looked up to the ceiling. The windowless attic room... I still felt spooked about that breeze which had come from nowhere, but had there been a desk in there? I looked at my watch. Sergio hadn't eaten anything yet. Did I have time to find Bernard's keys and look? Probably not, but I could shine my phone torch through the lock to check.

Absurdly thief-like, I tiptoed up to the shadowy roof space, stopped to listen to the dulcet sounds of Delius's *Cello Concerto* filtering out from the studio, then pulled out my mobile. Though the horrible dream about Vanessa shivered through me, I took a quick breath and pulled back the curtain.

'Ruth?' Sergio's voice made me jump from my skin. 'What are you doing?'

Glad of the gloom to hide my guilty cheeks, I turned around. 'I came up to see if you were ready for some brunch. Then I noticed this room. What's it for?'

He shrugged. 'I don't know, it's always locked. The landlord's own stuff?' He kissed my nose. '*Si per favore*. Maybe in half an hour? I'll come down.'

'Sure thing. See you in a while.'

I moved away with friendly wave, but I felt horribly winded. Sergio's evasive eyes hadn't quite met mine. Why was he lying?

I retreated to the boudoir, perched at the dressing table and lowered my head until my pulse – and my imagination – finally slowed. I'd felt bad for prying, so my mind was simply in overdrive, that was all. And my unease was silly; this multi-million-pound property was rented, of course it was. I'd naively never given it a second thought, but it made perfect sense for the owners to have somewhere to store their own belongings. Indeed, I now recalled seeing a couple of large tea chests in one gloomy corner. Maybe the other contents belonged to them too.

And yet that teddy's flinty eyes flashed in my head. It was definitely the one I'd seen in this room.

That isn't supposed to be in here.

Ignoring the queasy flutter in my stomach, I looked at the golden furnishings surrounding me. Perhaps she kept her work contracts and other documentation in here, including the 'heap' of manuscripts she'd described. The fitted wardrobes seemed the obvious place, so I stepped across and quietly opened the doors. I moved from one to the next, but to my surprise the rails and racks were all but empty. I chuckled nervously. So much for my heroic attempts to rise above her belongings. Where had they all gone? Plenty had found their way to my bedroom closets before Christmas, but surely not all.

Two items from a higher shelf seemed to wave at me, so I tiptoed up and pulled them out. The first was a framed professional headshot of my aunt. Though her gaze felt horribly knowing, I peered more closely at the fur jacket around her shoulders. It looked like the faux mink she'd worn the day she'd appeared at my uni halls. Where was it now? The second was a slim manuscript entitled 'The Folly'. I couldn't pinpoint what it was, but the name rang a distant bell, so I retreated to the bed. Taking a big breath, I prepared to open it, but the echo of footsteps approached, so I rolled it up like a magazine and stuffed it in my music bag.

Sergio stretched at the entrance. 'I could do with some fresh air. Do you want to join me? I have a fancy for some *Coppia Ferrarese*.' He tilted his head. 'It's the twisted bread partially resembling a croissant? We could walk to Olivine Deli and choose something for you too.'

Under Vanessa's supervision, I'd swatted up on types of Italian sourdough at some point, so he'd clearly misinterpreted my expression. It was actually astonishment: we'd never been anywhere outside the house together before.

'I'd love to!' I said. Yet the jolt of sheer pleasure soon turned to discomfort. Why was he asking me now? Why did he still have that same shiftiness about him from earlier? Was there something in the fusty twin room he didn't want me to discover?

I had no idea what I might find, but the imperative to search it went up another notch. 'But I promised I'd give my mum a call,' I continued. 'She'll get quite offended if I miss it or I'm late. Will you choose something delicious for me?'

'Sure. My pleasure. I won't be long.'

My heart thrashed. Olivine Deli. That gave me half an hour to return to the attic.

Chapter 77

I was short on time and panting by the time I reached the dusty curtain. The keys hadn't been on Bernard's bedside table this time, so I'd had to stealthily open its drawers. Thank God they'd been in the second one I searched, along with his mobile and various medals.

Nerves squeezing my chest, I took a sharp breath and turned the old lock. Once I'd stepped over the threshold, I snapped on the light and quickly glanced around the claustrophobic room. To check for what, I was no longer sure, but I blew out the air trapped in my lungs. As far as I could tell it was the same as before; there was nothing – and no one – hidden; no obvious reason why Sergio would deter me from coming in here.

But I had been right about the small bureau I'd absently noticed the last time. The old-fashioned school-style desk was the only one I'd found in the house, so perhaps I'd glean more about Vanessa's whereabouts after all. Keeping my eyes averted from the dolly's hostile stare, I perched on a spindled chair and lifted the lid. Bingo. This was clearly where my aunt kept her paperwork. The walls seemed to groan so I briefly stilled, then I swiftly fumbled through it, pulling out and peering at letters from production companies, a ledger headed 'expenses', theatre flyers and leaflets, but nothing with a recent date.

I reached further in and tugged out a couple of exercise books. Vanessa's extravagant scrawl on the front wasn't so very different to now, so presumably they were her treasured ones from school days. I had no desire to read her twelve-year-old homework, but as I made to put them back, something slipped out from the middle.

I frowned at my find. It was a slim bundle of weathered newspaper cuttings with a Post-it note stuck on the top.

The letter 'J?' was written on it.

Why the commonly used initial made me pause, I didn't know, but the hairs on my neck stood erect. Carefully peeling off the sticker, I took in the headline.

Mother and only child in drowning tragedy.

Gosh, a tragedy indeed. But when I read on, I discovered the daughter had 'miraculously' survived. The date was nearly forty years ago. Why would Vanessa be interested in this?

I moved onto the next one.

Girl, ten, who survived a horrific drowning that killed her mother when their car careered into a river is described as "clever beyond her years" for escaping through the window before running for help.

Then the following:

Bruising on mother's body is suspicious, an inside source says.

Then finally:

"Houdini girl" is taken in for questioning after a witness comes forwards.

Anxiety jangling, I pushed everything back. The time was ticking for Sergio's return.

I scuttled down to the lounge, curled up on the sofa and tried to push that 'J' from my head. But idioms pecked as I stared into space: curiosity killed the cat; nosy parker squashed tomato; ask me no questions…

And yet what had I discovered? Nothing save for a vague sense of unease. I sighed the agitation away. It was fine; I'd shelve it along with the rest of the flaming unmentionables which lined my belly. I just needed a plan for the day, something to shake off this underlying discomfort. I should have gone out for some fresh air with Sergio rather than chasing shadows. Perhaps I should go now – I could head for the deli and meet him on his way back with my arms outstretched. Only I couldn't do that, could I? He was the love of my life, but I was his dirty, hidden secret within these four walls. And it was me who'd instigated this fantasy, this affair, this relationship, so it was completely my own fault I was anticipating, testing and tasting heartache now so I'd know the full flavour when it descended completely.

'Ruth.'

'Sergio! I didn't hear you come in.'

As though he'd been reading my every thought, he moved from the doorway and crouched by my side. His gaze seemed as sorrowful as I felt. 'What's wrong?'

'Nothing.' I knew time was caving in; I had to make the best of each moment I had left. I lifted an eyebrow. 'At least nothing that a cup of tea wouldn't cure.'

'I'm on it,' he said. 'How about I impress you with my *cucinando* tonight?'

This was another first. 'Sergio Rossini the chef?'

'More a sous.'

'So I'm guessing you'll still need the head cook?'

'I will. If she's willing, of course.'

'She is. But how about the two hours of your time it'll take?'

'For you, anything.'

He stood and smiled, yet his eyes still looked sad.

–

It had been a lovely afternoon. True to his word, Sergio had joined me in the kitchen at four and helped prepare the pasta sauce by adding his '*l'ingrediente segreto della nonna*'. We'd had pre-dinner drinks together, we'd eaten together, we'd had exquisite sex on the lounge rug, and we were now entwined, stuffed and replete in every possible way.

'Everything OK?' he asked, lifting his head from my lap.

'How could it not be?' Then after a few moments, 'Why do you ask?'

He didn't reply for a while. 'Maybe I'm getting to know you a little.'

'Hmm. I'm not sure that's a good thing.'

Though I chuckled, the idea made me feel hot. How much did I know him? I'd become an expert in what turned him on, the tender spots below his ears and inner thighs, and how to tease him to distraction; I knew how to make him laugh, how to help him out of a dip and when to leave him alone; I'd also learned a great deal about his family, his childhood and early adulthood in Italy. But a line had been drawn after that. He had never offered and I'd never asked about his life after he moved to France. Other than the snippets my aunt had casually imparted over time, there was a gaping gap that was Vanessa.

Vanessa, Vanessa, Vanessa… It brought me full circle to the notion which had tormented me since this morning. Why had she kept the newspaper cuttings? Had the 'J' really stood for Joy?

Sergio tenderly cupped my face. 'What's going on in that beautiful head? Talk to me.' A small smile. 'I'm all yours tonight. Make the most of me while I'm here. I can be a good listener when I try.'

My throat swelled with sorrow. '*Make the most of me while I'm here*' felt horribly prophetic. And my thoughts were so crazy and confused, I wouldn't know where to begin if I tried. Could the 'strongest swimmer in our class' have been involved with the death of her own mother who 'got the end she deserved'? Is that why she was 'damaged goods' and had a 'spell' in a children's home? Then there were her words in the hospital: '*The water was so very cold. I felt her let go*'. Was that what my aunt had meant by '*I know what she did but I never let on*'?

And, though only God knew why I was connecting the two: what the hell had become of Vanessa's twin sister? The girl called Rose?

I revered to Sergio. 'Oh, nothing much. I'm just sleepy,' I replied. Then with a stab in my heart, 'Anyway, we don't do that, do we?'

'Do what?'

'Tell each other stuff. Be really honest.'

As though in pain too, his brow furrowed. 'I wish that I could, but it's—'

I quickly covered his mouth with my palm. 'It's fine. Stop.' Whatever it was, I did not want to know.

Chapter 78

Bernard brought us breakfast in bed on Monday morning as usual.

His expression inscrutable, he looked at Sergio. 'Don't forget you have your business meeting. We need to leave at ten.'

I could feel, rather than see, my lover's surprise. And when he replied I detected a note of alarm in his voice. 'Are you sure? On a Monday? That's short notice.'

'Yes, I sent you a text.' Bernard cleared his throat. 'A couple of reminders over the weekend, actually.'

Sergio sighed. '*Va bene.* I have no idea where my mobile is.' As Bernard left he kissed my forehead and pulled back the cover. 'I'd better find it.'

'Aren't you going to drink your tea first?' I asked.

His eyes had lost focus. 'Pour it for me, would you? I'll only be a minute.'

My mind thrashing with speculation, I watched him grab his robe and leave the room. A business meeting. That could only mean money, so maybe one with his accountant or bank manager. Oh God, was it my fault? Had Sergio gone way beyond his means by splashing out on the baby grand? He'd already have huge commitments with the rent and all the outgoings for this place – including the employment of a butler – and if Vanessa was leasing somewhere else...

Almost frozen, I waited for his return.

'Everything OK? Anything I can help with?' I asked.

His demeanour was so cloudy, it felt as though the man I'd intimately known for the last two months had walked out of his body and left.

He didn't answer my question. Instead, he headed for the en suite bathroom. 'I have to get ready,' he said.

−

Too buttoned up even to ask how long Sergio and Bernard would be, I sat on a high stool at the breakfast bar and tried to keep the frothing nausea at bay. It felt as though the grown-ups weren't telling me something for my own good, so perhaps I was still a kid after all. I waited for the click of the front door, but footsteps echoed back and Sergio appeared.

He softly pressed his lips to mine. 'Cook me something nice for supper? See you later.'

I inhaled to reply, but he'd already turned tail and disappeared.

It took a few moments to adjust. His parting kiss had been to reassure me, and the suggestion of food meant he'd return by dinner time. That meant a whole day on my own. Was I brave enough to resume my search of the house? God, I had no idea. On the one hand I needed to know when Vanessa would be back, yet on the other I was still reeling from my snooping on Saturday. Terrifying thoughts had swooped in and out of my head ever since. '*It's not something I'm proud of, but I had a spell in a children's home.*' Mum had *loathed* her mother, a woman not *worthy of mention*. Could Joy Parker really be 'Houdini girl'?

Then in the middle of the night Tim's suicide note had tumbled in. The way Mum had reacted on the day... Her offbeat questions about it since. Was this the 'truth' she thought Vanessa had imparted to me, the dreadful secret I'd passed on to Tim? It made sense. Her relaxed holiday demeanour had disappeared the moment Vanessa had mentioned swimming.

I wasn't sure what I'd hoped to achieve, but I phoned her last night.

'Hi Mum.'

'Ruth!' Then after a beat, 'It's very late. Is everything all right?'

'*No!*' I'd wanted to reply. '*Did you drown your mother? Is that why you were put in care? Is that why Vanessa had such a hold on you all these years? Has she threatened or blackmailed you?*'

That was silly, of course. My mum was a poorly paid solicitor's secretary; she had nothing to give in terms of money. And both women had spoken about their loyalty and tight friendship as girls. But why had she been so guarded and evasive when I'd asked about Vanessa's twin? Were the two things connected? I'd taken a breath to just ask, but the deepest dread had descended. It was none of my business. Honesty wasn't always the best policy. Maybe it was better to remain in the dark.

'I just wanted to hear your voice,' I'd said instead, realising it was true.

'Then come home soon for a visit,' she'd replied. 'You know how... how your dad really misses you.'

—

Too agitated to settle down for coursework or lectures, I spent an aeon in the lounge flicking through cookbooks, then an hour or so chopping veg and preparing a marinade for later. I pedalled on the spin bike for as long as I could muster, swam fifty short lengths and had a long shower.

It was still only three-thirty; time was truly dragging, yet when I finally sat at the piano, the queasiness eased and my thoughts became more alluring. Sergio loved me, I was sure of it; perhaps his future with Vanessa wasn't a certainty. She might be the one holding the purse strings, but money wasn't everything; sure, he'd have to move out of this amazing palace, but we could get a ramshackle cottage and devote a room which opened out to the countryside as his studio. Perhaps we could even squeeze this beautiful instrument in the parlour and play sweet music to the wildlife. We'd only need a basic kitchen to eat and a bedroom to sleep, and our lives would be perfect.

Pulling back from the keyboard, I deeply sighed. Who was I kidding? It was a child-like pipe dream. And anyway, what about Bernard? I was extremely fond of him too. His steadiness, lack of judgment, intuitive kindness; his efficiency, his cooking and cleaning skills.

I pictured his bunch of keys. There was something in the attic room I hadn't yet discovered, wasn't there? Why would he lock it otherwise?

Chapter 79

Watched by the solemn family on the wall, I found Bernard's keys in the same drawer as before. His medals and the phone were there too. Perhaps it was something to do with not being distracted at the wheel when driving, but it felt a little odd that he'd leave his mobile behind. But I had other urgent matters to attend to right now.

As usual I sprinted up to the top floor, but I was dizzy this time, so I shuffled to the studio and sat on my chair. I noticed the nudes had been rearranged and a couple of zipped art bags were propped against the wall, but I averted my eyes. Vanessa was already dominating my thoughts; I didn't want to add to them.

When the nausea had finally passed, I took a deep breath of resolve and strode to the room opposite. Though nothing had changed within, it felt danker, colder and creepier somehow. The knots in the old rafters looked like fathomless eye sockets, and even the teddy bear didn't seem so friendly today.

Rubbing the goosebumps from my arms, I focused on the weathered tea chests. As Sergio had said, they were probably for the landlord's storage, yet I still felt compelled to explore, so I lifted a lid and peered in. My heart lurching in my chest, I quickly recoiled. What the hell was that? I was tempted to run out, but I gritted my teeth and extracted the top items. They weren't dead animals as such, nor indeed a human scalp, but a fur coat, a stole and several wigs.

I gingerly brushed the mink jacket. Could this be the one from the photograph and Vanessa's visit? She'd said that was faux, but this most certainly wasn't. And the wigs? I wasn't about to touch them as they appeared so very real… but were they made from human hair?

Steeling myself, I poked into the second container. Akin to a child's dressing-up box, it contained hats, costumes and cosmetics from what I could glean. Despite my unease, my lips slightly twitched; God knows what horrors I'd expected, but I guessed they were outfits for the stage. Perhaps the house owner was in the entertainment business like Vanessa; maybe he'd leased it to her at 'mates' rates'.

A wad of theatre programmes to one side confirmed my suspicions, so I delved in again and extracted a rolled poster. Anticipating an auditorium banner, I idly unravelled it. Two versions of my aunt hip to hip gazed at me. I stared, disbelieving. Oh my God, she did have a living carbon copy. But after seconds of sheer terror, my eyes slipped to the blurb below the image: '*A moving portrait of two women joined at the hip whose extraordinary bond brings them fame but denies them love.*'

It was a play, just a play about conjoined twins. Yet I'd had enough. Something felt horribly off. As I began to back out a glimpse of pink caught my eye. Squinting to see what it was, I peered beneath the tidy bed frame. A handful of dead rose heads were scattered beneath it. Then, as if it had breathed in through the gaps in the floorboards, the distinct aroma of vanilla, jasmine and lily of the valley enveloped me like a second skin. Almost certain there was a figure beneath the rumpled eiderdown behind me, I bolted out.

I locked up with fumbling fingers, then squatted down and lowered my head. Seconds later I heard the sound of a clearing throat.

It was Bernard, hovering on the stairs with a tray. 'Everything all right?' he asked. 'You look pale.'

'Yes, I just felt a little light-headed from rushing up here.' Thank God he hadn't arrived a moment earlier. I slid the keys in my pocket. 'You're back then?'

'We are,' he replied. 'Where would you like to take your tea?'

—

The evening was strange and surreal. Sergio didn't mention where he'd been, and though his watch was noticeably missing, he didn't leave my side. His bonhomie felt forced as we finished preparing and eating our dinner, but his adoration didn't. Indeed, when we retired for an early night, it was as though he was absorbing every inch of my being, mentally photographing me and remembering it.

I wanted to shake him and yell, '*Why are you so sad? What happened today? Have you run out of money?*'

Yet deep down I knew those weren't the questions to ask. Those were: '*She's coming back, isn't she? I'll have to leave, won't I? Nothing will ever be the same, will it?*'

But it was preferable not to know, better to wallow in the sheer fantasy for as long as I could, to treasure the passion, the love, and to bottle it.

Chapter 80

When I woke in the morning Sergio was watching me, his face drawn and shadowy.

'She wants to see you,' he said simply.

It was exactly what I had expected, yet I still felt stunned, like I'd been dealt a knock-out blow. What did that mean? Today? Next week? Was Vanessa downstairs, somewhere in London or even in France?

'OK.' I replied. 'So—'

'Bernard will take you.' He made for the bathroom. 'I have to go out.'

Too petrified to ask what on earth was going on, I focused on my breathing. A million anxieties buzzed in my head, but one thought surfaced. My aunt wasn't dead; she wasn't beneath the quilt in that locked room upstairs. The notion shocked me and yet... Had that fear always been subliminally there?

Bernard appeared with his tray.

'What time are we leaving?' I asked.

'Shall we say at ten?' Then, anticipating my next question, 'Just bring yourself. It takes about an hour.'

'Yes. OK. Thanks.'

Despite his reassuring smile, I flew to my old room, pulled out the leather holdall and stuffed in the meagre possessions Ruth Parker actually owned. I felt marginally better having them ready for my return, but the most important item was my cello. Would it look odd if I took it with us in the car? But I had to have faith in Sergio. Whatever Vanessa wanted, he'd still look after my best interests, wouldn't he? *Wouldn't he?* Then why was he abandoning me when I needed him most, and why those soulful eyes? Where, exactly, was Bernard taking me? Was I even safe? I pictured the mobile phone in his bedside table. It wasn't his, was it? It was his missing employer's. Why on earth did he have it? Should I run away now while I could?

Suddenly desperate to shake the truth out of my lover, I bolted to the bannister and looked down. He was leaving, his dark head disappearing through the front door. Bernard looked up, his face fixed with that same smile as earlier. It made him appear odd, like a stranger.

One thing was certain: I didn't trust it.

–

Watching the world go by through the Bentley windows, I tried to absorb landmarks or signposts, but my mind was too scrambled to retain anything for long. What logical thought there was revolved in a small loop: where were we going? What did Vanessa want? Why had she asked to see me now, after many long months of silence?

Bernard negotiated busy A-roads, a stretch on a motorway, then a good twenty minutes along rural lanes flanked by fields speckled with sunshine, farm buildings and animals. I was thrown back in time to that journey in Normandy when everything had seemed golden and good, a sensation reinforced when he eventually slowed, entered an iron gateway and wended around the tree-lined driveway. But instead of a château, a handsome old property popped out at the top. Recalling Vanessa's long ago comment about a home in the countryside with a pavilion and a 'potager', I frowned.

Apprehension turned to annoyance. Like a minion to royalty, I'd clearly been summoned to her residence for an audience. She was doing it again, wasn't she? Dallying with me when she was bored and wanted a toy to play with until she found something better to distract her. I took a breath to finally speak,

342

but her manservant had parked and was gesturing through the windscreen.

'It was one of the first sanatoriums in England to be built specifically for the open-air treatment of tuberculosis. This one was private, so just the wealthy folk of course.' He pointed upwards. 'As you can see it was built on a hill to protect it from the winds, while still having the glorious views. See those large casement windows? They were fitted to admit a maximum amount of fresh air.' He glanced at me through the rear-view mirror. 'It was an important factor in the treatment of the disease.'

A blend of consternation, agitation and alarm loudly thumped in my ears, so it took an effort to tune into his words. We'd visited several historic houses over the past weeks and I hadn't heard Bernard speak at such length before. What was he saying? That Vanessa had bought an old sanatorium as her home? The Elizabethan-style building was huge, so perhaps it was split into apartments. There was no time to ask; he'd already climbed out and was beckoning me to follow.

He marched around a pristine lawn, then hopped up the steps which cleaved the high bank. I scurried to catch up and by the time I joined him, he was at a reception window and speaking a few words to someone who clearly knew him. Initially I supposed the man was a concierge, but my eyes and sense of smell knew better: a pale blue uniform, the tang of antiseptic and disinfectant behind the lemony air fresheners.

Reality finally settled on my shoulders: this was a private hospital, which meant Vanessa was ill.

Guilt plunged in, taking my breath. All those mean thoughts I'd had, the anger, even hatred. My self-centred, self-pitying behaviour. My life of luxury at her expense. Her bounty, her generosity, her kindness. And how had I shown my gratitude? I hadn't. I'd been too wounded and too proud to follow up my text after Christmas and say, '*How are you? I'm a little worried you haven't been in touch. Are you OK?*'

And even worse, so much worse, I'd stolen from her; I'd instigated an affair with her husband; I'd basically taken her place. Had Bernard told her? Was that why I was here? But there was no way to escape. His stance soldier-like, he was flanking me along a wood-panelled corridor.

He finally stopped at a door. 'Here we are,' he said.

I couldn't reply. I'd brought this shame on myself. Now was the time to face the music.

Chapter 81

Bernard ushered me inside, closed the door and left. It took several seconds to drag my eyes from the golden replica of Vanessa's 'boudoir' and force them look at the bed.

Rattling with dread, I tried for a smile. 'Hi. I'm so sorry I haven't been in touch or visited until now. I didn't realise you were... poorly. How are you?'

I struggled not to stare. Wearing a silky gown and her legs curled to one side, a woman was propped against a mountain of pillows. Had it not been for the strong stench of her perfume, I wouldn't have known it was my aunt. The skin stuck to her cheekbones, her face was tiny and pale, and her hair was hidden by a turban. Her green gaze was now a pale shade of grey; she looked so very old.

A disease was clearly eating her from within. Christ, her plethora of daily 'vitamins' had been medicine, hadn't it? Then there were her periods of lethargy and tiredness, which I had been blind to. How long had the poor woman suffered?

Remorse choked me again. I couldn't help likening her to the dead roses in the Wilton Place lobby. During those weeks they'd both been shrivelling, decaying. And dying? Oh God. Why hadn't Bernard or Sergio said something?

The old Vanessa chuckle made me start. 'Oh, come on darling girl, give me a smile. Now you're over the shock, let's have a nice catch-up and chat like the old days.' She laid a bony hand on the space next to her. 'Come and sit next to me. I want to look at you.'

It felt as if someone was squeezing my windpipe. *Catch-up?* Did she know I'd deceived her in the worst possible way?

'Sure,' I managed. I perched on the side, but she patted the bedding. 'Much closer, sweetie. I might look dreadful but I promise not to bite.'

I shuffled across to her scrawny arms.

'That's better, there's no need to be shy. We used to do this, didn't we? Just you and I. Wasn't it fun?'

She leaned in so closely, I felt her breath on my cheeks. For moments she studied me, then she traced my jaw, my eyebrows, my nose and my lips with dry fingers.

'I always said you were beautiful, didn't I, sweetie?' she said eventually. 'No one else saw it, but I did.'

Suddenly pulling away, she laughed, a child's peal of delight, then clapped her hands. 'Sergio thinks that he's the artist, but what a fine job I have done!'

A shiver trickled down my spine. 'Sorry?' I croaked.

Something didn't feel right. Clearly delighted by her own comment, my aunt continued to chortle and applaud. She abruptly stopped and frowned. 'Really, Ruth? Haven't you yet worked it out?'

'Worked out what?'

She yawned theatrically. 'Do tell me when to stop. It'll take all day to list everything.'

I was still dumbfounded.

'For goodness' sake, Ruth!' She counted on her brittle, cracked nails. 'Replacing those unflattering clothes, hiding your nasty underwear. Getting you fit and eating healthily. Pruning and preening and boosting your ego. Teaching you to entertain and cook. Educating you about art, geography and wine. Not to mention getting you away from that awful boy.'

The ground moved beneath me. 'What awful boy?'

'The one in room eight, of course. The word addict screamed out the moment I met him. If I'd have known that I wouldn't have gone to all the trouble of planting the—' She squinted. '—What is the common parlance? Ah, spice.'

346

I was struggling to follow. Gus. My friend Gus. 'You met him?'

'Only briefly.' She tutted. 'Don't look so crestfallen, darling. I did you a favour and he was more than happy to accept my hard-earned cash to do a runner. What did he say with the faintest of smirks? Something about his mother and it being an offer he couldn't refuse. He's probably in a ditch somewhere with a needle in his arm by now.'

The word 'spice' finally landed. '*You* put the joints I found in his—'

'Not personally, of course, but yes.' She stroked a strand of my hair behind my ear. 'I'm sorry about that darling, my little scheme went somewhat awry, didn't it?'

'What scheme?'

'To get rid of him, of course!' She sighed as though I was dense. 'The drugs raid? They were supposed to find them in his room and do the necessary to get him expelled or whatever the word is, but you got there first. Seeing you in the hospital was simply awful, and I did feel dreadful about that, but it all came good, didn't it sweetie? Like fate or serendipity. But we're going off subject. Come, I'll show you.'

Off subject? I was astonished, breathless, trying to process what she'd just said. Planting a dangerous, illegal substance in Gus's room. Meeting him and paying him to leave the flat, to leave me? Why the hell would she do that? But she'd already climbed from the mattress and was tugging me to my feet. Mischief shining from her eyes, she led me to a dressing table, sat me down on the stool and perched next to me.

'Ready?' she asked through the mirror.

I swallowed. 'Ready for what?'

With a flourish, she whipped the turban from her head. Patterned with a map of deep grooves and scratches, her scalp was completely bald.

'One minute!' She pinched her cheeks until she found colour, then opened the top drawer and scraped out her crowning glory of auburn hair. Swapping the wig for a blonde shade, she squashed it on her head. 'Voila! The finishing touch. Look, Ruth. Who do you see?'

Almost paralysed, I stared at our reflections. Vanessa was dreadfully wizened, yet the similarity was striking. And yes, I hadn't twigged at the time, but one of the nudes I'd glanced at only yesterday was not of her but of me.

This woman was still speaking. 'Look, sweetie, look at yourself. I painted you perfect and now you're me!'

She was right; superficially, I was her clone.

My mind feverishly whipped. Why had I never seen it? Those months of finishing school education; the clothes, the hair, the attitude, the style. And it had begun years before that: the bridesmaid's replica wedding dress when I was only fourteen. What had she said to me in France? *'Traditionally a bridesmaid dressed identically to the bride – the same gown and most importantly the same veil. Then if any evil spirits came to curse or whisk her away, the bridesmaid would act as a matching decoy and confuse the spirits long enough for the bride to become happily married.'*

Evil spirits, curses, *un diavolo…*

I groped to make sense of *why*. 'But I don't understand,' I whispered. 'Why would you—'

'Oh darling, don't you see? I've been poorly for a long time and now I've got what I wanted: longevity, lineage, a future, immortality of sorts.' She kissed my forehead. 'And it's all thanks to you. Do you remember the day we bonded in your mummy's kitchen?' She nudged me playfully. 'Now I'll always be thirty-three.'

Chapter 82

From guilt to incredulity, and all the jumbled thoughts in between, I'd gone through a whole gamut of emotions, but fear was now edging in. Vanessa's voice had been the reliable, reasonable one of old, but replicating oneself for *immortality* wasn't normal and that laughter had been off key.

I groped for reasons to draw the visit to a close, but she spoke again.

'As for the *love match*… It took a while, didn't it, but the result was just as I'd hoped and planned. More Anne than Jane, after all. Oh darling, don't look so alarmed. The power of attraction is a wonderful thing. And he's such a good lover, isn't he? The best I ever had!' She scrutinised me, then chuckled. 'From those pretty pink cheeks, I rather think you agree.'

Sergio. Good God, she was talking about Sergio. She'd *planned* it? Too shocked to answer, I simply gaped.

She picked up an ornate box and pressed something into my palm. 'I've wanted to give you this for so long,' she said wistfully. 'But I had to bide my time and stay away for the magic to work.'

Still reeling, I peered at the diamond solitaire. This woman knew about me and her husband. She condoned it. Good God, she'd orchestrated it by grooming me and withdrawing herself. What the hell? What the bloody hell.

I inhaled to say something, but she softly groaned, massaged her temples and moved to the window.

'These damned headaches,' she muttered, looking out.

Covered by protective metal bars, the 'casements' Bernard had mentioned wouldn't be opened for 'fresh air' anytime soon.

And now I looked, the lock on the door was code operated. My whole being felt icy. This wasn't a standard hospital suite, was it? It was a secure unit.

She unexpectedly turned and I flinched. Her expression lost, she looked at me blankly, but a moment later her dry lips stretched into a smile. 'Twinnie! Is that really you?'

She wasn't quite focusing on me. Spooked out, I swallowed. 'No. It's Ruth, remember? I'm not... I'm not Rose.'

Her eyes widened with alarm. 'We don't talk about Rose. She doesn't let me. Who told you about her?'

'Well, you did.'

'No! Never. We promised when she—' She seemed absent again. 'Rose. My Rose. Who told you her name?'

I pictured my mother the day she mentioned it. She wasn't just evasive, but downright lying. I steeled myself to find out more. 'It was Mum.'

'*Joy?* Joy told you about her?'

'Yes.' Vanessa was clearly bewildered; I was taking advantage of her confusion, but I wanted to know. 'Why wouldn't Joy tell me about her?'

'Because we—' She shook her head.

'Because we what?'

She dragged off the blonde wig and fingered it. 'I can't,' she said quietly. 'We promised.'

'You can. It's fine. You can tell me. Your secret will be safe.'

'Will it?'

'Yes.'

Her breath hot in my ear, she whispered her reply. But it was a struggle to process her words; my heart thrashed and a tinny taste was invading my mouth.

'Ruth?' Her gaze concerned, the old Vanessa had returned. 'Are you all right? Shall I call Daddy?'

Daddy? 'Sorry?' I managed. 'Who?'

'Daddy. Dearest Bernard, of course.' She rubbed my back. 'Really darling, after everything I've taught you, you are a little slow on the uptake at times.'

The portrait on Bernard's bedroom wall. The child with cropped hair, clinging to the woman's leg. That was Vanessa? Oh my God! All those breakfasts in bed he'd brought me and Sergio. The sex he'd nearly interrupted many times. That man was her *father*.

Then another bone-chilling thought: did Sergio know?

Vanessa seemed to read my mind. 'The watch you bought him was sweet, darling, but there are standards to keep and no one can live on fresh air. One needs to be sensible and remember that money makes the world go round.' She tutted. 'The best of everything, Ruth. Always! Clothes, holidays, restaurants, housing, cars. And apart from all those, even you should know most creatives need a generous sponsor or bene-factor, even if it is one's spouse.'

Putting a palm to her eyes, she stumbled to the bed. 'Yes, let's call Daddy. Lovely as it is to see you, visits take the very life out of me.'

As though he'd been listening to every word, Bernard quietly entered. Vanessa looked at him briefly, then turned away. 'I see you've brought Mummy. She was always your favourite.'

He didn't seem the least bit perturbed by her wacky comment. 'There were no favourites and Mummy died a long time ago.'

'Like Joy's mummy.'

Watching Bernard ease his daughter beneath the quilt, I waited with bated breath for his reply. Was this the moment my 'Houdini girl' fears would be confirmed, on top of what Vanessa had just whispered to me?

'I don't know about that,' he eventually replied.

'You went to the army and left me,' she said.

'I did, but that was my job and I always came back.'

She abruptly beamed. 'You came back when Mummy died.'

'Yes.'

'I knew you would.' She tapped her forehead. 'That's what I planned.'

'A little girl can't plan something like that, remember?' He cleared his throat. 'It wasn't your fault.'

Inching away, I gently blew out my relief. My mum wasn't 'Houdini girl', Vanessa herself was. Which surely meant that whatever had happened to her twin sister, my mum wasn't part of it.

Yet the whispered words, *We killed Rose* still clogged my mind like mustard gas.

Chapter 83

My whole being zombie-like, I returned to the Bentley and absently gazed through the rain-streaked window as Bernard smoothly drove me *somewhere*. He pulled up after a while and turned.

'Tea and cake?' he asked. 'There's a cafe at the back.'

I stared at him through burning eyes. Bloody hell; he was acting as though nothing was amiss. Yet I nodded, dragged my exhausted body from the rear seat and followed him through the double doors of a garden centre.

Vaguely aware of the vibrant bedding plants surrounding us, I greedily sipped my tea. God, I was thirsty. Hunger hadn't yet set in, but it felt as though I'd been imprisoned in that room for hours. I was still processing the multiple shocks. Should I feel pity, be terrified or resentful of the woman who once was my aunt? Bernard hadn't addressed me in front of his daughter, but he'd briefly muttered that she wouldn't be discharged 'this time' as we'd traversed the lawn to the car.

I focused on him now. The place we'd just visited was clearly a psychiatric hospital for people who posed a risk to the public or themselves. Had she been confined there before? Her fear of confined places and desire for open spaces would suggest so. The notion she might have killed both her mother and twin sister was unbelievable, but I'd just witnessed her 'seeing' them both just now. She was a seriously ill and dangerous woman.

Another theory struck. The windowless room in Wilton Place was clearly a shrine to Rose, yet that crumpled bed... Had Vanessa ever been locked in there? Those deep scars on her scalp and that weeping I'd heard... Had Bernard turned that old key for her own protection? The abstract of my aunt, the one that was her and yet wasn't, flew into my mind, bringing with it a new thought: had Sergio?

'Ruth?' Bernard's patient tone cut into my panicky musings. 'What do you want to ask?'

My fingers explored the dark knots in the wooden table top. Sergio. The man I'd completely trusted; the man I'd truly loved. Perhaps he'd been tricked or misled by his wife, but one way or another he'd betrayed me. That distinctive tang of her perfume hadn't been my imagination or an olfactory illusion, but from him and Bernard after they'd visited her. He hadn't been even remotely honest with me; even worse, he didn't accompany me today and help me through this trauma.

What had Vanessa said about money? It made the world go around. It paid for an artist to follow his calling. That's why he hadn't been truthful; that's why he'd maintained his silence. And even if a part of him had loved me, the missing watch said it all. He'd come here yesterday and chosen her over me.

Then another crippling idea: had my aunt rewarded him to be intimate with me?

I finally looked up. 'So you are Vanessa's father.'

'Aye.'

'And you had her and Rose?'

'I'm not following.'

Bile rose to my throat at the thought of Vanessa's whisper, but now was the time to finally learn the truth. 'You had another girl.' He frowned, so I quickly embellished. 'It's fine; I know.'

'Know what, love?'

'Vanessa "spoke" to her earlier...'

'Ah, that was Margot, her mum.' He smiled thinly. 'Hallucinating is part of her condition, I'm afraid.'

I briefly thought of my own spice-induced delusion, the very reason I'd got caught in this trap. 'Serendipity', Vanessa had called my hospitalisation. Bloody hell, *really*? Her mind-blowing account of planting the drugs to get rid of Gus – not to mention the rest of her manipulation – was still scarcely credible.

I reverted to her dad. 'She didn't sound very fond of her, of Margot.'

'Oh, she was, extremely.' His cheeks pinked. 'But Margot was... Looking back, I don't think she ever quite recovered from a difficult birth. But that's the benefit of hindsight. At the time I thought life was grand. We lived in army barracks to begin with, then she inherited a fair amount money from her folks and we were able to move out. But I was on the promotion ladder and had postings abroad, so I wasn't around as much as I should have been, and maybe Margot was one to put her own needs first. It didn't stop Vanessa adoring her, though. Clung to her leg when she was a toddler, then suffered from separation anxiety when she started nursery school. Truth is, Margot found her hard work.'

He pulled out a handkerchief, blew his nose, then fell silent.

I braced myself to ask. 'So when did Margot...?' The newspaper clipping had shown a Mercedes being dragged from a river by a crane, so I should have realised it had nothing to do with my mum's impoverished childhood. 'When did things change?'

'When Vanessa hit puberty. That's when it really matters what you look like, doesn't it? Especially with girls. She was growing into a beauty, but she couldn't see it.' He gave me an odd look. 'She needed someone else to say it, particularly her mum. So I suppose she switched her affections to me. I felt terrible when I couldn't come home straight after Margot's passing, but I didn't even hear about it for a time. I was on a covert operation and they had to organise my extraction, so she had a stay in Powys House until I came home.' He patted my hand. 'Thanks to your mum, she liked it there. Even wanted to stay and see the academic year out.'

I tried to bring him back to the point. 'Margo's passing: what did Vanessa mean by she'd planned—'

'That's just delirium, guilty feelings surfacing.' He seemed to read my very mind. 'I bet most kids hate their mum or dad at some point and wish them ill in their heads, if not verbally. My guess is she said something rotten to Margot before going to class that day and it's haunted her since.'

'Oh.' I was thrown. 'So, what happened to Margot?'

'An out-of-control lorry on the motorway.'

'God, I'm so sorry. That must have been incredibly hard for you and Vanessa.'

'Aye, but she was a fighter. When she left Powys House, she looked in the mirror and finally liked what she saw. She came top of the class at her new school, pursued her acting ambitions, was accepted at drama academy, picked up the French language at the drop of a hat. She didn't let her alopecia hold her back ever again.'

Alopecia. I pictured her bald head from earlier. 'So she's always had—'

'Hair loss, aye. Since she was small.'

I stared, stunned. I had no idea why this shocked me above everything else, yet it made perfect sense: the wigs in the top room and her turbans; that knowing look between the stylists at the hair salon; the bullying about her 'hair' and her comment about an autoimmune disease attacking oneself.

'How did the… the alopecia happen?'

'Treatment for a paediatric brain tumour when she was eight. The scarring and permanent hair loss was bad enough.' He squeezed the bridge of his nose. 'Then later she discovered the infertility. Remission for a long time, then the cancer came back.'

'Oh God. When was this?'

He dabbed a tear from his eye. 'Nine years ago.'

I nodded to myself. When I was ten; when she *ingrained* herself in my life. It made sense of her 'longevity, lineage, a future, immortality of sorts' comment, but despite the tragic circumstances, it didn't justify her exploitation, her grooming and cloning of me. Or why this man had indulged her by facilitating it.

'Frontal lobe syndrome,' he continued. 'Hence her neurobehavioral symptoms – confusion, forgetfulness, apathy, dysphagia, and more recently auditory and visual hallucinations, perhaps even psychosis, which is why she's safer in—'

'Psychosis?'

'It's an unusual side effect, but they say it can happen when there's been an episode or trauma in the past.' He shook his head. 'Her mum's sudden death, I expect.'

'I see.' I had already gathered what the answer was, but I asked all the same. 'Did or does Vanessa have a twin or a sibling?'

'No, love, she doesn't. What gave you that idea?'

I was no longer sure. 'The attic room at Wilton Place with the single beds,' I asked. 'Did Vanessa use it?'

'Aye. It was her quiet space for when her headaches got really bad. Sometimes the painkillers made no impact at all, so she welcomed the cool, and on those occasions, the dark.'

Yes, that day she'd been 'out of sorts'. When he'd appeared with a tray, there'd been a vial of pills on it. What had she said? 'Time for upstairs?' He'd nodded. 'I think so.'

My emotions spun again. From an early age Vanessa had been dealt a dreadful hand, yet despite all the suffering she'd donned that 'brave face'. This man had clearly been afflicted too. As her chauffeur-cum-skivvy, he'd devoted himself to his only child and that was admirable. I could pardon them both on some level. But the same couldn't be said of Sergio. I couldn't and wouldn't ever forgive him for his part in the deception.

'Why today?' I asked. 'Why did Vanessa ask for me now?'

He smiled sadly. 'She's getting increasingly confused and though she won't admit to any weakness, she knows her days are numbered.' He delved into his pocket and slid across the solitaire. 'She was so excited to give you this.' He had the good grace to blush. 'When Sergio stopped visiting, she knew something was afoot, so I kept her posted about, well, developments when I stayed with her at the weekends.' He held up a hand. 'I understand it seems odd, but she was delighted. She loves you both dearly. All she wants for her final months is for you to be happy.'

Part 5

Chapter 84

I caught the first available train to Manchester. Too shattered to even think, I stared at the transformed countryside through the carriage window as I hurtled back home. I had *transformed* too, but from what to whom? I had no idea. My only certainty was the need for my childhood bedroom and the safety of my dad's loving arms.

My parents glanced at each other with wide, worried eyes, but they didn't pry about my unexpected return home on a late May Tuesday, thank goodness, and as the days passed they sweetly clucked around me in the evenings, offering drinks and comments about the weather or snippets of local gossip. Mundane, but affectionate and secure.

I had no idea if Sergio tried to get in touch as I let my iPhone run out of charge. That lump of metal, that treasure, that lifeline, had once been so vital that it felt symbolic to let it slowly die like the woman who'd given it to me. As for her husband, he'd made his choice by abandoning me, running away and leaving me to face Vanessa by myself. Despite his declaration of love, he'd preferred money over me. Had he ever *loved* the real me, plain old Ruth Parker, and not the replica of his wife?

During each balmy June day I walked the paths of the glistening River Mersey, trying to exorcise the past and plan for the future, but so many questions remained unanswered, it was nigh impossible to mentally move on. The grooming or shaping of my life had started at ten, a light touch to begin with, but there was no doubt Vanessa had been an influence from that time onwards. What had I wished for under the magic cedar tree? To be her, of course. But at what cost?

The rot had begun earlier than that, though. I'd already been moulded by the distant, unloving and testy relationship with Mum. Or at least it had made me so malleable that I'd welcomed Vanessa's praise and attention with needy, open arms. From the snippets I'd learned, I understood Joy Parker was tortured by an illogical fear that the mother-daughter relationship would repeat itself, but was there more? What had Vanessa meant by her whispered words?

We killed Rose. I obsessed about this above everything else. Were they just the ramblings of a confused, dying woman? Possibly. But Mum had mentioned the name too. Who was Rose? Was she the bully at the care home? What had happened to her?

Occasionally I caught Mum observing me with a troubled frown. She lowered her gaze when she clocked I'd noticed, yet I was tempted to just ask. Perhaps I was viewing her through a different lens, but I admired her recent attempts to engage with Cad and I could now see that some of the harsh things she'd said or done as I grew up had been exacerbated, projected or misinterpreted by me through our lack of communication.

Dialogue and conversation, even simple talking was indeed the key. Could I, could we, do it?

My opportunity came at the weekend. Instead of sitting around the table for the usual Sunday roast, Tim, Dad and Cad went off to play a round of golf. I found Mum on the sofa reading a book, so I sat next to her, curled up my legs and took a breath. But she quickly spoke before I did.

'It's fine; I know.'

My shoulders tensed. The 'know' could have been any number of things. 'About what?'

As if she's had the same thought, a flash of alarm passed through her eyes. 'About Vanessa.'

I studied her grave, drawn features and I instinctively knew it was about her illness.

'OK.'

'Her father called me. He said she's near the end and asked if I wanted to see her.'

When this had been? From her taut stance, my guess was a while ago. And I suddenly realised she'd been wearing a long-sleeved top all week even though it was so warm. As ever she'd held in the turmoil, only letting a few drops seep out with a knife.

I inwardly nodded; I could never enquire about Rose.

'And do you want to see her?' I gently asked.

Her head down, she whispered something under her breath. Then she inhaled deeply, took my hand and squeezed. 'No, I don't think so. I think it's better to remember the woman we both loved, don't you?' She smiled thinly. 'That beautiful woman in the photographs.'

Chapter 85

A new week came around and I wanted to stop tormenting myself, I really did. But I'd caught Mum's muttered words and they simply added to my burning need to know: '*When she goes, the past can go with her, can't it?*'

What had happened at the care home? It was clearly something significant which had ricocheted throughout their lives.

Alone in the house, I mulled on the exchange with Vanessa about twins. I'd been blindsided by thoughts of Gus and his sister at the time, but she'd only mentioned 'twinnies', enduring elastic and bonds. Dad had said similar about my mum and aunt's friendship. In hindsight it was obvious: Vanessa and Joy were the twinnies.

We killed Rose.

The notion winded me yet again. Who was she? Did they really murder her? If they had, the crime had never been discovered. But could a child simply disappear?

Sitting cross-legged on my bed, I opened my laptop. Bernard had let slip the children's home was called Powys House and I knew the approximate dates of their stay. The internet was at my fingertips; a simple search would surely tell me more about a girl who'd gone missing.

I inputted a few keywords and was soon assailed by statutory guidance, safeguarding and an estimated hundred thousand runaways in any year, twenty-five of which were at risk of serious harm. Had Rose been *seriously harmed*? Did I really want to know? Yes, absolutely.

Steeling myself, I typed in 'Powys House', but all the results related to Wales. Pretty sure the Lake District had been mentioned at some point, I tried again, scanning through pages until I found one of that name.

I blew out a long breath. I'd expected an institutional, modern building of some sort but the handsome property was the stately home I'd noticed in the background of the attic room photographs. My heart raced; I was on the right track.

I peered at the two images on the screen. One was before a renovation, one afterwards. The mansion had been tarted up, doors and frames replaced, elevations transformed from a greyish cladding to white, and a pretty pavilion had been added to the walled flower garden.

I read the fine print:

> Once a children's home, the Grade II listed building was restored for private use in...

Bloody hell; did some poor family own a property where a crime had been committed? But that was surely my fervid imagination. There were reams and reams of poor missing kids, but no one connected to Powys House. Puffing out my relief, I idly looked further down the feed.

My eyes snagged on a headline:

> Trip turns to tragedy as children's home minibus veers into Derwentwater, Cumbria.

Anxious and nauseous, I opened the article.

> Employee drowns but two children survive.

Just knowing the worker was called Rose, I sucked in some air and continued to read.

Two girls, aged twelve, were taken to hospital and treated for shock and hyperthermia, but Jacob Armstrong, forty-six, manager of Powys House care home, was tragically declared dead at the scene.

Though there was no mention of Rose, my heart thrashed as I stared at the deceased's image. It would have been a tragic *accident* indeed had I not seen the similar headline in Vanessa's old school book.

'J' was clearly this man, Jacob Armstrong, and the children were the most proficient swimmers in school.

As if I was watching over their shoulders, I could clearly picture one twinnie write the letter 'J?' on a Post-it note and slide the cutting across to the other. Why would two twelve-year-old girls plan such a dreadful thing? I peered at Jacob Armstrong's benign expression and read the description of a 'much loved family man'. And yet there was something behind his dark eyes. Was this man *il diavolo*?

Chapter 86

The crunch of tyres from outside brought me back to today. Quickly snapping shut my laptop, I shook the shock from my face. I had to act normally; my mother must never know what I had discovered – and, worse, suspected. Yet when I checked the time, it was too early for either parent to be home, so I moved to the open window and peered out.

The Bentley was parked on our driveway. My instinct was to hide, but Bernard looked up. 'You're in then,' he called.

What the hell was he doing here? It wasn't OK just to turn up like this. But my anger faltered at his stony expression. Was it Vanessa? Had she died?

'I brought this,' he said, holding up my music pouch.

'Oh, right. One minute.'

When I'd left London, Bernard had collected my holdall and cello from Wilton Place before taking me onto Euston station, but the bag had remained in Vanessa's bedroom. It had sentimental value, but I'd assumed I'd never see it again, so I'd replaced it with a cheap one from Amazon.

I took it from him on the doorstep. 'Thanks,' I said. 'But you could have posted it.'

'I was passing. Right, I'm off to get petrol. I'll be back shortly.'

I frowned, perplexed. Why would he return? But the answer became apparent when his passenger climbed out.

I folded my arms. 'What are you doing here?'

Sergio glanced at the disappearing car. 'He didn't trust the removal people with his valuables.'

367

'Oh, so he's moved out?'

'Yes, he's going back to—' He shuffled his feet. 'Can I come in and explain?'

Part of me wanted to erase both him and Bernard from my life. I'd imprisoned myself in Wilton Place, but when I'd reflected on the past few months, there was a sense of them isolating me too. Yet I'd regret not hearing him out. Dispassionately listening was the thing, then coolly asking him to leave.

He followed me to the kitchen and sat when I gestured, but instead of speaking, he reverted to the artist of old, his face shadowy and remote.

Anger flew to the surface and it felt bloody good. 'For God's sake, Sergio, whatever you want to say, just say it.'

He raked a hand through his hair. 'I understand you're upset and quite rightly so, but it was so complicated, speeding so fast, completely out of my control. It went from a beautiful, incredible dream to the darkest, frightening nightmare. Then you made it all better and I pretended to myself it could go on forever. That was foolish, wrong. I'm sorry.'

'Upset?' My fury fired out. 'You deceived me for months; you weren't there when I needed you. You pretended to care for me when all the time you were complying with *her* twisted plans to make me some type of replicant.'

'Only for the modelling.' He sighed. 'Her illness was getting worse; she didn't always have the stamina even to pose, so she was keen to introduce you as a possible substitute.' He spread his hands. 'As you know, I wasn't happy with that, which was why I sent you—'

'But you managed to grit your teeth and do it anyway – and the rest – to keep me besotted and compliant. What for? So you could live in the lap of luxury, finish your bloody collection and pursue your dreams without having to lift a finger or pay for anything. Very honourable. I'm sure your *nonna* would be proud.'

He glared, then strode from the room.

'And don't think I don't know you bought that fucking piano with her money!' I yelled after him.

My lack of self-control was liberating. If he stormed out, I didn't care. But after a minute he returned and sat for some time with his head in his hands.

He finally looked up. 'I fell in love with you, Ruth. Fell in love for the very first time. From that moment I wanted to be honest with you but... I knew you would leave, so instead I stopped visiting Vanessa, hid from reality and lived the dream for as long as I could.'

Hadn't I done the same? Yet my rage still burned.

'*Wanted* is all very magnanimous, but you weren't *honest* on any level. Not mentioning the fucking butler was your father-in-law for starters.'

'I know, and I'm sorry.' He smacked his chest. 'But this was real.'

Did I believe him? Could I ever trust him again? I took a deep breath. 'So be honest now.'

'OK.' He rubbed his stubbly chin. 'I guess I thought Vanessa's fixation with you was a little... strange. That was why I remained in the studio when you stayed, why I was reluctant to engage, why I sent you away when you turned up. But she was disappointed I hadn't been able to... to achieve the last painting. I wanted to please her, so—'

'She wanted that, not you?'

'I did, of course.' He narrowed his eyes in thought. 'But she'd instilled that need from the beginning by encouraging me. I wasn't just talented but special; I'd be considered one of the greats, so I had to keep focus on the goal, dedicate myself to my calling and complete the collection. Then it would be displayed in full and the world would applaud.' He frowned. 'I understood she wanted the best for me but the pressure became increasingly debilitating. Then she left and I was completely stuck so... Well, you know the rest – instead of helping, your innocence and sweetness stunted me further. With Vanessa it was—' He seemed to search for a word. '—an obsession. Peeling back those layers. It was an artist's dream until—'

Il diavolo. Did he ever get to the nub and discover that?

'So the abstract…?' I asked instead.

'Painted after she was hospitalised. She's never seen it.'

His account sounded horribly familiar. Not encouragement but control by flattery and praise. Isolating him from family and friends. Putting him on that very high pedestal, then pushing him off to make him work harder to make amends. Not wanting the *best* for him, but to meet her own ends. What were they? To immortalise herself? To always be thirty-three?

Yet despite all that, I was glad she hadn't seen her doppel-gänger soul in the headshot.

I dragged myself back to Sergio. He was spreading his hands in a gesture of apology. 'And the money… She had inheritance from her mother's side as well as her own wealth. But I did pay for your piano.' His cheeks pinking, he shrugged. 'I sold a painting.'

'Oh right.' The art bag in the studio. He'd gone against Vanessa's command by parting with one from his collection for me.

'Yeah. I've got a couple more up for auction and the rest will follow. It would be good to have financial independence. Maybe return to France and start again. I still have my small place there.'

'That sounds nice.'

'And you?' he asked, 'Will you go on with your degree?'

'I expect so. At least something along those lines.'

'Music? Because you must, Ruth. Yes?'

I absently rubbed my stomach. I hadn't done a test, but I knew my morning nausea had been more than just anxiety. Was university feasible with a baby? Would I even have it? I still hadn't decided.

Sergio inhaled. 'So for me it is France or—?' New words hung in the air. 'Or I could stay and you could live with us.'

The golden bedroom in Wilton Place? No, never again. 'Us? I thought Bernard had moved out. You said his stuff's in the car.'

'We both have.'

'But your studio, the roof terrace…'

'Was only ever temporary. We moved there in September for a year. Vanessa said it was to be near her London doctor, but,' he rubbed his face, 'I don't know any more. And you're right, I should have come with you and supported you at the clinic. An appointment became available at the auction house and I accepted it. That was wrong; I'm sorry.'

But my thoughts were elsewhere. A lease during my first year at a London university. Coincidental or not? A shiver ran through me. When Bernard had escorted me from her hospital room, Vanessa called me back and placed a gentle hand on my tummy.

'You have my blessing. Be happy,' she'd said.

And yet she'd once told me that Segio had had the 'snip'.

Longevity. Lineage. Grooming us both to have her child? My God, how far did her manipulation stretch?

I shook the new shock away. 'Then where are you and Bernard now living?'

'A place an hour and a half from here. It's old, big, set in woodland. There's plenty of space for many grand pianos.' He smiled thinly. 'But in all honesty, it's very much Vanessa. She bought it fifteen, maybe twenty years ago; she had it renovated, decorated, had a folly constructed. Then all the furnishings—'

'A folly?' A disturbing déjà vu hit me. 'Is that a building?'

'Yes, in the walled flower garden. She liked to take down a flask of coffee and read her—'

'Her scripts. Or write one of her own, perhaps.'

What had Vanessa said in France? *'Traditionally it's a tower or similar constructed for aesthetic pleasure, one that has no real use. Some people build one as a monument. In my case it's a pavilion and my favourite place for contemplation.'*

A *monument*. But it wasn't just that. *The Folly* was the title of the manuscript I'd found in her wardrobe.

The before and after images from the internet flashed in my mind. One with a pavilion, one without, built on the very spot the 'twins' had posed.

I didn't need to ask, but I did anyway. 'Does this property have a name?'

'Yes,' he replied. 'It's called Powys House.'

Chapter 87

There was so much to analyse, deliberate and decide – Sergio, our baby, our future – but I didn't have time for that right now; I was itching to read what Vanessa had called a 'memoir of sorts'. Bernard soon returned with the Bentley, so I waved the men away, retreated to my bedroom and fumbled in my music pouch. Thank God the curled-up manuscript was still in there.

My heart thundered in my chest, yet I had to absorb what I could whilst I was home alone. Perching at my dressing table, I quickly turned the pages, scanning them for a mention of Rose.

After a few moments I stopped. My eyes weren't focusing, my brain wouldn't function. I needed to take several deep breaths and read the story from the start.

THE FOLLY

OVERVIEW: Two motherless twelve-year-old girls from different backgrounds become insepar-able. This is the story of the secret which binds them.

THEME: The unshakeable bonds of childhood friendship.

LIST OF CHARACTERS:

Girl Alpha: Confident, outgoing, open and spoilt.
Girl Omega: Bookish, reserved, sensitive, keeps her emotions bottled-up.
Him: the devil

OPENING SCENE:

INT. A SMALL WINDOWLESS ROOM IN AN OLD MANSION

The room contains two single beds. One bed is covered with a plush pink quilt, cushions and a plethora of teddies. The other is made up with a sheet and plain blanket, and a plump girl wearing glasses sits cross-legged on it, hunched over a book. The door swings open and three other giggling girls appear. They eat crisps and chat and play with the soft toys, but don't engage or even notice the other girl.

'Ruth?'

'Mum!' I spun around from the stool. 'You're home. I didn't hear you come in.'

'Sorry, I called you from downstairs. You must have been engrossed.' She glanced over my shoulder. 'Oh, your leather bag has turned up.'

Trying for nonchalance, I rolled up the parchment. 'It came in the post. A friend sent it.'

'That's nice of them, especially with the cost of postage these days.'

'Yes, it was.'

She hovered. 'So are we still on for tea?'

I had offered to cook dinner. 'God, yes, of course.' I peered at my watch. 'I didn't realise the time. I'll get to it now.'

'Lovely.' Mum pushed away the hair from her forehead. 'What time should we be at the table?'

'Will six-thirty be OK?'

'Dad will be home by then, so thank you, that will be perfect.'

Chapter 88

My respiration shallow, I set about my chores in the kitchen. Thank God I'd decided on a one tray chicken and halloumi dish that I'd prepped earlier. I only needed to scoop the thighs from the marinade, quarter the lemons, add all the ingredients and put it in the oven.

I was desperate to get back to Vanessa's story. I had glimpsed the name 'Rose', not within the narrative or the dialogue, but as a drawing. Could it possibly be true?

Once I'd finished chopping a side salad, I belted upstairs, but at the entrance to my bedroom I came to a standstill. Mum was at my table, turning the furled pages.

She quietly spoke without turning. 'Our dormitory in the attic. It was probably a storage closet or the like in days gone by as there were no windows. She's described it perfectly. Those teddies and cushions.'

I pictured the locked room at Wilton Place. Vanessa had clearly replicated it too, but I sensed Mum wanted to talk, so I silently moved to the bed.

'They were hers, of course. And she had this soft, padded quilt which looked to me like a heavenly baby-pink cloud. How I longed to lie on it or in it, or wrap it around me.'

She didn't need to say hers was the plain bed with the scratchy blanket. That she was a child who had nothing.

'She was immediately popular, the Alpha girl to whom everyone was drawn. It helped that she was so pretty, plump from the good life, gregarious and sporty and bright. In contrast I was spotty, overweight from bad food and unhappiness; I was introverted and kept my feelings to myself.' She glanced at me and smiled thinly. 'I wore reading glasses for my escape in books.'

I nodded. Omega girl. Like me.

Tension crackled in the air. I expected her to clam up but she took a sharp breath. 'I invisibly watched from the sidelines until—'

The hairs erect on my arms, I waited.

'Until the other kids discovered she wore a wig.' She clicked her fingers. 'It changed just like that. From then on they acted as though her alopecia was contagious. They taunted her, treated her like leper. One or two of the boys tried to pull it off. The bullying was truly dreadful.'

She fell silent for some time, so I cleared my throat. 'So you became her saviour.'

'No. *He* did. Her isolation made her ripe for the picking; he saw his opportunity to persistently yet patiently groom her. He listened, he cared, he gave her time and treats, he made her feel special. He came into our room to tuck her in, bid her good night, give her a chaste kiss and a cuddle before turning off the light and going home to his family. And all the while I was there in my single bed. Unseen. Unnoticed. Unloved.'

A word seared the air, but she didn't need to say it. Despite her roommate's appalling abuse – because I'd seen from the stick drawing that's what it was – she was jealous.

'Then the worst night came around. It was so black in that dorm, I always slept heavily, but I was woken by her muffled pleas for him to stop. I heard a grunt and heavy breathing, then the rustle of bedding and clothing, and finally a zipping sound. "My good and beautiful girl," he said, thanked her and left.'

My throat was so dry I couldn't have spoken if I'd tried. This horrendous rape was what I'd gleaned earlier from the drawing: a sketch labelled 'Alpha Girl' with a baby in her tummy marked 'Rose'.

Mum continued to speak in a monotone. 'I didn't fully understand what had happened, but from her shocking silence I knew it was bad. So I called her over, pulled back my bedsheet and held her tightly. When I woke in the morning, she was still dumb, frozen with shock, and my nighty was stained by her blood. I knew then I had to do something.'

'What was it?' I asked, steeling myself to hear about *two* Houdini girls.

'I took her place.'

'What?' I was completely thrown. 'I don't understand what—'

'I slipped under the pink eiderdown I'd so coveted and took her place.'

'Oh my God, Mum. Why would you do that?'

'When she finally *thawed*, I suppose, she was traumatised, panicky, unstable, made all the worse by her immaturity; she couldn't cope with it happening again. She'd lost her safe world – her mum and her home, the friends she'd made here.'

'But why didn't she report it?'

'Shame, Ruth. Feeling she'd somehow asked for it and brought it on herself. Not being believed. Besides, you don't inform in those places. I was tougher, more resilient and most importantly—' She inhaled deeply. '—it was my fault. The bullying, then the grooming and the abuse. Out of sheer envy it had been me who'd told the other kids about her baldness and operation scars.'

Bursting out of her composure, Mum suddenly gasped. 'She knew what I'd done, Ruth. It's here, in this scene, when Omega whispers "she has no hair; she wears a wig" to the other children. I had no idea until ten minutes ago.'

Vanessa's comment '*I know what she did but I never let on*' finally made sense, but I had no idea what to say to my mum. She had told tales on Vanessa, yet she couldn't have possibly known what would happen. And she'd paid her debt in a terrifying act of selflessness.

'So you became twinnies?' I gently asked, moving closer.

'Yes, we swapped, became one. And not just our beds or at night. I wore her clothes and the wigs and copied her make-up.

377

The other kids thought we were weird but it gave us a strange power.'

I nodded: the dressing up crates in the replica room.

'We continued to be twinnies even after he left.'

'Oh, he left?'

'Yes, him. Vanessa called him the devil, but I refused to credit him with that power.' She briefly looked at me. 'Yes, he got another job. We were at our happiest then, making plans for—'

She circled Alpha girl's stomach with a finger.

'For Rose?'

'Yes, our baby. Then he came back.'

'Oh God.'

'Promoted to manager this time.' She rubbed her arms. 'We'd hidden the growing bump beneath baggy jumpers, but we couldn't risk him finding out and somehow taking our baby.' Her expression hardened. 'Besides, the disgusting, snuffling pig deserved to die.'

'It's fine.' Swallowing, I took her hand and squeezed my reassurance. 'You don't need to explain. I read about his... his accident online.'

'Did you?'

I had given her a 'get out' card, so I was surprised when she grimly smiled and continued to speak. Yet I got it: now the floodgates had opened, splurging it all out was a release, therapeutic.

'Once we'd made that decision, it was exhilarating to turn the tables. Making him feel so special and handsome and loved that he had to devote all his attention to us. *"Please could we go on a day trip to one of the lakes? With a picnic, a blanket and some alcohol? We'd love to try vodka or gin. You could show us how a real man throws it back. We'd so make it worth your while..."'*

She sported a look of disgust. 'The views, the mountains and the hills were truly spectacular, yet there he was at the wheel, grinning and swigging from the bottle with a hard on, and complete putty in our hands. *"Get us nearer to the water, we want a better look. There might be somewhere private we can picnic...*" Then at some point on a narrow B-road with only a fence between us and the lake, we both knew it was time. One of us covered his eyes with a scarf, the other yanked over the steering wheel and unclipped his seatbelt so he'd smash into the windscreen, be concussed or at least stunned...' She shuddered. 'Well, you've read the rest.'

The silence yawned, but I had to ask. 'What happened to Rose?'

'I killed her.'

Trying not to react at the appalling word 'I', I held my breath and waited for more.

'Vanessa didn't want me to go on the outing. But I was the stronger swimmer. We'd repeatedly practised the lifesaving in case anything went wrong; I couldn't let her do it alone.'

'I don't understand. Why wouldn't she want you there?'

'She was worried about the impact of the van hitting the surface, the freezing water and the swim to the top.'

I shook my head, still perplexed. 'Sure, but as you say, you were—'

'To protect Rose. To stop anything happening to her.'

I pointed to the sketch. 'But Vanessa was pregnant, not...' My sentence trailed off as I gazed at her.

'It was me. I was Alpha girl, Ruth. Or at least I became her.'

Astounded, I tried not to gape. My mother had had a pregnancy before Tim? No, it couldn't be true. And yet her distraught expression told me otherwise. This was *the* unmentionable, wasn't it? She'd made Vanessa promise never to speak of it again and her only outlet had been the cutting. It made sense of her 'damaged goods', her post-natal depression, her inability to broach emotional issues such as Tim's sexuality. And particularly her difficulty bonding with a female child.

As I breathed through the shock, I mused the phrase 'our baby'. Vanessa's cancer treatment had made her infertile so the mother could never have been her. Was she already aware of it then? Is that why Mum had offered to share the baby?

Though barely a whisper, Mum spoke again. 'I lost her, our Rose. I could feel her let go when I swam to the surface. She finally came away later that night in our room. I don't quite know how many, but I was five, maybe six months on, so I killed a perfect, fully formed little girl.'

'You couldn't have known you'd miscarry.'

She looked at me with hollow eyes. 'But I did, Ruth. I wished it; effectively made a curse.'

Seeming to revert to the pragmatic mum I knew so well, she stood and brushed the creases from her skirt. 'Pipe dreams and plans were all very well, but I was scared about the future. About me. Would I become my mother? A teenage parent who despised her child, who disappeared for weeks at a time and finally drank herself to death. And would Vanessa really stand by me when she returned to her privileged life with her father? Honestly, I was relieved Rose had left us, but Vanessa was devastated.'

She handed me the parchment. 'I haven't read that far, but if she knew what I'd prayed for, please don't ever tell me.'

Blinking away the malevolent stare of that blue-eyed dolly, I inhaled and rubbed my own belly. Maledictions and devils only existed if you let them in. It was that woman – my grandma – who'd started the rot by making her child feel worthless and like 'damaged goods'. I would not allow history to repeat itself. Indeed, from now on I'd heal some of my poor mother's scarring by *showing* my love.

I held out my arms and drew her in. 'I'm so sorry for all you've been through, Mum. Always remember I love you. Very much.' Then, as though I was the adult, and she the child, 'We all make wishes, some of them bad, but none of us have the power to make them true.'

She gazed for a beat, then kissed my forehead. 'Thank you, love. If you say so.'

Chapter 89

Vanessa missed her wish to marry on Midsummer's Day, so it felt rather poetic that the same group of people gathered to say goodbye to her the same date, albeit five years later. Her father attended this time, of course, and though it was heart-breaking to witness his wretched, stooped stance, I kept my distance from him and Sergio.

Standing with my brother and Cad, I watched my parents make their way to Sergio's family to pay their respects. Had they always held each other's hands so tightly, or was this a new thing since Vanessa's death? Either way, their love brought tears to my eyes. How much did Dad know about Mum's past? Perhaps not everything, but he'd always adored her despite her damaged self-belief. Such genuine devotion was rare and incredibly precious, so perhaps that was why I still couldn't decide what to do about my future. Even as I threw a single rose into the dark chasm of my aunt's grave, I didn't know which way I'd go. Be alpha or omega? Elect for independence or a preordained life? For freedom or Sergio? Whichever it was, I knew I'd keep the baby.

-

When Vanessa's will was unearthed, I discovered she had left large bequests to Bernard and Sergio but Powys House to me. Perhaps I should have been grateful at my astonishing good fortune at nineteen years of age, but it felt too much like her final contrivance, so I railed against it, refusing to acknowledge the letters from the executors, let alone accept Bernard's offers to collect me for a visit. Yet deep down I knew that seeing it in person was the only way to decide my destiny, so after another week of insubordination, I finally gave in. I would take a trip to Cumbria, but I'd make my own way by public transport.

A tram, two slow trains, a stifling bus and four hours later, I arrived at the elegant front door. Clearly hovering in the hallway, Sergio immediately greeted me with cheek kisses and a delighted grin, then he gave me space to roam the house at my leisure. The ground floor salons and lounges were as airy, light and sophisticated as I'd imagined, seemingly free of phantoms too, but the acid test wasn't down here.

I found Bernard in the glossy, modern kitchen. 'I'm having a wander. Do any of the rooms have locks?' I asked.

'No. She didn't like them for obvious reasons, so she had any removed.' He rustled in a drawer and brought out a single key. 'Except this one.'

'The loft?'

'Aye.'

His expression was as deadpan as ever. Did he know what had happened within these old walls? Perhaps he suspected, but I was sure Vanessa had kept her promise to Mum, only breaching it by writing it down.

Once in the lobby, I remained glued to the herringbone parquet for several heart-thrashing moments. Although this property didn't have an open staircase, the ambiance, the furnishings, colours and decor were strikingly similar to Wilton Place, so I had to remind myself of one momentous fact: the attic room here wasn't a clone, a duplicate, a manmade twin. It was the real thing.

Popping my head into a replica boudoir, sumptuous spare suites, day rooms and bathrooms en route, I ambled upwards. When I finally reached the very top, I took a huge breath, strode to the only closed door and inserted the old key. As if refusing entry, the dead bolt wouldn't turn, and it took a second or two to realise it hadn't been locked after all.

Back in my fearful shoes from three months ago, I quickly flicked on the light and looked into the small windowless area. It contained two single beds, one covered with a plush pink quilt, cushions and a plethora of teddies, the other made up with a sheet and plain blanket. A plump girl wearing glasses was sitting cross-legged on it, hunched over a book.

I blinked the vision away. The warm room was empty and, save for what appeared to be an outline for a skylight, the walls had been plastered and painted. The exposed beams had been sanded and varnished, the old floorboards carpeted. Completely thrown, I unclenched my fist and looked at the manuscript I'd intended to leave hidden up here. So what now? Lock up behind me and throw away the key as planned, or leave the door open to let that dolly, those teddies and the children free?

My lips twitched wryly. Vanessa. She'd already made that decision, hadn't she? The hidden room at Wilton Place had been an effigy, a graven image, a likeness, a symbol of the dreadful dark past which could and should remain there. The whitewashed future was here.

Bernard was in the garden, poking a fire.

'Garden waste,' he commented.

It felt *serendipitous*, as my aunt would have put it. 'Is it OK to add this?'

'Aye.'

I threw on the parchment and we both watched the past turn into embers. But I wasn't there yet; I had to jump the second hurdle.

'I think I'll have a stroll in the sunshine,' I said.

'Very good.' As if knowing full well where I was headed, Bernard cleared his throat. 'Shall I bring you a cool drink? Something to eat? Or read?'

'Just a lemonade for now, please.'

Donning the wide-brimmed hat which matched my sarong, I ambled across the manicured grass. When I reached the pavilion, I raked back my sunglasses and studied the mansion's handsome façade. A child was buried in these grounds. My half-sister, in fact. Could I really bring up my own with the shadow of her always near? Could I exorcise her and the ghosts of the past forever?

Vanessa, Vanessa. I still hadn't decided whether she was good or bad, a saint, a sinner, a victim, sane or psychotic.

Why had she chosen me at the tender age of ten? Was it a desperate attempt to replicate herself whilst she was beautiful and before the cancer had a grip? Or did she see an unhappy child who'd needed a huge dose of self-worth and love like my mother had at the same age? Did she simply want a daughter? Or perhaps she wanted to punish Joy by subliminally taking the child she'd deprived her of?

I laid a gentle palm on my growing bump like she had. Or had she been earmarking me as the woman who would one day carry 'our' baby?

I shook each and every surmise away. Of more vital concern was my mum. Vanessa's death had undoubtedly released her, yet what if this beautiful property was sold and a new owner installed? Suppose they considered the summer house 'frivolous and without a purpose', pulled it down and found tiny bones which matched a dead man's DNA?

I stretched out my legs and chuckled. As if there was anything to decide! My rebellion had only been temporary; the 'sensitive soul' Ruth Parker was in the past and my aunt had gone; like evil spirits and curses, she'd only have the power to haunt me if I let her. Besides, her manipulation, or shaping, or whatever it was, now felt more like mellifluous choreography: my grand piano was waiting for me in the music room, Sergio's patio doors were open to the sound of birdsong from the woods beyond, and the organic fruit in the potager was ripe for the plucking. Who wouldn't want to live a country home with a folly, huge gardens and a vegetable patch? Be happy, self-sufficient and live off the land with babies and a man I adored?

Catching my handsome man's smile from his studio, I flushed and waved back. His *nonna* had come to Vanessa's funeral.

Somehow knowing I was pregnant, she'd done a rocking motion with her arms. Though I doubt she knew who the father was, Sergio had been watching and his expression had turned from puzzlement to sheer delight.

The breeze softly wafting around me, I contentedly sighed. Yes, being *chosen* wasn't so bad after all. My aunt was right; money did make the world go around; this glorious house was perfect and if I needed the occasional break, I had my chauffeur to take me out to a museum, a gallery, or for a dose of retail therapy. One thing was for sure; I'd never travel with the ghastly public again.

The Attic at Wilton Place *Reading Group Questions*

- When did you suspect Vanessa's generosity wasn't all that it seems?

- What did you make of the fraught relationship between Ruth and Joy? Did you have any sympathy for Joy at the end?

- Were you shocked or disapproving when Ruth propositioned Sergio? Or were you rooting for her?

- Was Clive a good husband? Was he a good father?

- Were you shocked to learn that Bernard was Vanessa's father?

- Had Sergio also been groomed by Vanessa?

- Was Sergio's weakness forgivable?

- Were you disappointed in Gus?

- What did you think of Joy's choice of taking Vanessa's place at the care home?

- Did Ruth make the right choice at the end? Did she sell out?

- Would you have made the same one?

- As Ruth herself mused, was Vanessa good or bad, a saint, a sinner, a victim, sane or psychotic?

- Sergio and Ruth bond over their artistic pursuits – what role do you think art plays in the book, and how does it fit with the role of money?

- What effect do you think sibling rivalry had on Ruth's relationship with Vanessa?

- How much do you think Ruth was brainwashed? How much agency did she retain?

- Why do you think Vanessa kept the attic at Wilton Place a shrine to her childhood trauma?

A letter from CE Rose

Hello lovely reader!

Thank you so much for reading *The Attic at Wilton Place*. I do hope you've enjoyed following Ruth's journey, living alongside her in Wilton Place and discovering Vanessa and Joy's dark secrets.

If you'd like to read more twisty, chilling tales about ordinary, relatable characters who get caught up in extraordinary situations, dilemmas or crimes, or who unearth deeply hidden, dark secrets, please check out my other CE Rose gothic-tinged psychological thrillers, *The House of Hidden Secrets, The House on the Water's Edge* and *The Shadows of Rutherford House*, or my Caroline England psychological suspense novels, *Beneath the Skin*, *My Husband's Lies*, *Betray Her*, *Truth Games* and *The Sinner*.

Book reviews are extremely helpful to authors, so if you have the time, I'd be very grateful if you'd pop one, however short, on Amazon, Goodreads, Waterstones, social media or any other forum you prefer. If you'd like to chat in person, hear my latest news or see photos of my moggies and other random things, my contact details are below.

Thank you again,

Best wishes,

Caroline

Website: https://carolineenglandauthor.co.uk
Twitter: https://twitter.com/CazEngland
Facebook: https://www.facebook.com/CazEngland1

Instagram: https://www.instagram.com/cazengland1/
TikTok: https://www.tiktok.com/@cazengland1
email: carolineenglandauthor@gmail.com

Acknowledgments

Huge thanks to:

Jennie Ayres, Keshini Naidoo and the rest of the Hera team for your top-notch editorial input and fabulous book covers.

My hubby Jonathan and my gorgeous daughters Elizabeth, Charlotte and Emily. Paris was sublime!

The Didsbury Aristocats Poppy, Lewie and Maisie, even if you do sit on the desk!

My brilliant friends and especially my cat-feeding, cake-making bestie, Belinda.

My fabulous, supportive local bookshop, E J Morten Booksellers.

My talented and insightful fellow writers at the South Manchester Writers' Workshop.

My early readers Sue France (AKA Cheshire's Queen of Connections) and Hazel James.

Cheshire Life editor, Joanne Goodwin - Vanessa may have had a central, double page spread, but you went two better and gave me four!

The wonderful book bloggers, in particular those who so generously stepped up to travel with Milly, Christie and Duncan on The Shadows of Rutherford House blog tour.

Every single fellow author, blogger, reviewer, reader or online book-group member who has championed my books.

Last, but not least, you guys – the fantastic reading public! Thank you so much for buying my novels, investing hours of your time reading them and posting such heartwarming reviews.